Jonas the Vampire

by

Alexandria May Ausman

Book cover design by Alexandria May Ausman
Editor: by Jon M. Ausman

Library of Congress Control Number: 2023921828

ISBN: 979-8-9890048-5-0 (ebook)
ISBN: 979-8-9890048-4-3 (paperback)

Published By:
Ausman & Cousins, LLC
1700 North Monroe Street
Suite 11, Box 284
Tallahassee, Florida 32303-0501

For author interviews: ausman@embarqmail.com

Das Kaiser Haus Series

The Rise of the Priceless (Chapters 1 to 10)
Metal Illness (Chapters 11 to 19)
Jonas the Vampire (Chapters 20 to 29)
Prince of the Elders (coming soon)

The Psycho Series

Cemetery Kid (Chapters 1 to 20)
Stop Calling Me Psycho (Chapters 21 to 33)
Motor-Psycho (Chapters 34 to 44)
Delusion of the Collar and the Key (Chapters 45 to 53)
Brutality's Prisoner (Chapters 54 to 64)
Aesthetic Akathisia (Chapters 65 to 74)
Metallic Burden (Chapters 75 to 83)

27 Masters Series

Anita the Benevolent (Chapters 1 to 7)
The Beast and the Witch (Chapters 8 to 16, coming soon)
High Priestess of Schizophrenia (Chapters 17 to 24, coming soon)

Book 3 Characters: Jonas the Vampire

Abelard: a submissive of the Haus
Agnete: mother of Christian
Annette: a Haus trainee
Barnum: an Elder of the Haus
Bladrick: an Elder of the Haus
Christian: the anger and lust shard
Claus: an Elder of the Haus
Cora: a FemDom of the Haus
Darrell: a child molester now deceased
Debbie: Meine Liebe's sexual psychopathic and sadistic
mother
Der Goldene Hund: the Voice or the Boss shard; the
Conscious shard
Drexel: an Elder of the Haus
Egon: Haus seduction Master and trainer
Emma: a black collar, aide to Jonas
Felix: a black collar door guard hired by Peter
Geraldine: a Haus trainee
Gretta: a House Elder, the Silk Queen
Grisham: a Dominant of the Haus
Heiner: Master of Geraldine
Hemmel: a Dungeon Master
Jonas: an Elder of the Haus
Justus: a deceased Priceless, brother of Milo
Leo: a Haus Dominant
Mad Max: the sadistic shard of Maximillian, aka the Heart

and Judgment

Mad Maxx: husband of Meine Liebe; a Das Kaiser Haus Dominant

Mad Maxx: the masochistic shard, aka the Brain and Guilt

Malfred: a wily Haus Dominant

Max: the Soul shard

Maximillian: the submissive name given to Christian by Peter

Maximillian: the seductive shard of Maximillian, aka the Libido

Milo: silver collar Haus seduction trainer

Olaf: House black collar; aid to Xavier

Peter: a Dominant of Der Kaiser Haus; best trainer of submissives

Rachel: the birth name of Meine Liebe

Robert: a House submissive

Rupert: a recently deceased Haus Elder

Russell: spouse of Debbie, a switch

Ryker: a House trainee

Vilber: House black collar; aid to Xavier

Xavicr: thc Fur King of the IIaus

Chapter 20: Femme Fatale

"I watched that gorgeous Geraldine open the door and go into the washroom. I looked down at this hex wrench she gave to me and thought, if only I had not masturbated like a thousand times before this glorious hour, it would have come in useful.

As it was, I assumed I was rendered "incapable" of anything more than appreciation for the sights that awaited me just inside that room. with a great deal of sighing, I dropped that key to my freedom into my breech's pocket. there was no reason to bother taking off, then putting back on, that complex device. Maybe, the next time though, I would allow my lust to run wild.

The visions of how grateful my Geraldine would be (and what she would give me for it no doubt) when Mad Max got Claus to save her from her lusty Dominant, put a smile on my face. I knew she likely meant she was willing to be my lover with only the promise of such a mercy, but I was honorable. I neither expected nor would I ask her to pay for the service without my end being completed. That would just be bad manners.

After I provided the service she requested though, then enjoying her as my true lover would be fair. I nearly had a skip in my stride as I headed inside the room following the trainees. This was the best day of my life, but not for

1

long I hoped (Mad Maxx chuckled with much bitterness and a frown at that, then paused, sighed, and continued. That behavior made me suspicious that the next part of his story was not going to be the sex-a-thon he hoped for, not by a long shot based on his unit language of sudden sadness.)

When I arrived all the girls were chattering about my scary" acting job to get them all in my possession. Annette laughed loudly and bragged that she planned to tell everyone she screamed, begged, and cried the loudest in my chains. The other girls all argued they would be the one to claim the honor of being the biggest victim of my brutal affections.

I laughed at them then said, "Are you going to practice this lesson I was invited to judge, or do I need to make all of you honest? I can take you downstairs, ja? Is that what you really want? Beware. I am good at what I do. You will not be so happy when the scars you bare do the speaking for you." I couldn't finish this empty threat without breaking up with much humor when the girls all looked at each other with sudden fear in their eyes.

Geraldine came up and slapped my shoulder playfully. "Stop teasing us. We are young girls. An experienced lover such as you Mad Max can make a maiden a whore in moments. Now sit there on the counter. Annette, you start since you want to be the biggest victim, ja." I kept *chuckling but did as Geraldine asked and went to this countertop and sat down eagerly awaiting my strip show.*

Annette, she pranced across that tile smiling at me with much coyness. She swung her hips and spun around as if she were seeking something in the distance. Then the pretty blond would turn her head slightly and capture my gaze, giggle then look away covering her mouth with her hand.

With her back turned to me she reached out and unzipped the back of her skirt. I nearly fell face first onto the floor trying to get a closer look as the garment fell revealing a pair of cotton panties with a fancy pattern.

She turned to face me still looking down with a mischievous grin, then pulled her sweater over her head. A cotton bra of the same pattern was revealed. there she stood in her white thigh highs, pumps, and matching underwear. Her skin was tight, smooth and her female parts barely covered by that cotton material.

I normally would have worried about my cock rising at this most fantastic scene, but thankfully, the masturbation releases kept everything nice and calm. I was able to enjoy the show, without paying the high price for admission (My Master laughed at that clever analogy.)

I had assumed that stripping to their undergarments was all I would get to see. You can imagine the gasp that I let free when the beautiful Annette reached behind her back and with only a quick movement her bra slid down her arms onto the floor (My mouth fell right next to it by the way. Holy shit, she was hot.)

I had not recovered from my teenage shock when that vixen then turned her back to me again, grabbed the sides of her panties, and slid them off letting them drop to her ankles. Meine Liebe, I would have been happy to die right there when she then bent down with that amazing bottom aimed right at my sight.

I could hardly believe the splendor before my eyes. I imagined the angels in heaven could not be more gorgeous than the female sexual organ in the flesh. I knew at once this was the thing I was born to try to possess.

All I could think about was grabbing her by that curvy waist of hers and thrusting my manhood into her with all my might. Even though my cock was quiet through this display, my mind went to a dark place full of animal wantonness for the mate with a female of my own species. The drive is hardwired in the male, and the female too. One does not need the parts to work for the lust to exist.

I was so busy staring (and drooling, I confess) that it took all the trainees giggling for me to realize Annette was speaking to me. my ears heard nothing but the distant sounds of drumbeats keeping the wild rhythms of my base instincts. I had been rapidly reverting to a less civilized creature while gazing upon the vision of my truest desires.

"Well? what did you think? Am I doing this seductive striping right? If you were a man that desired a girl, would you want me right now?" Annette crossed her arms under her firm, well-formed breasts while huffing in disappointment that she had to be asking me this three times (Poor girl had no idea that what she saw as lack of interest was full blown holy shit, I want you behavior. Mad Maxx howled at that while I kept my eyes on him with much suspiciousness. I worried he would work himself into another frenzy and my ass would literally pay.)

I cleared my throat and tore my eyes from the amazing naked Annette. "Ja, this was good, I think. Maybe you can spin a bit more and let the panties drop slower next time. Then when you bend, pretend to pick up your clothes, but do this with a bend of your knees, ja? This would give a much better view of what you wish to sell to your Dominant." I took a deep breath feeling extremely hot and faint while I gave this advice (that was beyond self-serving I admit).

Annette nodded, "Ja, I see what you say. You mean like this?" She turned and then bent down from her knees which automatically spread her bottom wide allowing a full view of her, uhm, potential.

I gasped and slipped while trying to put my weight on one of my arms (for support ja, not to tilt just a bit for a better view mind you), "Uhm, ja, that is perfect. Can someone crack the door and let some air in here? Why the fuck is it so stuffy? All I was saying was this was perfect, Annette. Do this and you are sure to be ravished by your lover." I grabbed my collar and pulled it out feeling it had somehow shrunk in the laundry.

Annette giggled with glee at her "passing grade" while grabbed her clothing. I tried to get myself more comfortable on my perch with much fidgeting and anxiety. It took all I had not to watch Annette putting her skirt back on. I wanted her bad.

The next trainee pranced about stripping and then the next in short order. I found with each unveiling of their gorgeous woman parts my shirt collar and cuffs seemed to shrink. It was getting very hard to take breathes thanks to the stagnant air in that damned room. I was obviously getting very turned on, but my cock was dead in his nest with no response mercifully.

My greedy eyes recorded each soft angle, curve, and fold of the beauties that danced for me in seduction. I knew masturbation material was not going to be a problem for a long time thanks to this private show.

I never looked away for a moment, nor forgot my role as the dutiful seduction trainer. I offered pointers (all designed to get me more of what I wanted, a good look), and constructive criticisms of their moves. I even got up at one point to demonstrate a better way to look behind at your lover wantonly without turning completely around.

At last, it was my gorgeous Geraldine's turn. As that beauty pranced my heart followed her steps with perfect balance. Her skirt dropped, then the shirt flew off and my eyes almost imploded with joy at what they scanned.

This time I did fall off the counter when in almost a single smooth movement she was able to expose her triangle of pleasure along with her large, perfect breasts. The girls all began chuckling at my "clumsiness." I got off the floor acting as if I were irritated.

"Fuck, what is so damned funny? This counter is killing my ass. I try to get more comfortable, and this slick surface sends me to a spill. " I growled out trying to cover for my dark thoughts that sent me spiraling to that gorgeous girl's feet.

I could see in the coy eyes and cat grin of Geraldine she was not buying my act. "Well get up ten. I need help here and you choose to play on the floor? You can see nothing from down there. I want my pointers like the other girls got, Mad Max."

I got up with vigor suddenly full of rage. "I will give you a pointer, Geraldine. Stop talking to me like you are my better. Do I need to slap you down? Make you suck my cock? That would shut your mouth then, ja. You are a trainee. I am Mad Max the Brutal. You forget yourself."

Her eyes lit with fire at my words, "Ja. I suppose you are correct. I thought you were better, but I see you are not. You are like all the other around here. Just a bully."

I felt my weird fire growing even higher. "Well, then we see eye to eye at last. I think this show is over. You are all capable of playing the whore your Master's want you to be. Soon enough they will take your favors with great pleasure until they can find a fresh conquest. Then you can serve without the bother of any further lust interest, nor the joy of true love. No one can love a whore, ja? What a fine life you have awaiting you on your knees till they desire your lips no more," I growled out in fury.

The girls all looked at each other in fear, and a few began to tear up from the cruel reality of my awful words. An uncomfortable silence fell over them. Geraldine

8

glared at me while watching the sniffing and wiping of eyes all around us.

"You happy now? They call you Mad Max the Brutal, and you know what? They are wrong. You are Mad Max the Cold Bastard. I cannot believe any of us thought you were our friend. At least the straight boys just fuck our bodies. You, cruel sonofabitch that you are, fuck our minds. You are just an angry little gay boy. Go dress in our clothes and pretend you are one of us. I would think you of all people could understand our pain and try to help us avoid such a thing as being nothing but a hole. Nein, instead you come in here and take out your anger on us as if we made your life the hell it is. Who the hell do you think you are," Geraldine yelled out full of her own furies.

I was suddenly thrown from myself hard into the wall. I watched while the seductive Max took over and a calm fell over our face. "First to answer the question you asked: I don't know who I am Geraldine. This living in the world of a gay man, but in the company with the females that I do not understand nor want to, well I apologize for my coarse behavior just now. This was the most unbecoming of anyone to be so ugly to such rare beauties. I do believe you are correct my love. I am just jealous that I am nothing when compared to the natural phenomenon all you are. Try as he might Mad Max cannot be half the seductress that even the least experienced of you are thanks to the advancements that

9

mother nature granted the woman. I beg you all for forgiveness that I surely don't deserve for that outburst driven by the foul demon envy." He bowed his head most gentlemanly to the disrupted trainees.

Geraldine's expression softened as did those of the other trainees at his most clever words, "Oh, well, ja that makes much sense. I never thought of this. Our showing off our gifts that we were born with must cause much frustration in you. I suppose we asked to much by our display?"

That suave boy walked over and took Geraldine's hands into his and lightly kissed her knuckles smiling with pure evil in his eyes. "Watching you gorgeous creatures is pure torture to my tormented soul indeed. Do understand, I am only human. I can feel the green-eyed monster too. I thank all of you for your patience with this unworthy instructor of yours. Ladies do remember, we are all in competition for the affections of the same gender, ja? It is tough to be in the enemy camp and view your arsenal which is so much more appealing than my own. You will put me out of business in no time, ja," he chuckled with humor as the girls all joined him in a relief sounding round of laughter.

I stood there, my mouth on the floor in shock and confusion. What happened to me? Why did I suddenly feel so angry at Geraldine? I was laughed at all the time, which was no reason for my temper to burn hot like that.

I leaned into the wall watching this seductive Max wondering what would have occurred had he not knocked me out of command like that. I hated to admit it, but I briefly wanted to, oh my God. I wanted to kill all the girls and I was going to do it too.

The world started spinning out of control as I began to lose my bearings. I watched myself staggering with sweat breaking out of my brow. The seductive Max flashed me a look of terror. He was being affected by my moment of intense confusion and inner terror.

The trainees came running at him as he began to fall backward in a full-on faint. They caught me before I hit the floor and dragged my nearly unconscious self to the counter. Annette and another girl turned on the facet and began to throw freezing water in my face.

I opened my eyes back in control. I looked up into the worried pools of Geraldine's beautiful eyes. I smiled at her weakly. "I guess your beauty knocked me off my feet, ja?"

She chuckled, "Looks like it. Well than I suppose I passed this lesson?"

I nodded with a bit of humor while slowly regaining my intelligence. "Ja. You all did a splendid job. Now I suppose there is nothing to do while Abelard finishes my

11

laundry service. Shall we paint each other's toenails and gossip like regular girls," I chuckled at that cliché remark.

Annette pushed herself forward in the crowd, "Nein, I say we have time for one more lesson. Some can start this and next week the rest can go. I don't know how much longer you will tolerate this burden of teaching us, Mad Max. I need help bad with the tolerating of touching in the oral sex."

That caught my attention. "Huh? Wait, uhm, I cannot have any of you trying the oral sex, uhm, I have to keep one virginity for the collar selection." She interrupted me.

"Not for you, Mad Max. For us girls. We need to not flinch and learn the orgasm through oral sex too, silly. It is not a virginity for us but required none the less." She crossed her arms stomping in anger as was common with her.

Geraldine shot me a look of apology, then said, "Annette, you go too far. Mad Max does not want to put his mouth on your nasty pussy. He is gay anyway. What the fuck would he even know about such a thing. I swear you are hell bent to run Mad Max off."

Annette glared at Geraldine. "That is not fair. I heard from my instructor that blow jobs and the oral sex with

12

females is similar. Besides, Robert told me that he was in the Dominant program years ago but dropped out. He said that all the trainees must be able to provide such a pleasure to both genders. Mad Max already has this training. Right Mad Max? This is the truth. Tell Geraldine."

I sat there slowly recovering from that weird experience of being tossed out of myself, listening while a verbal fight broke out among the trainees. Some were for asking me to do this favor, and others worried I would leave and never come back if they dared to insist.

I was unsure if I should feel super lucky or super scared. I had heard this was indeed a truth in the program, but so far, my Master kept me away from the females. I had no experience with such a pleasure (hell I had just seen a vagina for the first time only that hour.) I had plenty with the male version of the oral sex so how hard could it be?

I thought about the rumored sameness of pleasuring the intimate areas with a mouth (forgetting my earlier overblown anger, sexual interest, and anger nor fear can exist at the same time, remember that Meine Liebe) while listening to the girls argue.

After a few moments, I decided, what the hell, why not? I was more than happy to finally touch one of those gorgeous creatures (especially on their sex organs) with anything they would let me touch them width. They say the girls could receive this service without risking being soiled and it would bring them pleasure. That sounded good to me.

I also risked nothing. I no longer was considered to have the oral sex virginity thanks to my Master's rape during his collaring. The way I saw this, it would either be a glorious experience or an epic failure. Hell year, sign Maximillian up for that (Master Maxx laughed hard at that statement that made me flinch it was so loud and sudden.)

I cleared my throat politely. "Uhm, it is okay Geraldine. I will do this for all of you. Annette is correct. It is expected for the program. Like it or not, I have to do this anyway and become vastly experienced at bringing orgasm to both genders." I looked at the floor thinking of how much I hated giving the blow job, like you ja.

Though, I do like to get them from you, hey, why are you scooting way over there. Get back over here onto my lap Meine Liebe. Where the hell were you going?

Ah, you feared I was going to want you to do one on me right now. Well, in the morning, wait, it is morning, ja? Where are you going, I ask you? Get over here and stop trying to sneak off. Sit here, now. Where are you going to run? I could catch you, then I would be angry, ja?

I should thud you for acting a fool like that. Sucking a cock is not that big a deal. Why are you hiding your head in my arm? Okay cut this out, you are trying to make me feel bad for desiring my wife? I know better. Aren't you just the lazy thing?

Maybe you rather I take you the way I can find full pleasure? Uh huh, makes that blow job look like a good deal, doesn't it?

Tell you what. Let's play a game, shall we? You interrupt my fucking story one more time Meine Liebe, and I will make you put my cock in that pretty mouth of yours. That will keep you still and quiet I bet. If you still wiggle around, then I will flip you over and give you a reason to move around so much when that ass is on fire from my lust.

Ja, I see that got your attention, didn't it? So? Story? I think for now we will keep going but I am watching you. Damned brat. You make me pay for my raising. That is my curse to have to marry you as a child.

This was not my choice you know. You do realize we are only fourteen years apart in the life span. Today this age difference looks unbelievably bad, but not so much when you are twenty and I am only thirty-four.

That fucking contract I made with your Master Peter is always the fly in the ointment you see. I know you hate being with me in such a way thanks to this horror of immaturity when this adult lust comes for you. I am doing my best to overlook the perversion of this myself. It wouldn't matter if I did keep my hands off you. Debbie's criminals care nothing for your pleasure or comfort that is for damned sure.

I am as gentle as I can be but there will be pain no matter what I do to prevent it. You should never have been brought into this horror so young, not by Russell and not by me either.

Despite my fears of eliciting your hate for my crime against you, I hope one day, you will lust for me in return the way I want you. What cost would it be to receive the honor of reserving your harsh judgment. I would desire you give my clumsiness at this intercourse with you some time. I suppose I must ask this again when you have had time to think it over, ja?

I eagerly await your full maturity. I really pray it is soon for both of our sakes, but if not, then I can do nothing but ask for your forgiveness. There is no option here. I have to train you in the special services expected of a pleasure submissive.

It is too bad that I have so little experience with the female. You can bet Master Peter will not be kind to you when he comes to call on his rights. I will have to prepare you in every way for anything foul he may try to shatter your mind. Are we not the unluckiest of pairs?

Worst of all, we don't have long. He could return at any time. Why that look of surprise? You didn't know that? Well, now you do. We get our shit together as a truthful loving D/s pair or we fail Meine Liebe. Your Master Peter didn't know I was a real Priceless. He does know you are. That will work against us. I cannot have you lying to me or yourself the way that idiot Christian did. This happens to you; you will not get as lucky as he did.

Ah, that makes you wonder. You think to yourself, what the fuck is this crazy man speaking about now. Idiot Christian and lying to myself, well we both know you are Rachel, and that shit has got to stop.

On with the story…

"Annette squealed out in joy then pulled me off the counter taking my place with much speed. I backed up to give her space while the other trainees gathered around

to watch this vulgar display of clumsy teenage heavy petting.

The beautiful blond pulled off her panties and threw both her legs onto my shoulders pulling me with much roughness while demanding I put my mouth between her legs. I felt a bit of anxiety while shooting a nervous glance around at the eager faces all awaiting my "demonstration" of this technique.

Well, the issue was, I had no idea what to do with her parts. Everything I knew how to excite was missing, nothing looked familiar at all. I sat there staring into her vagina looking every bit the fool I was.

Annette got impatient with me. "Come on Mad Max. Where is your tongue work? I am ready, I tell you. I am relaxed and ready for my orgasm." She pulled on my upper arms sighing with frustration.

I shrugged then stuck out my tongue and went for it. Well, Annette let out a squeal alright but not in pleasure. She sat up and slapped the shit out of me. That apparently wasn't what she meant when she asked for my tongue work. I thought they said it was the same for both genders. Apparently not in everything (Mad Maxx laughed hard enough to turn red, then I joined him when I at last realized where he must have stuck his tongue to piss the girl off like that.)

18

Annette was cursing me most foully over my "slip of the tongue" when Geraldine leaned down and whispered in my ear, "That part at the top, which is like the penis for a girl, ja? Treat it like the tip of a man's cock. That will shut this bitch up and get her where she wants to go."

I nodded, then went to work as if this pretty blond in the right gender was Master Peter. Geraldine was a genius.

This worked perfectly. That girl immediately stopped yelling in annoyance. Her anger became moans of pleasure, then she grabbed my head nearly smothering me in her female folds.

Well, I didn't mind that a bit. I was more than happy to find my last breath within her musky sexual embrace. I continued to thrill the girl with my experience at oral tricks the work for the man and woman. Turned out the rumors about both genders being basically the same were mostly correct. There is some fine tuning, but overall, after the third girl I had a pretty good hang of this most satisfying service.

I thought when the pleased moans of orgasm in the pretty red head I was working over rang out, I would be done for that day. I sat back still on my knees before the swooning trainee while she yelled out my praises. I was pretty proud of myself, I admit it.

After all I had managed to watch a strip show and enjoyed the taste of a few of them without breaking my cock nor soiling a one to the circuit. My physical interest still had not stirred despite my most vigorous attempts fucking those girls with my eyes and tongue. It had been a most glorious day.

All the trainees got readjusted into their clothing. Some disheveled their hair and a couple used makeup to make bruises on their eyes or faces. Everyone laughed at the fake attempts to look like they had been tortured in the cruel chains of Mad Max the Brutal. I watched them full of relief that one day, I would be enjoying my life with the female at my side. Now that I had tasted a small tip of their favors, more was all I wanted. All I had to do is break my fucking collar.

We returned together to the laundry room with more than thirty minutes left of my time limit. Abelard had been working his ass off the entire time. I found my Master's laundry clean, folded, and packed in perfect order. I hated the laundry service a great deal, so this was a most pleasant surprise. This Abelard handling a distasteful chore while I fucked the girls with my mouth was something I could get used to. Shit, being a Dominant was great.

Abelard saw me coming and dropped to a kneel trembling. "I took care of everything. I beg you Mad Max release me for this day? I come back and find you tomorrow and find a reason to keep your favor in any service that guarantees my continued good health?" He shot a fearful look at the overly dramatic limping and disheveled females returning from there "torture" with me.

I smiled with evil, "Ja, see you tomorrow, Abelard. You are lucky I am sated for this day. Who knows what the sunrise brings? You are released for now."

Abelard shuddered. "Thank you for the mercy Mad Max." He got up and ran for his packed clothes bag and hauled ass right out of there fast as his legs could carry him.

Geraldine approached me then dropped to a kneel while I watched the frightened Abelard rush out of the room. "Mad Max, I think you left something behind. I would ask you to return to retrieve it. I must go now to my Master, or I would do this thing. Forgive me I beg your mercy." She kept her gaze to the floor.

I nodded feeling a bit confused wondering what I forgot in the washroom. "Uhm, okay, ja you are forgiven and released Geraldine. I see the others and you for more torturing next Wednesday. I found this a good distraction for a minute. We see how long any of you can last at the end of my cane, ja?"

Geraldine smiled, "We will be here Mad Max. Thank you for the mercy of granting us torture without the soiling. You are most brutal but fair." She got up and left quickly as Abelard had before her.

I glanced around at the nervous eyes watching me. I decided I had horrified them enough for the day. Besides, I had some plans to make. I was not happy to be sticking around to deal with the nasty coupling with Claus, but for the gorgeous Geraldine's safety I could handle it. I had already endured as bad with the cruel Xavier. One more horror, then when that beauty was safely in Mistress Cora's clutches, I could find my own peace at last. It was a decent thing to do for the girl that had been kind enough to give me the gift of the things I thought I would never know.

I walked out of that laundry leaving my packed bag behind to seek out this "thing" I left behind in the ladies washroom. I stopped dead in my tracks when I saw the beauty Geraldine rush into the door ahead of me. She was sneaking in there after telling everyone loudly she had to rush back to her Master's apartment.

Even the idiot Christian realized that the thing he forgot in the washroom was the intercourse with Geraldine. I reached into my pocket and grabbed that hex wrench smiling with glee. I was going to fuck that girl. I no longer cared about things like virginity nor breaking a collar. If I would be dead by the end of the week, then I was getting laid first.

I began rushing for that bathroom door, when to my horror Mad Max and this seductive Maximillian blocked my path. I could fucking see them like they were there for real. I gasped and nearly fell in an attempt to avoid running into them. I yelped in terror at this insane sight.

Mad Max smiled his creepy grin at seductive Maximillian who smiled at me with his usual polished politeness. "Where are you going there, Christian? Not to do what you are thinking, I hope. That virginity of ours is too important to throw away for a triste. The day will come. Do you even think what such an act would do to the girl too? Shame on your Christian, always the selfish one, ja Mad Max?"

Mad Max nodded to his partner. "Indeed Maximillian. This core of ours is the brutal thing. First, he kills everyone with that nasty anger of his, now he is going to rape the poor girl. Christian, get ahold of yourself and let us handle this situation, will you? You are too full of hate and demons to be allowed to make the decisions anymore."

I glared at Maximillian. "Ah, so that is who you are. The perfect submissive just like Master Peter wanted. I should have known that. Well Maximillian, go suck your

Master's dick and Mad Max go slap around some old Elder. As for me, I am going to fuck that pretty girl and neither of you can stop me. Get the fuck out of my way."

Maximillian shook his head while Mad Max sliced the air with his cane glaring with much authority in his cold eyes. "Cannot do it, my brother. You will kill the poor girl. How many more are you going to send to the grave? You killed your father, your stepmother, Vilhem, Ryker, Ben, and Milo. Now you want to kill Geraldine. Now that is too low. I really like her, and Mad Max does too. Hell, we all do. We will defend this one from your blood lust Christian. She doesn't deserve your revenge."

I growled out sending the passing silver collar running in terror at this insane scene of me yelling at "no one." "I ill no one, you demons. You killed them. Stop blaming me for it. I am the good guy and you are the demon. You are fucking with my head."

The black collars roaming the hallway also turned tail upon hearing me wailing out. Meine Liebe, a quick bit of advice here. If you are speaking with your inner demons, do it privately. Public displays of insanity are never a good thing, ja (I nodded in agreement at that truth. If only I had actually learned it. Sheesh.)

Mad Max frowned. "You can lie to yourself all you like. We all know the truth and, Christian, so do you.

That father hurt you and you needed to be defended from the thing you became. No one heard you screaming for aid, and no one cared. Two full years all alone locked in chains in that barn with nothing but the sounds of the horses, and our father's cruel whip. Until he brought that straight razor to end our torment. They let him out of trouble, you didn't even matter to the authorities. We helped you sneak in and tie him and his wife into their bed while they slumbered. We gave you that justice, but that need for killer revenge, it got into your blood," he said while glaring at me.

I growled out full of increasing fury, "Fucking liar. That fire was an accident. I was just having a bit of stress over the cutting is all. I never meant to kill him or her or anyone. Stop messing with my head I mean it. I remember more than you think. I just lost my temper was all, it could happen to anyone."

Maximillian nodded while smiling bitterly. "Well, that hate in you fuels your murderous anger, doesn't it? If that keeps up one day you kill the innocent over a silly slight. That would not be something you could live with. So far, the ones you have killed attacked us first, but how much longer till anyone becomes victim to your overwhelming rage."

I took off my hat and threw it at Maximillian. He easily blocked it and watched it roll uselessly away. "Get out of my way. I mean it you motherfucker. I am really starting to hate all of you bastards."

Mad Max laughed out loud, "No matter how much you hate us, we will keep you alive. We will makes sure you survive. We will not allow you to kill others or take our life from us. That is why you created us in the first place. Christian, you must understand, we are not judging you. We know you don't want to be the killer full of hate that you really are. We know you are tired. This brutal reality is not something you can deal with anymore."

Maximillian nodded at that. "You can fight us all you like. We are stronger than you are now. We will beat you and throw you the fuck out. Then where will you be? Oh, and death is not the answer any of us want to hear, so stop planning that silly suicide, ja. We know what you think we don't. We cannot allow Master Peter to win. We die, he will just get another to do the evil he has planned."

I scoffed. "You think you can throw me out? Out of my own fucking house? How the fuck do you think such a thing can be? The renters throwing out the landlord. Holy shit. I am beyond insane. Call the psychiatrist. This is not happening. I just want to go the fuck home. Someone, please wake me up. I am having a nightmare," I yelled out sending all the approaching collars running for the hills.

Mad Max swung his cane demanding my silence. "We all took a vote. It is decided you need to withdraw now brother Christian. Your too dangerous to be left in control until there is less stress, ja? Trust us, we are here to keep you safe from the brutal world, and the cruel world safe from you. Each of us will handle what you cannot and keep your hands from getting any bloodier. Now step aside. This thing with Geraldine is not going to happen. We will fight you to keep her safe. Know it or not, that is what you would want if your mind were not so colored with lust and anger." He and Maximillian took each other's arm and braced for my attempt to run through their combined effort to stop me from my intentions with Geraldine.

I let out a loud wail, then rushed them head on. They squinted their eyes, lowering themselves ready to handle my force, but at the last minute I dodged around them. I pushed past them and ran through the bathroom door before either of the evil Max could stop me.

Geraldine must have heard my railing outside in the hallway. She was standing there in the entry with a look of fear and shock when I pushed my way in. My face was drenched in sweat, my hat gone and my breath shallow from panic.

She appeared stunned for a moment then opened her mouth. "Mad Max? What was all that shouting? Did you get into a fight?"

I ran to her embracing her tightly. without a word I pressed my lips to hers with all the vigor I had been holding back since my introduction into the dark world of sexual congress with another. She melted into my arms, allowing her questions and fear to drain from her mind.

The kiss grew deeper and frenzied in only moments. She moaned out when I lifted her and carried her to the countertop. I pushed her to her bottom on it and she spread her legs while I tore her underwear off without breaking our kissing.

I grimaced then groaned in agony as my lustful intent awoke my manhood with a vengeance. That metal contraption suddenly shrunk as I began my growth spurt. There was no doubt no matter how many times I had spilled my seed, Geraldine would find me capable of finding more to give to her.

She reached down to grab my interest and gasped, "The hex wrench. Get that fucking thing off. Mad Max you cannot take my favor without removing it."

I nodded, breaking free of her wanton kiss. "I have it here in my pocket. I will need help, ja? Are you sure about this Geraldine? Once we do this, neither of us can take it back as we will be soiled." I began digging through my pants wildly trembling with both pain (because of that cock cage cutting me in two) and excitement.

She moaned out, "Ben already soiled me Mad Max, I lied. We were lovers in all ways. I have no virginity at all for many months now. That is why I must kill myself if I don't get away from my Master soon. He will sell me to the circuit when he finds out. You will save me, and I owe this to you for it." She began kissing my chest.

I suddenly awoke from my dream of lust. "What? You tell me the there is no virginity that you possess? You would let me soil my chances for freedom but give me nothing in return? Wait a second. You are an honorable submissive, ja? Equal service for equal service, but this is not a fair trade, is it? I take all the risks. Who put you up to this? A stollen hex wrench my ass." Anger began to burn in my chest with a fury I pushed myself away from Geraldine.

Geraldine sat up with a sudden look of hate. "You bastard. I know you got Ben tarnished. All of us trainees have hated you since the dungeons, you dumbass, priceless prick, not worth a shit if you ask me. Bet you didn't know I am the one that put Ryker up to that dress joke to make a fool out of you. Ben, and all of us, enjoyed your stupidity. Then I find out you ruined my lover by telling your master about his fighting you. You had that coming, asshole. Daring to insult him in front of everyone like you did. I wish he had killed you instead of killing himself. My revenge is taking your freedom from you, Mad Max. To sweeten my pleasure, Mistress Cora promised me if I was able to soil you, she would purchase me. I will see you rot in that collar. I am going to tell everyone you raped me even if you never lay a finger on me. Might as well do the crime because you sure as shit are going to do the time. You are one stupid sonofabitch. You feel right into my trap without me even working hard. Don't look so sad, Mad Max. I will think of you fondly all my life because I know you will have to take it like a woman all your days. Now come take the only pussy you will ever get. Then you can get back to sucking cock like a good little gay boy." She pointed at her exposed female parts.

I grimaced at my stupidity. It was time for me to face the brutal truth. I, Christian, am the monster, not the other Max boys. They were my shield to protect me from those that want to try to harm me, and to save me from my willingness to kill all of them.

Another thing the Maxes were right about, I couldn't be trusted to run my show because of that nasty temper of mine, Meine Liebe. It is downright murderous.

Oh well, bye-bye Geraldine.

I rushed to the vengeful girl with that hex wrench in my hands. Before she could say another word, I grabbed the sides of her mouth and forced it open. I then shoved that metal tool down her throat and let her go.

"Here Geraldine. I was right in the first place to refuse your most generous offer. Ben gave this to you; he wanted you to have it. Wouldn't be right for me to take the gift that represents his true love. Now, you two can be together for all time, like you promised each other, ja?" I backed away as she fell to the floor, her eyes filled with terror as she began to choke.

I watched as she grabbed her neck and tried reaching down her throat gasping and clawing for air that would not come. For several moments she gasped, gurgled, and struggled wildly. I didn't move nor take my cold, murderous eyes off that cruel bitch.

I realized at last, she was no better than Ben, Ryker, Vilhelm, Milo or anyone in that Haus. All of them wanted to use me to get what they desired. They all deserved to die. Especially, that boy staring at his reflection without sympathy for the dying Geraldine.

Felix came through the door just as the pretty trainee took her last breath. He gasped and ran to her trying helplessly to revive the dead girl. He shot a look of horror at me.

"You did this? What the hell Maximillian. Why?" He shook Geraldine's limp frame.

I smiled at him full of demons. "I grew tired of the sound of her screams, Felix. They no longer brought me pleasure. I told you I am a man of mercy. I give her the freedom she deserved and a tree in the orchard shall be something to remember her by." Mad Max and Maximillian walked over to join me.

Mad Max frowned. "Now you leave Christian, or we make you leave. This shit must stop. That girl didn't deserve this, and you know it."

Maximillian nodded, "Ja, this was a waste. She was so pretty and young. Damn you Christian. Plus, you lost that hex wrench. What a fool. We could have gotten out with that thing…at least for a moment."

I grinned wider, still glaring with insanity at Felix. "Now boys, calm down will you. I got this under control. Felix is going to keep his mouth shut or he will find a tree next to pretty Geraldine, ja? Speak up brute, I am worn out from my busy day. Torturing girls and killing backstabbers is arduous work. This thing, she works for Cora, great work catching that rat black collar with eyes and ears in the wall. I wonder if Master Peter will find you so useful when he finds out this plan almost went down, ruining his well laid strategy in moments."

Felix dropped the dead girls head as if she burned his hands. "What? Nein. This is a clear case of your breaking vows of monogamy again and stupidly losing your virginity fool. Now you will never break that fucking collar."

I shook my head still grinning. "Nein. Please check that the device is still in place, Felix. I couldn't soil this girl nor break my vows with her in any way. Lift her skirt and check for yourself. She lacks the tools to release my own, nor to do any penetrating. I break no vows. I suppose Mistress Cora forgot about the chastity device. This cold bitch was willing to claim rape even though I could prove otherwise, why bother with the gossiping? That couldn't be good for my Master nor his trusty inside source of information."

Felix groaned, "Ja. I hate to say this, but you have a point. Still let me see the chastity device with my own eyes in case this gets out somehow. I need to be able to claim with honor nothing happened here other than a bitch found her peace. Oh shit, why did she do this?"

I chuckled full of evil. "That is fine. I show you my tethered cock you pervert. Then you check that girl's virginity. It is not there, I fear. She is but a trainee and already fully soiled. That dishonor gets a girl put to the circuit, ja? Good enough reason to feed the orchard." I undid my trousers and showed Felix the device was indeed locked tightly, with that key hidden deep in the stomach of a dead girl. She was telling lies no more.

Felix stuck his fingers into Geraldine's corpse making a face of disgust. Then his eyes went with in shock. "Shit, just as you say. This girl is very seasoned. Oh, my God, Mistress Cora sent this creature? Why would the girl do this for her?"

I scoffed. "Was the fine Mistress's stable collar that took this girl and stole her from her Master. She was trying to hide this crime from being likely discovered. If I raped her, then Mistress Cora would never have to pay for the lost collar price, and the girl would be sold as a Haus slave since it wasn't her fault. If her story were a truth then I would be put to seed normally, but with this fake priceless collar, locked in chains and passed around the Haus like a whore. This about right, Felix? What I cannot figure out is how this conspiracy escaped your watchful eyes. Getting lazy, are you?"

The one-eyed collar growled, "Fuck you, Maximillian. I cannot watch everyone. I thought with Ben gone, well you had nothing to worry about with Cora. Looks like she wasn't through with you though. How can I tell the minds of others?"

I smiled at that. "You seem able just fine until lately. Oh well, this rodent snuck under the fence but never reached the garden. No harm done, ja? We better get out of here before someone sees us with the recently suicidal Geraldine. She told everyone she went home. I made a big scene in the hallway, so everyone ran away. No one saw this, not even you or me."

Felix nodded then followed me out. Neither of us looked back after leaving Geraldine, my first love, dead there on the bathroom floor. Just like every other thing I ever wanted in this life, a nightmare come to truth.

I grabbed the laundry bag while Felix watched around us to make sure everyone was still spooked enough to stay away. We took off down the hallway together when I was roughly pushed out of myself by the Mad Max.

He glared at the one-eyed collar with coldness. "You need to get the fuck away from me Felix. This will cause the tongues to wag. This we don't need, get." Felix peeled off cleanly but moved only a pace or two away and stood there watching us head for the stairs.

Then suddenly Mad Max stopped, dropped the bag glaring at Olaf and Vilber with hate. "I see no one around Olaf. Maybe your mouth writes a check your cock cannot sign? Here I am lover boy." He turned around and shook his ass at the immediately fuming door guard.

"You little sonofabitch. I will show you how a grown man can fuck." He came running at Mad Max.

That evil boy dashed up the stairs making sure to allow Olaf to capture him just at the top of them. I watched in horror as Olaf backhanded Mad Max knocking him to the floor nearly out of his mind from the blow.

Olaf stood over the prone boy undoing his pants. "First I will make you suck my dick then I fuck you Mad Max. Priceless my ass." Vilber let out a jell of fear.

"Olaf, stop this insanity. You touch that boy and they will put you and him into the orchard. Are you ready to die, fool? For what? A piece of ass?" Vilber came running up the stairs to try to restrain Olaf who was already rolling the groaning Mad Max over to his back for his lustful attempt.

Felix saw this assault from his hidden place and came running alongside Vilber to aid in pulling Olaf off Mad Max. They both reached the brute just as he dropped to a kneel grabbing Mad Max by the back of the head to force his cock in his mouth.

"Get off him, Olaf. Now," Felix yelled out while frantically breaking the doorman's grip on the evil boy's head.

Olaf turned and struck Felix in the face. Felix began to stagger at the top of the steps. I rushed up to and flung Mad Max clear. With a smooth movement I reached out and grabbed the back of Felix's boot and pulled it towards me with all my strength. This was just enough force to trip the confused black collar. He let out a scream as his feet went out from under him.

His neck broke by the second step on the way down ending his horrid wailing for mercy. The sound of his falling down that staircase was like someone hitting a watermelon with a hammer. Loud, hollow, and cloddish. When he finally came to his rest at the bottom, the one-eyed collar was no more. Bye-bye Felix. I know you were behind Geraldine and Mistress Cora, you fucker.

Olaf and Vilber held still in stunned silence looking down the stairs at their dead brother collar.

I giggled wildly then said, "Oops, someone had a little spill there. Don't let that spoil the party boys. I am still here Olaf. Ready to teach me that lesson or did you find your satisfaction in being a pupil in the class of don't fuck with Mad Max 101?"

Vilber shot me a look of shock. "You killed him. You tripped Felix and the man is dead, but you sit here laughing? I told you this is a demon Olaf. Let's get the fuck out of here. I value my life. This thing if full of things from somewhere hot I think."

Master Peter had heard all the racket outside his door. He had been napping so he missed the main show but showed up for a possible encore if Olaf insisted on pushing me that way. Mad Max stood above me looking down shaking his head while clicking his tongue just as Master Peter came running out into the hallway.

"Christian? as that necessary? You killed Felix before we had a chance to question the bastard. Damn, two in less than an hour. Aren't you tired? I know we had to kill him before tomorrow at one, but could you pace yourself here? I worry that you will get too accustomed to hanging out so you can murder anyone that pisses you off. What an evil thing you are. Now move over for Maximillian to clean this mess up, oh unless you wish to kill a couple dozen more. Maybe you're not done throwing your shit fit?" He shook his head in frustration at me.

Maximillian walked up next to Mad Max. "Fuck, another one. God damn it, Christian. Felix? Really? Where the hell were you when this happened, Mad Max? I thought you had this in hand."

Mad Max shrugged, "I was looking for my hat, get over it Maximillian. This killing we agreed on remember. That rat would have told on the affair with Claus and we all voted or, where were you? Off trying to fuck someone when this happened, whore?"

Maximillian stuck his nose in the air. "Shut up psychopath. Move over Christian. Let me handle this shit. Glad you found you hat. Keeping up with our perverse fashion is way more important than that cocksucker that fell down the stairs." He pushed me out of his way, sending me rolling across the floor from his force.

I finally stopped then looked at Mad Max giggling, "Is he always so bitchy?"

Mad Max shrugged. "Gay, you know. They can be so fucking prissy and touchy. Hey, what was it like getting to touch the girls so intimately? I bet it was heavenly. You can tell me. What did day taste like?"

I nodded. "Sure as the fuck was. Best thing I ever tasted. Kind of gamey but I like the flavor of the wilderness you know?"

Mad Max rolled his eyes. "Christian, you are insane, but I thank God for it or I would be no more, ja?"

Maximillian glared at us. "Shut up. I am working here."

That sudden outburst caused the stunned Master Peter, Olaf and Vilber to snap their gaze at Maximillian still laying there on the floor next to a kneeling Olaf.

Master Peter appeared terribly upset. Did that fool really love Felix? No way. "What happened here? Speak up Olaf, Vilber. I call the fucking guard right now if someone doesn't tell me why the fuck my Felix is lying dead at the bottom of this fucking staircase."

Maximillian shot me and Mad Max a look of irritation then gasped dramatically (Mad Max was right, what a queen), "Oh Master. Thank God Olaf and Vilber got here in time. Felix went mad. He attacked me at the top of the stairs saying he was going to kill me. He said he was the only one for you and I was in the way. I struggled and he hit me, see this bruise on my face (he shot a look of caution at Olaf who had rapidly caste his eyes to the floor.) Olaf and Vilber pulled him off, but he tripped trying to swing at them. It was an accident, but one of Felix's caused Master. Please I beg mercy for Olaf and Vilber. They are my heroes. I dare not think what would have become of me had they not come running to aid my desperate struggle."

I looked over at Mad Max who made a stroking motion with his fist and rolled his eyes at that bullshit acting job by Maximillian. I had to agree, really? No way Master Peter would buy that story. Besides, Olaf and Vilber hated me. They surely would report the truth and get me whipped or worse.

Instead, Olaf nodded, "Ja. Maximillian reports the truth, Peter. Felix was screaming that stuff. Vilber and I come to protect your Priceless collar. He was swinging at Vilber while I was here to see if Maximillian was gravely injured. I saw Felix trip with my own eyes. It is a tragic accident of his own fault."

Vilber looked at the floor sniffing back tears (pretend tears, by the way). "This is what happened, Peter. Our brother was mad with jealousy. He often spoke in whispers of his obsession with you. I suppose the madness of watching your happiness with Maximillian got to him at last."

I couldn't believe my ears. The door Guards that hated me were siding with me. They could have gotten me in a shit storm but instead picked the side that was about to win. There was no doubt at last that the two of them realized I was a true Priceless and not one to fuck with. Good thing too. I was ready to send two more to the bottom of the stairs, maybe three if any one of them fucked with me.

Master Peter dropped to his knees next to Maximillian who was groaning, feigning injury, "Oh, my love. Did this brute harm you? This is horrible. I cannot trust

41

anyone. Every fucking person in this Haus is trying to fuck you or me over. What the hell am I to do."

Maximillian smiled with mischief. "Well Master, it is not my place to say but Olaf and Vilber should be rewarded for saving my life. This is a great service and incredible loyalty they showed toward your glorious power. They can surely be hired in Felix's place to offer me personal security. just until, well I am done with my training and collar selection, ja?"

I shot a look of horror at Mad Max. "Is he fucking joking? Get the fuck out Maximillian. You are a fool." I ran to push him out of the way, but Mad Max caught me and held me even though I was kicking to break free of his grip.

"Stop this struggling, Christian. Maximillian knows what he is doing. I told you to trust us or so help me God I will toss your ass myself." He pushed me back hard into the banister.

I watched in disbelief, as did Vilber and Olaf, when my Master nodded. "This is a great recommendation, my love. You need protection and I need loyal black collars. Olaf, Vilber, what do you say? This honorable position comes with the benefits of eating in the Great Hall, access to the single men and women of your class, and of course extra income. The work is sometimes long but the

42

compensation is better than even Xavier granted either of you."

Vilber looked at Olaf unable to respond. "Ja, we would be indeed honored to accept this lofty position, Peter. Though we are unsure we are worthy of your favor," said Olaf while shooting me a look of extreme confusion.

Master Peter chuckled. "You can thank your champion, Maximillan, for pointing out your qualities. I will leave him in your gentle care for the next years until he makes it to the collar selection. Come by in a few hours for your oath of loyalty to me and vow of secrecy to my Home. For now, I need to take my collar inside and clean up his wounds. I thank you again for saving him from that unworthy worm Felix. Call the Guard and have that trash removed to the orchard. I want it out of my sight." My Master offered his hand to Maximillian who took it, appearing grateful while he shot a look of triumph at the door guards.

I watched the two Guards walk down the stairs to take the one-eyed black collar to fertilize the tree; I warned him I would find him. I was shocked at this turn of events when I heard a voice behind me, "Well, that was some weird shit, Mad Max. What did I miss? I got stuck working on the knots we will need to escape when Barnum leashes us." I turned around to face jet another Max.

This was the one I saw tie the elaborate knots that suspended the dead Milo and tied my father and his wife, while they slumbered, to their bed just before I lit it on fire.

He was wearing the same outfit as the rest of us, but around his clothes were chains of many lengths and widths. His wrists were tied with rope that had been severed, and a ball gag hung around his neck just below his collar and leash. I realized with horror this creature was the bonded Christian from the barn.

He was one of the oldest of the Maxes and could escape from locks, knots, and chains plus he could tie them well too. Years of nothing else to do taught this tough shard the skills of freedom from restraints of any kind.

I stuttered, "You, uhm, there was an accident or two."

This boy giggled. "Ah, Mad Max, I thought we agreed Christian gets no more time in control. Let me guess, Felix and who else? Leo? Agnete? Oh, I know, wait, no there is that Olaf, then who?" He watched Olaf and Vilber hauling the limp Felix off while slowly nosey silver and black collars began to fill the hallway one again.

Mad Max growled, "Fuck it was that fine girl, Geraldine. Can you believe that shit? What a waste."

The boy frowned "Oh hell, I wanted to fuck that girl. Why her Christian? I thought you liked her. I know I sure did."

I nodded. "Well, turned out she didn't like me, uhm, who are you again. I forgot."

He laughed out loud. "Ah, why I am Goldene Hund, Christian. Did Felix or Geraldine hit you in the head? How do you forget your oldest friend? I been with you for all these years and keep the boogeyman away, but still, you never learn my fucking name? Would hurt my feelings if I had any." That made him and Mad Max howl with laughter.

I looked down at the drop to the floor from the banister. "Oh ja, I recall you now. I suppose that one loses some memories from the confusion madness causes, ja? Did you by chance vote too to keep me from controlling my own life, old friend?"

He kept giggling but nodded. "Ja. It is time for you to go to sleep and let us handle this mess we are in. You cannot stop killing everyone or trying to kill yourself. You keep splitting us up too. This keeps up, well, schizophrenia hell for all of us. Christian you are too dangerous with all that hate and anger you carry. You never would let anyone help you with it, now it become you. It is nothing personal. For the record, I think your awesome."

I nodded at Mad Max and him, then ran like the wind knocking Maximillian right out onto the floor, taking possession of myself with all the strength I could muster. I gasped as the air filled my lungs and the nothing faded into the warmth of living flesh around me.

I grabbed my Master Peter with sudden viciousness staring into his eyes with insanity behind my own. "Master hurry, call the doctor. I am going insane. Help me, they are coming. If you don't help me, they plan to take me hostage and I will be no more. Don't let them get me."

Master Peter's eyes went wide in terror. "Maximillian? What the fuck? My love, you are babbling. Come inside. I think it is all this stress. I think Felix hit you too hard. You just need to lay down for rest."

I groaned as I saw the Mad Maxes smiling, gathering up in force like a huge pack of wolves. They were coming at last to take control away from the angry, murderous Christian.

I wailed out in terror at the sight of the dozens of personalities I had created in an effort to avoid the cruel realities I never had the guts to face. "Oh shit, there are too many of them. I am fucking doomed. I got to get the fuck out of here." I tore from Master Peter's embrace and took off down the stairs fast as the wind.

I understood at last I had always been fleeing from the most deadly an enemy anyone could be cursed to have, namely myself.

Chapter 21:

Max-A-Million

"I ran down the steps with the Max's in pursuit of me. I glanced back to see Master Peter yelling for Olaf and Vilber to "catch his collar" that without a doubt he believed had gone mad. I took off down that hallway knowing just what had to be done. This Mad Maxx thing had to be destroyed.

Olaf and Vilber dropped the dead Felix and took off after me. I waited till they were too far from the door to turn back. Then I made a turn, took a deep breath, and then took off full speed. I was heading right into my pursuers all of them. No one expected this shit.

I let out an insane wail which stopped Olaf and Vilber in their tracks. I pushed past the terrified men while they tried without success to grab my wiry ass as I flew by them. I braced myself for the collision with the Maxes gathered together behind the big brutes Olaf and Vilber. I could see they were ready to capture what those two could not.

They were out of luck too. I smashed through them. I gasped in horror when I saw the "personalities" I smacked into shattered from the force of my busting through the barrier they were trying to create. All the Max's began to wail with me at the loss of their brothers that lay in pieces all over that floor.

I couldn't believe this insane shit I was seeing. Oh Meine Liebe, I knew right there and then I was hopelessly mad. It was clear the end of Christian had come. I couldn't allow the Guard to come take me away to wherever they sent the ones that lost their minds. If this wasn't proof that I was gone then I couldn't think of anything else that could prove such horror.

I didn't stop my wild flight. I poured on the speed headed right for the door of the Haus, that for the moment was unguarded. I heard Master Peter screaming from the top of the stairs when he realized what I was planning to do.

"God dammit. Stop him Olaf and Vilber. The boy is headed out to his death. Someone call the Guard. Tell them Peter says don't shoot his collar. He is coming out the front door. He is ill and doesn't know what he is doing. This is a horror. Please, someone catch him before it is too late. Fuck me," my Master yelled out sounding beyond panicked as he watched this show, helpless to stop my progress toward sure death.

Even he knew it was too late to stop the bullets that would be ringing out in only seconds when I see the sun in my face at last. I was committing suicide by doing the one thing forbidden all collars no matter their status. I was trying to escape the Haus.

I hit that big wooden door with all my strength. It felt so good when it opened, and the bright sun blasted into my eyes. At that moment I felt like a miner that just come from the darkness of his world After many hours of hard labor. I covered my face with my arm to protect my unseasoned vision from the blinding glare.

I didn't hesitate to stride right out of the entry of the Haus's front door into the warmth of the daylight. I was immediately silenced my wailing by my awe of a world I forgot even existed. It was truth I had seen it briefly during the fire but had not been able to appreciate such a thing that day.

I stopped in my tracks. I kept my face covered, unable to tolerate the strong natural light. I stood there marveling at the forbidden sights of green grass, the blue skies, and the smell of the living After so many years locked away from it, just as the first bullet screamed past my head.

I smiled with thrill when I heard another one impact the earth just in front of my feet. Then another flew by grazing my velvet jacket. I flinched slightly when I felt the heat of its deadly speed burning the material into my skin. I wondered why these idiots were such bad shots. Three bullets went by, and I was still among the living.

Then another bullet came flying. This one hit me on my left upper thigh. I let out a scream from the sudden agony that was both burning and sharp. I grabbed my wounded leg and fell to my knees. I heard the killing bullet miss me. It would have made connection with my head. Thanks to my taking a painful kneel, it passed just seconds too late to end my torment.

I was panting out in pain and sweating from the heat of the sun roasting my light sensitive skin there on the ground when a shadow came over my kneeling form. I thought with some interest that the clouds covered the blinding sun. Then the shadow put all its weight on me crushing me flat to the earth below.

I heard a voice say. "Hold still. They will not shoot you long as I am with you. Do not struggle nor stray and I will get you out of this nightmare. Stay with me Maximillian this I command." I felt this shadow grab my upper arm and lift me to my feet with much strength.

I could see nothing thanks to the years of haunting the dimly lit hallways and dungeon cells. If it had been overcast or I had thought of grabbing a pair of *sunglasses, well let's just say my plan was foiled by this stranger and the fact that I was nearly blinded by the light. (*Okay and these black collars paid to shoot escapes couldn't fucking aim to boot. Damn. How the hell could they miss? Fuck I was in black velvet, breeches with the complexion of a corpse. That is something you don't see every day. You'd think day could hit a target that obvious, ja? I nodded my head at his description chuckling at the idea that most likely it was that very reason they missed. No one knew what to make of the sight of him running out the door then stopping while looking like a teenaged Dracula. Probably stunned the shooters just enough to save him.)

*I was unable to think because of that horrid pain in my leg from the bullet. My rescuer dragged me along with him. I narrowed my eyes and tried to look at him (*I knew it was a male by the voice or perhaps a female with your problem maybe. He laughed at that, not funny.) *I could tell he was tall, strong and could make out his hair was long like the females.*

I could not distinguish more of this stranger before my stomach began to lurch. The world was spinning. I looked down at my leg to see blood pouring from the wound down my stockings into my shoe. The pool of my fluid was making a squishy noise with each step I took. This made me even more faint.

The terrible bright light suddenly was removed as the two of us went through the door. Olaf and Vilber grabbed my arms snatching me away from this man with much rigor. Master Peter was there too, looking into my face with much anxiety.

I felt confused and unsure of the sights or sensations all around me. I thought maybe the bullet in my leg and loss of blood had made my mind dull. I felt myself lifted off my feet and being carried but I was unsure who was doing this. I heard much commotion all around, the sounds of many voices, whispers, and my Master's shouting at someone.

Then suddenly I was floating away from the pain, rising above the boy I possessed. Mad Max grabbed me and pulled me from my position above myself. He glared at me angrily.

"You near got us killed, Christian. This is over. Der Goldene Hund says you are to be bonded for this disruption. I pray it is not too late. Maximillian goes to suffer the agony you caused fool. I for one will not miss you," Mad Max said with much anger in his tone.

I shook my head feeling very confused. "Der Goldene Hund would not do that. I am his best friend Mad Max. You lie."

53

"You are my best friend Christian and always will be. You did me much honest service, but the time has come. This brutality is twisting you up. You can no longer tolerate the job I created you for. I apologize my dearest friend. I should have made more to help with the pain sooner. I was just a kid. Now I see the error of this. Forgive me. I will release you when this task of freedom is achieved. I thank you for taking the burdens that I could not. The stress and pain of this horror life we live has filled you with hate without direction. It has colored your vision of all things my friend, made your memory weak. I should have step in the second I realized you had forgotten that you are but a copy of the original Christian. You have become the shard of impulsivity, lust, and anger. This endangers us when allowed to run untethered. I have come to chain you down and hopeful it is not too late to save me." I turned to face the bonded boy known to us all as Der Goldene Hund the real Christian Axel.*

He smiled at me with loving bitterness in his expression. My memory of the way I came to be suddenly flooding over me. I saw the helpless Christian Axel hanging from the chains in our father's barn. He was crying from yet another whipping. This was many months since our mother left us in the night as she went chasing after a more exciting life. My father blamed me for her leaving him. He thought the stress of having a kid made her mad even though she had a history of disappearing suddenly long before she met and married him.

Agnette was always known as a moody woman, given to ideas of grandiosity from time to time. The woman was known to do anything of pleasure to excess. She drank too much, spent money too freely, had a lengthy list of lovers, and was always looking for the next big thrill. Her family was wealthy, so they could afford her ever-changing ideas of what could bring her happiness. The woman was often called "a maniac" when describing her ever changing obsessions.

My father had been one of her flings that managed to corner the clever Agnette. He was a man of no fortune of his own. He saw my mother as his ticket to a good life. He was happy to claim paternity to her growing belly despite the fact that he knew he was likely not the truthful sperm donor.

At the time of her discovery of pregnancy, Agnette was well known to be sporting a new lover, a man of well born status in a place called the **Das Kaiser Haus** *(I gasped loudly at that revelation realizing with horror what he was going to say next. Master Maxx smiled with wickedness and nodded.)* **He was called Peter.**

Everyone knew this Peter was the biological father of her unborn child. Agnette was put into a bad spot when this man refused to marry her when informed of the unwanted life they had created with their lustful triste. Peter saw the idea of fatherhood as hindering his rise to the top of power within the Haus.' He told Agnette to find another idiot willing to take responsibility for what he had recklessly done.

Agnette, realizing she needed a fool that was willing to do anything for a taste of the easy life she could offer him, found this idiot in Gerard. Before her belly even was swollen, she married him to cover her embarrassment.

A healthy male child was born to a mother that didn't want him and a father that had no blood interest in the baby. This neglectful situation continued until Christian's sixth year. That was when Agnette's wanderlust reappeared. She abandoned Christian to suffer the wrath of Gerard when he discovered her betrayal. She took her fortune and left him the responsibility of raising a kid that was not even his own.

In his disgust, Gerard took this "pain in his ass" to the barn on his property and chained him up away from prying eyes. He didn't want anyone to see the boy looking less like him and more like his truthful father every day.

I suddenly recalled that when I first saw Peter and Maxx I though them a father and son team. Guess I was right, yuck.

After two years of isolation, beatings and bondage, the straight razor attack came when the absent Agnette suddenly reappeared with orders to return custody of

56

Christian to her care. This order came too late to stop the "cracking" of the boy's mind from all that time of severe abuse at the hands of Gerard and his cruel new wife.

Ta pass the many hours alone without anyone to speak to in the chains, Christian spoke to himself for company. He spent many hours working on ways to break out of the knots, chains, and locks the Gerard kept putting him into. Each time he escaped the brutal Gerard would use a more secure method.

One day, Christian broke out and ran away. He was only a little boy of six and a half. He ran to the first house he could find. The old woman inside this home took the frightened boy inside and gave him a Goldene Hund stuffed toy. She told him this hound could scare away the boogeyman that made the little Kind cry like he did.

The police came and returned Christian to his father Gerard. The beatings and terror increased. Christian had hidden the stuffed toy hound in the straw and when he could escape his bounds he played with this thing, his only possession. Then one day, Gerard caught Christian with the toy.

He took this hound and tore it to pieces while Christian wept and screamed. That night in the chains the pieces of this hound come back together like magic and grew into a boy that looked just like Christian in the chains. This Christian said, the Golden Hund came to be his best friend and help him escape the boogeyman, Gerard. He knew the Christian was very tired and scared.

So, in an act of truest friendship, the Goldene Hund switched places with Christian, taking his place and pain in the chains. It became this way for the day until the attack that led to Christian's return to his mother Agnette and the ultimate revenge on Gerard for all he had done to us.

When Christian's wounds healed enough, he and Der Goldene Hund returned to Gerard's farm. We snuck in and tied him and his evil wife to their bed while they slept. When day awoke day found themselves too far bonded to escape as we finished keeping them restrained.

They cursed us, screamed, and begged. We heard nothing of their pleas for mercy, just like Gerard had taught us with his own deaf ears. Der Goldene Hund himself lit the match that set their bed alight. We smiled hand in hand while the evil couple burned alive in that bed. Then we burned down the rest of that farmhouse too, watching every second with much delight.

The police took us to the insane asylum for this criminal act, but we were only eight years old and just turned too. Thanks to that and our silence of our alliance with each other, they let us go home in one week. They told our mother it was the stress of our wounds that caused a temporary insanity. That was all. Nothing unexpected with so much abuse of that little boy, ja?

Well, Christian would not know of this true rumor until he was already in the collar of the man that could claim him for more than his submissive. A secret told to him by Ryker, and confirmed by Felix, when he discovered the identity of my mother that day just before his death.

I had forgotten, thanks to the shock of it no doubt, that he told Mad Max that if Agnette was my mother and she only had one son, he personally knew who the father was because Peter had told him. That is the real reason we had to kill him by the way, couldn't have him telling my Master I knew the truth.

I closed my eyes at the revolting realization that Master Peter was most likely the father of my Master. Not that I didn't understand the disgusting situation of a biological parent sexually abusing their own child, but really this was horrific news.

It was the stress of this horrific discovery of Master Peter's true identity the few days before Geraldine's murder and the understanding of this conspiracy that caused Christian to go amok like that (which was figured out easily when you knew who this Master really was to us.) Felix and Ryker had accidently told us why we were sold to the Haus and selected as a "fake priceless."

Our biological father, Peter, had always known we existed. He had originally denied his son to keep his kinship to me from impeding his rise in the Haus. Then, when that rise required a "Priceless's favors" to help with his ascension, Peter knew where he could get the pretty male needed for the job of seducing the all-gay Elders of the Haus. Hell, he had made the boy he had in mind for this role himself.

Master Maxx laughed bitterly while shaking his head. I will never understand the revolting nature of some human beings Meine Liebe. I know this abomination you understand with your own personal terror of it. Well, so do we. Master Maxx pretended to gag, then I mocked his behavior. He hugged me tightly while we laughed holding each other in an empathetic hug of kinship only a child/adult of sexual abuse by a biological parent could utterly understand.

It was pretty obvious what had happened. Master Peter went to my mother and talked the greedy bitch into selling the kid between them into the dungeons without revealing to anyone my true identity. Then he went to Xavier and tempted him with the promise of my favors for all his life if he would convince the other Elders to level me Priceless without any evidence of such a thing.

Xavier took the deal and I to this day still do not know how he got the others to go along with this bullshit. Likely, the old sadist scared them into it, or they actually believed it. Whatever the reason, they did, and my fate was sealed, as was theirs.

My Master got the dungeon Masters to allow me to fight them, and even encouraged it by constant and chronic isolation, beatings, and cruelty that was uncommon for the slave collars. This made me more difficult to manage than normal and turned off all potential Dominants that come to purchase a collar for their own from the new crop of potential submissives.

When the time was right I was old enough that Peter could justify the cruel consummation of a collaring on a twelve-year-old but not younger than that) my own fucking father came in and purchased my collar for his own use. He then could be sure to not only train me for this job he wanted done, but could assure my loyalty, control what I heard or didn't in rumors and hide the fact I was not really a priceless. This worked except for one tiny mistake.

I am a Priceless and was one long before the Haus come for me. Try as he might, I had managed to discover all his secrets (and mine). This meant he never intended for me to break my metal. He made this horrid contract with me only to be assured no matter what happened I was in his employ for all his natural life (okay Meine

Liebe, I may need to use your bucket for a moment, I think I am ready to vomit, you too? Ja, at least Peter is not as ugly as Debbie; still, yuck. Ja, let me go puke before you do. I ate more than you did.)

We did take a brief potty break here but to be honest the puking threat was just a joke. I snuggled back into his lap wondering if I could ask a question. He saw my looking at him with inquiry.

He smiled then kissed my nose making me giggle. "You wonder if your Master Peter knows I know, ja?"

I nodded smiling with relief that he could read my mind daI didn't want to have to listen with his dick in my mouth remember.)

Master Maxx got that look of wickedness in his steel blue eyes. "Nein, I never tell him that I know who he really is. You never tell your enemies what secrets you possess of theirs, ja? I play a game on this father of mine. I never tell him I have this mental illness they call Schizoaffective Disorder nor of my PTSD either. I even got rid of the fucking psychiatrist that wrote that shit down to try to stop me from Medical School. Fuck that guy. I didn't survive all I did to have some bastard with a degree tell them I was a fucking psychotic. I admit I am a little crazy, maybe, sometimes, but a fucking schizophrenic, no way. I also never told Peter or my mother I know of their love for each other, or that I am the result of it. I knew after I figured out this horror that Agnette was playing a game. She wasn't leaving, she was hiding out till I was done taking down the Elders for her lover. I realized the two of them were still fucking around behind everyone's back. Likely all the "walks" he was taking in the orchards were his sneaking off to sleep with Agnette. Violating their own son in the morning, then going to fuck his mother by dusk. Wow, now if that don't make you puke nothing will."

I glared at him with my mouth open at that denial that he was nuts and not schizophrenic. I wasn't nearly as nuts as Master Mad Maxx and they called me schizophrenic.

He saw my look, "Oh hell no. Don't you start with me. I put that diagnosis in your records to get you out of that fucking public school only. I said it because it almost worked to get me kicked out myself. You cannot go to that place, Meine Liebe. If they see the way you are treated or behave, they will take you away from me. Then they lock you up for having stress like your Master does. We are not schizophrenic, damn it. We are just a bit different. That is all. You know what? I think there is no such thing as madness even. I think maybe the things we see and hear just mean we have more powers of perception than others do. Who is to say we are not superhumans? Well, maybe we are. You ever think of that one?"

I smiled, feeling better that he had an explanation for the weird shit going on in my dark little world that I could live with. I nodded while letting out my breath with relief.

Thank God I was not crazy. I was really worried there for a bit. Master Mad Maxx (who is telling me a story that has the same shit going on in his mind therefore has nearly [if not] the same diagnosis) said we are just superhumans. Now that made perfect sense. I can read minds, and so could he. I can go through walls (well my shards can), fly sometimes, float above myself, live in a dream, see things no one else can and hear the electrical grid. See not crazy, enlightened (Oh boy...YIKES).

Master Maxx pulled me close and cleared his throat, "Well the good news is that we will never have cause for family reunions. I mean your HusDom's father just fucked my mother and step-father-in-law. My wife is fucked by her mother and stepfather. Your HusDom's father fucks his own son and you. That makes my head hurt. Wait, hey I just want you to know you are commanded to never fuck my mother and I won't be fucking yours either. We must draw the line in the sand somewhere in all this horror. This messed up family of ours has real problems understanding boundaries, ja?" He rolled his eyes then covered them with his hands rubbing hard in frustration.

I nodded while giggling at the insane dark humor in his sudden outburst.

He glared at me in a playful sternness. "Do you think that funny? That is fucked up is what that is. Well let's agree that our devil children never meet their grandparents, any of them. We tell the demonic horned creatures we spawned that the elders of our all died in a fire, ja?"

I smiled with diabolical joy. "Ich Hole die hot dogs. Du bringst die Streichhölzer mit. Machen wir diese Geschichte zur Wahrheit Meister." I blurted out forgetting myself. (Translation: I'll get the hot dogs. You bring the matches. Let's make this story the truth, Master.)

I began to wince; sure I was doomed when he laughed out maniacally. "Das klingt nach einem tollen plan für mich. Allerdings bratwurst mitbringen. Es schmeckt besser als hot dogs. Igitt." he kissed me on the nose making me giggle like a child. (Translation: That sounds like a great plan for me. However, bring bratwurst. It tastes better than hot dogs. Yuck.)

Master Maxx and I laughed for some time until finally he went back on with his story, which is more twisted than he is himself.

"I stood there staring at der Goldene Hund feeling bad that I had gotten so out of control like that. He had always trusted me the most of all of us and there I was nearly getting us killed. Ja, it was time for me to rest for a

bit. I knelt before him shaking almost in tears over my bad behavior of the last several days.

Der Goldene Hund put his gentle hand on my shoulder and whispered in my ear, "Look here Christian, I plan to reward rather than punish my dearest brother."

I looked up and saw the army of Max's approaching. At least fifty of these boys, all a copy of the other, came forward into a V formation. I watched in awe (as did Mad Max) while the boys on the left and right merged into each other, one after another.

This went on until only three were left. The one in the front and one boy on each side of him. That two on the left and right then merged leaving only the single Max. His eyes had been closed. When he had absorbed the very last extra Max, he opened them smiling the gentlest smile I ever seen on my face in all my life.

Der Goldene Hund smiled back while Mad Max shot a look of confusion at my kneeling self, "What is this? Fifty make one. I don't understand," yelled out Mad Max appearing upset by this strange sight.

Der Goldene Hund chuckled. "There were too many of us. I collapsed them into one Max, just Max. This boy holds all the restraint needed to guard our dear overworked Christian. He will keep the leash on him and hold our empathy, patience, love, conscience, and kindness. The two of them can keep each other in check, Mad Max. We had spread our good emotions too thin you see. That wore out Christian here. Now Max and Christian, they work together. See I give your leash to Max for the holding, and you get his in return." I was handed Max's leash while he took my own while still smiling at me with kindness.

"Tis an honor to walk with you brother. We can do much good for Der Goldene Hund and be an effective team, ja? You tell me what you want, and I will share my own desires with you. Together we find a way to get our wishes without hurting the plans of Mad Max and Maximillian, ja? This is the way, equal service for equal service. This you agree to Christian," said Max to me with a soft voice that sounded like a bird wings when they take off into the sky for flight.

I nodded with sudden understanding of the wisdom in all this, "I accept this agreement brother Max."

Mad Max rolled his eyes. "Ja, we are fucking crazy. Oh well, let's go check on Maximillian. I am sure that queen is in there pissed off we are not in there telling him how sorry we are that he suffers. You know without constant stroking that fucker get all hormonal."

Der Goldene Hund giggled. "Mad Max you are a hateful bastard. Have you seen Mad Maxx your own brother? I have been busy with a plan that includes him for Barnim…"

Mad Max interrupted him. "I saw him following Jonas After that fetish Vampiric Elder rescued us from the bullets in the yard. Mad Maxx is likely off in the chains waiting for his beating over all the terrible shit that Christian did today to be sure. I think we forget Barnim the sensual sadist for now. First contact has been made with Jonas. He cared enough to pull us to safety, so he saw us. He is within our grasp. I think we better practice biting a neck to drink blood, ja?"

All of us (including Der Goldene Hund) gagged at that. "Oh hell. That is who grabbed me and pulled me inside? This tall long haired man is the Elder Jonas," I blurted out with my typical impulse.

Der Goldene Hund nodded, still appearing a bit sickened by Mad Max's statement. "Ja Christian. Though I wouldn't call him an Elder as he just barely became one. The youngest of them at only the required age of fifty-five. He ascended earlier this year when old Rupert died remember?"

Mad Max nodded. "Of course, he don't fucking remember Der Goldene Hunt. Sonofabitch thought he was you, didn't he? Gott Verdammt this means we only have the six of us now, right? Good thing, it was getting pretty fucking crowded in our head. Hell, Maximillian was starting to scare me a bit he was crowded so close. That whore maybe would have rubbed off on me all the wrong ways if that shit kept up."

Der Goldene Hund sighed. "You sure do whine a lot for a sadist Mad Max. Make yourself useful and find that fucking other half of yours, that masochistic Mad Maxx. I tire of hearing your bitching."

Mad Max growled out while tipping his hat at Der Goldene Hund, "Well your wish is my command, Master Hund. I go now to find that pussy boy that cannot get enough of my caning." He chuckled with evil, then tore off to seek out his alternate shard Mad Maxx.

I looked at my brother Max, then toward der Goldene Hund. "What will we do about this thing, that discovery of our Master's relationship to us? How can we, this will not do." I moaned out suddenly remembering why we had tried to commit suicide in the first place (you know kin. The stressful to find out you were sold, then bought, raped, and then fucked literally by your father all this time, ja? I nodded in agreement that would indeed be a good reason to want to die. Debbie sure made me feel that way. I totally understood.)

Der Goldene Hund frowned as did Max. "Dearest Christian, this evil is neither one of our makings nor desire. The guilt of it therefore is not our own to bare. Let this go and forget it if you can. There is no shame in trying to survive. This unnatural sex with the man was a source of problems from the beginning. Other than Maximillian the pansexual of us, not another, including me is interested in the male for sex anyway. Let Maximillian handle this horror of sex with Peter. I created him for this horrible task of gay sex enforced upon us you know. He contains all the training to overlook all personal discomforts or abhorrence. Maximillian sees no color, gender, boundaries, nor relationship when it comes to providing for the pleasures of his Dominant. I made Mad Maxx take the whippings for this dishonor of the things we do to survive. Then I sharded the Mad Max to balance the scale. He keeps control of the anger caused by all this horror through well trained torturing of willing victims. Your new task is to create a list that our child Frau will need to possess in order to break her own metal. Max will help you to select her for us by being sure she is strong enough, and more than that will be better off, not worse, for the curse we bring with us. That means she will likely be in a situation worse than the one we offer her in return. That is going to be tough to find. In the meantime, we all work together to bring this Haus to its knees so that we can get out that door legally and find this Frau that will end this shameful situation our father has put us into. Then, we break the power of our Master/Father/Abuser for all time *and kill him for not wearing a damned prophylactic when he fucked our mother the day we were conceived."*

Max and I nodded at those most wise words (but how did you know I planned to kill Peter? Maybe you can read my mind, creepy little Demonseed Frau of mine. By the way, don't fucking answer that. I am already scared enough of you. I think sometimes I would have been better off to fall down the stairs myself than to collar your angry, bratty ass.)

I opened my eyes feeling groggy. I saw Mad Max standing there with Christian and someone I never saw before. They were holding each other's leashes and smiling at me. That made me feel a bit pensive. I assumed Der Goldene Hund had dealt with our little "Christian out of control" issue at last.

I felt faint from the pain medication in my system but otherwise I thought I would probably live despite fucking Christian attempting to get us killed. I had worked my ass off to come with a plan to get rid of Felix while putting Olaf and Vilber in our debt. Shit he almost fucked the up royally. What an idiot (I looked up with a start realizing that Master Max had just switched on me. His voice was a bit different. It had a higher pitch to be exact. This is some really creepy shit to watch trust me.)

Master Peter came into the room accompanied by the brute Olaf. "Ah look here. My love Maximillian is awake at last."

I groaned out realizing I had missed my appointment with Claus. "Master, how long have I been out?"

Master Peter shot a look at Olaf of worry. "Only a few hours, Maximillian. The bullet was only a flesh wound. Nothing serious was injured. You got incredibly lucky. What the hell happened? you went insane on Me, but seem okay now? How are you feeling? Anything I should be worried about?" He sat on the bed next to me stroking my cheek lovingly.

I could see Christian and Mad Max making gagging faces, but I did my best to ignore them and do my job. "I guess that Felix hit me harder than I thought. hat outburst was uncalled for Master. I beg your mercy and request punishment for it immediately. It shall not happen again."

Olaf shot a look of fear at my statement. "Peter, I normally would never speaking out in the home of a Dominant nor dare to tell him his place, but this boy just saw his old friend die after the man struck him hard enough to set off such madness as we all saw. I would beg you to show the mercy of allowing the outburst to go with only the punishment he already received of a bullet in his leg."

I nearly choked on my own spit over Olaf's attempt to save my ass from a thudding. Master Peter shot a look that at first appeared irritated but quickly softened.

"Yeah, there is wisdom in your words Olaf. I hope that you and Vilber are better at protecting my Priceless collar from his youthful stupidity in the future though. If not, then he will be joined downstairs by two black collar door guards. I let this one slide Maximillian but no more of this bullshit trying to get away. We discussed this. Break your collar honestly," Master Peter growled out full of anger.

I nodded, keeping my gaze down, grateful for both the mercy of no thudding and that I had not missed my seduction opportunity with Claus. "Understood Master. Thank you for your mercy to this unworthy boy."

Master Peter's look softened to a smile. "Ah, but you are most worthy, my love." He leaned down and engaged me in a deep passionate kiss.

I glance over to see my brother shards covering their mouths pretending to vomit at this incestuous display. I closed my eyes, so I didn't have to put up with the obvious judgement they were passing on me. I was there to do this job and I would be damned if the immature antics of those misguided shards interfered with it. Though I have to admit, now that I knew who Master Peter really was to us, I would have rather been stuck being fucked by the disgusting Leo.

Master Peter pulled back from his kissing me. "Olaf, can you go collect more ice and find a walking cane for my Maximillian? Thank you for this service." He watched the black collar rush off to mind his orders then looked back at me.

"We are alone. Tell me about this bullshit with that trainee Geraldine. I heard they found this girl dead in the washroom near the laundry. I asked around and heard she was sweet on you. They found her soiled, and I was questioned by her Master Heiner if maybe you could have done this foul deed of stealing his consummation virginity. I bet you are grateful for that cock cage now. I checked to be sure and found it still in place. I know you didn't do this criminal act, but I think you know who did. Did this girl say who soiled her to you?"

I frowned then took a deep breath feigning sadness. "I cannot lie to you Master. The dead brute Ben, of Mistress Cora, did the act. Master Heiner is owed the lost collar price by Mistress Cora. I would have told you sooner, but I only heard of it today when this trainee confessed it to me while I was doing laundry service. She left saying she was going to her Master, and I saw no more of her. I guess that is why she told me, she was, oh poor thing, she killed herself I suppose. So sad. That Ben was a real bully. Too bad he didn't end his life sooner or Master Heiner would not be without his rights and lost income."

My Master crossed his arms and narrowed his eyes suspiciously. "This is the same story I got from a trainee called Abelard too. He said he overheard this trainee tell you she was heading to her Master, and she was upset that some boy had taken her favors against her will. But she can no longer be questioned about this."

I nodded while remembering Christian catching Abelard in the hallway and ordering him to say that if anyone asked if he saw anything odd in the laundry today. Good thing Christian had enough insight to think of this cover story.

Master Peter sighed loudly as if tired. "Well, I know you pine for the affections of the female silly as that is. I suppose I can show a little mercy for this obsession you have with having the female for a penetration experience of your own. I think maybe that will lower your stress level a bit and help you focus more on seducing the Elders as you are supposed to be doing. To give you this relief I will let you see the list of Mistresses' biddings on your final virginity. That will give you something to look forward to and maybe stop this speaking to soiled trainees in public. That could have been a scandal that ended you if not for your cock cage being found intact you know. I command you never to speaking to any females in public or private from this point till I say otherwise. Not even your own damned mother. This is a directive."

I looked over to see Mad Max, Christian, and the other boys' mouths open in shock and obvious horror at that cruel directive. They certainly weren't happy to hear this shit. I was not worried. Getting to keep a tab on which beautiful Mistress would be our lover for a single leashing of all our wildest dreams would just have to be enough to sustain us for now.

I nodded. "As you wish Master. Thank you for your wisdom and mercy."

He chuckled. "Nein. I show you no mercy and this you know. I have to ask where my Maximillian is? This boy I am speaking with is too good to be the truth. He never argues, and does his job without hesitation nor complaint? Well, okay he can stay in my bed then. I think soon I will have a use for the pleasures he can grant me like no other can. For now, I let him rest though. Sleep my love. I will see you in a few hours for my rights. I need to attend to the oaths and contracts of Olaf and Vilber or I would have you right this second. Any argument over that, like maybe your leg hurts too much?"

I shook my head. "Nein Master. This leg injury is not your fault, nor does it excuse my owing you service. I will be here awaiting your pleasure at your leisure."

Master Peter's eyes went wide. "Well slap me and call me surprised. I see the perfect submissive before my old eyes jet again. Good. I say stay this time, and that is a directive. Leave the bastard Maximillian that give me headaches wherever you keep hiding him. I have finally decided I like you better. At least for now. Maybe another day I yearn for the fight but this time, I am tired of chasing you Maximillian. That understood?"

I nodded as I watched him leave to attend to the newly employed security team of Olaf and Vilber.

Mad Max spoke up, "That scene was disturbing. No wonder we are bat shit crazy, ja? How is that leg? Does it hurt much?"

I looked at that sadist bastard with irritation. "Why don't you get in here and find out for yourself, Mad Max? I am not gonna describe it for your twisted thrill. Who the fuck is this guy with Christian, and why the fuck isn't Christian like chained the hell up or something?"

Christian glared at me. "This guy is Max. He is my brother granted me by Der Goldene Hund, Maximillian. I ask you to not be rude and speaking like neither he nor I am standing right the fuck here. We can answer for ourselves you know, prissy boy."

Max pulled Christian's leash and shot him a warning look. "That was a cordial thing to say to our brother Christian. He is in pain. That makes anyone irritable, ja? Besides this trouble is of your doing I seem to recall?"

Mad Max growled out, "Enough of this banter. Are we going to be capable of this nasty coupling with Claus tomorrow or not Maximillian? How bad is that leg? Will it interfere with sealing our deal with him or not."

I sat up and groaned as the agony of that "flesh wound" near sent me to a faint. "Fuck it is pretty bad, Mad Max. I may need you or Mad Maxx to get us there. Then once the sex gets serious, I can handle it as long as you are ready to relieve me the second that old fucker cums. I cannot take this pain like you boys can."

Mad Max nodded. "Okay, I can do this for you, but be careful Maximillian. When you go to suck his cock and grab his hoddensack, don't squeeze too hard when the pain spasms come. You may grind them to dust, this bastard is so old."

Christian gasped out loud. "Damn, Mad Max. Has anyone ever told you what a twisted fuck you are? That was fucking dark."

Mad Max chuckled then looked at me smiling that creepy grin of his. "Ja, Christian. Your mother said that when Xavier was fucking me. It is okay though, because your father personally trained us to suck a cock and tolerate penetration. Your mother was of course impressed with the sexual ability she witnessed as that ancient schwuler fucked her boy. Damn, and it bothers you that maybe I am a little bit twisted? I come by it naturally. It runs in the family, dumbass. So, fuck off Christian."

I moaned in pain. "Shut up. Stop this fucking arguing like children. I have a headache. Fickin mich."

It was then that I heard the phone ring. I laid there quietly trying to listen in to discern the nature of this call. I am not sure what made me think I needed to know the identity of the caller, but something told me this was not just a "how you are doing" discussion.

I was barely able to make out my Master's voice in the next room as he said, "Jonas. What a pleasant surprise to hear from my old friend. What? Oh, ja, I was going to come see you in a few days to thank you for this kindness you showed by saving my Priceless collar. He had a bit of a spill earlier today and roughly hit his head. He was not himself. What? Oh, you would be? Well, uhm, this is kind of sudden. I had not expected, nein, of course I am willing to bargain with a man of your honorable position, but my Maximillian is in bad shape so it may need to wait more than the usual seven days if we come to an agreement. You do agree with that, well then, I am listening. I will hear what you are willing to offer then I will tell you what I hope to obtain. Ja let the negotiations begin then."

I stopped listening at this point and looked at Mad Max. "Get to Der Goldene Hund. Barnim is not next, it is this auto-vampire Jonas. Shit. I am not doing this one. I cannot stand the sight of blood. Gross! This one is the one for you Mad Max."

Mad Max shook his head appearing revolted. "Forget that bullshit, Maximillian. I am not okay with drinking any blood. I go ask Der Goldene Hund to see what he suggests. This is a bad seduction. I don't care if we do get stuck in the silver. I am not fucking doing this that the vampire wants. That is too fucked up even for me."

Christian giggled. "I can do this one. I will slit his fucking throat. Now that will surely be his desire come to truth, ja?"

I rolled my eyes. "Okay that leave out Christian too. How about you Max?"

Max shrugged. "I cannot do anything without Christian nor he without me. He wants to kill Jonas and I want to forgive him. I am not sure that is going to help seduce the vampire though?"

I groaned. "Can Der Goldene Hund do it himself maybe? Wait, I forgot, get Mad Maxx to do this one Mad Max. This should be right up his alley, ja?"

Mad Max chuckled then cut the air with his cane. "Ja. If he doesn't then I beat the fucker half to death. If he does, then I do the same. Either way he will be okay with it. Dumb bastard does like his torture. Nothing could be more self-harmful then drinking another's blood or whatever the fuck these vampire people do."

I smiled. "Good, then go see Der Hund. Have him do the research on what Mad Maxx needs to know about this seduction. I will attend Master Peter, then first thing in the morning, you take over and let's do some recon before sealing this deal with Claus. Oh, and find Abelard. I want you to hand over all our used laundry service to him. We will need that two hours to seduce our latest lover Jonas as we make him ours. This could work, I hope. Now all you go unless you wish to stick around and see the perversion with our father?" I watched all three of the shards haul asses out of that room like it was full of killer bees at those words.

That night I got through the horror that had plagued us since the day we mistakenly agreed to Master Peter's collar. It was indeed harder to endure his lust and sexual congress now that we knew of his paternity to us. I did my best to remember this was really no different than all the other horrible sex with the men. After all, we didn't care for it before we knew, so nothing had really changed but our deeper understanding of how revolting it truly was and is.

I awoke the next morning to find a walking stick leaning against the wall and my Master already off to do whatever he did during the day. He left a note reminding me of my studies, and a list of services he required completed. I looked them over seeing a request for me to meet with a new seduction trainer called Egon around twelve thirty. I smiled thinking the timing was perfect for my secret trip and triste with the Elder Claus.

*I stood up and nearly swooned from the pain. Mad Max entered the room and switched positions with me relieving me as promised (*I turned to see if another change would come in Master Maxx, and yep it did. His gaze at me was the one I recalled from his torture sessions in the chains. I realized at this point he had been doing this the whole time. I just never noticed till now. To think I thought he was just being moody. Shit no. He is unstable. There is a difference.)

I grabbed the walking cane and quickly changed into a velvet outfit that had a burgundy wine undershirt. I assumed if I was to run into this Jonas during my recon,

I would want to remind him of his fetish in any way I could.

I took off out the door and was immediately hailed by Vilber and Olaf. I limped with the aid of that cane to see what these two idiots wanted.

Olaf looked at the floor appearing nervous. "I don't know why you put in that good word for us with your Master to grant us this great job working with him, but I suppose I owe you an apology for all the mean shit I did to you, Vilber too. We apologize and hope there are no hard feelings between us?"

I chucked full of the demons. "Uhm, what mean shit? Oh wait, you mean holding me down while Xavier raped me. Oh no, you are talking about beating me up till I couldn't fight you as you clipped me in his chains so he could torture me. Are you speaking of that desire to put out my eyes with a stick? Or thinking I am possessed by demons? Nein, I know you are sorry for spreading all the shit that was private all over the Haus about me. Ah, wait, I forgot, you are apologizing for threatening to rape me. Nein, you're vowing to do this in front of every fucking silver and black in the place right. That mean shit?"

Olaf groaned and Vilber covered his eyes with his hands. "Okay, okay, ja all that. I admit we have been pretty nasty to you. Yet still you spoke up for us, made us the heroes so that your Master hires us. We admit we owe you for that." I interrupted him.

"Fucking right you owe me Olaf and you, Vilber. You owe me your complete loyalty. You will keep anything you see or hear about me to yourself, including from my Master. If he tells you to follow me, you will agree but go hang out somewhere else and tell him you watched and I was compliant with his orders. That there was nothing out of the ordinary. This you understand?" I glared at them both with hatred over the long history I already had of being the victim of their cruel treatment.

Olaf and Vilber flinched then stared at me in disbelief. "You would ask us to betray your Master and our oath to him? hat we cannot do," said Olaf almost as if he feared Master Peter could somehow hear him even suggest such a terrible thing.

I shook my head. "Nein. I don't ask you; I demand it. You fuck with me, and the death Felix found will look like a mercy. I happen to know that I am worth more than a million of you, either of you. I can scream a word and the chains would be a kindness you wished for. Or you can be smart and do what I tell you and your reward will be great one day soon. To prove this is possible I ask you Olaf to make a request for something only a powerful Dominant could give you. By tomorrow this thing will be yours. Go ahead, ask me for this thing of rare pleasure."

Olaf chuckled. "Oh, hell Vilber, calm yourself man. This kid is insane. I thought for a moment there he meant this crazy shit he said. Okay, Maximillian, I will play this game with you. I want a woman with blue eyes, long red hair, and huge boobs. She must be heavy set; I like them with meat on the frame. I want her to suck my cock then let me fuck her till my dick falls of. She must be a pleasure submissive of rare experience, so I am thinking at least thirty-five or more. I even have a name, Tamina of Master Malfred's house. He never shares her so good luck and since she is silver there is no way I can ever have that beautiful woman for my lust. You get me a night of wonder with her, then I do whatever the fuck you want for all time Mad Max. Now anything else we can do for you, you creepy bastard?"

I glared at Olaf with hate while addressing his stunned partner. "Vilber, Olaf said what his desire is, but I hear nothing from your mouth."

Vilber gasped, "I don't like this game."

I turned to stare at him. "Asking ain't getting now, is it?"

Olaf snorted, "Sure as fuck isn't. Quit being a pussy Vilber. I say my darkest desires. You say yours, damn you. There is no fucking harm in it."

Vilber nodded but appeared nervous as he said, "I always wanted to sit in the Great Hall and dine with a Dominant like we were equals. Just once to say I did it."

I nodded. "You have a name too or any Dominant will do?"

Vilber looked at the floor. "Even a fresh one would be more than I could ever dream. Now I am done with this stupid game. Get on your way Maximillian and laugh at us pathetic black collars and our wishful thoughts. That is what this is. You got your revenge by humiliation. Good for you."

I snickered evilly, "Ah, how wrong you are, Vilber. I already told you both, one day I will break my metal. When I do that, my revenge is to see you two buried just outside this door. That my friends will happen. You don't know who you fucked over, but one day you will be sorry for it. No apology can ever change that. See you boys tomorrow morning with your requests. Ciao."

I limped away from the door guards that were shooting confused looks at each other. I looked at Maximillian that was following me for this recon toward our submitting to Claus's lust. "Did you get all that? We get this woman and make sure that Claus brings Vilber to supper, ja? Then these guards will no longer be Peter's men but our own."

Maximillian nodded in approval. "Ja, I heard it. Brilliant plan of yours. What if Claus balks at breaking the rules so harshly for two low black collars?"

I stopped my stride and stood there staring at him in irritation. "Maximillian, you are a fool. You tell Claus this must be done so we can continue to see him behind Peter's back. He will do anything to keep his "Priceless" collar under his lustful thumb."

Maximillian took a deep breath of sudden understanding. "Ah, fuck, which is indeed a stroke of genius. I never thought of that."

I clicked my tongue. "Uhm, I know that. I am the brains, and you are the, well, the bitch. You just lay there and take it and I will do all the strategy, my lovely whore." I chuckled while Maximillian threw me a look of anger at that true assessment.

"Fick Dich, Mad Max. Did you talk to Mud Maxx about Jonas speaking of weirdos?" Maximillian walked next to me as we moved toward the large hall of fancy sitting furniture (we hoped to find Jonas sitting there reading like we had heard rumored he did from time to time. He was allegedly a vampire, so the collars tended to talk about his sightings like he was the real fucking thing or something you know.)

I nodded with some amount of confidence. "Ja, he will do it he says. However, you and I have to get the nightmare shard into position first. He says he couldn't seduce a fly to land on his arm even if he put honey on it." I chuckled at the truest assessment of my brother shard. What a nut, ja?

Maximillian chuckled too. "Okay. I have no issue with the tease as long as I don't have to stick anything in my mouth other than his cock."

I groaned. "I wish you had a cock in that mouth of yours right now Maximillian. Then I wouldn't have that fucking visual your words elicited, asshole."

Maximillian smiled at me. "Tell me, does that leg hurt much? I bet it does, ja? All this walking must be a bitch. Good, you can stay in there for the rest of the day as I refuse to re-enter since you call me names."

I rolled my eyes as we entered the "fancy furniture Hall." "Fuck you are truly a prissy gay. I just realized the panties you put on this morning for Claus's lust are bunched up but somehow you are the one feeling it not me. Shut the hell up and keep an eye out for Jonas. We work together like Der Hund says, ja?"

He nodded at me while we strolled through the Hall as if we were merely passing through when suddenly I hear the voice I now recognized as that of Jonas, The Vampire Elder.

"You there, Maximillian, over here. Come here boy. I call to you." His deep voice demanded from left of our stride.

I turned towards the sound and saw the Elder sitting in a large medieval-appearing chair holding a thick book of old leather bound quality in his lap. His long black dyed hair was laying loose about his shoulders and his well-manicured goatee and moustache appeared to have been colored the same shade of black, like that of the Raven bird, ja? He had a sharp nose with deep brown eyes that appeared almost as black as his mane.

He was wearing a fancy black suit with a red button up undershirt and shiny black shoes. He would have given Bram's Dracula a run for his money if he had only donned a cape to match his fancy suit. I was immediately creeped the fuck out.

I approached him as he demanded, feeling a bit worried maybe this guy really was the living dead ghoul of legend though his skin was not pale enough. I thought maybe he could use some white makeup to make his unsettling appearance more believable, ja?

He was smiling at me with teeth that either really had been filed to sharpness or I needed more medication to stop the hallucinations (either was possible I must admit.) "Ah, you are even more impressive to look at when not laying on the ground bleeding in the yard. I didn't think such a thing would be possible." He chuckled at that most disturbing statement.

I nodded but kept my eyes to the floor. "I thank you for the mercy of your kindness in saving my worthless hide. I was out of my mind from a blow a moment before. I suppose I also owe you my apology for being a bother."

He leaned forward looking around to make sure no one was hearing him speak. "Ah, well, watching a stunning creature such as you come out into the light cowering, then taking the bullets as if not afraid made my decade Maximillian. What is your real name? I am curious to know the one you had before this given at your collaring."

I looked up at him in shock. "Uhm, I don't think that is a proper thing to discuss Master Jonas. I believe that boy was dismissed."

Jonas chuckled. "Ja, but not really, right? You tell me your secret and I will give you one of my own. Don't make me order it, Maximillian. I want you to tell me of your own freewill."

I felt my mouth go dry and throat closing as I said, "Christian Axel."

Master Jonas smiled with sudden glee. "I love this name much more than that bullshit one Peter gave you. I will call you Christian Axel, but only in private I swear. Now for your return of this service. I am interested in something besides a onetime leash with the power-driven Peter. I think you will understand what I can do for you if you are willing to be my secret lover. If not, then you are not the Priceless I think I saw out in that yard taking a bullet like the true force of nature he really is."

Maximillian let out a gasp in shock. "Oh, Meine Gott. This is too easy; Mad Max. Something is wrong here. This man is dangerous. Call Der Hund. This has to be a set up."

I tossed an irritated glare at that over emotional schwuler boy Maximillian while I responded to the Vampire Jonas. "This secret you share I dare say is a thrilling fantasy, Master Jonas, But I do believe your testing me could result in my meeting up with my Master's tawse in chains. I thank you again for the generosity you showed by pulling me from my temporary madness. I believe we will see each other soon enough for a leash. That is all I am authorized to agree to."

Master Jonas scoffed "I don't agree to Peter's request. That fucker is looking to put me in his hip pocket. I told him nein. I will continue to refuse his demands. There will be no leash, my Christian Axel. This is why I am coming to you directly. It was a chance meeting to see you walking by, but I would have found you to consort over this matter sooner or later, I think. This is fate instead telling me I must have you for my own pleasure. Name your price and be my lover."

I looked around to be assured no one heard me, "If I said I want what my Master demanded Master Jonas, then what?"

The Elder Vampire smiled with a wicked grin. "Ah, I told your Master hell no because what I want from you cannot be given in a single showing. I will need many infusions for all the rest of my days. Now granting you an unlimited favor for unlimited pleasure of your mind, physique and blood can grant me, that is a trade of equal value. You say the word, and I vow it shall be yours. All the darkest power I wield will be at your command and in return you grant me the immortality of your kind's legend, Christian Axel. Do we have a deal then?" He held out his hand allowing me to notice his long nails were also filed to points, just like his spooky teeth.

I trembled but took his hand. "Ja, I agree to this, but you must allow my Master to believe you gave in to him. Otherwise, he will cause trouble. I ask you to call him and agree but on the arranged leashing I will not allow the couple. This way honor is kept but my Master is satisfied he got his price for the pleasure you never got."

Master Jonas closed his cold, clammy hand around my own and pulled my shaking self close to his sinister looking mouth. "You have much more diabolical plans than I even imagined. I like this style of yours. I thought you only a submissive try to control the power of this Haus. Well, this kind of courage turns me on. I will be happy to join your growing army of faithful followers Priceless Christian Axel. I can even get you an audience with Drexel and Bladrick after him. All I ask in return for aiding you in your bid to rule this Haus of despots is that every week you come to see your Master Jonas and give him a taste of you. Beware, I am a greedy bastard myself. This extra I sweeten our bond with will cost you your soul."

I nodded. "Well Master Jonas, then I will sell it to you. Better you hold on to it than the Devil who also will lay claim at some point. Good luck holding on to it when old Scratch comes for his due."

Master Jonas laughed with glee. "I love you already dark Christian Axel. I will call Peter this afternoon around the time you are sending Claus to cross dresser heaven, ja? I keep him busy for you while you wrap that poor little sissy around your demonic fingers." He winked at me while I stood there stunned into silence.

He let go of my hand. "Nein, Christian Axel, he didn't tell me. I have been following you for a few weeks. I saw this beautiful creature one day in the hallway in the most remarkable clothing fashion. I had to have him for myself. I noticed he was speaking to no one but the demons in his head. I realized this was a Priceless. Only they do that. I knew one many years ago who did the same. I knew at once this was the Maximillian of the gossiping around this Haus. I saw the leashing of you to Claus. I live across from him and I share a single wall. That man is a loud fucker. I heard him speaking of his inability to meet your demands. Then when you left, I checked your schedule of classes outside Peter's apartment and realized the only time you could sneak away for a secret tryst with Claus was at one. That class had an instructor that mysteriously killed himself. I merely stalked you and used my math skills to deduce your movements, my love. Now I wonder, how will you meet our agreement if Claus has your Thursdays?"

I smiled at my new best friend, the Vampire Jonas. "Ah, well I just got a two-hour opening on Wednesdays. I cleared my schedule just for you and maybe a friend?"

Master Jonas smiled with much joy. "Ah you are aware of Bladrick's fetish. Kill two birds with one stone. What a clever boy you are."

I tipped my hat at the Vampire. "Maybe, but it seems I can learn a few tricks from you, Master Jonas."

He looked at my injured leg. "I will teach you all of them long as you pay my price."

Chapter 22: Closet Secret

"I stood there feeling extremely nervous about that strange look in Jonas's eyes. It was definitely one of lust, but somehow a different kind of it, it is difficult to explain it. It is obvious that caused me more than a little discomfort. I again worried maybe this Elder was the real undead creature of the legends.

Maximillian (The fucking crybaby he is, damn) was grabbing my arm acting like a crazy boy, "Mad Max. See that look he has. He plans to drink all our blood then turn us into a fucking walking corpse. We got to get the fuck out of here."

I shot a look of anger at that prissy boy. "There is no such a thing as a real vampire," I said to that dumbass.

Master Jonas, he of course heard this thing I uttered without my realizing I spoke out loud (damned Maximillian distracted me). "Ah. This you think is the truth. That there is no such a thing as the Vampire? Well, maybe I can make a believer of you, Christian Axel? I am the very creature of wish you show disbelief."

I let out a gasp in terror that this man was obviously more insane than us. "Ha, very clever joke. Sure, this game of role play I am happy to serve you in. This is the one where you are a Vampire and I am just a stupid boy that has no idea of the danger he is in, ja? Now, I think I need to bid you adieu. I must apologize for my rudeness Master Jonas, but I was on my way to attend a service for my Master Peter. If you can be kind enough to release my audience, I will be ready to provide the special services to you and work out the return service agreement during the "false" leashing." I kept my eyes on the floor thinking this guy was a real freak, you know?

Master Jonas sat back and chuckled at my statement. "Ja, it is a yoke. A game of the role play. If that is what you need to believe, then so be it. All I care is that you come to me of your own freewill and give me the immortality I seek from you. The Priceless of legend is just within my claws at last. This dark gift I will never allow to escape, that you can be assured. You and I will talk sooner than you think. I will not wait much longer for this exchange to begin. I already grow too old as it is waiting for another chance to possess the forbidden silver's unnatural powers as it is. I tasted you already to make sure you are what I thought I saw in the yard. Not only are you the true thing, but I have already developed the urgency for more like a druggie craves his chemical addiction. I will have my Christian Axel fix soon, one way or the other."

That was a weird and disturbing thing he said right there (don't you think? Yikes). "Uhm, I don't understand, Master Jonas? You tasted me?" I was ready to run from this psychotic bastard at this point (I hated that prissy

Maximillian may have had a point when he said we were in over our head.)

The Vampire nodded his head. "Ja, that wound in your leg. You bled all over the place. I got some of that magic that runs in your veins on my hands. I tasted it to see if you had the power within it, as the legends of the Priceless claim. I woke up this morning and I felt the youth, vigor, and vitality, which has been steadily declining over the last few years, back within me. Only a little lick and I am already stronger. I cannot deny my eagerness to find out what a full meal of this glorious power you hold can do."

I gulped, finding my throat had gone dry. "Oh, you want to drink my blood like the vampire in literature. I guess I thought that you expected I would be drinking yours." I shot a look of concern at Maximillian who looked like he was ready to faint in terror, not helpful I must say.

Master Jonas's eyes went wide, then he began to chuckle at my ignorance. "You are too precious for words, Christian Axel. Nein, I don't want you to drink my blood. That will do no good for me, now will it? I seek to live forever, not to slowly die of anemia. The legend is that if you couple with the Priceless it will bring on an unnatural life span. If I couple with you, it will buy me more years of breath. Drinking directly from the tap should bring back my youth as well. I intend to take both from you. I thought you understood what I am trading my service for. I suppose you misunderstood so let me spell this out so there is no complaint later, Christian Axel. I am granting you all my power in this Haus, and an audience with two more Elders, for the true immortality you give to me in your complete submission as my lover to my dark lust and baser desires. I want this willingly, without despair or disgust, and I want it for all time. This price you ask of me is not too much to pay for such a marvelous eternity you grant in return. This is why I turned down your Master Peter's request. Ha, a onetime infusion for what? My loyalty to that pig. Never."

I stood there unsure if I should flee, fall on my knees begging Master Jonas to slit my throat and finish me off, or accept this fucking weird offer (now that I fully understood what he wanted, maybe drinking his blood was not such a bad thing in comparison.)

*Maximillian suddenly shoved me to the side and took over the tongue (*I stole a look at Master Maxx and yep, you guessed it, he suddenly changed, fucking weird but cool too. I was starting to get a kick out of it. How the fuck did I miss it before.) ***"Dearest Master Jonas, it would seem to me that the power in this Haus and audience without promise of their compliance is not a true equal service for the one you require from me. I think if we are to negotiate a more honest trade, then I would need more than what you are willing to grant. It was a real pleasure, but I think I must pass on this most thrilling offer.***

Though I thank you for considering my unworthy person for such an honor. Have a most glorious day, Master Jonas." I turned the hell around and began leaving this nightmare before that psychopathic dipshit Mad Max got us in any fucking deeper into this weird shit.

Mad Max was a bit stunned by my shoving him out of the way, and my leg was killing me, but I ignored them both moving like I was expecting Master Jonas to turn into a bat to bite my neck any moment.

Then to my shock I see Mad Maxx running at me from the direction I was fleeing. That crazy masochistic bastard was bruised to shit, and sweating like a whore moving faster than I ever knew he could run. He smacked into me, throwing my ass to the floor while he took my place.

I heard Master Jonas call out my name. "Maximillian, I didn't release you from my audience. Get back over here or you will not like the results boy," he growled out sounding truly angry.

I stopped my retreat and stole a look at Mad Max who was helping Maximillian off the floor. "What the hell man. Run you fool. He wants to drink our fucking blood. That is insane. He wants to kill us. Get out of here. We agreed to handle this situation for you," yelled out the furious Maximillian at me.

I shook my head then mumbled to him while slowly limping back to the chair of Master Jonas. "You fool. We have no choice. Without this insane Elder we cannot break our collar. If he wants to drink our piss then we increase our water intake, you prissy bastards."

Mad Max glared at me with disbelief in his expression. "Now I see everything. You would do what this whore Maximillian finds too dangerous and disgusting. The floozy Maximillian lets our own father fuck us, Mad Maxx. He maybe knows what he is talking about if he says nein on this insane Elder's demands."

I see Maximillian push Mad Max hard. "You pick now to insult me? Aren't you the stupidest fucker. How is that helping this situation? Look Mad Maxx, this is serious, don't go speaking to him anymore. He will cut our throat and drain us into a bathtub for his pleasure."

I ignored them both. Der Goldene Hund was clear in his directives. He said we had to capture all the Elders to escape this hellish Haus. Like this or not, we had to make this deal with Master Jonas.

I saw this situation much more clearly than my brothers could. If the thing the Elder wanted was dangerous, revolting, and likely to cause much injury, then the price extracted should be equal for our trouble. I had come to pull this sinking ship from the bottom of this ocean of disaster before the two idiots Mad Max and Maximillian fucked the deal beyond repair.

I stood before the fuming Master Jonas with my eyes to the floor. "You dare to deny me, Maximillian? Do you think that wise, my love? I can have you killed with only a yell. If I wanted to take you to the torture chamber below, cut your belly open and drink you dry, no one could stop me. I offer you a great deal and you storm off like an insulted spouse. Speak up now or I will make you wish you had been able to collect the correct bullet yesterday in the yard." His dark eyes blazed with fire which likely could burn me to the ground if he aimed it correctly.

I nodded. "Ja, you can do all those things to me and more, I am aware. However, if you do, then the Priceless you seek will be no more. How long do you think it will take to find another? How many years did it take to find me? Do you have all the years left without the immortality I can grant you to wait for one more open to your dark affections?"

This caused Master Jonas to become even more agitated. "You arrogant bastard. You hold me hostage with your words. How dare you?"

I looked up at him throwing my own blaze. "I dare because you play me for a fool. You want much and offer little in return, Master Jonas. Surely you can do better than this shit you are trying to get away with. I thought you were clever. Go ahead, try harder to catch my favor. I grant you eternity with my crimson treasure and you wish to give me a lollipop for the stick of your needle? I think not. Equal service is demanded. Either grant me such as this, let me go in peace or you call the fucking Guard. I have no time for your games. You are not dealing with an idiot like you apparently are accustomed to. I warn you. I fear neither torture nor death. Both are my pleasure. The fool is you to not recognize this."

I stole a glance at Mad Max and Maximillian that stood there with their mouths hanging open in shock that I yelled at this powerful Dominant like that.

Maximillian shook his head, "Oh shit, we are so dead."

Mad Max nodded. "Seems that way, oh well. Look on the bright side. At least we can take off those uncomfortable panties you put on us, Maximillian. They are chafing our hoddensuck. You keep forgetting they exist because you don't have any." Maximillian swatted Mad Max on his upper arm with much irritation.

I refused to break my hateful gaze into the now softening one of the Vampire Jonas. "Well, well, you are even more than I ever hoped. No wonder just a tiny taste makes me lust for you with eagerness I have never known before. I see you're truly worth the price of your metal. Unlimited years and youth are indeed a high prize. If you think my return too low, then you name what more it would take for you to come to me willingly."

Once again, my brother shards mouths dropped in surprise as I said, "I need the voting counsel in my back pocket as bad as I need the Elders of the Haus. I will come to you willingly and give all this you ask if you grant me your power, aid me to grab Bladrick, and Drexel's votes, and help me capture each member of the ones that hold the vote in collar selection or rule making. I will collect Barnim on my own, but you will give me every other motherfucker in this place of nightmares come to truth. Meet my demands or you can go haunt the cemeteries for fun until at last a grave there claims you for her own."

Master Jonas smiled with wickedness and crossed his arms. "Basically, you demand I become your loyal partner in taking control of the power of this Haus. Is this what I am hearing from you, Christian Axel? You once again earn that name. The perfect one for the amazing boy I see before me."

I nodded, still glaring with much displeasure. "You can see it that way, it matters not to me if I get the price I demand. Your loyalty and work to gain this control can allow me to wield my authority without discovery. I want to change this place and the way it works and break my metal while I do this. Right now, I can gain the power with time, but to dare to use it would result in my Master or others figuring out my deception."

Master Jonas's smile got so wide I could see all his teeth. "Ah, this price you ask is very expensive, more than even what you demand from Claus."

I took a deep breath. "He only asks for a life worth of pleasure. You ask me for unlimited ones. Unlimited lives for a single one of supreme power are not so high a price to pay."

He nodded. "This is truth. I would tell you I need to think about this in an effort to keep you from seeing my desperation, but that would only waste time I do not have. I will meet this price. I agree to my silent partnership and compliance with your every command in wielding the complete power you will hold in the Haus. I will aid you to obtain, with only Barnim excluded from my list of targets, but I desire to add one more single stipulation since the price has become this high."

I rolled my eyes with feigned irritation (because I effectively just took the step that in an abbreviated time would result in my complete control of the Haus and I fucking knew this very well. Whatever this crazy fucker wants he was going to get, he had to know that.) "Ja? What else can I possibly do for you now the I agree to allow your couple and the drinking of my blood? Oh, I know. You wish me to check you for the fleas when you morph back from being a bat or wolf, maybe?"

Master Jonas's mouth flew open in surprise and then he began laughing so hard he almost choked. "Oh, Meine Gott. You are fucking hilarious. I am adoring you more every second, precious Christian Axel. I will remember that one, very clever. Nein, though if I start shape shifting such a service could come in handy, ja? Jonas laughed again. I want to remind you I demand this to be willing. I want a true lover of you, not a compliant one. For all that I am going to grant to my beloved, I expect romance from this arrangement. I waited all my life for you. I expect the dark fantasy to become one of forbidden reality. I don't wish to just fuck you; I desire to make love to my Christian Axel and for him to love me back."

I looked at Mad Max and Maximillian to see if this was even possible. They both shrugged, then began glancing around the room refusing to make eye contact (fucking useless bastards). I wished immediately Der Goldene Hund was around. I sure needed his expert advice. I decided if none of us could do this thing Master Jonas asked of us, maybe he could create another of us that could. After all he made that schwuler boy and the psychopathic brother of mine, didn't he? Anything was possible, I hoped.

I nodded. "Okay, ja, I suppose that can be done. I vow to meet your desires without qualm or hesitation. You return your oath and release me to do my tasks. I thank you for the mercy of it."

Master Jonas smiled with much happiness. "I grant my unwavering allegiance to you, my love. We will become one heart in no time. This is a fine day. I grant your release to attend your tasks of attempting to rule the world. I am grateful I captured you on the way to the top rather than trying to thwart your fall off the other side. You are a brave one, I give you that. If I had not come along, both in the yard, and in your plan, you would have grown a strong tree in the orchard no doubt. You just saved your life and found your freedom, though it will be a bit of time before you realize this."

I smiled with understanding. "Oh, I do realize this, Master Jonas. The thing I learned in my years of bondage is how to pick an unbreakable lock. As I said earlier, have a most glorious day, my friend."

He gave the hand signal that I was free to go. I turned and strode off forgetting that my leg was in bad shape. Sometimes, that happens. I don't notice pain like I should. That has resulted in some stitches being ripped, and a few more days in a recovery bed than expected. Thankfully that day I had my brothers running behind me yelling at me to recall our injury.

"Stop moving like there is a fucking fire, fool. You'll bust that wound back open, Mad Maxx. Fucking dumbass," hollered out my brother Mad Max.

I slowed my stride and remembered to put my weight on the cane to relieve the pressure of my weight as the two caught up with me.

"I cannot believe that just happened, nor the fact that Mad Maxx did it and not me," bitched Maximillian.

Mad Max chuckled. "Don't worry there, whore. You will get the chance to suck the Vampire's cock to make up for the loss of sticking your nasty tongue in his ear. You mistake being a sperm pocket for being seductive. Any old bitch can lie there and be a hole you know."

Maximillian was super pissed by that crass statement (and I agree he should have been as it was pretty nasty; you know.) "I have had enough of your insults, psychopathic creep. I am going to stick that cane of yours up your ass and then we see who is the hole." He pushed Mad Max who then slammed into my back making me stagger forward a bit.

"Cut this out, you bastard. Quit crowding me. For God's sake stop fucking talking. Just shut the fuck up," I yelled out in incredible agitation at the Max boys acting like horses' asses.

Every fucking collar silver and black dropped to their knees around me, immediately trembling over my sudden outburst. There was silence, as I demanded by accident, and everyone gave me plenty of room to travel down that hallway. I staggered in a painful limp as I passed all of them feeling a bit sheepish that I scared them all like that. I wasn't talking to them, but I wasn't going to tell them that I was yelling at my inner demons either. I decided, best to move the fuck on.

I got down that hallway in record time considering my impaired left leg and the use of that cane. when we got far enough away from the kneeling crowd, Mad Max approached and kicked me from myself. It was his right to take over. It was getting close to time to prepare ourselves for the new seduction instructor and the couple with Claus.

I turned to look at my brother Mad Maxx with some awe at his handling of the Vampire Jonas. "I still cannot believe you were able to do that brother. If this man is honest, in less than a few months we will own this place. More than a year earlier than we thought possible."

Mad Maxx and Maximillian smiled at that glory. "I didn't mean to show either of you up like that, but the agreement you made with him seemed a bit pale compared to his demands. Forgive me my arrogance to interfere where I am not the most skilled. I go now to the chains for my unruly behavior."

109

I rolled my eyes at that most cliché statement from that masochistic bastard. "Christ, come on Mad Maxx. There is no time for masturbation right this minute. I know fucking well you get yourself all worked up taking that thudding. You are as crazy as...well okay we are all Gott Verdammt nuts, but I am working here. Go rest with Christian and Max. Leave the business to the grown-up little baby girl."

Mad Maxx flipped me the bird while I and Maximillian chuckled while turning the corner in the hallway. I nearly tripped and fell over Annette curled up holding her knees sobbing in front of her Master's apartment door.

I stopped dead in my tracks at the sight of the pretty blond. It had only yesterday I had the pleasure of watching her prance naked, then taste her with my employment of oral sex. I then promptly murdered her best friend for daring to try to soil me in a plot for revenge. Okay, well Christian did that, but you know all of us get the blame.

I cleared my throat unsure what to do if anything. "Uhm, Annette, are you okay? Anything I can do for you?" I worried maybe she was weeping over the death of Geraldine.

Annette looked up, appearing startled. "Oh, Mad Max. What are you doing here? I heard you got shot trying to commit suicide After they told you Geraldine killed herself. This must have been just another gossip lie." Her eyes were red and puffy from many hours of sobbing.

I looked down in feigned sadness. "Uhm, I did get shot and you heard correctly. I was saved in my bid to end my pain for my lost love." I thought what the fuck, better she thought me in painful mourning than her thinking the truth that I was Geraldine's brutal fucking killer.

Annette nodded, tearing up with fresh water in her eyes. "Ja, I loved her too, Mad Max. I was devastated but I know I must keep going. You trying to honor her so was very romantic and I for one think for a gay you're the best friend any of us could ever have desired. Thank you for caring so much for us worthless girls. We never forget what you did for her and all of us."

I nodded then dropped my gaze feeling poorly for having to say what I said next. "Ja. I was going to tell all you on Wednesday, but since you and I are here now. I tell you and you can tell the others. I must withdraw my tutoring for your seduction courses. I have received a directive to end all contact with females until further notice. I don't care about my own punishment for breaking such an order, but my Master would hurt any girl caught with me. Maybe even have her put to the lawn. This I cannot allow. So, will you tell the girls for

111

me? I will miss all of you more than you can ever know. I will never forget the fun and laughs we shared." I felt a pang of regret thinking of the fact I told her the truth. It was strange to think I felt my heart break. I didn't even know I had one of those things.

Annette nodded and sniffed loudly. "I am sorry to hear this, Mad Max. Now I am depressed in a triple way. I lose my best friend Geraldine, then my Master put me out of his threesome with my sister collar while telling me I am too fat, and now I lose my Mad Max too."

I almost fainted at her second statement. "Annette, I think maybe I am having some blood loss. Did you say your Master put you out of a threesome because you are too fat? Wait, I thought you were a virgin anyway. Threesome means..." she interrupted me.

"Ja, Mad Max I know what a threesome means silly. Women have three virginities too. You only need one to make collar selection. I still have my anal virginity and I never completed a blow job either. My sister collar and I fuck our Master regular, but lately he is more interested in her. I was falling behind in my ability to seduce you know, and now I am gaining too much weight, I am losing him." Tears rolled down her cheeks heavy as rain.

I looked at this beautiful girl trying to seek out this imaginary fat one her Master claimed. "I think you

Master needs glasses, or a head examination Annette. Your figure is perfect, and beyond beautiful. He throws out a treasure. I wouldn't cry over the idiot ideas of a madman if I were you. So, what if he doesn't recognize the glory of Aphrodite on Earth he is so blessed to own? Another, wiser Master will purchase that collar at selection and this one will be left stroking his forehead and own cock in despair at losing the gift he could have had for all his days."

Annette's face broke into the most beautiful smile I ever saw. "You mean all this you say about me, Mad Max? Say yes and I will never have cause to question my desirability again if a lover of your caliber says such kind words to the likes of me." She wiped her eyes of their rain.

I chuckled with much bitterness over this sad situation. "Annette if only I could have been so blessed to call you my very own, I would never let you leave my bed. I would hold you in my arms for all my days and curse the reaper when he came only because I could not lay my eyes on such rare beauty with my eyes closed by his scythe."

Annette let out a gasp, then stood up rapidly grabbing my wrist and dragging me after her. The suddenness of her doing this sent me into a confused shock. She stopped after only three paces, opened a door and pulled me inside after her closing it behind us.

She hit a light switch to reveal this was a small closet outside of her Master's apartment. She grabbed my upper shoulders forcing her lips to my own. I admit I was happy to let her kiss me with this most unexpected wantonness, so I didn't fight her off in anyway.

The kiss got increasingly frenzied when with sudden terror I realized Master Peter forgot to attach the cock cage. I was at full erection in my breeches, my dick nearly ripping the lace panties in half that my boy Maximillian laid out for the Claus seduction.

Annette noticed that there was a lot more of Mad Max than when she had last kissed me in the ladies washroom. She felt my, uhm, interest pushing into her belly as she rubbed herself all over my chest and waist.

She pulled herself from the kissing and looked at me with a smile. "I once told you to stop looking at my ass in the laundry room and called you a gay boy that would never get the nasty sex you wanted from me. I apologize for that now. I see that you are maybe a lot of things, Mad Max, but you are not a gay."

I groaned out at the realization this was that pretty trainee I was eyeing the day my brother Ryker called me back to the utility closet for my biggest mistake. I had forgotten her, but she had remembered me.

Then before I could stop or even understand what the hell was happening, she reached into my breeches and by so doing freeing my cock of its material cage. When she did this she yelped out, appearing surprised.

"Holy shit. Ich hatte die Gerüchte gehört, aber is das normal?" She stared at my manhood in what appeared to be fear. (Do I really need to translate this one? Take a guess at what she said. Mad Max is fucking huge, like over nine inches huge and likely was at thirteen too. He is a big guy okay, big guys are well big.)

I shook my head panting and terrified that this kiss was getting out of control fast. "I don't understand what you mean is this normal. Please Annette, we need to get out of here before someone sees us. Stop playing around. Get off me and let me out of this closet, I have things to do." I tried to push her back while grabbing my breeches to readjust myself.

She shook her head. "Nein. I won't have you throw me out too. I thought you said you would do anything to have me for your own."

I nodded. "In another life, I wish to be so lucky. But in this one I am forbidden your favors. Forgive me Annette, but I can only love you from afar. Thank you for helping to remind me of why I must break this collar. I will think of you till the end of my days."

Annette swooned at that, then with great suddenness pushed me into the wall, forcing her mouth to mine again. I pushed on her trying to pry her off gently (I didn't want to hurt the girl that was making me feel so wonderful after all, ja.) She wrapped her left arm around my shoulder and neck pulling herself up like a kid on her mother's lap.

I tried to break her kissing, but she kept forcing her mouth to mind with wildness as I again felt her grab my interested cock pulling it from my breeches once more.

That was it. She was going too far with this game of hers. I grabbed her shoulders to push her roughly this time ready to voice my anger. I never got that chance.

Annette pushed forward onto my lap with suddenness, letting out a loud moan while throwing her head back with her eyes closed. I was struck stupid immediately as the sensation of intense pleasure rolled up my spine from my groin. This feeling was so intense I was confused by it. It took several seconds for me to finally realize I was inside Annette.

She groaned into my ear, "Take me Mad Max. Ficken mich, now."

Her words, the rapture of being inside the correct parts overtook my senses. Mother nature's drumbeat pounded into my ears calling out my innate urge to copulate with this willing female I was already penetrating.

I spun her around and forced her back into the wall without breaking our couple. She yelled out loudly encouraging my mount, "Do this Mad Max. I need this. You need this. Give me all your love."

I didn't need to hear that twice. I immediately did what comes naturally. I thrust with abandon entering her with all my force and every available inch of my sex organ. I was completely unaware of my unusual size, nor did I even care if I hurt this girl. All I could think of was the incredible pleasure this behavior was causing me.

Each of my harsh, unskilled, brutal thrusts caused her to wail out loudly. At first, I thought this meant I was doing what she wanted (okay, as I said to be honest, I really didn't care, I was only thinking of Mad Max.) I hate to admit this, but she did beg me to stop at least twice. I must also say I did hear her complaining I was "too rough" and "too much" for this couple with her.

Luckily for her, I was a virgin. Thanks to that mercy (for her, not me) it only took maybe five or six of these pounding strokes to send me bucking into spasms of orgasm.

Unlike the ones I was accustomed to during masturbation, this climax was so powerful I nearly passed out from the explosion of intense gratification. I knew immediately this kind of joy could only be found within the sex organ of a woman. I needed more of this.

I panted and moaned out in thrill while Annette slapped my face angrily. "Gott verdammt, Mad Max. That hurt like hell. Get off me, you pig. I think you broke my pussy with your monster cock. Shit, I am ruined, you bastard. I need to see if I am bleeding. What the hell is wrong with you? No wonder they put you in a fucking cock cage. You need one, you animal." She appeared that she was not as satisfied as I was by the results of her seduction (Mad Maxx laughed hard while I glared at him angrily siding with Annette, he was too fucking rough.)

I finally pulled my spent manhood from the girl After she berated and wailed of her damaged status for a few more moments. I readjusted my now incredibly happy cock into the horrible panties and beeches while Annette checked her own organ for rips or tears.

A strange sleepiness was overtaking me. I yawned, then slowly the fog lifted from my lust driven teenaged brain. Oh shit, I just lost my last virginity. If anyone found this out, then I was trapped in my metal.

*I closed my eyes and called out for **Christian** to come. This girl had to go. I got trapped by yet **another fucking** plot. This time it worked. Fuck, how could **I be so stupid?** I looked at Annette with intense anger at her trick of seduction and crocodile tears. I felt anger at myself for falling for the oldest trick in the book.*

*I looked up just in time to see **Christian** and **Max** arrive nearly out of breath. **Maximillian** came running too. All the boys that arrived had looks which were priceless. They all realized I got laid and they missed it.*

*Annette finally stopped her bitching about this "rough sex" I had with her then looked at me with much seriousness. "Mad **Max**, you cannot tell anyone this happened. I would be ruined and so would you. I didn't mean for this to get out of hand, I swear it. If my **Master** knew what I just did, he would put me to the lawn. I will never tell anyone. It is a secret with my **Master**, but I am collared with a vow of monogamy, Mad **Max**. This thing we did is illegal at my age, so I am sworn to never speak of it. Now I broke my vows with you. I am dead if you do not show me mercy. You may be trapped in your metal, but at least you live for another day. What the hell was I thinking? I am so fucked. Oh God, I don't want to die, Mad **Max**. Please, please, never tell. I will do anything. Swear this to me and this secret goes to my grave too." She fell to her knees prostrating herself while weeping heavily that she was afraid to die.*

I looked at my brothers wondering if we could trust this girl to be telling the truth. They all shrugged then looked at Christian.

Christian stared at her a moment then said, "Okay, test this girl. If she is telling the truth she has a collar name. Ask her to tell you her metal name. Do not believe it unless it is typical for simple metal. If she is lying, we will know and she dies."

I nodded. "Annette, you give me your metal name so we can swear this secret proper by blood."

She sat up still sobbing. "I will be happy to cut off my own hand if you ask me. My metal name is Niemand which I soon will be for real."

I looked at Christian who was smiling. "She is called nobody. This is a proper simple metal name. This girl is truthful. Make the blood oath and get the fuck out of here you lucky bastard. Fuck, I wanted to be the one. Why didn't anyone call me."

Max and Maximillian nodded at that both shooting my smiling face a go to hell look of jealousy. I got laid and it was awesome. Ha, even if it was so fucking fast, I was not sure it actually happened.

Annette and I cut our hands and swore a vow of secrecy to this "accidental soiling and oath breaking" in our own blood to our collar names. She kissed my cheek while we checked each other for any signs the needed to be cleaned up to keep this act hidden.

"You were just awful at sex Mad Max, but I am grateful for it anyway. I love my Master and this experience taught me to appreciate him more. He is good to me, but I lately been neglecting his affections. I want you to know while I never speaking of this horror again, I will always remember you as my friend though I can never look at you again, nor you me." She frowned and teared up a bit.

I kissed her forehead. "Don't cry, Annette. I will never stop thinking of the gift you give me without any expectation of return. You may not understand this, but you did more for me this day than anyone ever has. For that, I will never stop loving you. If ever you are in trouble, you can call Mad Max. He will owe you a favor."

She smiled bitterly. "I pray I never need to call it in. If I do, I will remind you that you said that. Now get out of here. I leave in a bit. We cannot leave together. Thanks again Mad Max. Much luck with breaking your collar. If you do it, then I ask you to remember me fondly in the hallways as you pass by."

*I nodded. "That you can count on. Goodbye, Annette."
I stuck my head out and found the coast clear.*

*Without another word I slipped out of that closet and
headed for the apartment hoping to clean myself up
before my next tryst. Only this time I would be playing
Annette's role, yuck.*

*I headed up the staircase being glared at by my newest
men (though they didn't realize it yet), when Olaf yelled
out, "Your Master said not to leave until he got back. He
went out for an errand."*

*I nodded that I understood gratefully that Master Peter
wasn't home. If I was quick, I could cover my
indiscretion (okay major fuck up, but damn was that nice,
ja) before he could figure out I was now fully soiled.*

*I rushed to the washroom and scrubbed my cock until
it was nearly raw, terrified somehow, he would be able to
tell I had found the pleasure of a woman. As I polished
my manhood the boys, including Der Goldene Hund,
came calling demanding details of my thrilling
experience with the female.*

*"This was pure bullshit. I was supposed to be the one
that got to have sex first," again whined Christian.*

Maximillian scoffed, "I am the one around here having earned that pleasure. I always have to do all the dirty work. You'd think just once I would get to be the one penetrating."

Mad Maxx laughed, "Well, you would likely fuck the wrong hole schwuler. At least Mad Max could tell the difference, ja?"

Maximillian growled out, "That was bullshit to say. I know the difference. Christian got to give the oral sex to the girls. Now Mad Max got to fuck one. What does Maximillian get? He gets to suck and be fucked by the cock. How is this fucking fair?"

I snorted with humor, "Shut up queen. You love it. You are just mad no one is fawning over you. Annette wanted me to worship her not the other way around. That I was happy to do for her. You on the other hand are nothing but a drama loving bitch. She was looking to stoke the cock not a prissy ego. She wanted to have a man between her legs. That automatically leave you out."

All the boys began snickering as Maximillian's ears burned with redness at my insult. "Oh ja? Maybe you can go see Claus on your own. Then when he's done with you, let's see who the woman around here is, ja?"

I scoffed, "Get over it Maximillian. You can have the next one, I promise. As it was, I didn't know this was gonna happen. It got out of control is all."

Der Goldene Hund frowned at that. "Ja, it did Mad Max. This could be serious. I hope that Christian is right about letting this girl survive. If she speaks, we are finished. Listen up all of you. I don't like this order to avoid the females any more than any of you, but that girl yesterday almost finished us. This one today took down my sadist like he was butter, and she was the flame. If we got lucky and Annette was true, then we may survive. No more fuck ups or shall I say nein to fucking the girls until we break this collar. I mean this. It is a directive. Don't speak, look at, or think, wait a second, okay you can think of them, but nothing else." He pointed at all of us while we dropped out heads in shame that the girls made us stupid like they do.

I nodded in agreement with this directive. "Ja, Der Hund, I swear it was amazing, but I couldn't stop myself. This power the females have is dangerous for the mission. If that girl walked in here right now and dropped her panties, I would fuck her again and not give a shit who caught me doing it."

Christian perked up at that statement. "Shit, it was that damned good. Fuck, I missed this," he yelled till he was red in the face from his frustration.

The door opening and Master Peter came in, thus ending our "meeting of the Maxes." I quickly fixed my clothing and cleaned up my mess before rushing out to greet my Master.

I dropped to a knee as he walked past me to the couch sitting down glaring at me with some anger in his expression. "Olaf and Vilber said you were out most of the morning. Where you been my love?"

I kept my eyes to the floor. "I took it upon myself to attempt to gain interest from Master Jonas for a leash."

Master Peter's eyes went wide in surprise. "What? You did? Well, I suppose you heard the loud phone call and knew he said nein to my desired payment. I didn't hear my phone ringing, so I suppose you were unsuccessful. Too bad, we needed him badly. He may be the youngest, but he is the most well-connected man in this Haus. If we could have owned him, then you can almost guarantee the council's favorable vote for Dominant at collar selection. I was saving him for last thanks to his most known disagreeable character. He is head strong, stubborn, hard to please and cares not for what anyone thinks. He even goes too far by openly flaunting about his fetish, that sick thing he is into. I almost felt sorry for my beloved Maximillian having to endure his nasty affections even if only for one night."

I nodded. "I understand Master, but I was willing to do what is required of me for this plan. I did my best to engage him with much prancing and silliness. Maybe I tried the wrong techniques. I am not well seasoned at this seduction game, I fear. Perhaps worthless in fact."

Master Peter chuckled at that self-assessment. "The Elders are purely gay, my love. Nothing you do could be wrong when trying to seduce any of them. You are an Elder's dream come to truth. A young boy, beautifully built, blond hair, blue eyed and tight. This is all they need to find lustful desire for you. If you fell, had a seizure, pissed your pants, and called out for your mother they would swoon like you were a God. You will find you are perfectly designed to play right into their ultimate gay fantasy."

I took a deep breath and tried not to puke over his horrible words as I replied, "I understand, Master. This is just too bad for me and good news for them, ja?"

My Master nodded. "Ja, for a boy not interested in the man it is indeed a tragedy for you. How is that bullet wound of yours today? You were drugged terribly last night and were a disappointment to my affections. If we get lucky and this seduction attempt takes its hoped-for effect, I could not think of a leash until that shit improves. You're worse in my bed than ever. I don't mind ripping off these Elders a little with over blown brags of your fake artistic expression in sexual ability, but

Maximillian as of late sex with you is worse than fucking a corpse, you are so unaffectionate." I winced at that true assessment.

Of course, it can be hard to fake interest when it is your father fucking you. "My leg is fine today. It was likely the pain killer last night Master. I was groggy, and the weeks before I had been a bit worried about this whole seduction thing. I am getting over this. I apologize for it and will vow to try harder to please you. Thank you for the mercy."

Master Peter nodded. "Well good. The truth comes out at last. That is all I ask around here, Maximillian. Just be honest with me. Then we work together like a proper D/s relationship does. If it bothers you, then it bothers me too."

I shot a look at the Max boys that all put their finger in their mouths faking a gag at that bullshit. Didn't bother my Master to fuck his own boy, but sure as shit was disturbing to his son.

He wanted nothing more than for me to tell him the truth. He had to be kidding. All he did was tell me lies from the very beginning. Sure, he had to rape me in bonds because the Guard was outside the door. What a crock of shit. I wanted to strangle this bastard, but I knew killing Master Peter would only get me a bullet in my own head. Nein, I would finish this thing, turn it on him, then take my time making him pay for what Agnette and he have done to me. There was no doubt my life was over, but before I went to hell, I was going to give my father a taste of my pain.

Master Peter looked at the clock on the wall with a sudden start. "Oh hell, it is nearly time for you to meet with Egon downstairs. I left the apartment this morning forgetting to put on your chastity device. I am getting old, I suppose. Anyway, good thing you are so lamed up no one would question you today. Still, I will go get it and put it on before you leave for your lesson. From now on you will remind me about this. I cannot always keep up with your best interests. Time for you to take some initiative, ja? That is a directive, Maximillian." He got up to retrieve the cock cage.

I admit I trembled a bit in fear that at any moment he would look up and just know I had fucked while he put that fucking thing on me. I did my best to cover my relief when he didn't appear to notice a damned thing amiss. There was no physical change in me now that I was no longer a virgin. No one could see the difference in me like I thought they all could. This fear that somehow, I was different was all psychological.

Obviously, I sit here with you now with a broken collar. So, it is obvious that Annette never told a soul. She was honest and I was grateful that I lost my virginity to that beautiful blond. It would be the first of only two before you Meine Liebe. It was certainly not a great experience, and I barely knew it happened.

However, it did. I found that I was indeed straight and could find incredible pleasure in sexual congress if the gender was correct. Best of all, I didn't have to kill someone to get something I wanted for a change. That made the whole experience (even if brief and clumsy, okay and the girl was unhappy with me) something that would keep me dreaming of you for the many years to come.

Did you just scoot away a tad? Don't you lie. Get back over here. why do you try to sneak off every time I speak about the sex with a woman being magnificent you act like I am going to attack you over a memory. Okay, you know what, come to think of it, you are pretty smart. I did think of fucking you a moment ago. Still, get your ass back over here. If I want to fuck my wife I will. Get over it. Now, where were we?"

I took off for the torture rooms down the stairs of the Haus to find this Egon who had agreed to take over Milo's role since his untimely suicide, poor bastard.

Anyway, I got down there and found this idiot hanging out in the shower rooms. I think you know this is not the kind you take in a bathtub, think whiskey, yuck. He was watching a couple of trainees dealing with getting used to this nasty fetish. In particular I never could stand this particular fetish of Roman showers. The smell you know, barf.

I stood at the entry nearly ready to offer my services as the one puking thanks to that gross scene when finally, the fool saw me standing there. He told the second instructor his appointment had arrived and left the struggling trainees to his care.

I followed the heavy set middle aged black collar to the end of the hallway. He poked his head into the "branding" room and saw we had privacy with no one currently using the space. I came in after him trying to figure out how to get his loyalty and silence for my Thursday trysts with Claus. This was gonna be tricky no doubt, but I was sure I could find a way. Everyone there needed a favor or two, and now I was one that could get that done for them.

I watched the clock slowly ticking away the moments while this braggard when on and on about his prowess as a seduction and domination trainer. I had to stifle several yawns during his long-winded crowing. I finally tired of this game.

After about ten minutes of it without an end appearing in sight, plus I had a date to get to), I interrupted him as politely as possible, "Gott Verdammt, will you shut the fuck up. Christ, you are giving me a headache. (What? That is polite for me, I am a sadist remember? Damn, quit giving me that look, Meine Liebe.)

Egon stood there with his mouth agape unsure what to say to my "polite" outburst. "Uhm, excuse me? I uhm, well I think we need to first work on your language. You cannot seduce anyone with a mouth like dat."

I chuckled at that. "I beg to differ Egon. My mouth has seduced plenty, sometimes more than one in the same hour. Look, you had your fun bragging now it is time for me to find out what it would take to keep your silent, if that is even something you can do, and claim that I come here every week for a lesson you never give me."

Egon's eyes went wide with that. "What? Are you offering to bribe me to say you are in my class, but then never show up?"

I nodded with a big evil grin at him. "Ja, you heard that correctly. I don't need your aid, but my Master would not listen. I wish to go elsewhere and study for my real classes. What will you take for this trade? No one need to be the wiser."

Egon shook his head wildly. "Are you insane? Even if I did agree, someone would be the wiser when you fail

your Dominance testing. Without training in seduction, you will fail that section fool."

I rolled my eyes at that. "I will not fail that part. In fact, it is the one thing I have already aced, much to my disgust. Again, I ask nicely. I am willing to trade and turn a blind eye, but if you insist, then I am happy to retire you from this job for good."

Egon gasped, "Did you just threaten me? I should call your Master or the Guard for that."

I nodded now clicking my tongue at him. "Ja, you should but I notice you are not. So, what the hell do you want in return for this favor. You're wasting my fucking time acting like a eunuch. Tell me so I can agree and move the hell on."

He looked around as if expecting to find ears growing from the walls, then took a deep breath. "I have a fetish that I am not allowed to engage in thanks to my level. I can watch it all I like, even train someone to do it, but I am forbidden."

I groaned at that. "Oh? What is it? Do you like to fuck sheep or have hamsters run up your ass? Gott, I hope not. I am having a good day and so help me if you say either of those nasty things, I will kill you right here and now to protect my fucking lunch in my stomach."

Egon's eyes went with in shock. "Oh Meine Gott, nein. Nothing weird like that. Shit. I don't even want to meet anyone that is into that shit. Do you know someone like that?"

I rolled my eyes and stood up ready to punch this time-wasting bastard. "Nein. I also am not a dating service if you are looking to fuck someone who does like those things. Your fetish dumbass, speak it so I can puke and get to my studies? Ja?"

Egon looked at the floor "Well, I uhm, like the chains, electricity, and thudding. It is kind of my thing. I had a secret girlfriend for a while that did this for me, a beautiful silver collar but she found a new lover. Anyway, if you could arrange it so I could get one hour a week in the chains for a little torture, then I overlook this hour and call it even."

I smiled with full on wickedness at this news. "You don't say? Does the gender of your torturer matter to you?"

Egon shook his head, "Nein. I mean it is not the torturer I am interested in; it is the pain."

I sat back down and stretched out my legs flashing an evil grin at the other Maxes standing there with their mouths on the floor. "Well, this is turning out to be the best fucking day of my Gott Verdammt life, Egon. You have my attention. Now let's talk about the details, shall we?"

Egon narrowed his eyes. "You mean you can do this for me? I mean I know your collar is Priceless but getting someone to do this for a black collar and keep their mouth shut, that is nearly impossible. How can you be sure they would be trustworthy?"

I clicked my tongue. "I swear to you Egon, the person I have in mind for this favor is someone I would trust with my own children and has been seeking just this kind of arrangement for some time now. Tell me do you have your Wednesdays free?"

Chapter 23: Jonas the Vampire

"Egon nodded, "I can get any hour I wish free for such a thrill if I know it in advance. The day of the week is not a problem, any of them."

I grinned full of demons. "You say you can train one to do this thing you want, ja?"

Egon laughed. "What are you planning, Maximillian, to get a trainee in here to cut me up or fry my ass? I think not. I would want a thudder of at least some skill."

I shot a look at Maximillian that was making horrid urgent noises and motioning toward the late hour on the clock. "I can meet this request Egon, personally, for your pleasure and my own. I have great skill with the cane, but you can train me with other tools for a bit of variety, ja?"

The middle-aged seduction trainer's eyes went wide, and a smile came over his expression. "Wait, you would do this for me? If you are serious, I don't know how I can ever re-pay you for such an honor of it." His eyes were shining with awe for some unknown reason to me.

I sat up with a bit of confusion at his odd statement. "Uhm, ja I would do this myself. I have some free time on Wednesdays for now but that may change without much notice. We can work this out I am sure either way. So, we have this deal or nein?"

Egon smiled with glee. "Fuck, ja. I never imagined in my wildest dreams to be at the end of a pleasure tool with a Priceless collar. I think I may faint from my luck. Tell me this is no dream? If it is, then I never want to wake up. I not only will keep your lack of attendance a secret, consider me your loyal collar from this day forward in equal trade for the gift of your powerful affections."

I growled with much irritation. "I agreed to thud you fool, not fuck you. That is out of the question. Besides, my dance card in that area is currently overflowing, much to my disgust. I will never add no nasty black collar to it."

Egon's eyes went wide with terror. "Nein. I am sorry Maximillian. I didn't mean to offend you with my cryptic words. I see you don't know the legends of your silver. This is not a surprise to me. None of your kind last long enough to hear all of them. They say that the thudding skill of the Priceless is so sublime it will take the sufferer of their torture to a secret world of unimaginable delights. I would never expect to couple. That is the furthest thing from my mind. I am not the pansexual nor gay anyway. I swear my interests with this agreement were honest and pure."

I calmed down when he said this. "Oh, okay then we have a deal. I am happy to have a loyal black collar under my command. I give you this hour of, uhm, torture till you find this secret world you're seeking. I must go now, and I see you on Wednesday around ten. We will meet here and make sure to bring a lock for the door that only you have the key to. We need not get caught, ja?" Weird, huh? All this bullshit about a Priceless, damn maybe they think I could fly or bring back the dead too.

Egon giggled (ja, like a wife, straight my ass, girly boy). "I will be here Maximillian. I swear I cannot believe my luck today."

I got up and rushed to the door. "Well, I was having one of them kind of fine days myself until now. See you next week Egon. I will bring my cane; you bring your screams." I winked at that swooning idiot, then hauled ass to the backway up to the top stairs apartments.

I could not go the normal way with Olaf and Vilber still unconvinced of my abilities to destroy them (yet). I reminded Maximillian to mention the needs of the door Guards during his couple with Claus. We needed those favors quickly or it would not be long before my deceptions were discovered by Master Peter.

I made it to Claus's door with one minute to spare. I was sweating, out of breath, and my wounded leg near killing me from the running around on it for hours like that. I didn't even have to knock. The door came open and Claus reached out and grabbed me by my arm pulling me inside with much roughness.

He slammed the door and come at me faster than I would imagine a man of his advanced years could move. He snatched my hair on both sides of my head kissing my mouth with aggression. I didn't fight this frenzied display of lustfulness, figuring the sooner this was over the better you know? I shot a look at Maximillian when this old creep began pawing at my blouse trying to rip it open without unbuttoning it first (shit that was stupid, I didn't want to have to sew them bastards back on).

Ta my shock (and horror) that fucker grinned then left. I swear Meine Liebe, I could have killed him for sticking me with this disgusting schwuler sex business. I knew it was retaliation over my getting to fuck Annette but, Gott damn it, Claus was a nasty bastard.

We never even made it to his bedroom. He took me right there on his living room floor like an over-eager soldier back from many months of war without any distractions for his baser needs. I got through the foulness of his requests for oral stimulation then harsh penetration by reminding myself I was gonna beat this old sonofabitch with my cane soundly the second I got a chance at it. It was not quick intercourse either. That fucker wanted to take his time and enjoy it. Can you believe that shit? Oh well, sucks to be us, ja, Meine Liebe?

Anyway, when at last Claus was spent of his lust (at my fucking expense, Maximillian was so dead), I was at last released from his foul touching. It was while we were re-dressing when I noticed he was wearing the panty hose and lace panties under his trousers as Master Peter suspected. I scoffed at this loudly but kept buttoning up my shirt (counting them buttons to see if any was missing, that idiot pulled off three of them. I hate sewing. You can do all that for me from now on, that is a directive. I wish I had you around back then, okay for more than the sewing, I admit that. Hey, get back over here in my lap. I told you to stop trying to sneak off Meine Liebe.)

Shit, where was I again? Oh ja, so I scoffed loudly, and Claus heard my sound of disapproval. He looked at me with some confusion.

"What? Did I do a bad job in our couple or something? I personally think that was my best performance ever. I never enjoyed sex so much. I am already looking forward to next week with joy. If only I was younger, I would ravage you again. Maybe twice more in the hour I have." He chuckled, then looked my still half-dressed self-up and down with lustful intent (Okay, just fucking yuck, you know).

I shook my head. "Nein, I am not complaining Master Claus about any of that. I notice you still hide this obsession of yours from the sight of everyone. You fear their judgement. That I find revolting." I started buttoning my clothing faster in case he decided my charms of making him younger were already working and he came at me for seconds, yikes!

Claus frowned at those words. "I told you Maximillian, I cannot just go prancing about in my beloved dresses like you can. I am a man of respect and power. An Elder Dominant of the highest class. If I come out in my gowns and makeup, I would be a laughingstock."

I chuckled then grabbed my hat that had been flung to the far end of the room in his frenzy. "Well, that is a funny thing. I never knew that a lion worried about the laughing of the hyenas. I thought the big cats kill them mangy dogs when the get too close to them. That is natural though. You think what you do is not natural I suppose. There is no higher predator than the lion among the animals. They know it too. I know damned well they don't hide quaking in their dens when those hyenas pack up to attack them. They stand their ground and kill the canines and eat them for their dinner. I believe you are incorrect to fear the misguided judgement of these below you but what would a dumb boy like me know? Clothes are only material and fashion is meant to be a pleasure. If you deny yourself such an amusement worrying about the giggles of people you can legally murder, well, who am I to say you are wrong for this mercy you grant them at the sacrifice of your own freedom. I suppose you are a bigger man than I ever will be. I personally would use your power until I silenced every Gott damned snicker I heard behind my back."

Claus looked up at me with a startle. "Oh Meine Gott. What you just said, this was wisdom I never thought of. You're right. I could put anyone into the orchard if they dared to laugh at me. Maximillian, my love, how did I ever live without you? I have been a fucking fool. I struggled all my life to be the top power of this Haus and still I waste what I fought to have. Come here my love, I want to hold you in my embrace until my time with you is up. I will do my best to draw the strength I need to break my chains of doubt and finally be myself without fear."

I did as he commanded cursing Maximillian for the millionth time since this whole bad scene began. Suddenly I remembered my task. "Master Claus, I need to call in my rights to favors from you. I know it is a bit soon as you only just received my special services as I promised." He interrupted me smiling while stroking my cheek in his embrace (again let me say, yuck).

"Ask my love and it is yours. I am most pleased with your services to me. You're an amazing lover, the best maybe I have ever known. I feel like a young boy again and am already feeling pain that I must let you leave me

shortly. I will pine like a lost spouse for my Maximillian until at last I have you again next Thursday." He smiled with much kindness in his gaze.

I nodded. "Uhm okay, I need aid in being capable of seeing you without detection. This arrangement will not work until I buy out two black collars that you know. They were in Xavier's employ. The Haus calls them Olaf and Vilber."

He ran his hand along my chest appearing a bit irritated at hearing those names. "Ja, I know these two names. What is it that they ask to keep their tongues still of your daily movements?"

I sighed, keeping my baleful eye on Claus's wandering hands worried a bit that he would rip off another button any moment. "Well Olaf asked for a night of passion with the silver collar of Master Malfred's home named Tamina. Vilber requested to share a meal and the company of a Dominant in the Great Hall.

He scoffed. "These black collars ask much. I am not too surprised though. They think a great deal of themselves since Xavier once trusted them so much."

I winced. "You cannot meet their demands then? This is not a good thing. Without their allegiance I will be *discovered in a short time slipping away, Master Claus. Master Peter is no fool."*

Master Claus grabbed my chin forcing me to look into his stern wizened face. "I didn't say that the favors they demand cannot be met. I only say they ask a great deal more than either of them is fucking worth is all. You can rest your fears my love. I am the fucking power of this Haus the last I checked. Didn't my gorgeous Maximillian only just remind me himself? I will contact Master Malfred immediately. This Tamina and Olaf can meet in my own secret cottage for this arrangement this very night by eight. As for this Vilber, you tell him to be at the Great Hall at the same time and wait at the entry. His Dominant date will fetch him from there. Now, I am aware you will need to leave me within only a few moments, but I would request a couple of favors of you myself." His expression softened as he looked me over while there in his arms.

I took a deep breath. I was grateful he could capture the door guards but not happy to hear he required more than he already took from me. "You know I can deny you nothing, Master Claus. You possess my heart and my loyalty just as I possess yours."

That statement made the old Elder nearly swoon with joy. "First, I ask for a kiss before you go. My other desire is your promise that when next we see each other outside my time holding your leash, I can gaze upon you with

143

adoration, and you will openly appreciate this attention in front of anyone that witnesses this public display."

I chuckled. "I have no problem with either of these things you wish of me, but I must warn you Master Claus, Master Peter is a jealous man. Brazen flirting with each other may set him into a nasty humor." Not that I gave a shit. I was more than happy to piss in Master Peter's shoe with everyone around to see such shameful behavior.

Master Claus smiled wickedly. "Well Peter is lucky I am an Elder and cannot directly possess my truest desire completely. If the rules allowed me to own submissives, be assured Peter would be growing a tree in the orchard, and your collar would be in my hands. I am a jealous man myself, and I think he has no idea how far I would be willing to go to have what my position of power allows. If he punishes my beloved for following my wishes, then you tell me and I wouldn't want to be him when Claus gets his revenge, ja? Peter allowed my leash with you and that is no secret. By Haus law I am permitted to show my interest, respect, and thrill upon seeing the collar that I had once enjoyed so thoroughly, even if I am supposed to never gain such joy again."

My eyes went wide at hearing that open affection was legal after a leash night was spent. "Oh, this I didn't know. Well, if you are willing to defend me from my Master's displeasure over my expression of yearning for you, Master Claus, then I will be happy to grant this favor you ask me for." I smiled with evil back at him relishing the thought to not only would my flirting with Claus piss Peter off, but it would likely get him reprimanded for attempting to stop it.

The Elder chuckled. "Ah, you are a devil Maximillian. I see the eagerness in your eyes to see Peter whipped for punishing you. He should have informed you of this rule though. You are aware that leashes are usually kept to one time only and Priceless collars rarely are leashed out at all. Spending the night with a pleasure submissive that was so desired one Dominant traded much for the thrill of it, can lead to unquenchable lust for that collar that belongs to another. Many a secret affair, like our own, have begun this way. It is ridiculous to assume after a coupling of two people there will never be any unresolved desires between them. Therefore, the Haus allows for open displays of tenderness and even expression of wishful intent to help keep some of the sneaking around to a minimum. The punishment for any Dominant that corrects the unrequited lustful expression of his collar for a spent leash Dominant is five lashes in the rooms below. I think maybe Peter may be in for at least a few dozens of whippings over his inability to follow the rules, but what do I know, ja?"

I began to laugh full of demons at this clever old bastard's desire to see Master Peter knocked down a peg or two. "I think I may be falling in love with you, Master Claus," I said jokingly.

Master Claus took on an expression of seriousness. "That is my intent Maximillian. Now, for the second favor I requested. My kiss?"

I nodded then engaged him in the passionate kissing he desired. This time I was able to endure his heavy petting without any feelings of disgust. Master Claus was offering to make my putrid existence a bit more tolerable for only the payment of my appearance of compliance to his lust. For this even I, the sadistic Mad Max, could tolerate a little molesting without penetration for such a fine trade. Though I was still gonna kill Maximillian for his dirty trick of leaving me to be fucked by this guy.

When the hour was up, Master Claus allowed me to leave, but was too upset to see me to his door. I was young and unaware of the true power I wielded over the heart of my conquests. I viewed his lack of attendance to sending me out of his apartment personally as evidence that he cared only for using me as a sex object.

I had no idea he had taken off to his room to grieve heavily that I was never going to be staying for good. This strange behavior of rushing away the second my time was up with him would replay every time I left him over the next few years.

Master Claus never learned to tolerate the pain of seeing his lover walk out his door for all the time of our affair. His fear that each of my visits was the last time he would possess his darkest fantasy likely caused him much unnecessary torment until the reaper finally came calling for him almost four years later.

I must say it was a silly thing for him to fear. Meine Liebe, you will agree that I am many foul things, but one thing I am more than anything else is a man of my word. I promised to be his secret lover all his remaining life, and I remained so till he took his final breath, even after I broke my collar. If he was alive to this very day, well then, I would still be visiting his apartment to meet his lust every Thursday at one.

Who would have guessed this old, hardened Dungeon Master of an advanced age would be so damned sentimental and soft hearted for the likes of a scarred up, disturbed kid? The man may have been beyond hideous looking, and his touching was indeed beyond revolting but I must admit he spoiled me quite a bit. I would find over time he was not opposed to granting anything my dark heart desired.

Ta think, I managed to seduce this cross-dressing, old buzzard simply by thrashing him till he faced up to his own reflection. If that is not insane then I don't know what is. Well, I suppose stranger things have happened in my life and before I end this story you will agree I have had my fair share of the most bizarre of situations occur.

Well, I high tailed it from Master Claus's apartment After making sure the coast was clear for my rapid retreat. I was almost to the back staircase below when Master Jonas appeared out of nowhere. I almost screamed in terror when the Vampiric seemed to materialize out of thin air. I fell to a kneel unable to get my terrified mind out of a whirling pool of pure panic.

Master Jonas found this fright of mine hilarious. "Christian Axel, what the hell are you doing groveling on the floor like a scared child. Get the hell up and demonstrate that bravery that makes my blood hot and heart pound in my chest with desire for your love."

I was panting a bit from my running away from Master Claus's apartment and the startle Master Jonas had caused me. "Uhm, I apologize, Master Jonas. I didn't see you standing there, is all. I suppose I thought I had been caught sneaking off from, uhm, I just thought you were Master Peter."

Master Jonas chuckled again at my stupidity. "Not even close. I would be offended if you mistook me for that pig even in your panic to leave the scene of your crime, but I understand. such a thing that your doing is extremely dangerous. To be caught would be most unfortunate for your continued good health. Ah, but this is of no consequence since it is not true. I wanted to catch you before you managed to escape my path fleeing back to the safety of your Master."

I stood back up doing my best to calm my shallow breathing. "Ja? you required my attention for something, Master Jonas?"

He nodded. "I wanted to tell you that I arranged for this shame leashing with your Master as you asked me to. It is set for next Friday night."

I felt my stomach turn a bit at that news. I was aware I needed to gain the affections of this most powerful Dominant but the idea of how this had to be done, oh fucking yuck. I nodded at the news and tried not to let him see me turning green with my disgust at it.

"Uhm, thank you for the mercy of letting me know this, Master Jonas. You are most kind to do so," I mumbled out feeling my lips had gone numb with the terror filling my veins.

Master Jonas caused me to flinch when he broke out in a loud deep laugh at my response to his statement. "Oh Meine Gott, kind? I think not. I don't chase you down to tell you this because I am being nice Christian Axel. I am here to demand that the day you come for this leash, you engage in no other coupling from the morning until I possess your collar that night."

I looked up with a startle at that weird directive. "Huh? I don't understand. Why would you even care? I

149

thought you realized I cannot allow you intercourse while it is Peter that holds the leash. If I did, then the favor you owe would be his to claim."

Master Jonas nodded. "Ja, it would be if I were a man that felt any honor toward that stupid bastard. The truth is that I know what a creep he really is. He is not a man of honor. I owe none of it in return for such a waste of human existence. I will do whatever I wish with my leash night and enjoy my rights. I give my favor and oath of loyalty to you, not him. I look forward to getting my darkest desires met with his fucking permission this one time. Every time after that, what he doesn't know doesn't hurt him, ja?"

My eyes went wide at this most disturbing news, "Forgive me for saying this Master Jonas, but if you betray Master Peter by making this vow you never intend to keep. Then why should I believe the one you swear to me?"

Master Jonas smiled in a way that chilled me to the bone. "Christian Axel, you dare to question my true honor? I swore my oath of loyalty to you to gain your real love. You will need to learn to trust me, or you will fail to earn the immeasurable services I repay you with."

I nodded doing my best to appear strong but honestly, I was scared out of my skull of this Vampire man.

"Trusting you was not part of the agreement, Master Jonas. I said I would give you my couple, blood, and romantic interests only. So, at the risk of losing your interest by insulting you once again, I must demand to know why I should believe in a man's word when he is so quick to betray his promises to another."

Master Jonas's expression turned dark and fucking scary I admit when he grabbed my arm pulling me close to his face where only I could hear his words. "Because I was within hearing distance strolling in the gardens the day Agnette told your father of your conception, Christian Axel. I know who you really are and the extent of this horror you endure. Peter is a man that would be so dishonest as to use his own blood in such an abdominal way to obtain power. He will never receive my honesty. He deserves none. It is my pleasure to see the victim of his cruelty rise and destroy him. I would have aided your quest for freedom if only your asked for my help. However, since I will be put into many uncomfortable situations over this bid for the darkest of vengeance, I decided to ask for a taste of your unnatural gift to make it worth my while. Then upon meeting you, I find myself enslaved to the most amazing creature on earth. I must have you for my own, in all ways and I will. Now question my loyalty to you again and I will forget that I am lost in your eyes. I am a patient man, and I understand gaining your love will take time, but I will not tolerate deception from you. As I just told you, I know this streak of dishonesty runs in your family. Beware, I can be violent beyond your imagination little Christian Axel. Do not test me boy."

I began to tremble in his clutches as his words rang out in my ears. "You know who I am? I don't understand." I attempted to deny the truth that was too painful to hear spoken out loud by another (and had gotten Ryker and Felix a place in the orchards, to be truthful).

He sneered at me with what appeared to be disgust. "Don't even attempt to play me, Christian Axel. You know fucking well what I am saying to you. I heard Agnette tell Peter she was to bare his child. I heard that bastard tell her to find another fool to claim her belly. I found that disgusting. What father would deny his own offspring. I hated that man for all the years until one day not long ago I see this beautiful boy of my darkest dreams wandering the hallways yelling at no one. I asked around and found this Priceless collar belongs to that rat bastard Peter. I then discover the Priceless is an interest of Xaviers, and Agnette is trolling with that dumb fucker. It took only a bit of snooping to discover the bullshit the three of them hatched to attempt a Haus takeover using their own fucking kid. I wondered what sort of monster you must be to agree to such a disgusting arrangement. I began to follow you out of morbid curiosity. I realized with horror that you had no idea of any of this. That is why I pulled you with a bullet in your leg from the yard.

You found out didn't you, Christian Axel? In a moment of weakness, you decided you couldn't live with it."

I shook all over feeling I may display an unmanly tearful breakdown at hearing what I didn't want to face, "If you knew I wished to end my life over what I learned then why the fuck did you save me? It was my sincerest desire to end this thing that should never have been."

Master Jonas's look of indignation softened slightly though it was still quite stern and full of fury. "I was not going to save you. I admit that. I watched you staggering in the sun full of the bravery ready to face your end, but vishing for death is not true bravery, is it? Living with the horror, now that takes real courage. I suspected that Peter made a mistake thinking he was clever passing off a fake when he possesses the real thing. I decided to save you to see if you indeed were the Priceless, I suspected you were. Even after being given such a blow from a brutal reality, you sought me out and demanded my loyalty in exchange for becoming my lover. You have no qualms about doing whatever you need to do to gain your revenge. I fell in love with you that very second. You can be assured my adoration of you was hard won and not taken lightly. I will aid you in every way to take over this Haus and crush your enemies. I will enjoy watching the look on their faces when the nightmare the greedy Peter and Agnette created from their own kind backfires on them both."

153

I dropped my gaze, still fighting off the tears of despair that threatened to make me look a fool in front of this Elder. "If this information was discovered so easily by you, then surely others would know by now who I really am. If so, then I will be destroyed soon. If not by my Master himself to hide the deception, then by another looking to stop his rise."

Master Jonas shook his head, never breaking his glare at me. "Nein. It was not easy to discover. It took me more than thirteen years to put this all together, Christian Axel. All your life only me, your mother and father know. I believe you destroyed the other one privy to this information or perhaps Felix was really that clumsy? Jonas chuckled with wickedness. I appreciate your style of doing what must be done to protect yourself. I would have done the same. I can assure you. I am the only one in this Haus that knows the entire truth of this nightmare."

I looked up with a start. "You have enough dangerous information that you could use it to blackmail my Master into a lifetime of my enforced favor to your every whim. Why the fuck would you not just go around me and get what you truly desire? I can promise that would cause him much pain. This fight is not yours and I find it hard to believe watching my Master and mother getting there just desserts would be enough for you to get involved in this fray."

Master Jonas tightened his hold on my arm while fire began to light in his dark eyes. "Ah, you are correct. I could go and see Peter with my secrets. He would force you to come to me, give me all a man could ever take from another. However, I hold in my hands the most powerful Priceless I have ever been so blessed to see. The demons of revenge, horror, and agony run in your veins. I want you to willingly allow me to share in the forbidden power that kind of hate generates. I don't want a slave, Christian Axel, this I already told you. I want your passion and your affection as a true lover. I can have all I want. All I need do is keep my mouth shut and give you plenty of reasons to love me the way I want you too."

I nodded. "Okay, this I understand but then I must be honest with you in return for your own truths. I will not love you, not for real. I am not lustfully inclined for the man. I will do my best to play the role you desire, but it will always be false." I gulped down with fear realizing being a liar at that moment may have been a better plan than showing honesty.

Master Jonas let go my arm and backed up smiling at me with confidence. "You think that love is driven by sexual desire, Christian Axel? I realize your youth has you at a disadvantage in understanding there are other paths to true love that do not require sexual attraction to bring you to it. In time you will find a romantic passion for your Jonas, even if at this moment you have no belief such a thing is possible. I only ask you to be open minded

155

and come to me willingly. It is my job to build the fire of amour within your heart that will heat your desire for my affections. Allow me to do this unhampered by the false understanding of this amazing emotion. The feelings of romantic love have been badly injured and twisted up within you from the gross misuse of you by others all your life. I can repair such damage; this I also can promise you. All I need is your willingness to try, your complete trust in me, and a little time. This was my stipulation that you agreed to. Remember?"

I nodded, still keeping my eyes to the floor over this most uncomfortable confrontation with my inner demon. "Ja, I remember. I am a man of my word. I will keep my agreement and do as you ask for next Friday. The way I see it, I have no choice but to trust you anyway. If you wanted to end me, you would have done so long before this moment with all that you already know. You will find no further questioning from me, Master Jonas."

He laughed hard again then pulled me close kissing my forehead without bothering to care who may be slinking around to witness this display. "You call me Jonas not Master Jonas, Christian Axel. I am not your Master. You are the Priceless collar and my true love. You have not yet figured out you are my master, and I am your helpless slave. Now, you get home to Peter's apartment and clean up fast from your tryst with Claus. I sent that dumbass father of yours on an errand to buy me time for this discussion. I also assumed because you are new at this sneaking about you didn't think to shower before leaving your lover's bed. Next time do that before leaving his embrace. Forgetting to cover up evidence will get you caught quickly, my love. Don't ever forget that important fact again. Now go, get home and shower. Hurry up, I will see you on Friday." He motioned me to flee, which I was more than happy to do.

I ran down the stairs then up the hallway back toward the front of the Haus. Sweat was pouring down my face from the pain in my leg and the vigorous activity of my gait. Terror gripped me while I recalled Master Peter's words regarding his discovery of Ryker's evidence left from my couple with him the day of my brother's death. I had forgotten that if Master Peter decided to call special services, Claus's use of me would be readily evident. Shit, how could I be so stupid not to think of that.

I almost ran up the stairs to my Master's apartment without recalling to inform Olaf and Vilber that I had met their requests. I had to stop on the third step and limp back to the now glaring door guards risking wasting more time. I had to give them the directions Claus gave of me.

"Well look at this Vilber. Looks like Egon worked Mad Max over pretty well. Did his thudders hurt that much? Shit, you'd think you a bit tougher after feeling the lash of that brutal Xavier," chuckled Olaf as I closely approached the two so no one would hear what I was about to tell dem.

157

I rolled my eyes at his attempt to engage me in useless banter. "Shut the fuck up Olaf. I come here not to be insulted but to give you news of interest I believe."

Vilber shot Olaf a look of cautio., "Leave Mad Max be with your nasty words, Olaf. Why must you encourage him to set Peter on our asses? I am in no mood to join this collar in a thudding from Egon."

Olaf scoffed, "Fuck you are a pussy, Vilber. Oh, okay, what the fuck do you have to tell us that we give a shit about, Mad Max? Did Egon grab your ass while he swatted it with his tawse or something?" He chuckled at that disgusting guess of my interest in discussion with them.

I shook my head growling with much irritation at this bastard hating that I needed his allegiance so badly I would have to endure his presence above the ground until my metal was no more. "Nein fool. I come to tell you to be at the garden cottage of Claus at eight sharp tonight. There you will have the night to enjoy the favors of the beautiful Tamina without prying eyes or chance of discovery. As for you Vilber, be at the entry of the Great Hall at this very same hour and a Dominant will retrieve you for your requested dream dinner date. I will keep my Master busy without his needing your services for this one night. Now, tomorrow morning when the sun awakens the world, your loyalty belongs to me, Mad Max, for the rest of your days as agreed."

You could have heard the foundation of the Haus settling when I said this to the two stunned brutes. They stood there staring at me in disbelief for several moments before Olaf finally recovered his tongue.

"What? Nein. This must be a joke, it must be. Those things we asked for are not only illegal, but they are also impossible to obtain," said Olaf with some fear leaking into his tone. He worried it was truth. If I wasn't kidding, that meant I had the power of the strongest in the Haus at my command. He was starting to understand I could have him destroyed if I wished.

I smiled with full on wickedness at that dumb bastard. "Ah, but you go tonight at eight and see if I tell lies. Enjoy the woman of your dreams. Fuck her till your dick falls off Olaf. I be seeing you in the morning. Vilber, I believe I will see you in the Great Hall at supper time, ja? It will be a pleasure to have you working for me boys. Now I must go, I am a busy man, ja?" I turned and rushed up the stairs leaving the shocked guards to awe at the power they were realizing I held in my hands.

Thankfully, Jonas was telling me the truth. Master Peter wasn't in the apartment when I staggered through the door. I was trembling in anxiety of being caught in the act of my affair with Claus. This caused some clumsiness in me until at last enough of the hot water and liberally applied soap, along with other more personal cleansing procedures, had washed away all signs of my betrayal of my collaring oath of monogamy.

I quickly dried, redressed, and cleaned up the terrible mess I had made of that bathroom. It seemed I dropped, knocked over, or displaced every fucking thing in that room during my terror driven task. I had to calm myself down. Acting like a scared kid was getting me nothing but more work to add to my already impressive list of daily shit I had no time to complete.

I was about to rush to grab my biology books for a bit of studying for the Friday exams when I saw Maximillian come slipping in with a look of victory on his face.

"So? How'd that business with Claus go brother Mad Max? You lucky boy, two lovers in only one day. One you fuck, the other fucks you. I am so jealous," he snickered at his cruel statement.

I turned around full of anger that he left me to handle Claus's couple like that. Without a word of warning, I plowed that schwuler motherfucker right into the wall. He struggled while I grabbed his throat throttling that bitch soundly. Our struggle ended up knocking everything off Master Peter's bathroom counter into the floor from the force of it.

"You Gott damned son-of-a-bitch. You left me to deal with that nasty shit. I am going to fucking kill you for this," I yelled out with much fury as I choked that prissy shard with much pleasure.

Maximillian choked out, "Let me go, Mad Max. You deserved that. I am sick of your making fun of me for doing my fucking job. This taught you a little empathy, didn't it? Penetration and oral sex with the man is not fun, now is it."

I squeezed him tighter, turning him blue. "You cocksucker. Teaching me empathy for your worthless self? Is that what you call what you did? Who are you to punish me, you stupid jackass. How about I flip you over and fuck you up the as. There is your empathy, you motherfucker. You think you're my master? Ha, you are nothing but a fucking pressy little schwuler hiding behind your delusions of power," I screamed out as I watched Maximillian starting to dim and fade nearing a shattering in my grip. He was about to be no more.

"So, I am just a prissy little schwuler with a delusion of being your master, am I. Well, isn't that interesting news to hear, Maximillian," I heard the voice of Master Peter roar out behind me.

I let go of Maximillian immediately and dropped to a kneel. My brother shard gasped and ran from the scene, no doubt grateful (despite the horror of what Master Peter heard me say) for this interruption of my near murdering of him. I trembled in terror realizing that my Master thought I was referring to him, and not to my submissive brother shard Maximillian.

Meine Liebe let me take a moment to say, if you are gonna try to murder one of your shards, then make sure to do it quietly. Also, would be smart to make sure all the breakable shit is tied down. Masters don't understand you are not speaking to them since they cannot see what you do. It is something I had to learn the hard way.

I nodded at this most valuable information. Too bad it was another lesson I never really learned.

Master Peter stepped into the bathroom staring in fury at the broken mess on his floor and his shaking collar kneeling in the center of it all. "What the holy fuck is wrong with you Maximillian. You break up my house, talk about me most foully behind my back, and you lie about all of this I see by feigning a respectful stance for me. You need to speak up fast or I am going to make you sorry you were ever born."

I hear Maximillian scoff at that as he came at me with speed. "As if we weren't already that. Move over brother. I will fix this shit." He pushed me with strength out of myself sending me sprawling across the floor.

I looked up at Master Peter pretending to be in psychological torment. "If you want to know then I will tell you. I ran into Master Jonas on my way home from my lesson with Egon. He says he purchased my leash for the upcoming Friday, and this upset me. I know it should not bother me, but this man is not only disgusting he frightens me. Then I was almost home when I overheard some chattering collars whispering in the Halls of your affair with Master Grisham. You say that you love me, but you sleep around and trade me like a whore to these foul Elders without a care for my feelings about any of it." I did my best to appear very jealous though I was full of shit.

Honestly, I was hoping that rumor about him and Master Grisham was true. If he could find another lover maybe he would stop fucking me. That would suit me more than fine.

Master Peter's angry glare immediately went to an expression of surprise. "Oh, my. I uhm, Maximillian my love there is no truth at all to this thing you heard about me and Master Grisham (shit, there went that hopeful fantasy, ja?). Even if it were that is none of your business. I didn't vow monogamy to you. As for trading you off like the whore, this is unavoidable. You have no idea how much it pains me to watch my prize befouled by these beasts. If I could assure your broken metal any other way I would do it. This you know. So, this silly jealousy you demonstrate is uncalled for. I am not sleeping around on you or indifferent to your pain, my love. I love you more than even a parent could love his own child."

I took a deep breath wincing at that most foul and truthful parallel he claimed was similar to his love for me. If this is how every parent loves their children the way my father loves me, yikes! If he were correct, you'd have to ask yourself how the fuck has the human race survived all this time.

I did my best to appear relieved while shooting a hateful look at Mad Max still laying in the floor his mouth open in shock at my bullshit acting job and that horrid analogy Master Peter just used. "Then I can do nothing but beg your forgiveness for my most unbecoming display of injured affections based solely on wild fears in my head and phantom whispers of deceit I hear gossiped in the halls. I throw myself upon your mercy, Master. Do with me as it is your right."

My Master's expression softened as he approached me still in my kneel. "What am I going to do with you, Maximillian? How can I punish my beloved for demonstrating jealousy for my complete attention? I love only my Maximillian and find all my interests with him is a dream come true for your master my love. I am flattered and cannot fake anger over this honor you show to me. You can clean up this mess and I accept your apology. In fact, I am going to prove you are my only desire right this minute." I looked up with honest disgust watching him undoing his pants walking toward me hand singling me to stay on my knees.

I immediately realized I had just talked him into finding his lust at my expense, shit. Well, I suppose having to suck your father's cock there in the bathroom floor because you got him to believe you jealous of his attentions, is better than a thudding, not even. I would have rather suffered in Xavier's chains a thousand times. Yuck, just fucking yuck.

After I brought my Master to his apex, he no longer demonstrated anger at my bad behavior. He left the room ordering me to attend to the task of picking up the broken things and sweeping up the chaos Mad Max and I had made of the floor.

I closed the door and shot a look of fury at Mad Max still sitting on the floor looking disgusted. He had been stuck as a witness to the revolting blow job that saved our ass from the chains. I glared at him beyond furious since it was his own fault that shit happened in the first place.

"What the hell you acting so grossed out about brother? I do believe you sucked a cock yourself today. Not so fucking high and mighty now, are you," I said while crossing my arms at him.

He stood up appearing pissed I brought out the truth like that. "You bastard. You abandoned me to deal with Claus's couple. That is not my job, Maximillian. You are the one that does the nasty sex with the man, not Mad Max. I see you didn't even balk when your own father sticks his dick in your mouth. You love the taste of jism, and we all know this, you whore."

Now that was going too far. I had no choice but to do the job I was created to do. I was sick and tired of being treated with no respect for being good at what I do. One can even hate the work but still be an expert and worthy at the employment of it.

I scoffed, "I am stepping out of this boy, and we can settle this bullshit right now, Mad Max. I will not spend one more minute listening to your insults. I have had it with you." I jumped from the boy watching as he fell to the ground in a deep, mindless trance without anyone inside to run the show.

I squared up with the sadistic Mad Max while he pulled out his cane ready to thud me the second I was within range. I grabbed up a piece of broken glass from the mess on the floor. I was going to cut that vicious shard's throat and send him back to hell where he came from.

Just as the battle of the Maxes began the walls shook with the furious yell of our core Der Goldene Hund himself. "Halt, you sonofabitches. Drop your weapons and kneel. I didn't command this bullshit. Mind me this minute or I will destroy both of you where you stand without restraint."

Mad Max and I did as Der Hund ordered immediately. I was scared to death when I saw Der Hund enter the room with Mad Maxx, Max, and Christian right behind him. This was bad. Our core was beyond angered at our constant bickering. I was terrified to find out what he planned to do to end this open hostility. I could see in his eyes, he had something in mind, yikes.

Der Goldene Hund removed one of the broken chains from his outfit then called for Max and Christian to approach him. I watched still shaking in my boots while Mad Maxx come over and dropped to a kneel next to his brother Mad Max.

"My dearest Christian and this new creation Max are my bridge between the old me and the one being birthed by this painful path I endure. See how they hold each other's leashes and compliment the other perfectly. Max holds my forgiveness and ability to love while Christian my anger and innate lusts. They never argue with each other because they are in balance. You foul beasts do nothing but fight amongst yourselves. Each of you were created to protect me and aid me in my survival.

167

Maximillian, your job is to take the sex I cannot tolerate. Your behavior of leaving my shard Mad Max to do the task your specially designed to handle is not forgivable. It is not your right to punish Mad Max for perceived slights. His shard is sharp tongued, clever, and without empathy. The terror tasks of planning murder, deceptions, and cruelty is his job, not the finer points of gay sex. This thing you did today could have cost me everything. Mad Max didn't even know to clean the fuck up after such a foul deed. You would have known better."

I suddenly felt shame come over me as I realized Der Goldene Hund's words were correct. I hadn't thought of anyone but myself and revenge on Mad Max. He was not aware of all the nuances of sexual congress with the man, nor even the woman. I thought of his brutal, thoughtless thrusts on poor Annette.

Mad Max was not refined enough for the physical employment of providing or taking penetration, shit, why didn't I realize that? I had been blinded by my need to force him to find the very thing he doesn't possess, understanding for the pain we cause another.

In fact, I was aware Mad Max's lack of empathy protected Der Hund from hesitating when a brutal, cruel, or unfair situation arose. Sometimes, deep regret or feeling sorry for one's enemy can get a person killed when they cannot do what must be done to survive.

Der Goldene Hund could read my thoughts. "That is right. You see the error of your way, don't you Maximillian? Well too fucking late, isn't it? We got lucky and that getting so blessed included a horrid act to add to the ever-growing list of abominations with that twisted father of ours, didn't it? good enough for you Maximillian. However, I can feel that shit too my friend and I would like to know what right you have to force me to endure something that never needed to happen? You knew fucking well that Mad Max would retaliate. That is what he fucking does. That is his Gott damned job. You're lucky he didn't kill you."

I turned my head and looked at my brother Mad Max that was keeping his eyes to the floor "I apologize my brother for refusing to save you from Claus's lust today."

Mad Max glared at me. "Go fuck yourself schwuler boy. I will kill you next time I get the fucking chance. I will shove that apology right down your throat as a chaser for all the dicks you ever put there."

Der Hund railed out loudly shutting even the angry Mad Max into a cower immediately. "That is a fucking enough. I hear no more of this shit today. Come here Max and Christian. My loves you know what to do. I bind you for all time. What was two will become one." I watched in awe as Der Goldene Hund took that chain and tied Max and Christian together there back-to-back to each other.

Then all three of us Max shards gasped as the bonded Love and Lust shards melted into a glob of glowing goo. It was amazing to look at but also somehow disturbing to realize only moments before that glittering glob had been two boys that looked just like us.

Der Hund smiled then looked at Mad Maxx. "Come to me, my Masochist."

The tormented shard got off his knees and approached Der Hund. "Open your mouth my brother. I will feed you the most passionate emotions humans can possess. Your meal of your brothers will enlighten you. From this point on you will recall the taste of such pleasure and will desire nothing less and else. This will push you to crave more. Your appetite will bond you to my leash. Your desire to end your unquenchable hunger will force you to seek all possible carnality in all that I target."

I watched trembling in great terror as Der Goldene Hund scooped up handfuls of the shimmering gelatin and forced it into Mad Maxx's gaping mouth. That Masochistic shard began to glow from his head to his toes growing brighter with each swallow of that stuff. He had closed his eyes and seemed to be in rapture despite the repulsion of eating his own brothers.

When one third of the pile left of Christian and Max was inside of Mad Maxx, Der Hund stopped his force-

170

feeding behavior. He ordered Mad Maxx to return to his place and kneel and called Mad Max forward.

Der Hund did that same with the Sadistic shard without stopping until only one third of the pile was left. The same thing happened with Mad Max as did to our brother Maxx. He glowed brightly and seemed unable to hide his thrill at this horrifying dinner he was devouring.

He was then released, and my turn came. I was terrified, I won't lie. I didn't want to eat that stuff nor be forever cursed as a slave to emotions of passion. I had been free of such a burden all that time with Christian and Max handling the load without my breaking under the weight of it.

However, I could not deny any commands of Der Goldene Hund. His wishes are law. I opened my mouth, and Der Hund began his task of feeding me what was left of my liquified brothers.

I felt the surge of intense pleasure and despair immediately. I both desired and was repulsed, loved, and hated, felt merciful and vengeful all at the same time. The heat of these strong emotions set me on fire with their intensity. I looked down to see I glowed just like the goo that now ran in my veins.

I felt extreme depression when the final handful was fed to me. There was no more to engulf. I knew immediately I had to find more of it no matter what I had to do. I had to have more of that stuff.

Der Hund smiled at me with that gentle expression he often demonstrated. "Now my brothers you all have a deeper understanding of what it truly means to be human. I leave myself in your skilled hands once more. We must meet this request given to us by Jonas the Vampire. I realize that it will take all three of you working as a team to accomplish what he desires. With a piece of Christian and Max as a bridge in each of you, we can be romanced and return it when the service is fair and equal. Mad Maxx will tolerate the bloodletting. Maximillian will provide the seduction and endure the Vampire's lustful couple. Mad Max you will attend all other tasks such as conversation, strategy, and when required, vengeful behaviors. Come Mad Maxx. We leave these two to attend to the mundane. If I come back to find any further arguments that lead to punishable behaviors, I will not be so understanding. Get along or find yourself out of this family of Maxes, I mean it." Der Hund motioned Mad Maxx when they followed the core of us all out of the room without another word.

I looked at my brother Mad Max feeling the urge to lick the floor where that glowing stuff had been laying. He looked at me and grinned full of evil.

"Okay, you can lick the floor on the left and I get the right." He took off to do what I was already contemplating. Damn him, I didn't want to share.

We spent the next several moments licking the ceramic tiles like two alcoholics that dropped the last beer on earth there onto the floor. Finally, we both realized there wasn't anything left of that amazing goo. All we were accomplishing was to behave like mops collecting dust and hair on our tongues.

I sat there in some despair at having no idea where to find more of my desire. "This sucks Mad Max. I cannot stand it. I don't know what bothers me more, that I just ate Christian and Max or that I wish to eat them again."

Mad Max groaned and sat down next to me staring at the tranced-out boy laying on the floor. "Well, that doesn't surprise me that you say that. I know the one thing that bothers you the most is the fact that you are not constantly eating some boy. Prissy cocksucker."

I was stunned by his insult. After just being warned by Der Hund to cut our arguing. "Why you dirty fucking psychopath. How dare you? At least I am making them feel good. No one likes you. Why don't you go find Egon and beat him so you can stroke your cock to his screaming, you freak."

173

He chuckled, "Now that's an idea. Thanks brother. I go now to this boy and see if I can get a release to wander around and find Egon for my cane. If not him then maybe Abelard?"

I couldn't believe this guy. I couldn't even piss him off by calling him what he is. Shit, he seemed proud that he is a psychopathic freak.

"Nein. I need to study dumbass. Then tonight we got the Great Hall. You can take over then and keep an eye on Vilber. I am curious to see what poor bastard he got to play a Dominant at this bullshit favor for that brute." I got up and entered the boy and stretched immediately as the fog cleared out of my brain. Then was pissed to recall I had to still clean up the mess from earlier. Well, at least I didn't have to mop one big spot on the floor, yes? My Master, Maximillian, laughed at that one.

The rest of that amazing day went quietly. I studied best as I could trying hard to ignore Mad Max talking off and on about how incredible the penetration of Annette had been. To be honest, I pretended to be irritated by his chattering about it, but in secret I loved hearing all the details. That girl was hot, and I was still very angry I didn't at least get to see it happen. though I was promised the next girl. So, I did my best to be satisfied that my day would come.

It seemed like time flew by. Before I knew it my Master came to me to take my leash to follow him to the Great Hall. There was a knock at the door just as he finished affixing my chastity device.

I was readjusting my beeches when I see a delivery man give my Master a large black box with a black bow and ribbon. I wondered if this was a gift from one of the Dominants sent to my Master in a token of respect over the loss of the black collar in his employ (Felix remember? Most knew that Felix loved Master Peter, so his lost loyalty because of his death would be something other Dominants in the Haus would respect.). To my surprise, and Master Peter's as well, this package was addressed to Maximillian.

My Master handed it to me frowning, "The delivery collar says this is a gift from Jonas. He desires you to have this token of his affection."

I almost died of terror. "What? Why would he do this," I yelled out loud more to myself, fearing betrayal of course, than to Master Peter.

"Calm down my love. It is not uncommon for interested Leash Master's to shower their prospects with tokens of their affections. Apparently, your attempt to curry this Jonas's favor this morning captured his fancy more than I expected possible. I know his demeanor on

175

the phone today was vastly more agreeable than yesterday, but damn, he already he is trying to woo your desire to serve him to your full capabilities. You better be careful when you allow his couple with you Friday. If you are the dead fuck you are with me, after he goes out of his way to attract your willing return of his lust, well, it can go bad for you. I maybe pick up my Maximillian cut up and beaten."

I shivered at that. "Really Master? He can cut me up and beat me and you do nothing in retaliation?"

He chuckled at that. "Nein. If you lay there like the statue forgetting this ain't Drexel (the Elder into statues and mannequins in case you forget) fucking you, then you get what you deserve. Now open the damned present. I want to see what he gave you, Maximillian."

I opened the box to find a long black jacket of velvet lined in crimson silk. The jacket was quite handsome and fit perfectly, though I was unsure how he knew the correct size. Master Peter was pleased with the token. He thought it fit with my unusual 18th century dressing style. He liked this addition to my look so much he even demanded I put it on and wear it to the Great Hall that night.

There was a note in the box under the coat. "May this gift warm your heart and blood. ~Jonas."

Master Peter wrinkled up his nose appearing grossed out. "Damn. This Jonas is a real sicko, you know. I hate that we need his help so badly to accomplish our goals, Maximillian. Thank Gott it is only for the one night. Can you imagine the horror if this guy had collared you instead of your Master Peter. The nasty things he wants to do with you and your blood. I cannot even think on it without gagging."

I glared at Master Peter (Mad Max was behind me and it was his turn to take over, so he was sticking around). "Ja, finding sexual interest in one's blood, which is disgusting, isn't it? I would think it may be the most revolting thing one can do." I said making a thinly veiled reference my Master's hypocritic statement regarding Jonas's depravity.

Mad Max pushed me out of myself growling under his breath, "Shut up, Maximillian. You will get us caught fool."

I rolled out of the way still wishing to slit Master Peter's throat, catch the blood that spilled out, and call my new lover Jonas for a toast to the Vampire's continued good health. Anyone that hated my father was now a best friend of mine.

Master Peter took my leash, and we left the apartment without any further difficulty thanks to my pushing that prissy out of my way. I noticed the door guards were two brutes I had never seen before. Apparently, my new black collar men managed to bribe a couple of relief fellows. I smiled with evil thinking of the look on Olaf's face when he showed up at Claus's cottage to find the sexy Tamina waiting naked to fuck him silly.

Then I saw Vilber standing at the entry of the Great Hall looking around with nervousness as my Master and I approached.

"Vilber? What the hell are you doing hanging around here like a buzzard? Don't they feed you enough at your own dinner time? Shit, get the fuck out of here. I think you have other tasks to attend without making your betters have to enjoy their meal staring at your ugly face," said my Master while he awaited the black collar attendant to come retrieve us for seating.

Vilber hung his head after flashing me a look of anger (he thought me a liar, of course). "You are correct, Peter. I apologize for being such an eyesore. I will be off now." He began to leave when I saw something that made me gasp, then drop to a kneel immediately bowing my head low.

Claus the Elder and most powerful Dominant of the Haus had arrived. He was wearing that white gown covered in rhinestones that I had told him was my favorite. He was in full drag, even wearing makeup and pumps. I, of course, dropped in full protocol as was required by Haus Law for all silver collars when an Elder was present.

Master Peter was startled by my drop to the floor but the appearance of the "bigger than life" showgirl looking Elder caught his attention more than my fall to my knees.

Vilber was trying to retreat (as was also protocol for the black collar around an Elder) when Claus yelled out. "Vilber, where are you going, my love. I am sorry to be late. It took a bit longer to get dainty than I expected. I am grateful you had faith I was on my way. Now take my arm and lead me to our table for our dinner together. I look forward to all the gossip and a fine meal with you."

Meine Liebe, the smile on my face was bigger than if the Devil himself would wear if he managed to collar a Pope. Vilber shot me a look of thrill, then took Claus's rhinestone riddled arm with pride that made him shine brighter than the sun. He not only was supping with a Dominant in the Great Hall, but with the Head of all the Dominants.

Claus paused a moment then shot a look at my Master that seemed a bit bored. "Ah. Peter. You will join Vilber and I at our table. There is no one in this Haus whose gossip is of more a thrill than you. I desire that

Maximillian sit at the table within my sight. I wish to enjoy a beautiful scene while I digest my meal and there is not any sunset that can compare to that Priceless collar of yours."

Master Peter gasped at that. "Why of course, my dear friend Claus. I would be honored, as would Maximillian to be of service to your pleasures." My Master tugged my leash hard, motioning me to stand and follow.

Den before this odd party mix of Elder, Dominant, Black, and silver could follow the stunned black collar server to a table another voice called out from behind me.

"Ah, Claus. It is good to see you. Are you heading to dine? I was looking forward to seeing if you wished to sup with me. Looks like you're already very occupied. I will find my company elsewhere then. Maybe tomorrow you would be so inclined to honor me with your friendship, ja?" I didn't need to turn around to know who owned this voice, I had come to recognize it even without the use of my eyes to verify the owner.

It was Jonas the Vampire.

Chapter 24: The Power Dance

"Claus turned around as did Master Peter. "Ah, Jonas, my friend. Nein. Nein. Come join us at my table this night. There is always room for my dearest friend and neighbor anywhere I go," said Claus sounding genuinely happy to see his brother Elder.

Jonas came forward and took the beaming Elder's other arm sending Vilber into fucking black collar Heaven with glee. Master Peter stood there staring at me looking confused. I shrugged my shoulders, appearing just as shocked as he. We followed the Elders while I could almost hear the stunned thoughts of my Master. He was trying to figure out how this boy he called a "dead fuck" had managed this level of seduction. I had managed to capture him a seat, and the attention, at the table of the two most powerful men in the Haus.

What I wanted to know, was what the fuck Jonas thought he was doing here. His openness about his attraction to me was surely going to get this affair he wanted with me caught before it began. I wondered if maybe I had fucked up daring to trust this odd man.

Then again, maybe he was really a Vampire and that is why he didn't fear getting me killed? I sat down in the chair next to Master Peter and across from Claus and

Jonas. I kept my eyes down hoping he was the real thing. He would need to resurrect my corpse once Master Peter had the Guard blow my fucking head off for double crossing him.

I was terrified but I could see that Vilber was in seventh heaven. When the cross-dressed Elder asked him to pass him the vine from the center of the table, that black collar nearly cum in his trousers right there and then. He truly moaned out in pure thrill, mumbling something about it being his pleasure. or some shit like dat.

My Master kept trying to get my attention with his eyes. When I evaded this private tactic, he reached under the table and swatted my thigh. I flashed him a look of wonder and he raised his eyebrows. I assumed he was asking me what the hell was going on.

I shrugged but then dropped my eyes immediately. I felt faint and hot. This was maybe one of the most uncomfortable positions I had been in, well me, Maximillian has been in worse. (Mad Max began laughing hard at that off handed insult to his brother shard and I hate to admit it, but so did I.)

Master Peter didn't seem satisfied I was as confused as him. "So, Jonas and Claus my two greatest friends. I am beyond honored to share this supper with you. I am not sure I am worthy of such honor though." He was fishing.

Claus looked at Jonas with much wickedness, then to my Master. "Oh well, I could lie and say it was because we desired your conversation Peter, but no need to do such a thing. I invited you because I wanted to gaze upon that amazing collar of yours. I never enjoyed anything so much in all my long days as the fantasies he fulfilled for me. In fact, I must say I feel like a new man since my hot, sultry, passionate, night with him in my arms." Claus was no doubt trying to push my Master's buttons with those words, yikes.

Master Peter nodded, "Ah, well this truth I can believe. Maximillian is the most amazing of all submissives this Haus ever has known. I see he did indeed cause a change in you, my friend. You partook of his legendary power, and I see this is a new outlook on life I assume?" He ran his eyes over the gown Claus was sporting.

Claus giggled then looked at Jonas ignoring my Master completely. "Jonas, my old friend, if you have not enjoyed a leash with Maximillian you must hurry to obtain one. I am practically two decades younger from a single couple with the boy. I know with your skill, in a single night, maybe you can extract a lifetime extra, ja?"

Jonas smiled back then looked at me with open lust in his eyes. "I like the way you think my dear Claus. I already have worked out my own night of romancing of the forbidden silver. I have this Friday all for my very own. I pray I can unlock the puzzle of his power in only the twelve hours of darkness I have to work with."

Claus clapped in glee (really? what). "Ah. What I wouldn't give to be you this Friday. This collar will take you to a world you only dared to dream of. I swear I awake every morning in a sweat thinking of my own precious night with him. Do me the favor and think of me at least once during your partaking of this wonder on Earth."

Jonas chuckled sounding quite sinister, "Old friend, if I were to think of you during my ravaging of this gorgeous boy, my manhood would run backward looking for a place to hide. Your ugly mug is the last thing I want to see when I have that right there to be looking at." He pointed at me saying this real loud.

I thought for sure Claus would be insulted but instead that Elder laughed. "You have the point there, Jonas. Damn, my own reflection couldn't be more cracked looking if I dropped the fucking mirror. How the fuck did I get old Jonas? Maybe I should have taken up your worship, ja?"

Jonas nodded. "Ja, about one hundred years ago when you were a young Frau fresh out of your mother's kitchen. As I see it, it is too late now. You don't want to be alive for a thousand years and stuck in your seventies, do you?"

Claus laughed even harder. "Damn, you are rough on me tonight, Jonas, you vicious bastard. Nein, no way I want to be around that long as this old Hag I have become. Now, if I could only find the female Priceless. A night with her would arrest father time and send him running in terror of Claus."

All the Dominants at the table laughed at that. I wondered what the hell that meant, but since I am not a girl, not my problem I suppose. I said nothing but kept my face towards that table in shock that Jonas openly told Claus of his leash. Neither of them seemed upset about the other's interest in my affections. The same could not be said of Master Peter. He was showing definite signs of irritation of Claus's open bragging of his enjoyment of his leash rights.

"You wouldn't even fucking know what to do with a female Priceless you old schwuler. Likely, she'd still give you some age defying ability when the two of your shared makeup secrets, ja," laughed out Jonas most cruelly.

I winced at that in-your-face insult. To my shock, Claus laughed so hard he nearly choked. I shot a look at Vilber. He looked back and shrugged also unsure why the most powerful man in the Haus was allowing Jonas, the youngest and newest Elder, to speaking to him like this.

Master Peter reached under the table and swatted my thigh again. I looked at him unsure what he wanted this time. He smiled while holding my gaze.

"Well, a female Priceless is a myth, we all know this. I have the closest thing to such a mystical creature right here in my loving hands. You will soon see that Claus tells the truth, Jonas. One night with my treasure and nothing else you ever known can satisfy again. I am so blessed it is mine for all time," he bragged out, making me angry that he said such a lie. I was breaking my metal, and he wasn't gonna feel blessed when I slit his throat after that, Gott damned him.

Jonas nodded, "Ja, the female is of no use to me anyway. I set my appetite on something tabooer. This thrill I seek will do me much good, I think. I have been feeling my age lately. I bet not much longer though. This Priceless will give me back my youth and vitality."

Claus winked. "And vet dreams for years after to go with that stolen time of yours."

That was all Master Peter could take. He reached out and grabbed my leash near my collar. I did my best not to fall onto the table from the force of his dragging me toward him. I almost yelled in shock as he pulled roughly, making me sit down like a kid would sit on Father Christmas's lap.

As I helplessly followed my leash the chain hit the plate in front of me. It made a lot of racket causing the Dominants at every table to glance – not like they weren't already sneaking looks and whispering at the strange scene – at our dinner party participants. The tongues were starting to wag big time with so many broken rules (silver and black at the table with Elders was bad enough; now a silver using his Dominant as a chair, oh hell it was so fucked up you know)?

I felt extreme shame that he made this move of possession like a child grabbing his toy before another can touch it. This was not the smart thing to do when he claimed to be attempting to seduce the top powers of this Haus. He had allowed Claus's taunts to make him jealous.

While I was in a hurry to witness Master Peter in an uncomfortable spot, I didn't enjoy being held in his lap like that. Jonas and Claus's humor had observably dimmed almost immediately at this most immature move on Master Peter's part.

If this had been the extent of his bad manners maybe the Elder's would have merely glowered without intervening. Master Peter didn't stop there though. He grabbed the back of my head clawing a handful of my hair then compelled my face to his planting a most disgusting tongue kiss on me right in front of them as he had done before with my mother present.

The first time he pulled this bullshit, it served its function well. This time, it backfired on him. Jonas cleared his throat loudly.

"I think you let the Priceless sit in his own chair. I demand you release our eyes from suffering your rapture Peter at our expense. I cannot speak for Claus, but I for one cannot thrill at the sight of this beauty with your ugly lips all over it. If your intention was to demonstrate Maximillian's skills, then I would advise using caution at this overselling technique. I am already well sold, and the deal is already struck. I believe, however, that is not what you are doing, I would not assume to insult your intelligence. That would lead me to realize this is a vulgar display of jealousy over this treasure among us. For your sake, I hope this is not the case. You know the punishment for interference with a spent leash's right to pursue this object of desire by fantasy looking and speaking. Such bad manners are unwarranted anyway, now are they? After all, your eagerness to leash him out to us, is proof you care so little Christian Axel that you sell it to Claus and now to me for almost pennies. I for

one am thrilled to pay such a low price compared to what Maximillian is honestly worth," the Vampire growled out then took a long pull on his wine glass shooting a look of disgust at his brother Elder Claus.

Claus nodded then glared at my Master sternly. "I agree with the wisdom of Jonas in this. Let that Priceless go to his seat. I do not wish to watch my love pawed with hands that are not my own. You can violate him at your will in your own time when I am not around to have to endure the pain of it."

Master Peter let go of my hair and leash motioning me to return to my chair appearing beaten. I got up and moved swiftly, grateful the my "lovers" saved me from the humiliation and horror of dealing with enforced public incestuous behaviors (I mean Claus didn't know but Jonas sure as fuck did).

Claus's look softened to the of kindness as he shot a big smile at me. "Wait, Maximillian now that you are off Peter's lap, stand up so I can view this wonderful outfit you wear. I want to engulf you with my eyes which will help to quench my hunger for you. I dare say, it will have to be enough to fill my yearning for the rapture of your embrace. Jonas, you should run away now, toss your bid for that collar transfer with Peter for Maximillian. If you are a fool as I was, you will find food tasteless and the wine dry for the rest of your days After your conquest of this sublime creature forged of the forbidden silver. Heed my warning brother, the legends are true."

Jonas smiled with evil intent at those words while gazing at me standing there demonstrating his "gift" jacket. "I am looking forward to becoming a prisoner of love as you have become Claus. Better to have tasted the fruits of the Gods once and pine all my life, then never know the joys of it at all. Besides, maybe this Priceless will not break his metal. If that is the case, he will belong to another soon enough. I can always hope for a second leash, or you know what? Maybe he will escape that silver. That would be even better. I will woo his affections and one day he will be mine willingly, ja?"

Claus gasped then giggled. "Jonas, you are an awful man. I saw him first. I will woo him and when he is judged Dominant, he will choose me as his lover not you. The boy could never wish to slumber next to a man always looking to bite him, ja?"

Jonas laughed at that. "Some people like to be bitten, Claus. Maybe I will take you upstairs and show you privately how nice that can be. You are looking mighty eatable in that white gown. I have never seen you look so handsome and full of life. That kind of turns me on."

The two schwulers began to howl at their "fake" flirting with each other. I sat back down finally calming a bit. I shot a look at Vilber who was still enthralled that he was the one man in all the Haus that every collar and Dominant wanted to be that night. Okay, maybe a few wanted to be me or Master Peter. Supping with two Elders was something few if any Dominants ever got to boast of in their lifetimes.

It was then that two old men came into the Hall. The crowd hushed and everyone's eyes darted about with anxiety, excitement, and confusion. I immediately hauled ass from my chair and took to my knees. The Elders Drexel and Bladrick had arrived, and they were suspiciously looking for Jonas.

I kept my eyes to the ground as the great men approached the table greeting their brother Elders with typical manners expected of their status. I could not believe this was happening. Jonas was proving to me he was a man of his word when I heard him insist that they join the table dinner party.

Bladrick, the eldest of the elders at eighty-one, spoke for him and Drexel. "Ah Jonas, you sly dog. You call us to sup so we may gaze upon this beautiful sight. How can we ever repay you," he said with a deep, rusty voice common for a man of his advanced years.

Jonas chuckled. "Well, to be honest I had no idea Claus was going to be so fancy dressed. He is quite the vision though I must admit."

Drexel nodded. "That he is indeed. I will have to paint you Claus in this very gown. It is becoming and matches your eyes perfectly," said the oddest and second youngest of all the elders, he being only in his sixties. Ja, remember he likes to fuck the statues and mannequins, or so that list told me anyway.

Claus was blushing of course and completely enjoying his newfound attentions. "You boys sit down and stop trying to stroke my hoddensack with your silver tongues. That can wait until we are alone, ja?"

Again, laughter broke out among all the Elders at that innuendo statement. I was still in my kneel of respect, but I stole a look at my Master. He was sitting there staring at the four of them with his mouth open in shock. If Barnim showed up, then my Master could boast something no Dominant could (well unless they were in big trouble with the Haus and the Elders called to exile them). Master Peter's status shot through the roof just by this one public display of this favor shown him by these powerful men.

Drexel and Bladrick were seated when Jonas noticed, at last, that I was kneeling at my Master's side on the floor. "Maximillian, what are you doing? Stand up my love and get back in your seat. I don't wish to have to gaze at the floor my whole meal looking for my pleasure. It is okay, Bladrick and Drexel would be lucky to see the beauty I will be possessing soon enough for my thrill."

I stole a look at my Master who motioned me to mind Jonas's command. I took a deep breath to steel my nerves then stood to take my seat. Bladrick and Drexel, who had been chattering to each other, gasped in unison staring at me wide eyed with their mouths open appearing surprised.

I trembled slightly as I sat, thinking their behavior was because something was wrong with the way I looked. I quickly dropped my gaze trying to see if my outfit was out of sorts or perhaps I got dirty kneeling rapidly like that?

Luckily, Jonas was there to save me from my thoughts of insecurity. "Ja, told you, didn't I? Gorgeous. His pedigree and skill can already be verified by Claus, and I get my own taste this Friday coming. That forbidden pleasure there can be yours all you need do is ask. Oh wait, where are my manners? Peter, you're not opposed to leashing that amazing Priceless of yours out to a couple of sad old lonely men like Drexel and Bladrick here are you? I bet they both could use the gift of a couple with one that can grant them fresh life and vitality, not to mention a view of beauty in perfection while they steal the years away from the grave." He smiled with that razor mouth of his appearing to enjoy his breaching of proper protocol of keeping leashing requests private affairs.

Master Peter sat there appearing too stunned to respond for a moment but then he nodded. "Uhm, ja, I think if they were to call on me something can be arranged that all parties can be happy with." He dropped his napkin as he went to wipe his nose (which he always does when he is nervous, watch for that tell behavior Meine Liebe. Always a bad sign for you. Your Master Peter doesn't like to be in a position of powerlessness as he was that night. His company outranked him you know.)

Drexel and Bladrick stared at me openly with smiles of debauchery that made me shudder despite myself. "Bladrick my brother, I can call and make this arrangement for us both if you wish it to happen."

Bladrick nodded. "More than you can know, Drexel. I had heard the gossiping, and I saw Xavier's condition, but I had no idea, ja, make the arrangements, brother."

Now understand Bladrick and Drexel were not really brothers, but Bladrick was so elderly that he could no longer couple properly. His fetish was that of the voyeur. This you heard of. Nein? Oh Well, Meine Liebe, which is when someone gains pleasure from watching the sexual activities (any kind of them from stripping to masturbation or even full sexual coupling) of others.

194

It is a pretty common fetish, and most people, even the normals, engage in it. It is not considered too unusual for a person to watch the things called X-rated films or look at the magazines of pornography. That is a form of light voyeurism, but Bladrick's fetish was a bit more significant. He liked to be in the room and liked the participants in his viewing to know he was watching them. More than that, he liked to direct their behaviors, this you understand, ja?

Drexel had a most unusual fetish. He had no need to engage in sexual activities with another living creature. Thanks to this, over the years, Drexel had joined up his own odd interest's with Bladrick's to up his thrills.

In other words, Bladrick would watch and even direct Drexel in his sexual activity's with his statues and mannequins. The two men had become a team of bizarreness that in truth hurt no one since both men were consensual and no living creatures were otherwise involved.

At least that is how it was. That night, I realized with utter disgust, Drexel was looking to find a little more warmth in his next fantasy lover and Bladrick was ready to find a way to join the fun.

Fucking yuck you know. How the fuck did I get so unlucky? I mean what the hell is wrong with someone just wanting to fuck another without all the weird shit? Bad enough I am a male. They got to go adding in more obsceneness to that. Fucking you own kind, sexing the statues, stroking the dead cock while watching that nightmare, drinking another's blood to find your orgasm. Why? Just why?

Sex feels pretty fucking good without all that bullshit added I thought, but what did I know, ja? I was just a stupid thirteen-year-old boy that could think of nothing but the blue skies and Annette's beautiful eyes.

Okay, sorry Meine Liebe but I always wanted to say that, on with the story.

Jonas laughed at the newly arrived Elder schwulers inability to keep their eyes off me, "Claus, your date has been noticeably quiet. You ignore his affections which is so impolite. You know what I think? Let's have the Hall play some music and you two can dance the waltz to make this up to him, ja?"

Claus turned bright red at that suggestion that he dance with Vilber. "Ah you are so bad, Jonas. Maybe my date Vilber wouldn't want to be seen with an old gal like me. I am so old my knees may creak louder than the music anyway."

Jonas looked at the moon eyed Vilber. "Do you hear this? Your date feels she is not appreciated by you. After

all the arduous work done to be pleasing to your eyes. Vilber, for shame on you."

Vilber nearly choked in terror. "Oh, nein. I apologize Master Claus. I think your gorgeous in that dress. I thought I was too unworthy of such bliss to even sit in your radiance. I would never have dared to believe I could be so blessed to hold you in an embrace and glide with you on the floor to music. I would likely die of a heart attack caused by my rapture the second you swayed to the rhythm of it."

Claus almost fainted from pure delight that Vilber was making such a fuss over him (smart move on Vilber's part, give that brute credit there.) "If this be truth then I must have this dance with you. Call the attendant and make the music so. I want to dance till my toes blister. This is the finest night of my life, and I have had so many."

Jonas, Bladrick, Drexel and Vilber all smiled while the old cross-dresser swooned and carried on. They all gave him many compliments on his gown, makeup, and large diamond jewelry while awaiting the music to be pumped in through the speakers in the Great Hall.

Then, at last, one of the classics by German composer Richard Strauss designed for a waltz permeated the air. Vilber stood up and offered his hand to the giggling

Claus, asking him for the dance. I swear I thought I would die of pure shock watching this unimaginable scene play out.

Everyone stopped eating their meal to watch with awe as the black collar, which was forbidden to even be in that room (much less at that table), began to beautifully dance with Claus through the room. Vilber was without a doubt, in heaven, and Claus seemed to be sharing a cloud just below him near the pearly gates.

I stole a look at Master Peter. He glared at me, then rolled his eyes making sure the others could not see it. I shrugged letting him know whatever the bosses wanted they apparently got. I then turned my attentions back to the dancers, privately smiling that this "low brow" behavior was upsetting to my Master.

He was such an arrogant prick. Well, most of the well-borns are. They think themselves better than everyone, and to bother with the likes of Vilber would be viewed as "slumming" and "beneath" them. I admit, I personally thought it a beautiful thing the way Claus didn't care about Vilber's status, and Vilber accepted Claus with an open heart. (Fuck Master Peter and everyone like him passing judgement on others like that, the hypocrite. I nodded that I agreed with him on that completely.)

Drexel, Bladrick, Jonas, Master Peter and I sat there watching these two souls become more enraptured in this courting behavior with each passing moment. The other Dominants in the Great Hall had initially been casting looks of disgust at this open disregard for the well-entrenched rules of the Haus. I noticed after only a short time of their witnessing the joy of this simple pleasure created for Claus and Vilber, the gazes of discontent dissolved.

I watched with much humor as slowly Dominant couples of every gender mix began to join the cross-dressed Claus's lead. Soon, many couples were swaying and twirling to the wild sounds of Strauss's symphony.

I was so enthralled by this scene I nearly screamed in terror when I felt a tap on my shoulder. "May I have this dance?" I looked up into the sharp toothed smiling face of Jonas.

I shot a look of terror at my Master who was sitting there with a dumbstruck look on his face. "Uhm, I think I must decline Master Jonas. Thank you for such an honor, but my leg, it is still weak from the incident yesterday."

Jonas's smile widened. "Ah, then you can lean your weight on me, Maximillian. I will carry you in my arms if need be. I desire to hold you in my embrace for all to see.

I am sure Peter will grant his permission, ja Peter? Do you have issue with my stealing your treasure for a moment for my own selfish pleasure?"

Master Peter's face went red with underlaying jealousy. "Ja, of course, Jonas. Be my guest. Maximillian get your ass up and mind this Elder. He wishes to dance, then you will dance with him. You get over that injury that you did to yourself and please him well. Go!" He then kicked my chair with some aggression.

Jonas frowned at that. "There is no need to be ugly, Peter. This boy is seriously injured. I understand his hesitation and appreciate his loyalty to his Master's favor. You would be wise to do the same." He held out his hand requesting I take it.

I winced but stood up, taking this strange man's hand as I was commanded to do. Jonas pulled my limping self behind him till we were in the center of the swaying dancers. I almost fainted in shock when he grabbed me around my waist and pulled me to him in a tight embrace. I tried to turn my head to glance at my Master, but Jonas reached up, putting his hand on the back of my head. Then like Master Peter earlier he forced my lips to his kissing deeply without care of the witnessing of this inappropriate behavior.

I trembled in extreme terror, just as I felt myself thrown to the floor. Maximillian had been hanging around to keep an eye on things. When this "heavy petting" business began, using his best judgement, he took over handling the situation as this was his job.

I initially attempted to pull away and struggle against this Vampire man. He would not let me free of his intimate embrace nor did he grant me any ease of it. I could not budge his strength (which was impressive, but again I was only a thirteen-year-old boy). I gave into his frenzied mouth kissing assuming Master Peter would kill me soon enough. I realized there was no need to worry about having to deal with the whispers and laughter from the other collars over this embarrassment in the hallways tomorrow. The dead cannot hear.

The music suddenly switched to one of a faster rhythm. Jonas pulled back from his oral attack and dipped me backward, causing me to gasp in utter surprise. Then without a moment's hesitation, he twirled me with great skill, leading a rapid paced dance across the floor.

I was helpless as if hypnotized by his spell. He would reach out holding my waist, arms, and clutched my back all in perfect tempo with the music. I moved with him, spinning, twirling, and dipping in splendid grace as if a puppet being worked by the most perfect of string Masters.

Around us, there were gasps of awe and most of the other dancers retreated to the sides to watch this most talented demonstration of flawless mobility. Jonas may be a Vampire, but that man missed his calling as a dancer of the highest skill.

When the song ended so did my trance. Jonas pulled me once more into his embrace, smiling into my panting eyes with wickedness rising in his expression. He let me down and kissed my neck while the crowd of Dominants all around us applauded in appreciation for our wonderous display.

He whispered in my ear, "If Peter lays a heavy hand on you over anything done or said this night, you will tell me and I will thrash his ass till he wishes for death, Christian Axel. He doesn't know it yet, nor do you, but you are mine." He pulled back with those words and still holding my hand led me back limping to my chair.

I sat down still unable to catch my breath nor think a coherent thought. This was getting out of hand. I couldn't understand what was happening to me. I didn't even notice my leg agony during that wild dancing. Nor did I fight this man hard enough when he kissed me. I think I may even have liked it, at least a little.

Master Peter was beyond aware over what he witnessed (as had practically the whole fucking Haus.)

"Well Jonas, no one can dispute your ability to make it appear Strauss was thinking of you when he wrote his music. However, I think in the future, you will remember that this collar is my property. There is a vow of monogamy between Maximillian and me. I don't like to share my things." Jonas interrupted my Master as he took his seat, appearing more than a little irritated.

"But you do share your things for the right price, Peter. I did nothing that breaches this collar's oath to you, fool. I only took a taste of my purchase, which is not illegal. Say another word in argument with me over my right and we can settle it downstairs, ja?" Jonas glared at Master Peter not even attempting to hide his contempt for the man.

Master Peter cleared his throat and wiped his nose (again, beware that behavior, Meine Liebe, not ever a good thing.) *"My dear Drexel and Bladrick, I would like to throw my case of injustice at your feet. Are these liberties Jonas takes with my property not a forbidden pastime? He has not even paid for his leash yet."*

Bladrick looked at Drexel then to Jonas, finally settling his sights on me. "Well, since our brother Claus, the head of us all, is not present to make this call. I assume since I am the next in command, I will make this judgement. I say Jonas is within his rights, Peter. If you don't want your Priceless pawed on by another, then stop fucking leashing him out. Otherwise deal with the behaviors such a beautiful creature will elicit in the ones that share in the favors he will provide them. You know the rules. A leashed Dominant is allowed to openly show interest, woo, and even embrace the object of their couple, or even a future couple, as long as others are around to witness nothing but superficial affection is shown. I see a kiss and dancing with my own eyes. I didn't see any intercourse nor deep molestation occur between Jonas and your silver. No rules nor vows of monogamy were broken. You granted Jonas the right to use this boy for his pleasure once. Therefore Jonas is well within his honor to be overly familiar with him from this point on. You will drop this request, or I will allow Jonas his right to punish you for embarrassing him over his partaking of the rights of his relationship with that Priceless collar of yours," he growled out sounding furious.

Master Peter's eyes went wide with surprise. "What? You mean that it is perfectly legal for Jonas to paw and kiss on my Maximillian for all his days in the metal over one leashing? This cannot be correct. I never heard of such a…" Drexel interrupted him this time.

"Uhm, ja it is correct, Peter. You never held a single collar for more than a year that I can recall. So, you never learned the rules of the promised or spent leash for Elders. You certainly never held any collars that were this coveted by so many, none of us have. While it is not common for a spent Dominant leash to desire such open

204

interest in something they can likely never possess again, it is their right to do it. Jonas, Claus, and eventually me or Bladrick can chase your collar with gifts, open wooing, romantical advances, and even kiss or touching him superficially all we like. Wishing for, and chasing is not getting, is it? We are all Elders, Peter. We couldn't hold your Priceless collar for our own even if we could kill you off and steal him for our own lusts. So, get the fuck over it. It is not that fucking hard to have realized holding such a gorgeous boy with such perfect qualities under a bunch of old men's noses would lead to much unrequited desire. If you didn't think this through before you got greedy to see our payments for our turn at using him for our pleasures, then that is your problem. In fact, I am only speaking for Bladrick and myself, when I say there is no need for any bullshit arguing over a price for this leash you will grant us. I agree with this price, even though it is unheard, and so does my brother. Now, come here Maximillian. Since you are now a promised thing, I want my taste of this prize and so does Bladrick."

I shot a look of horror at Master Peter who was turning green himself at this order. "Wait, I uhm, didn't say what the price is, perhaps I ask too much Drexel."

Drexel scoffed. "If Claus and Jonas can afford it, then Bladrick and I certainly can. We are richer and I dare say almost as powerful with our influences in this Haus. You said you would permit a leash, we said we accept your price. This bullshit of haggling over the details can be handled later. Enough of this stalling. I said come here boy. I want my taste," he yelled at me across the table pounding his fist down making all the China ware rattle with the force of it.

I got up without another moment's hesitation when I saw Jonas motion me to mind this command with his hand gesture and glare of caution. I realized at once the dangerous position I was in. If I ignored this angry Elder another second, it was going to go bad for me.

I decided Master Peter would just have to get the fuck over it. I knew an Elder could see me put to the orchard with only a word. If this man wanted to bend me over that table and violate me all night, I either complied or found my place next to Ryker, Villhem, Felix, Ben, and Geraldine.

I knelt before the Elder Drexel but gasped when he snatched my upper arm pulling me roughly forward almost onto his lap. "I cannot taste you on the floor boy. I am too old to bend down that far. Get up and give me your lips now." He grabbed my hair and planted his nasty kiss on me.

Jonas could be heard chuckling in the chair directly behind me while that vile man pushed his foul tongue into my mouth with wanton vigor. I did my best not to puke as I tried to balance myself to prevent falling onto

Drexel. I had no choice but to use his seated knees to hold up my weight, unable to rise, but unable to rest comfortably on my knees while this humiliation went on for what seemed to be forever.

It may have never ended if not for the tapping on Drexel's back by Bladrick. The schwuler pulled out of his kiss but held my head tightly in his clutches appearing out of breath.

"What the fuck do you want Bladrick. I am busy Gott damn you. Can you not see with those thick fucking cataracts of yours," he growled out while leaning back down to kiss me again.

Bladrick put his old claw over Drexel's nasty maw. "I want my turn. You take too long, Drexel. I will be pushing up the flowers in my grave before you finish. Give me my chance before you make the poor boy throw the hell up with your near toothless mouthing on him."

Drexel shook his head violently. "You old coot. Get your hands off me. You are like a dog that chases the tires but cannot do shit with it once it catches one. Let me test the skills of this treasure and you will just have to be satisfied by watching, which is all you can do anyway."

Bladrick pushed Drexel harshly. "You bastard. My mouth still works simply fine. Truth is, I am surprised you are spending so much time touching something that can actually feel it. Let that living creature of myth go and I will show you the proper way to enjoy the softness of the flesh you despise."

Drexel let me go so rapidly I teetered a moment then fell backwards. I let out a loud yelp spilling onto the floor when my injured leg failed to catch my sudden drop. Bladrick jumped up yelling in fury.

"See that is what happens when you treat your playthings without care, Drexel. This one cannot be glued back together. Use some fucking tenderness for a change will you, clumsy baster. The Elder schwuler and Jonas rushed over to aid me in getting up off the floor.

Truth was I had opened back up my wound in the fall and all that vigorous dancing didn't help, I am sure. I looked down to see a large wet spot of blood spreading across my thigh as I took Jonas's hand, he offered to pull me to my feet. He saw the fresh injury at the same time I did. Of course he did, vampiric sonofabitch that he is.

"Gott Verdammt. Look what you did Drexel. This collar is bleeding from your fighting with Bladrick like a couple of kids. This wound needs immediate attendance, or he will be no good to any of us. Peter, you go tell Claus we are going to your apartment and call for the Haus doctor for this treatment of Maximillian now. We will

meet you there. Come, Drexel, Bladrick, aid me in getting this collar up the stairs safely, ja?" I was suddenly surrounded by the three Elders that towered above me like a nightmare come to truth.

I let out a gasp as Jonas pulled me to my back and Drexel grabbed my legs. Bladrick cleared the way while the two strong Elders hauled me out of the Great Hall like they were trees and I the hammock between them. I tried to search the crowd seeking the figure of my Master.

It was impossible to see anything. Everyone in that Great Hall was pushing forward trying to glace with curiosity at the silver collar being taken away. They wanted to see the thing the highest powers of the Haus desired to such an extent they would bother to hand carry him home.

Bladrick had to keep pushing the nosey Dominants out of our way, which was slowing down our progress to the hallway, and staircase. There was true chaos that broke out all around us. Silver collars falling to their knees before the group of Elders, black collars trying to retreat, Dominants following behind like groupies wanting to get an autograph of a famous band. I began to feel faint, sick to my stomach and beyond frightened at this confusing scene.

Jonas looked down into my scared eyes with a smile of calmness. "I got you Christian Axel. You will be okay. It's only a flesh wound. It will heal, but the wound that should worry you is the one in your heart cupid has left with his arrow, ja?" He winked while I swooned with oncoming darkness caused by my blood loss.

I was out cold before Jonas and Drexel got me to Master Peter's door. I didn't come back from my unconsciousness for the rest of that night and several hours the next morning. I definitely had overdone it. The doctor was there staring into my eyes when at last I found my way back to the world of the living by one the next day.

He shook his head at me. "I told you to take it easy, Maximillian. You young ones think you're immortal, ja? Well, you may be more advanced at healing but even the kids have limits. You lay in this bed for another day, then go easy, I mean it. Nein with the dancing and tomfoolery you been up to. Don't be foolish. You lost much blood from that gunshot. It will take time to recover this fluid, ja? I already had to give you a transfusion. I do not wish to go seeking another. That shit is hard without proper facilities. I go now but mind me. Next time maybe I smother you with your own pillow rather than be bothered working like a damned field doctor on the battlefield" he scoffed out while packing up his doctor's bag.

I nodded, "Ja, I apologize for this. Thank you for the mercy of it."

He snorted at that. "Mercy? Such a thing is a myth around here, Maximillian. You have been shot in your leg while trying to commit suicide. I realize I have been treating you for increasingly dangerous injuries several times over this last year. You're becoming quite the brutal boy and you better be. Only the most savage will survive long in this fucking Haus. I am no killer, or I would give you the gift of truthful healing. You have more than earned such a kindness no doubt. Since I can only patch you up, then listen to my advice this time. You stay off that leg. See you in two days for the removal of the stitches." He left the room angrily slamming the door behind him.

I looked over at my brothers Mad Max and Mad Maxx. They stood there glaring at that hateful doctor with looks of disgust.

"I should stick my cane down his throat. Smother us with a pillow? Who the fuck does he think he is," growled out Mad Max with much irritation.

Mad Maxx chuckled, "I didn't realize he was into breath play. Pervert is what he is."

I shook my head. "What the hell happened? I was stuck kissing the nasty Drexel, then it kind of went fuzzy. Did either of you see what happened after dat?"

Mad Max nodded. "Ja. That spooky Jonas hauled us back to Master Peter's bed, Maximillian. Our stitches come open and we lost too much, hey, get the fuck off me freak." Mad Max struck Mad Maxx with his cane sending his brother shard fleeing to the other side of the room.

"What the hell, Mad Max. I didn't do anything," yelled out Mad Maxx while he rubbed his backside from the sting of the swat.

Mad Max scowled, "I don't like being crowded. Now I want to know, what the hell happened with that dancing shit. Maximillian, I thought I saw, I cannot even say it without wanting to vomit. You fucking whore. Did you dare to find some interest in that creepy bastard? He is brainwashing you, fool. I am beginning to be sorry I didn't call you to fuck Annette. You're getting your job confused with our truthful desires."

I glared at that sadist, "You wish you saw something other than me doing my fucking job, pervert. You never give me an inch of credit for anything. Maybe I am getting very good at this acting interested, ja? Didn't think of that did you. Der Hund said we have to capture these sons-of-bitches anyway we can. The loyalty of this one called Jonas, is required to look romantic. This is not my command. I do what this freak bastard asks and look what happened? We have Drexel and Bladrick in our sights. I refuse to answer to your fucking accusations, taunts, or displeasure, for being the fucking best of us all at my job. You are jealous, is all. What good were you? I seem to recall I had to toss you out and save this mess before your stupidity got us trapped in this fucking metal."

Mad Max shook his head. "That is bullshit. I was handling that gross kissing just fine. You had no right to interfere. Your too much of a whore. You wanted to be kissing that gross man and every one of us knows this. That is the truth of why you pushed me out of the way. Admit this Maximillian, you gay slut."

Mad Maxx snorted out loudly. "Leave him alone, Mad Max. Maximillian did what Der Hund told him to do. Der Hund and Christian Axel gave him the role of handling all the sexual, seductive stuff with Jonas. If I didn't know you any better, I should be asking you at this point why you are so angry about this. It seems you are the one interested in more than just getting through this horror of the seduction of this Vampire man. After all, Maximillian is the one trained to handle sexual abuse without attraction or interest. Yet, I hear you complaining when you didn't have to endure such a nightmare of same sex affection yourself? Makes the mind wonder who the gay slut among us is really, ja?"

I chuckled at that most true assessment. "Ja, Mad Maxx is right. Why do you have your panties in a bunch over this? I did the job and Jonas is well pleased. I even got the full attention of Drexel and Bladrick. They were fighting for our attention, stupid. You saw that. They will be a piece of cake, then only Barnim is left. Our metal good as broken. Like my brother Mad Maxx, I must question your apparent insult at this situation myself."

Mad Max glared at both of us with unbridled fury, "Ficken dich."

Mad Maxx laughed hard at that but stayed across the room far from that cane of our sadist, "That is what I think you desire more than anything else, pervert."

I began laughing along with my brother Mad Maxx while Mad Max turned red with much anger. See he could hand out the taunting but never cared for it when turned on him. My wild giggling must have been heard by Master Peter in the living room. I was quieted to terror when he came through the door with a murderous look on his face.

"So? You need not stop this laughter for my comfort, Maximillian. I am dying to hear what is funny about

laying up in my bed. You are worthless. You cost me money and embarrass me in the Great Hall behaving like a hormone driven spouse. You practically threw yourself at Jonas. Drexel and Bladrick won't stop bothering me, calling every fucking hour wanting to know when I am granting a leash to you. There are more fucking gifts, offers for leashes, and demands I sell your collar out right to another, waiting in the living room. You have piles of this shit sent by your many suitors from Claus and Jonas to even the fucking new Dominants All are begging to capture your affections. It is disgusting." He crossed his arms while looking down his nose at me.

I looked away quickly recalling what Jonas told me to do if he tried to strike me for accepting the attention of his flirtation. "I apologize for this most undesired side effect of my attempts to follow your wise commands. I am neither powerful enough nor is it my place to refuse the orders of an Elder. I look to my Master to protect and defend me from myself when my unseasoned tactics designed to meet his pleasures lead to discord with him. I can only throw myself upon your tender mercies, Master. I am not capable of controlling the actions of my betters. I am helpless against it thanks to my low ranking."

Master Peter's hateful look softened immediately at this truthful reminder that I was the submissive in his D/s relationship with me. Only the Dominant had the power to protect and defend us from the outside influences of the world. It was my role to lift him up, but his to use the

power I granted him by doing such a thing. He knew
better than to blame me when his plan for raising his
status had unintended consequence for his property.

Understand this Meine Liebe, if you loan out your
things, then when they come back scratched, damaged, or
the other now covets to have them constantly for their own,
it is your fault, not that thing you let them hold a while.
Jonas and Drexel were correct. If Master Peter didn't want
everyone desiring his Priceless collar, then he should have
kept me home where they could never see the treasure he
possessed, ja?

I looked at the floor then back at Master Maxx with
much sadness in my gaze. He stroked my cheek appearing
to know what was on my mind.

"Awe, Meine Liebe. You think I allow these criminals
to do what they do to you because I don't love you like
Master Peter didn't love me, this correct, ja?"

I nodded feeling despaired that he was right. I realized if
what he was saying was true, he was lying about loving
me.

Master Maxx pulled me tightly into a hug then took a
deep breath. "I want to kill every man that has ever touched
my Frau, including Russell, and soon your Master Peter. It
drives me to near madness whenever I think of it. I had

much difficulty in the beginning dealing with this horrid jealousy, but finally I remembered one important thing. I will say this one time, then never again until that collar of mine is broken. I will kill as many of these bastards as possible one day. If I had been successful in getting you safely to the Haus, we would have had to use your favors by leashing just as Master Peter used me. It is the only way to be sure of a unanimous vote. We are at a dangerous disadvantage because we cannot use your beauty and grace to seduce the vote in this way. I had feared this from the start but finally realized a proper solution. For you to qualify for the vote, you must be tested first. I have been carefully promising leashes to the right Elders to be collected during the administration of this testing. Now, this will make the Elders that come for their leashing rights not only wild with impatience while they wait the long years, but it assures their desires when unleashed upon you will be most brutal. For that, all I can do is apologize and remind you it is only for this one time in your life you must endure such savagery. Your own Master still endures the promises made during his own rise to Dominant in a few of the leashes to this very day. You will be mercifully protected from that kind of horror. But then again, you are not. Over the years I train you, you must suffer the many sexual assaults of the men that pay your mother for the thrill of it. This was something I found going on when I arrived, not a new thing. Now I control these men and vetted the worst or dangerous. Either way you or I go, the Haus or Debbie's basement, you would be subjected to hideous sexual exploitation, and I would be cursed to watch it happen. This is the way of our kind Miene Liebe.

We are not the blessed ones. I will do my best to keep my heated anger under control, and I ask you to do the same. When you break my metal, I will be happy to aid you in killing anyone you wish vengeance upon, and perhaps I will destroy a few of my own choosing. I ask you to do your job, and I will do mine, without feeling or shame. If you feel the weakness of despair, come over you because of this abomination we call our lives, try to focus on the love one day we will have all our own, without another fucking bastard between us. Then we both can say nein to hideous lust from the monsters that touch us against our wills, ja? Try to recall Meine Liebe, I am not anymore free than you. My body isn't my temple either. Not till you break that collar and we have our children together."

I nodded, trying to keep the tears from welling up in my eyes. I finally realized what Master Maxx was trying to tell me. He had broken his collar, but he was still an enforced prostitute just like me thanks to the betrayal of our own parents, my mother, and his father.

I realized he wasn't asking me to do anything more than he himself had suffered. Master Maxx had made it clear; he was suffering not only my own fate but pain that he could not stop mine easily. He had done whatever it took to get this far.

"Then we understand each other, ja? I will go on with the story or maybe you rather sleep a bit? I am not sleepy, but this I leave up to you." He kissed my forehead lovingly, he is the Maximillian shard at this moment in case you are wondering, that's why I didn't get swatted.

I nodded. "I am awake Master."

He smiled. "Okay, where was I again? Ah, ja, Master Peter was angry that I gained much admiration around the Haus. He had planned to raise his status in the Haus, but instead it was the name 'Mad Max the Brutal' that was on the rise."

"Ja, I suppose I should be thrilled with your ability to do what your Master commanded. Still, it causes me much pain to watch my prize slobbered on by these old men," breathed out Master Peter as he relaxed his stance of defense.

I nodded. "You should be the one they salivate on Master if you think watching it is bad. These men are disgusting. I again beg your mercy, Drexel and Bladrick, even this Jonas are nightmares." I did my best to appear grossed out. Not that this was hard to do since I was indeed revolted by the whole bunch of them, Claus included.

Master Peter chuckled, "I don't know what got into me thinking you enjoyed this foul attention they all give you."

I shot a look of abhorrence at him. "Really? Master, you thought being passed around in public like a whore was something anyone could find joy in. If you know such a person, I would love to meet him. Let that idiot do this job and leave me to my books."

My Master sat down on the bed next to me and reached out to caress my face. I unintentionally reacted to his disgusting touch. Okay, I meant it but didn't mean to let him see it. He frowned at that, then sighed with irritation.

"I don't understand this sudden behavior of balking at my affections, Maximillian. What is wrong with you? I thought we got past all this already. It is my pleasure to embrace and couple with my Priceless collar. You're most industrious at seducing the targets I select for you, but you fail to provide me my desires. What did this doctor say about your activity restrictions? Did he say you cannot engage in carnal congress? I think not. Stop this behaving as if I disgust you as if I were nothing more to you than the old Elder's that I leash you too." He took a handful of the hair on the side of my head pulling it harshly to hold me still while he began his sexual assault on me.

I endured his harsh lusting as best I could. I usually thought of the girls, or as of late Geraldine or Annette, but oddly this time at least twice, the dancing in Jonas's arms crossed my mind during Master Peter's brutal couple with me. I began to wonder if maybe I was finally losing my mind.

Not that it would be much of a surprise if I were. After all, the man forcing himself on me was my father. I was a secret lover of a seventy-two-year-old crossdresser and trying to seduce a mannequin lover and his voyeuristic partner. Finding sudden interest in the creepy, but debonair Vampire in this mix of monsters, was not too farfetched I believe.

When Master Peter finished his interest in me, I laid there staring at him redressing himself wondering if fucking his own kid disgusted him even a little. If it did, he sure as shit didn't show it during his lustful exploitations of me. I admit, his vigor and thrill at it seemed pretty damned honest to me. Never took him long to find his orgasm. Nor did he ever bother to return even an offer of return, not that I would take it even if he did.

I thought to myself that if this perverted, selfish, arrogant bastard wanted to continue this horror show of incestuous affections, so what if I did fall for Jonas as the Vampire said he'd make me do? It would serve Master Peter right if I ended up running away with one of the targets, he himself insisted upon.

I decided fuck it. I was finally ready to open my mind to the idea of a lover (a true one, not just sex you know) *that may not be one of my sexual preferences. The couple with Annette (and the devouring of my brothers Max and Christian) had awakened a sudden yearning within me. I could not fully understand it, but it was clear I was desirous of feeling needed, wanted, and genuinely loved. Sure, I wanted the female even more now that I had a taste of the pleasures of mating with one.*

However, until I could be free for such a dream to come true, it looked like Maximillian would have to be less picky. I was eager to find solace in the arms of anyone regardless of gender, which could offer some relief from the sickening relationship I had with my Master. His appalling use of me as a thing for him to find his sexual tension relief had caused me to feel worthless, used, and above all, it created self-loathing.

When Jonas spoke to me, kissed me, and held me in his embrace while we danced, I felt important, sure, and confident for the first time in my life. These feelings were like a special kind of medicine for a soul that had been diseased since I can remember. I found myself wondering what he was doing that moment. I had a growing desire to be near him, so I could experience the sensations of being "special" and adored like only he had been able to do.

When Master Peter left the room humming some tune with happiness, and likely feeling more relaxed now that he re-marked his territory, the Max boys came out of their hiding places.

Mad Max could hear my thoughts about Jonas earlier. "See Mad Maxx, told you he is gay. He is totally fucking gay, this one. He is thinking of Jonas's eyes. Fucking bullshit right here. I am not putting up with this. If he starts up a real affair with the Vampire, we will be bats by the summertime. I don't want to sleep in a coffin. The girls don't like that shit you know. Call Der Hund. We need to get Maximillion on a leash here."

Mad Maxx shook his head. "Shut up Mad Max. I think Jonas is great. I am starting to really like him a lot. I think he is kind of sexy with those sharp teeth of his and the long hair of the female. Snappy dresser too. I am turned on with the idea he might even give me a good thumping the way I like it. Maybe a few sessions in his chains can erase a lot of sins, ja, I bet it could."

Mad Max stood there with his mouth on the floor that my brother Mad Maxx sided with me regarding our deeper interest in Jonas. "Are you fucking kidding me. Oh, Meine Gott. Well, guess we already have gone batty. Did that fucker bite you when you danced with him, Maximillian? Nein. He has put you both under his Vampire powers. I read somewhere those undead bastards can put spells on their victims. I am calling in Der Hund. We are doomed. This guy is the real fucking thing. We are going to be condemned to the darkness, slipping round tombs, drinking blood of virgins."

I began giggling at the insanity "Did you hear that Mad Maxx? You know what? I think Mad Max is right. I suddenly feel the lust for the sweet crimson of one that never tasted the pleasures of the flesh before. Whatever shall we do?" I threw my hand on my forehead pretending to swoon with the horror of it all.

Mad Maxx chuckled loudly, "I tell you what we do, starve to death. There aren't any fucking virgins in this place, and I don't believe I ever saw any takeout deliveries."

We both were laughing at the now terribly angry Mad Max when the door to the room opened again. I quickly covered my nakedness with the blanket unsure of why since my Master was the one that disrobed me in the first place.

Olaf and Vilber come into the room to my surprise. They kept their gazes to the floor while I narrowed my eyes at their rude invasion of my privacy and Master's bedroom. Damn, didn't even knock, the fucking brutes.

I glared. "Well? What the fuck do you two want? I believe you got what you asked for. If this be true, and we know it is, then I ask again what the fuck are you doing here bothering me."

Olaf looked at Vilber who reached out and closed the door then he said, "We come to swear our allegiance to you properly. I would like to add my personal apology for all the nasty shit I have ever done or said to you."

Vilber nodded, "That goes the same for me. I never can thank you enough in this life for what your favor has done for me. Yesterday, I was Vilber the black collar nothing. Today I awoke to find I am Vilber the most desired black collar among his class in a the history of this place. I can take my pick of lovers, everyone wants to give me a favor, and I have a place of highest respect among them all. I never dreamed of such a thrill as I got last night at the Great Hall, in the embrace of the Head of the Haus, Claus himself. Then today I found there are even better things. I get to serve at the feet of Mad Max the Brutal Priceless of future legends. You will make me famous; I will have immortality." He dropped to his knees kneeling with much grace while dropping his eyes.

I turned my attention to the bastard Olaf. "Seems your partner recognizes greatness better than you. You apologize without sentiment behind it I suppose?"

Olaf dropped, not quite as graceful but he was truly a brute, to his knees next to Vilber. "I do accept that you are a man of your word, and one of untold power. I bow to you and as I say swear to do your bidding till the grave seeks me for her lover. My Tamina was more than I ever imagined, and the night with her will live on with me for all my days."

I nodded, still appearing stern. "I accept your vows to serve me with stealth, vigilance, and I expect you to keep all my secrets, even from Master Peter. This you both agree to?"

They nodded and said in ja in unison.

I smiled at that. "You may rise then. I have something I need done right away."

The guards got up appearing curious as I sat up in my bed. "I need you to seek out Egon. Tell him I am moving our appointment from Wednesday to today. Have him meet me below in two hours ready to suffer at the end of my cane. I have need to start my "special training" right away. No fucking questions and speak to no one else about what I say."

Vilber nodded. "As you wish Mad Max, I will keep your Master busy while you attend to this thing with Egon. I also would like to offer a few other names of loyal black collars that with only a little caressing could be valuable allies to aid you rise in this Haus."

I smiled at Vilber. He was a smart one to see through to my plans, It was time to start building my army, war was coming.

Chapter 25: Seduced Seducer

"I would be most grateful to those willing to be loyal to me, Mad Max, Vilber. You speak to these men for me, find out their requirements for their bowing to my requests. Bring me the list and I shall see it done." I winced while trying to sit up straighter, my leg was not in undamaged shape.

Vilber nodded. "This I can do and have completed in a few days. Anything else before I withdraw to find Egon?"

I glared at Olaf. "Ja. I will only say this one time to the both of you. If you ever betray me, even once, I will see you torn limb from limb by the dogs in the yard. I have demonstrated my power to you, I am not a man to be crossed. My temper is short and my mercy shallow. Serve me with honor and honesty and you can be assured I share all that I obtain with those that aided me to the top. Fail me, and I would not want to be you. Now get the fuck out. Next time knock Gott damn it. Rude brutes."

The door guards got off their knees and took off to attend my orders. I groaned in pain but forced my feet to the floor. I needed to get a shower to get rid of Master Peter's foul lust and dressed for my meeting with Egon. The doctor told me to stay in the bed, but he was not trying to take over the Haus. I had no time for rest or healing. I would have to toughen up or die trying.

I was not handling the pain well, so I looked at Mad Max. "I did my part with the enduring Master Peter's sex with us. It is your turn to handle the boy brother. I need some time away from this horror. I will hang around just in case, but I think our Master is spent from requiring any special services for a while. I believe it safe to switch with you even before this cleaning up. You simply handle pain better than me."

Mad Maxx scoffed "Why not ask me to handle the boy, Maximillian? I am the best of us all at pain management. Hell, I even like it and you know this. I am not ashamed to admit that."

Mad Max chuckled. "We need to shower, dress, and make excuses to leave the apartment. We don't have time for masturbation you fool. That is why he calls on the best Max of all of us. Egon is asking to be at the end of our cane, not beat us with it. Go stub your toe or something, that should keep you busy for a bit freak."

Mad Maxx growled, "Fuck off, Mad Max. Will you let Maximillian decide this?"

I looked at the Maxes shaking my head. "I already said Mad Max is the one that should handle this brother. Stop this bickering like the spouse. I think we should wear a dress even if we do look the fool. That way when we act moody, argue constantly, and seem difficult to please we can at least be dressed for the role."

I shot a look of anger at Master Maxx for making that most untrue assessment of the female.

He saw me make that face and laughed till he was red. "Sorry, Meine Liebe, but look what the hell do we Max's know about women? Nothing. All we had to go by was rumors, myths, and the few days experience we gained in the bathroom with a handful of teenaged girls. I know better now, but not at thirteen. Truth is that men are far pissier and harder to please on average than any little girls, ja? I can kiss you and calm your anger. Your Master Peter, well good luck getting that old bastard cooled off when he gets his fury on." He ruffled my hair making me giggle.

"Mad Max pushed me aside and took the wheel. I headed to a quiet place for a rest with Mad Maxx. I was spent from the many hours of seduction, pain, and the horror of another sexual assault from Master Peter. I was more than ready to recuperate in peace even if only for a brief time.

I went to the shower doing my best to ignore that angry wound in my leg. I damned myself for getting shot in the first place. Fuck, I had been so stupid to lose it like that. I could have been killed before discovering the truth of my hard labors.

In only two days, I had nearly seduced all the Elders. I had taken control of the Haus through the most powerful of them all. I even controlled the black collar guards in my Master's employ and was well on my way to adding many more men to the ranks of those who served Mad Max's interests. I wouldn't have wanted to miss this by lazily growing a tree in the orchard. What the hell was I thinking?

I was careful to keep the water and soap off my injury. The doctor had carefully wrapped the gunshot in bandages but there was still some seepage of blood visible. I groaned realizing this would stain my breeches. There was no avoiding it, but I did add a bit of new gauze to do my best to keep the flow staunched.

Once I was cleaned and well-dressed, I concealed the cane into my clothes after removing it from my hiding spot in the bathroom. I was ready to visit with Egon, but I still needed the excuse to leave. I hoped that idiot doctor had not spoken to my Master about the restrictions he had given to me. Not that the doctor asking me to relax and stay in bed had stopped Master Peter from using me most foully anyway.

I limped out of the bedroom, doing my best to appear healthy enough to leave the apartment. I decided not to attempt full deception in my requests for dismissal. I would simply ask Master Peter if I could go to the torture rooms below. I thought he may allow me to go if I informed it was for "studying" you know.

He was reading a book on the couch when I approached him and dropped to a kneel. That fucking hurt by the way. "What the hell, Maximillian? Why are you out of bed? I thought the doctor said to rest. Get back in there, fool, before you kill yourself."

I shook my head. "Forgive me Master, but I am bored to tears. I thought maybe since I am for the moment slowed, I could use this time for study of the fetish tortures. If you would allow me the mercy of going below to sit quietly for observation, I would be most grateful." I kept my eyes down trying to ignore the throbbing agony in my thigh caused by the strain of my position.

Master Peter chuckled. "Ah, well I think even the walk down so many stairs could be a strain on you at this point, Maximillian. However, I would like to hear how grateful you might be if I overlook that and allow this distraction?"

I sucked in my breath keeping my wits about me despite his disgusting request for a repayment promise. "Uhm, I would not dare to assume to know how to fully demonstrate such a thing without your input Master."

He laughed out loud at that. "You are asking me to tell you how to show your gratitude? I thought I had spent more than the last year doing that. I tell you what Maximillian, you can go for two hours of this observation, if and only if when you return you can show me the affection you wasted on that fucking Jonas while dancing with him last night." He reached out and grabbed my face to look in my eyes.

I was a bit nervous by this behavior and unsure if this was in the category of needing to be reported to Jonas as he told me to. "I am not sure I understand, Master. Are you asking me to dance with you when I get back?"

He squeezed my jaw. "Nein, I want you to kiss me like you did him. I want to be treated like your lover, not your job. I told you this a thousand times, Maximillian. I am sick to death of feeling like I am one of fucking Drexel's mannequins when I am with you. You can go, but when you leave the torture rooms, leave the cold fish Maximillian there in those rooms. Return to me as a wanton lover or I will make you hate sex with the man even more than you already do. I don't give a shit if you fake interest, but you better start making me feel you desire my coupling. I mean it. This is your last warning. If you can do it with these foul Elders, then you should have no problem doing that for the one that loves you, ja?" He glared at me with full fury, and jealousy there was no doubt, at what he perceived as me slighting him in my seduction of the old Elders.

I started to argue with him about this, reminding him that my "acting" interested was his own doing, but I needed out of the apartment. "As you wish Master, anything else?" I almost choked on them words but thought "what the hell" I could always ignore his request or hand it off to Maximillian later you know.

He smiled at that then leaned down and forced a deep kiss on me. I closed my eyes and endured the disgust of it but still was unable to demonstrate any passion on my return. He pulled back, appearing irritated by my lack of heat from his attempt at affection.

"See this is what I mean, Maximillian. You go now and think about what I said. When next I kiss you, I expect you to kiss me back like you mean it. I give you two hours to get this shit under control. Come back like that, and I will take you back downstairs for a personal hands-on lesson in what you merely watched before. Get the fuck out and don't come back as this thing you are. Bring me a fucking pleasure submissive of impressive sexual artistic qualities, not just a pretty boy without an ouch of sensual skill worth having. I mean it."

I got up, and began to head out, but stopped dead at the door sighing. "Master, forgive me but I believe I will require the chastity device. You directed I remind you before I ever leave this apartment without you present." I wanted to kick myself for this, but I knew I could not be trusted if I ran into any willing girls. I didn't need him to come looking for me if he recalled it after I left.

He smiled with pride. "Very good, Maximillian. I wondered if you would disobey me. Come here and let me tether my rutting buck, ja?"

I groaned a bit but did as he told me. I really wanted to throw this thing into a fire. but I realized after that serious offense with Annette, I had a weakness that could not be controlled. I thought I had apparently gotten lucky with her. There were too many in that Haus hoping to see me trapped in my metal to dare take any more chances with my overwhelming sex drive to find pleasure with females. Like it or not, that fucking metal monster was my only defense. (Master Maxx sighed loudly and rolled his eyes.)

After I was safely in my sexual restraint device, I took off from the apartment with as much speed as my limp would allow. I had to lean on the railing to get down the many stairs, but I managed to do it without falling to my death, much to my surprise.

I saw Vilber and Olaf speaking with two black collar males at the door. I nodded at them, and they flashed looks of acknowledgement. It was their job to watch out for my Master's interference with Egon downstairs.

I headed for the dark, dank staircase the led below chuckling at all the silver collars kneeling as I passed them. I noticed the black collars were oddly bowing too, and the few Dominants I passed stopped to smile at me, looking me up and down with what appeared to be eagerness. That was a bit unsettling. What the hell was going on, I wondered.

I was grateful to be free of so many eyes when at last I made it to the old doorway to the downstairs rooms of torture. I let out a scream of terror when I opened that old wooden thing and there stood Jonas grinning at me with that pointy toothed smile of his.

He chucked in pure humor while watching me gripping my chest having my near heart attack from his startling me. "Christian Axel, you sure know how to make a man feel sexy, ja? I hope to make you scream for all your days just like that, but in pleasure not fear. Are you heading down my love? If so, I think I will join you. I am in the mood for a little pain entertainment."

I was panting, having trouble catching my breath from his scaring me like that. "Fichen dich. I thought for sure you were Death come sneaking up to embrace me with his boney touching. Shit Jonas, you shouldn't sneak up on me like you keep doing. I won't have to worry about being shot in the yard, I will die of a heart attack instead. Are you following me or something? Everywhere I go, I run into you these days. It is making me nervous."

Jonas laughed. "Uh ja, I am following you Christian Axel. I tend to obsess about things I desire. I will go thousands of miles to track down an ancient book or piece of art that strokes my interests. I am like a blood hound tailing you with the utmost vigor and thrill." He grabbed me without warning and pulled me close to him while rudely reaching down the back of my breeches.

I gasped in terror at this brazen public groping of me, when suddenly he snatched my cane, which turns out was the reason he grabbed me in the first place. He pulled it out of my hiding spot and held it up to my face grinning like a cat about to eat a mouse.

"What do we have here? Ah, this was Milo's cane. I would know this thudder anywhere. I wonder what you did to Milo to gain his most coveted tool. This was a gift granted him by his brother Justus. You would have to take it from his dead hands to obtain it. I wonder if that is what my most vicious Christian Axel has done. Tell me, my love, did you kill Milo with your couple like you did Xavier or with your bare hands as you did to Felix?"

My eyes filled with terror at this Vampire's accusations "Why would you accuse me of such a horror. I kill no one. Milo gave me this cane before he took his own life. He said he thought a Priceless should have it, that is all. Give this back to me. It is mine."

Jonas nodded with an expression that told me he wasn't buying it. "Okay, you can try to lie to me Christian Axel. Doesn't matter to me how you killed that old silver collar. What interests me is that if you get caught with this, the punishment is severe enough you may not survive it. I don't want to see my treasure wasted like that. I need your love and blood to stay young and satiated. There is nothing wrong with protecting my source of pleasure. I hope to enjoy your forbidden powers for many years to come. If I don't keep my eyes on you, you'll end up like Justus, and all the others before him. None of you live to adulthood, not one. I intend to see you live to be an old man, and I will be there too because of it."

I frowned at those words. "What is this really about? You don't really care if I did kill those men. Are you trying to trap me in my metal? That is what this is, isn't it? Are you blackmailing me? For what? I told you I give you everything you asked for without threatening me. I am not stupid you know. I know you want to use me like everyone else. I will never be the fool to even entertain for a moment you cared for me otherwise. You can be assured you'll get your fucking romance, fake of course, but then you were warned that I would never love you for truth, weren't you? I will even tolerate your freakish fetish Jonas, but you will never see me be an old man. The second I break my collar I will not be here in this fucking hell hole, which is for sure. You say to trust you, but then you show up and interfere with my plans to escape this hell I am in."

238

Jonas laughed deeply while letting me go and handing my cane back. "That you plan to leave this place the second your free is exactly what I want to hear Christian Axel. I assure you; I am not attempting to keep you from breaking that collar. On the contrary. I want you to bust it in two. No other Priceless collar has lived long enough nor have any ever escaped their metal. This Haus is too greedy. They always use up the poor Priceless, unable to hold back there urges for the payback they would get if they would merely be patient and let the forbidden silver mature and break free."

That was a weird thing for him to say. 'What? I don't understand. I have to pay back the Haus to break my metal. Are you speaking riddles, Jonas."

He looked around to make sure no one could hear his whispering to me. "I knew Justus you know. I was a young Vampire back then. I tried to get to him before the lust of this Haus sent him to the yard with their demands on him. Everyone wanted their taste of the forbidden, it drove him to his death like all of them before him. I reached him too late. I have spent all my life waiting for another Priceless to be collared. The legends of your level are significant, and all truthful. The reason there has never been a female of your kind is because it takes a male Priceless that broke his metal to find one. You will survive to break that collar of Peter's, that I will swear to you. Then you will go into the world and find your mate. There are many legends about this mythical female only you can discover. It is said you will be drawn to your Priceless mate by a love so strong even threat of death will not be able to end your yearning for her embrace. You will know she is the one the second you lay eyes on her and she will bring your inner demons peace. When you blood bond her to you at her maturity, you'll transfer the last of your forbidden silver power to add to her own incredible abilities. Then she will be capable of things many believe to be supernatural. There is a legend that to couple one time with the female priceless can heal terminal illness, restore full health and vigor, automatically grant her lover a full decade of new life, and in time can even turn back the internal clock."

I had to scoff at this kind of bullshit belief of the crazy Vampire. "Ah, so that is what this is all about. You don't want me; you want my Frau? Gosh, as you said, you sure know how to make a man feel sexy Jonas." I chuckled at my most rude comment.

He shook his head angrily. "Nein, I don't want your fucking Frau. I am not interested in females, Christian Axel. I want you as my lover. I believe I have made this very clear already. I am not stupid. I refuse to fall for the lie that my affections will ever be satisfying enough for you nor to the extent you will give up your bid at breaking your collar. I already grant you my powers in this Haus and brought you the powers of Drexel and Bladrick as promised in return for your becoming my lover. I will further sweeten my offer now. The experience of taking a single taste of a forbidden silver female of legend is a fair trade for what I can do to make your dreams come true. I can even overlook the lack of charm a woman possesses to keep my interest for a one-time conquest that offers so many long-lasting age defying gifts. I will keep you alive, and even make sure that collar of Peter's is busted for your promise that I get a leash with your Frau before she breaks her own metal. Once she does, her powers and your own are gone from my clutches forever. I am not a fool. Without your collars neither of you would submit to my desires willingly. You'll only desire each other. To further break my heart, I know when you escape your metal, you'll leave your Jonas seeking this soul mate of yours without any other thought. I will be left to age and rot alone. I am willing to accept that fate if, and only if, you are willing to repay me for my sacrifice by giving me the youth, extra years, and healing a leash with your female Priceless can restore to me. I will even throw in the promise to make sure her own metal falls away when her selection vote comes. I am a man of my word, Christian Axel. You would be wise to consider my offer and take it without hesitation. It would be easier for me to trap you in that collar and use you up like everyone else intends to do. However, I do love you. When you love someone, you will sacrifice all your own happiness just to see them comfortable and content themself. I am willing to see you free, to prove my affection for you is honest."

I stood there unable to comprehend what the man was saying to me. This business about legends, a female

Priceless, and leashing my own dream of a Frau all my own were a bit much for my unseasoned brain to understand. The only thing I truly heard was that this powerful Elder was promising me that he could see my metal broken. All I had to do was promise a leash to a future Priceless Frau that for all I knew didn't even exist. I didn't even hesitate to vow it, thinking I had made the best deal of my young life. With Jonas on my side, I was sure my collar was as good as gone.

I looked at Master Maxx harshly. "But I do exist Master. You said I am a female Priceless collar. That means you are going to leash me to this scary Vampire, doesn't it? Oh no, he is going to bite my neck and drink my blood or will he die of old age. Wait oh no, vampires can't die, can they," I said almost frantic in terror at this new horror I was starting to understand.

Master Maxx reached out and popped me harshly with his cane (Mad Max is running the show so yeah, I should have kept my fucking mouth shut, shit). "For starters, ja, Jonas still lives Meine Liebe. Second ja I am a man of my word. when your testing comes, Jonas will be the first to call in his leashing rights."

I shuddered and stared at him wide eyes, tears welling at the idea of a Vampire coming to bite my neck.

Master Maxx saw my look of terror and chuckled. "Stop acting like a scared little girl meine Demonseed Frau. You will maybe like sleeping with Jonas. He is a most skilled and romantic lover. As for his blood drinking business, well I got through it, didn't I? You are much more vicious and stronger than I ever dreamt of being. Knowing you, you may break that old bat Jonas into two and take back the blood he dares to try to extract. I swear Meine Liebe, even the Devil quakes in terror of the day your twisted little soul goes back to hell. He fears you are the one that will take over his realm. Early in the morning I swear I hear old Scratch praying to God asking for you to stay healthy and alive as long as possible to keep you away from him. Master Maxx laughed hard at that. Even my own violent demons kneel in fear of you. I don't know if all the legends of the female Priceless are truth, but there are a few that I now can swear to. I did know you were the only one for me the second I met you. I can only think of your embraces day and night. Last, but most important, I do find my peace when I am with you. I cannot imagine my life without Meine Liebe anymore. I am your helpless slave, ready to serve you in this life and the next. No matter what happens, I will always be with you, fighting at your side, loving you with my whole heart and soul. With that in mind, who is to say old Jonas won't find his return to youth and vigor from his single leash with you? I know you certainly make me feel wonderful but do understand this; he will never touch you, nor will anyone else without your approval the second the council votes you Dominant. I did affirm this leash promise to him from our bargain all those years ago but do recall he has to keep his side of our agreement. He already swore he would aid us in making sure that vote for your breaking my collar is ja and not nein when I went to him with the news that we were wed and the blood bonding is done. This thing will not even happen until you have passed your testing many years from now. Do not let it stress you. Jonas is already sixty-five years old. He may not even live long enough to collect his leash rights, meine Frau. Now on with the story ja or do I make you put my cock in your mouth for speaking out of turn again?"

I quickly turned back around and snuggled into his lap shutting my trap and averting my eyes in silence. He chuckled at my obvious answer of "no thank you please" and continued with his story…

"Now, getting the vote swayed my way was the easy part as you have learned. If that was all I had to worry about, this story would be over right here. The trouble was there was so much more to breaking a collar then just a vote of ja by a bunch of middle-aged farts. The difficulty was getting the audience with those bastard council members for their approval without getting myself killed or failing the last four sections of the Dominant testing. Remember, I told you that was the hard part.

Jonas smiled his evil toothy grin at me. "This is a good day. Now, where are we headed Christian Axel? You have

Justus's cane and appear eager to thud someone. Who is the lucky victim?"

I glared at him with suspiciousness. "I think you are going too far with your nosey questions, Jonas. I bid you adieu. I will see you on Friday next week I believe." I tried to push past this bothersome Dominant.

He held out his arm blocking my path. "Nein, I think I will come with you, and you will cease this bullshit telling me what I can and cannot do. I do believe until that metal is busted your still under my command. You promised to be my lover and I take that seriously. I am not a weak conquest like Claus. I decide when and where I take what I am promised from you not fucking Peter. If it were my wish, I could pick you up and carry you to my bed right this minute and you would submit to my lust without argument. This is not the way to win your heart I am aware, but it is within my power, Christian Axel. It does you no good to incite my anger over something that is supposed to be a thrill. So, I ask again, where are we headed? Don't piss me off by forcing me to demonstrate my resolve in this matter." He crossed his arms and shot fire from his dark eyes at me.

I stepped back feeling a bit of fear at his demanding I tell him of my plans. Thudding for a silver collar is forbidden unless for training or pleasure with a Dominant. Understand this thing with Egon was personal for my own interests. That carried a punishment of scarification and several days in the dungeon.

I looked at the floor stressing out as I heard myself say, "I am heading down to have Egon train me to thud properly. It is his pleasure, and I require perfect skill. It was my plan to learn this service so well it would be sure to bring Barnim out of hiding to witness it."

To my surprise Jonas didn't fume as I expected he would. He beamed with a smile of pure delight.

"Ah, that is a brilliant plan my love. It is truth that Barnim loves to watch a thudder of extreme skill work over a victim. His social anxiety keeps him away from everyone but if rumors of such a skilled display of torture were to reach his ears, there is no doubt he will venture out of his apartment to view such a pleasure just as you suspect." To my shock he pulled me close and kissed my forehead, again ignoring all the prying eyes watching us speaking there in the crowded hallway.

I trembled a bit wishing this scary Vampire man would just slink back to whatever dark place he came from. "Ja, well, Egon is waiting, and I have a curfew. I don't wish to be rude, but I must be going Jonas. Thank you for the addition of our agreement, and for all your help." I took off for the door this time not giving the Elder a chance to hinder my journey.

I gasped when I saw Jonas following me quietly as I limped down the rock staircase. This guy was worse the lint on a wool suit. He wouldn't get the hell off me. I was running late so I decided to stand my ground After I found Egon. I worried the black collar trainer would leave thinking I was kidding about my agreement with him.

I found the over-eager Egon standing at the Branding Room door holding his private lock, and a smile on his face when he saw me. Then that expression of glee melted to that of horror when he noticed the Elder Jonas swooping in rapidly behind me.

I could see in Egon's eyes he thought I betrayed him to an Elder. He frowned in anger and backed up at my approach. "Mad Max? What the hell are you doing down here? Our lesson isn't until Wednesday." He tried to cover his ass, good try, but even I wouldn't have fallen for that bad acting job of his.

I stopped and shook my head in disgust. "Give it up Egon. Jonas knows about this. Don't worry. He is on our side. There will be no punishment for this thing we do. You just must trust me. Now, we go inside out of the view of everyone to talk, ja?"

Egon's eyes went wide while he stared in disbelief at Jonas that towered behind me like a damned creepy version of Jack the ripper. *"Oh, uhm, ah, ja, okay, I unlock this door. We use this room."* He was trembling so badly he dropped his keys three times on the floor trying to unlock that damned door.

Jonas shot me a look of humor and I chuckled at the clumsy fear that Vampire elicited in the black collar trainer. When the lock was open at last the three of us hurried inside and closed the door behind us.

Egon backed to the wall keeping his eyes downcast. *"Look Jonas, I don't know what Mad Max told you, but it was not my intentions to break the rules. It just sort of, well shit. Look do your worst. I don't care anymore. I am a fucking fool for thinking I had gotten so lucky. Good things never happen to Egon. I should have known this was a set up."*

I growled at Egon's accusations that I was a dirty stool pigeon that had set him up. *"Fichen Dich, Egon. I didn't betray you Arschloch. Jonas already figured this all out. I told you he is here to watch not punish you. Stop being a dick."*

Egon looked at Jonas seeking approval from him that I was telling the truth. *"Ja, Egon, I am only here to aid you in training Mad Max. I want to see him become a thudder of exceptional skill for my own selfish pleasures of watching a Priceless in action. You do your job, and I will not breathe a word that any of this ever happened or happen," Jonas said coolly with a friendly smile on his face that somehow still appeared sinister. It is all though sharp teeth of his you know.*

Egon appeared beyond thrilled. "Oh, my Gott. This cannot be happening to worthless old Egon. I am getting the forbidden pleasure of enjoying the thud of a Priceless with the honorable Elder Jonas here to witness my joy. Did I die and go to Heaven or something?" He swooned once again convincing me he was anything but a straight man.

I growled out in irritation. "I can sure as shit make sure you find that mythical place kneeling before Gott if you keep acting like a smitten Frau Egon. I don't have all fucking day you know. Let's get this started. You waste my time, as usual."

I didn't have to warn him twice. Egon wanted this thudding bad. He practically had torn off his clothing and was naked, sweating like a whore, and smiling in anticipation before I could even stretch out my wrists properly. I watched with a bit of humor and Jonas openly chuckled while the man rushed to put on his cuffs so I could clip him in the chains.

I secured my willing victim and without another second's hesitation began my thud. Jonas watched this show for a bit quietly. Egon alternated between yelling out in agony and offering pointers on a smoother deployment of my swat.

This went on for about ten minutes before Jonas, who had been leaning against the wall watching, approached me. I was standing behind Egon welting his thighs when the Vampire suddenly reached out and grabbed my wrists before I could release my swing.

"Nein, Mad Max. This is your bow, and Egon is your musical instrument. Your aim is impeccable, but your stance and smoothness of motion need practice. This is art, not labor. You look like the lumberjack trying to cut down a fucking tree. You should appear like a violinist playing the rarest Stradivarius. Close your eyes. Now, use only your ears and listen to the beautiful sound of Egon's song. Let his notes of pain merge with your soul and move with him in perfect rhythm. Your wrist is too tight. Loosen this and your mind with it. Allow me to guide you to the target as you learn to control the tool of this symphony." He stood behind me holding both my wrists in his hands demanding I keep my eyes closed while allowing him to use me as his puppet in this thudding.

I did as he commanded. He wrapped his fingers into my own, bending my limp wrists with much skill as he swung my arm and struck Egon. I heard the black collar wail out in agony louder than he had since I began. The sound of it excited me deeply within. I immediately felt peace and comforted by it. I had not felt like that since the day Ryker had run screaming from the burning closet so long before.

I wanted more of this. I focused immediately on the graceful movements this creepy Elder was employing that made Egon cry out like that. Jonas turned us slightly then with much elegance smoothly deployed another thud using my arm.

Egon yelled out in a fury then began to beg to let him rest a moment. The sounds of his torment incited even more eagerness within me to torture him with vigor. The more he pleaded and cried the more pleasure I received. I thought, I could do this all day. "Ja, this was something I really could use more of in my life.

Mad Max ran his hand down my arm making me tremble. I was now more worried he may thud me rather than fuck mc. Either way, I was not interested. I was good just keeping my fat mouth shut and listening. He grumbled sounding a bit disappointed when I didn't respond with more than a mild flinch.

Unfortunately, there is only a bit of usable space on the flesh for a proper thud. It only took me twenty minutes, with the aid of Jonas, to work over every available spot of his safe zones. He was panting, wailing *loudly, and begging for us to stop by then. He was welted and bruised as hell.*

I was unwilling to face it was time to end the session. I continued to strike any spot of unmarked canvas on Egon's skin like a young dog overkilling his prey. Had it not been for the Elder being present to stop me, I likely would have beaten Egon to death without care.

Thankfully, since finding willing victims for torture is hard to do so you try not to kill them you know, Jonas held my unexperienced ass by my leash. He pulled me away from the sobbing black collar and gave me a harsh backhand to "wake me" from my sadistic trance.

I held my burning face feeling a bit sheepish that I had become as blood thirsty as easily as I had, and in front of this Elder too. Not good or so I thought anyway. Jonas laughed while I grumbled watching him release the blubbering Egon from his bounds.

Egon fell to his knees moaning in agony. "Ah, thank you so much for your mercy, Jonas and granting me such a pleasure Mad Max. I am a happy man at last." I stared at this nut in confusion.

He was crying like a newborn babe and thanking us for the pleasure of torturing him to a point of near faint. I swear I will never understand the mind of a masochist. I spent many hours trying to discover the secret to their fucked-up desires talking with Mad Maxx. I still don't get it. Whatever their issues, Egon's pleasure was congruent with my own. So, who really gives a fuck why he likes it. Long as he was happy to come back for more of that fun.

Egon rested there a few moments. Then he smiled with gratitude and pride when Jonas commanded me to aid him in helping this black collar re-dress. I was not happy about having to serve this bastard, but Jonas outranked me by a million miles. He had also been generous in his demonstrating for me the proper form and wrist work for the professional thud. I decided to keep my complaints about dressing another collar to myself. I assumed I owed him at least that much.

Egon informed me that he would use arnica oil and ice to quickly heal the welts and stripes. He thought he would be ready for another session in three or four days. I was unhappy to hear I had to wait so long but Jonas nodded his approval that this was an acceptable number to expect.

I watched as Egon left the room, slowly but appearing full of radiance like that of the brightest sunny day. The man must have thanked us at least a million times before at last he and his constantly running mouth were gone.

I laughed when Jonas looked at me snorting. "If only we could thud a tongue. I swear I would break Egon's over my fuckin knee. Does the man every shut the hell up?"

I shook my head. "I imagine he even speaking in his sleep, Jonas. He seems to love his, what did you call it? Oh ja, his song is more than either of us ever could. I just hope he knows better than to do any singing to the wrong ears."

Jonas grinned with an expression of confidence. "There is no need to worry about that old black collar talking out of class, Christian Axel. Egon is as honest as father time. If he gives his word, then you can depend on it. You pick your loyal men wisely, my love. They don't come any finer than Egon or Vilber."

I shot a look of surprise at him. "Huh? Vilber? I don't understand what you mean…"

He held up his hand smiling with mischief. "Don't, Christian Axel, just don't. I am not where I am in life because I am an idiot boy. Claus didn't suddenly develop a taste for black collar guards. Vilber was there last night because you put him there. I imagine this was a payoff to gain his loyalty. Smart move, and wise choice is all I was saying. Just when I think you cannot out do yourself, I find yet another amazingly brilliant move. Intelligent, beautiful, cunning, strong, and naturally skilled at everything you attempt. No wonder I cannot stop thinking of you. I swear it is driving me mad. I daydream constantly of killing Peter and running off with my gorgeous Christian Axel, far from here, somewhere warm perhaps where you need no clothing." He chuckled while looking me over with lust in his eyes.

I laughed nervously. "Uhm, ja, well I think I would like to ski occasionally. I would miss the snow in a hot climate."

That made Jonas roar with laughter. "Oh, my love. Your dark humor kills me. When the hell was the last time you even saw snow? You know nothing but these stone walls and dim hallways. You couldn't even walk across the grounds to be shot properly thanks to your lack of seeing any natural light. Now while I find that pale skin of your very sexy, it is not good for a young man to never feel the grass on his feet or wind in his hair. You know what? Ja, give me that cane to hold before you get caught with it, and then you take my hand and follow me. I will not hear any stories about you needing to get home because of some fucking curfew either. I know damned well Peter gave you at least two hours out, or you'd not been so lazy about letting Egon go." He held out his hand demanding my cane, okay well the late Milo's cane.

I looked down at this thudder with sadness in my eyes. I was feeling despondent about giving up my favorite thing in the world. I dared not anger this Vampire. I needed his loyalty too much to quibble about a material possession that made me feel less anxious. I would just have to get over it. I promised myself when I broke my metal, I would buy a thousand of them and keep one handy every day.

Jonas smiled with kindness on his face when I gave it to him without complaint. "Awe my poor Christian Axel, you look very upset. Please, you must believe me. I don't confiscate this thing from you out of cruelty. Eventually Peter will catch you with it. Then where will you be? I promise to keep it safe for you. You can have it anytime you like or even come to see me and practice in my apartment where no one can ever catch you at it."

I nodded. "Ja. thank you for your mercy and offer of protection Jonas. I am grateful for it despite the way it may appear."

Jonas laughed. "Okay now take my hand and come with me, again, no argument." He reached out and offered his clawed hand to me.

I winced but took it without quarrel. He began pulling me at a rapid stride back through the torture chamber, to a dark hallway, then out a door right into The Orchard. I gasped when the overcast sky came into my full understanding. All around us were fruit trees and bushes of various flower types.

Jonas smiled at my look of shock and surprise for a moment then began pulling me out further away from the exit of the Haus. I whimpered while looking around wildly in terror and tried to break free. I wanted to get back inside before the black collars started shooting at me again. I no longer wanted to die, and this idiot was trying to send me back to where he found me.

Jonas held my hand tight chuckling with glee at my obvious distress. "Calm yourself, my love. I am with you. They won't shoot if you stay right at my side. I caution you, do not stray or even let go my hand. If you do, then they will open fire."

I looked around with terror trying to see these phantom snipers. "Oh, my Gott. Please Jonas. Let's go back inside. I haven't even gotten my stitches out from my last stroll in the yard. I am not in the mood to be fertilizer for the fields today."

Jonas laughed hard. "Where is that bold boy I love so much? Stop struggling and enjoy this gift I am giving you. You must learn to trust me, Christian Axel. I said I would never let anyone harm you. I want to see your beauty in the daylight, indulge me this pleasure. Tell me you have not dreamed of such a thing as seeing the sun, the clouds, the trees, as you once did as a child."

I nervously kept swinging my head in every direction, but I could not deny being outside was one of my greatest desires. Jonas was making this happen. Even if only for a short time, even if only a few paces from that hell hole Haus, I was in the real world. I could not calm down completely, but I certainly was starting to marvel at it.

Suddenly, Maximillian came out of nowhere and knocked me out of the boy to the ground. I was so pissed. I waited for years to be free and this whore was stealing the experience of it. I chased after the two of them beyond without looking for a way to get back inside. I wanted to smell the fucking flowers and feel the wind.

I pushed Mad Max out and called my brother Mad Maxx because I could sense, Jonas was going to want something more than a polite thank you. Only the selfish sadist Mad Max would expect Jonas was just being a kind heart for this amazing gift he granted us.

I had been trained to know better. Nothing in the fucking Haus came without a price, and this was going to be an expensive trade, of that I had no doubt. It would take me and Mad Maxx to pay this bill we were making by accident.

Jonas smiled as he pulled me close to him and wrapped his arm around my waist like a lover would. He walked slowly allowing me to use him to aid my own limping gait. I ignored his adoring looks and lustful smile best as I could. I focused on the sights of nature I had been forbidden for so long.

I wanted so badly to break loose from this Elder, throw off my shoes and run barefooted through that beautifully manicured landscape full of colors. The air was fresh and felt good in my lungs. It filled me with a need to flee and never look back.

Jonas seemed to be reading my thoughts. "Christian Axel, I warn you. Never come out here without me at your side. These black collars are trained to kill. You will not get lucky if you ever pull what you did the other day. Promise me this and I will return a promise to you. I will bring you to this natural beauty from time to time, to help keep the dust of the Haus from clogging your veins. Peter should be doing this kindness for you, but that selfish bastard takes no time to woo you. He thinks love can be forced. I know that is not true. He expects much without consideration for the need to allow for any freedom of choice. My love, I want you to choose me because I am the one you want, not just because I want you to."

I nodded feeling a bit strange by all his flirty talking. "Uhm, I told you I am not interested in the man, Jonas. You already admitted you know the second I am free I am off to seeking my female mate. This thing you ask of me, well it is not fair to you nor possible for me."

He stopped then looked around appearing to be seeking something. With a sudden smile breaking across his face he turned to me. "Come with me now, over there. I will show you something."

I nearly fell when he lurched forward pulling me along with him by the waist. He moved briskly causing me to feel faint from the rising pain in my wounded thigh. We approached a thicket of trees clumped together with many bushes that created a kind of "private outdoor room."

I was helpless to stop him as he hauled me into the opening of this place. I was too far from the Haus door to flee, especially with my bad leg, back inside without getting my head blown off. I didn't bother to fight him when he forced me to sit on the ground next to him against a tree.

He smiled then reached out and took my hat off. "That is better. Now I can see your face better. You are very handsome, Christian Axel. I am hopelessly enthralled. The frosting is gorgeous, but the cake underneath is so scrumptious it will cause a man to sell his soul for a mere taste." He stoked my cheek with much adoration in his dark eyes.

I frowned and looked down at my lap on that one. "My Master said I am like the wedding cake. I am all frosting, and my cake is dry and unappealing." For some reason that really bothered me. I am still not sure why.

Jonas sighed loudly. "My love, Peter is a bitter man. He has no more care for his son than to put him in another man's care. Instead of beating this man to death when he damaged his most precious child, he leaves the little boy to claim retribution. Then for your courage, strength, and resolve, he repays you by selling you into his bed to be used for his perverted interests. He tells you lies and abuses your gifts. None of that is your fault. Look around you, Christian Axel. Who do the silver and black collars bow to? Mad Maxx, not Peter. Who fights for a taste of your favors? The Elders. You have captured every heart, dark desire, and soul in this Haus. Peter is jealous that others can see the treasure he possesses but has done his best to tarnish. No matter what he has done, your silver shines through so brightly it blinds him and draws everyone else like moths to a flame. I for one cannot believe my luck to be sitting here with the most magnificent human I have ever had the pleasure to meet. I know everyone from Claus to the worms below the foundation wish they were me right now. Funny though, all I can think is how all I can wish is the I were another person. Anyone but me. What I wouldn't give to be someone that you desired as much as I do you."

Ah that sly old fox. He knew what to say to stroke the fires of an abused young boy who thought very little of himself. His kind words rang in my ears like the sounds of a dove cooing, calling for his lost mate. I was enraptured at this strange, romantic speaking man despite my abhorrence of a same gendered touch.

I looked up. I gazed into his adoring eyes trying to find the answers to the confusing emotions rising within me. They were not lustful, but they were not love either. It was something else, something closer to reverence or idolization. A trance like the one I had been in when we danced came over me once more.

This man was confident, strong, commanding, mysterious, cunning, and universally feared. His very name was synonymous with "controlled recklessness." He did what he wanted, when he wanted, and how he wanted, without an apology or explanation. If Jonas wanted something he took it. The fact that he was giving me the choice to turn him away unrequited made me feel unique and special. I viewed him as a representation of everything I was not but wanted to be.

He leaned down and pulled my face to his kissing my lips with initial gentleness. I closed my eyes and let him lead me wherever he wanted to go. He pulled away immediately and frowned.

"Nein, I told you Christian Axel. I won't make you be my lover. I am not Peter, Gott Verdammt. You don't desire me, I understand that. I ask you to desire my company willingly or walk the hell away. I cannot stand feeling as if your disgusted every time I touch you. That would hurt your feelings if I did such a thing to you. Claus may not care, maybe no one else either, but Jonas, well he would rather be alone than force himself on another. You are not my whore. You're to be adored, held with tenderness, and desired above all things. If you can never feel the same way, then so be it. Sex, that is only a function, and I can deal with your dislike on that level, but this mechanical behavior over other expressions of affection, not interested." He sighed and looked away, appearing terribly upset.

I sat there unsure what to do. I didn't find any interest in his touching me in any way at all. How the fuck could I fake it so that he didn't know? It was then my brother Mad Maxx showed up and knelt next to me.

"Maximillian, look at him. This man means more to us then anyone we have ever known. He saved our life, protected us from several severe punishments with his good advice, has kept his word, and is willing to give us the choice to say nein to him. He said to love someone is to be willing to sacrifice your own happiness so that the other can find comfort and joy. So, do that. Sacrifice our happiness. Ignore what we desire from a lover. It is truth that he is not the right gender for our lustful interest, he

263

is scary as hell, and he is not even the right age. However, focus on what is worthy about him and when you kiss him or allow his couple think of who he is, not what he is. If this you can do then so can I." Mad Maxx stood up and grabbed Mad Max before he had a chance to push me aside and try to re-enter the boy. Damned fool almost got us in trouble again.

I looked over at the grieving Jonas. "I think I finally understand, Jonas. I am just a young man, many things about this complex life are still fresh to me. You say to me you wish you were anyone but you right now. You wish to be someone; anyone I would desire to have at my side. Well, then you can be assured you are the right person for me. I can think of no one I would rather have with me this moment. If you can give me time to learn the proper way to adore you the way you have earned from me, then we will be starting the romance you asked me for."

Jonas turned back to me with a look of joy that was quite beautiful to be honest. "That is the one thing I have, time." I leaned forward and for the first time in my life with a man, I initiated the kiss of passion.

This time Jonas became frenzied with lust within only moments. He grabbed my arms pawing and tugging until I was in his lap straddling him fully clothed, thank Gott. His interest in a couple was more than evident, but I recalled that Master Peter would be looking for trouble upon my return. So, there is an act that does not leave clear evidence which could lead to discovery.

When Jonas began to try to undo my breeches, with much skill I might add, I pulled away from the lustful kissing. "I cannot allow this Jonas. I apologize but I must ask you to follow your own good advice regarding this affair."

He was panting in obvious torment at my denying him his pleasure. "Ja, ja, I understand Christian Axel. This is not the proper place for such a loving act anyway. I wish to do this right, not in the weeds like animals. Forgive my getting carried away like that, you're just so…I cannot seem to keep a hold on my lust when I hold you is all. This can wait, ja, I can wait. Your worth however long it takes."

I smiled at that statement, then realized there was one way to attend to my lover that Master Peter could never trace. I felt Jonas shudder and then he moaned out in rapture when I dropped to his lap to demonstrate my skill with oral sex.

I had much skill at this act by now, and Jonas had apparently not been attending his baser urges often. It didn't take long for him to find his climax. He yelled out in pure ecstasy then rubbed his face harshly mumbling out many compliments to my ability to bring him to the brink.

Then he reached down and pulled me to his face for another series of passion filled kisses. I was surprised by this still wanton filled behavior. I just assumed like all other men, once he found orgasm, he would cool his lustful interests.

It was then I felt myself hurled from the boy by Mad Maxx. I hit the ground at Mad Max's feet confused at this strange hijacking. I started to stand up and complain when I realized why my brother did dis.

Jonas was kissing more harshly, becoming more frenzied than before I gave him the blow job. I backed up in terror as this Max was wondering if we were about to see our own murder by this Vampire.

Jonas was near chewing my lips off with those sharp teeth of his. I winced against the sudden pain that ran up my thigh as he and I writhed against each other in our passion filled embrace. He felt my shudder which appeared to set him into overdrive. Then in a smooth quick movement he bit down on my bottom lip harshly.

I tasted the iron from the fast welling of blood rushing to the surface of this superficial break in my tender flesh. I moaned out in some fear when he began sucking harshly on my lower lip recovering the small amount of my fluid that leaked from this minor injury. I thought any moment he would bite me again, only this time somewhere not easily hidden from my Master, and maybe deep enough to cause me much agony.

Instead, he pulled away panting with his eyes closed and a smile on his face. "This can wait too. I only wanted a tiny taste, for a meal of you I would need a cleaner, more controlled environment and proper preparation. I do not wish to kill my goose that lays golden eggs with infections from nasty teeth and no antiseptic, ja?" He released me from his grip, and I retreated from his lap to sit beside him grateful that I only ended up with a bit of blood and his jism on my breath. It could have been much worse. The man was lusty.

He readjusted his trousers after I relieved him of his urges. Then he sat up smiling at me with a sated, foggy look in his dark eyes. "That was an amazing taste of the pleasures to come, Christian Axel. I am well pleased, and I must say I feel romanced the way I always wanted. You are a man of your word, and a Priceless of the highest quality. I am grateful for both. I have always been extremely patient, but I must admit it will be hard to wait until Friday to deflower you, my love."

I almost scoffed. "What? Uhm, no I think you misunderstand Jonas. I cannot give you my penetration virginity. I need that for the collar selection."

He smiled with much evil in his pointed smile. "You are the one that is misunderstanding, I believe. I am not referring to that kind of virginity, Christian Axel. You're my lover now, which for a Vampire is also called the Donor. I will take from no other while we continue our secret affair. You have never fully fed one of my kind before, so that makes you a virgin. It is the fourth secret virginity each of the Haus members have since it is a penetration that will cause blood to flow and the first time traditionally leaves a scar.

I shot a look of terror at my stunned brothers. "A scar? Wait, I will survive this penetration, right?"

Jonas chuckled. "I have not lost a Donor yet. But there will be pain. This you will get used to."

I groaned. "I was once told that lie that about penetration elsewhere too." I sighed with much dismay that my good intentions with Maximillian were coming back to bite me, since the bloodletting was the task Der Hund assigned to me, shit.

I was refitting my hat while Jonas stood offering me his hand to pull me to my feet when a voice called out. "Why Jonas, are you back there catting around? Shame on you. Come out at once and bring your lover. I want you to meet a friend of mine."

My eyes went wide in terror, but Jonas didn't seem to be the least bit frightened. He grabbed my hand, roughly pulling me to my feet.

"Follow my lead. Don't speak unless I speak to you first. This woman is a nosey bitch. I got this handled. Don't leave my side, they will shoot you." He dropped my hand and snatched up my leash while rolling his eyes.

I followed behind him in automatic high protocol thinking I had heard that voice somewhere before. It was familiar to me but from where I could not recall. I saw Jonas step out from behind the tree and light his face up with a fake smile. I limped out of the bushes behind him suddenly recalling the owner of that voice.

It was Gretta, and Leo was with her as usual.

Chapter 26: Midnight Mistake

"Gretta and Leo both gasped as Jonas pulled me out of the secluded spot by my leash. The look on their faces told me Master Peter would be hearing about this indiscretion last, after every other bastard in the Haus got the scoop.

Gretta recovered her tongue while Leo stood there with a sheepish smile spreading on his chubby face. "Ah. I had no idea you were enjoying a leash with Peter's Priceless collar, Jonas, forgive our intrusion." She covered her mouth, appearing most humored that she had run across us in this way.

Jonas scoffed. "I am not enjoying a damned thing but a stroll in the orchard Gretta. I would thank you to keep your twisted ideas to yourself, if you value that overactive tongue I like to add."

Leo's eyes went wide with terror while Gretta appeared unaffected. "Oh? I just assumed if you two were in the bushes like that, well, there is no reason to fear. I am a woman well able to keep a secret Jonas. Leo can as well. I wanted to introduce him to you. I fear this was not the right time though. We shall move on and let you get back to your strolling then." She shot a look of mischief at me that sent shivers down my spine.

The two began to leave but Jonas bellowed out in anger. "Get your asses back here Gretta and whoever the fuck you are. I will not have either of you rushing off to besmirch the fine reputation of Peter's Priceless just because he had to sit the fuck down for a minute. Look at his leg, Gretta. There, see the blood. This submissive was shot a few days ago. Maybe you heard of this."

Gretta and Leo squinted their eyes staring hard at my bleeding thigh. That wet stain was rapidly spreading at this point, thankfully, and this was the only time I was glad to be bleeding like that, trust me. The injury was most evident and neither of them could deny the observable proof of it.

Leo looked shocked. "Ja, I heard but didn't believe it. This boy is heavily bleeding, Jonas. Gretta, I would think this is serious. No wonder he had to sit down."

I almost sighed a breath of relief when Gretta nodded. "Why did the Haus doctor allow this damaged submissive out of bed. Jonas, can this collar even walk?"

Jonas shook his head. "The stupid physician let the collar out of bed. I found him near fainting in the torture rooms. I took him out for a breath of fresh air. At first, it seemed to clear his mind, but this bleeding started getting worse. I had him sit down to see if maybe it would stop with some pressure. Now I think I will need aid getting

271

him back to the damned door. I thought of how great it would be to try to take a little advantage of Peter's injured Priceless, but had I known I would get into such a tight spot with my sport, shit, I don't need him dying on me. Peter is a damned fool letting this treasure wander without any aid. If he expires then Peter will likely expect his collar price returned. I didn't shoot him. Why should I be responsible, you know? That is what I get for being a bit sadistic and well too lusty. The collar is too sick to even get any fondling out of him. Shit, this was a complete waste." He pulled harshly on my leash causing me to stagger and groan a bit.

I would have been pissed by what he was saying, but I knew he was lying for a reason. If Gretta and Leo thought he was up to no good, best to admit he was. Then with the half-truth out there he spun the rest with lies of my incapacitated health to cover the truthful carnal affair. It was a very clever ploy I admit, and I could see it was working. Leo and Gretta bought the whole story, lies and all.

I made sure to play the part of a confused, intensely injured person by moaning just under my breath as if in much pain. I trembled a bit and whenever Jonas took a step I would stagger and limp, appearing startled. This acting job worked perfectly with the explanation given. Gretta and Leo immediately offered to help Jonas get the Haus Priceless safely back inside.

Leo pulled one of my arms over his shoulder and Jonas took the other side. I continued to stagger slowly, dramatically appearing to fade in and out of my consciousness. Then I felt Jonas reach behind me and grab my ass. This inappropriate behavior made me steal a look of confusion at him. He winked at me smiling with a "we are getting away with this bullshit" expression.

I nodded and continued my "significantly injured" behavior. Gretta was rushing ahead of us loudly announcing to no one to "get out of the way." If I had not been in so much danger of a session in the chains over being caught in this most compromised situation it would have been hilarious to see.

We all arrived through the exit door without me getting another hole in my flesh. I was sure grateful for that, let me tell you. Jonas and Leo let me stand on my own the second we were back in the dank halls of the torture chamber.

I stood there leaning up on the wall sweating from that horrible panic. I took a deep sigh of relief believing the worst of the danger had passed. It seemed no serious harm had been done. Gretta and Leo were fooled, and I had not gotten shot. I looked up and saw a large clock on the staircase entry way.

Immediately, a shiver went up my spine. It had been two hours and fifteen minutes since I left Master Peter's apartment. I had lost track of the time in this whole drama scene. Shit, I just knew I was so fucked. My Master surely would cut me in two over this insolence.

I slumped with terror. "I must go. I am late. Master Peter is going to kill me. What the hell was I thinking." I began to rush away but Jonas grabbed my upper arm holding me tightly, giving me a look of caution.

"Peter will have to wait. You are not well Maximillian. Your color is off, and you can barely walk. Gretta and Leo can also verify this. Relax here a bit before trying to walk up all those stairs. I will come with you when your vitality has recovered and explain this situation to him." Jonas growled out while pushing me back against the wall with much strength.

I shook my head wildly. "Nein, there is no excuse for this insolence. I will be punished severely for being late. The later I am the more lashes I get. Damn you, let me go. I have to hurry, or my ass will look worse than my leg." I tried to push my way out of his grip.

Jonas looked at Leo. "Help me hold this collar. He is delirious with blood loss. Gretta, may I request you to go to Peter's apartment and call him down here to us. This needs to be handled here and now before Maximillian hurts himself over dumb commands that will get him injured further."

Gretta smiled with thrill that at last she was important to this Elder (what an ass kisser, ja?), "Ja. I am happy to do this for you, Jonas. Leo, stay here and keep this Priceless quiet. I will be back shortly." She practically ran up the stairs with speed I didn't know that woman had.

Leo smiled with perverted glee as he came forward and put his hand on my chest pinning me to that wall. "You just be still, Maximillian. There is no need for this struggle. Gretta will get your Master and Jonas will please him with a proper understanding of things out of your control." He rubbed his hand slightly doing his best to cop a feel of my flesh beneath my blouse.

I rolled my eyes at the disgusting attempt to take advantage. "Get your filthy hands off me Leo. I can fucking stand up without your aid. Remove yourself or I swear I will render your hoddensack useless with my knee to it," I growled out in irritation at his foul touching.

Jonas's eyes went up with at my statement. "Maximillian, which is rude of you to say to this man. Where are your manners?"

I looked at Jonas with much fury. "My manners are reserved for those that mind their own. This foul thing is rubbing my chest, and I don't believe that I was shot there, nor do I stand with it. I want his hands off me or I will be happy to take the lashes for breaking him in two."

Jonas shot a look at Leo's offending grip on me. "The collar says he doesn't wish to be pawed. I think you go too far with your attentions to him. Perhaps you are attempting to steal a taste of what is not yours? You will let him go Leo."

Leo frowned but removed his hand from me. "He is truly out of his mind with the pain. I understand this, but I swear I will do nothing but attempt to aid him. This was not the inappropriate behavior he is claiming, this I swear to you Jonas. I am a man of honor. I would never take what is not granted to me. I am not a thief."

Jonas nodded with a diabolical smile crossing his lips. "Today you are not. That I agree. Let me make this clear to you Leo, this Priceless, I am claiming him as mine. You keep your fingers and everything else off my things or you will find the offending item broken. If I ever hear of you attempting a leash, or molesting Maximillian behind everyone's back, well my friend, you can consider it the last pleasure you ever have." He reached out suddenly and grabbed Leo by the hoddensack.

Leo screamed out in surprise then vailed in agony as Jonas twisted his "jewels" in his iron grip. "I didn't hear you, Leo. Did you understand my words? I mean what I say."

Leo could barely breathe, his eyes bulging out of his head while he whimpered, "Ja I hear you. I never touch Maximillian again."

Jonas emitted an evil chuckle, "Nor even ask to?"

Leo gasped out looking more like a blow fish then a man. "Ja. Ja. I don't even know his name. Please, Jonas, you're going to rip off my hoddensack. Let me go. I swear I will never bother with this collar again. You have my word."

Jonas released Leo's sex from his torture with a loud laugh. "Good, then we understand each other. Now we can be friends, ja?"

Leo fell to his knees gripping his pain riddled manhood nodding as he breathed out in a near whisper. "Ja, ja, friends. Hahaha, I would like that very much, Jonas."

I stood there staring at the writhing Leo in pure shock. Jonas pushed the anguished Leo with his boot, forcing *him out of his way. The Vampire then approached me, his expression turning to one of deep concern.*

"My love you are very pale. I am afraid this was too much excitement too soon after your injury. I am worried your blood will be too thin and weak when my leash night comes next week. I must insist you get more rest in preparation for our mystical coupling. I don't desire my lover to be nearly drained before I can claim that glory for myself." He stroked my cheek gently looking deep into my eyes.

His words and actions were causing me to tremble as I recalled this strange fourth virginity he spoke of earlier. "As you wish Jonas. I will follow your instruction and be ready to grant your pleasures without failure." I tried to look at the floor to avoid this man's gaze.

He grabbed my chin roughly forcing me to look back into his face. "Do not look away from me, Maximillian. You don't know it, but I am about to take you to a dark place of forbidden pleasures as much as you take me. This is a willing expedition to a place only the bravest dare to go. I need you as healthy as possible for this journey. You will rest or I will hear the reasons for your disobedience. I am not a merciful man. I wouldn't test my resolve to have what I desire if I were you."

I felt my trembling grow more intense as the seriousness of my situation finally sunk in. This Vampire wanted to enact dangerous puncturing, and bloodletting on a regular basis. I would do well to get to researching if there was any fucking thing in the written word about it. What the hell was a Donor, and how much trouble had I gotten myself into with this scary Elder by agreeing to be his secret lover.

He could read the fear and panic in my eyes. His fierce expression softened with the suddenness of a Spring storm. I gasped in pure terror when he leaned forward and engaged my lips with his own kissing in a frenzy as he had outside in the Orchard.

Jonas appeared to become enthralled with the passion of this public embrace. I cried out in fear when he grabbed me around my neck, pinning me to the wall with his weight. His other arm ran over my flesh pulling and tugging at my clothing in pure wantonness. I knew that Leo was still on his knees watching this display of near copulation right there for everyone to see.

My stomach was flip flopping, threatening to send its contents to the floor as Jonas pushed my head to the side. He rushed in with his mouth licking and kissing the right side of my neck moaning out as if enraptured.

I could barely breathe, and my heart was pounding to break free of its rib prison. My knees began to fill with weakness, and I was sure I was gonna piss my pants from the pure panic filling my every blood cell. I thought Jonas was going to rip my throat out right there and then. I hadn't been this scared since my father came come at me with that straight razor.

Then real terror gripped me when he began to suck in mouthfuls of my flesh and bite down lightly each time before releasing. He was not breaking my skin yet, but I could tell he was working himself into a place of no return.

Until this most disturbing behavior I had stood very still. I didn't even move my arms from their place at my sides. I just let him have his way keeping my eyes closed praying he would stop if I didn't encourage him. I realized this technique of appearing only compliant, though not willing, wasn't working to get him to cease this time as it had before.

I was afraid to anger him by saying nein, but more terrified of what he was going to do if I didn't. I raised my arms and gently tried to push him off me. I didn't say anything, but I did make it clear I wanted him to quit his mishandling of my person.

Jonas responded by squeezing my neck more tightly and moving faster with his suck and biting actions. This sent me into a full-on terror. I began to struggle wildly in his grip begging him to stop. When this failed to produce an end to this nightmare, I began to scream for help.

I heard Leo gasp upon hearing my cries of distress. He got up and ran away, likely didn't want to witness my murder, I assumed. That really set me off into believing my life was about to be drained by this Vampire man. I added my feet into my battle against Jonas, kicking at him wildly in blind panic.

It was at that moment I felt Jonas being pulled off me. I was swinging and kicking without attempting to aim. I hit one of the two people that were working to restrain the lusty Vampire by accident in my terror driven flail. The man yelled out in anger but recovered quickly returning to his task of literally saving my.

Jonas let out a loud roar as he gave into his assailants. He released my throat and pulled back from his biting me. I fell to my ass sweating, panting and still crying out in fear. I watched without understanding what was happening. I saw that Peter and Leo were there holding back the fuming Jonas from his passion driven attack on the Priceless collar.

Slowly, I began to realize that Gretta had returned with my Master as Jonas told her to. Leo had been at a distance keeping an eye on the situation that appeared to be rapidly getting out of control. He rushed to them informing my Master and Gretta of Jonas's turbulent state and my fast-deteriorating safety in Jonas's embrace with much terror.

Master Peter had demanded Leo aid him saving his collar from getting his throat ripped out by the Elder Vampire's overeager blood lust. The two of them had forcefully restrained Jonas pulling me free of his interests.'

Jonas was without a doubt beyond livid at this interruption of his affections. "You will release me this moment worms. How dare you even think yourselves correct in this dishonorable interference. You have no right," he yelled out in his booming voice.

Master Peter let him go immediately, as did Leo. "You were aggressively molesting my collar, Jonas. This is illegal. I only do what I must to protect and defend what is mine. That is my right by contract with this submissive."

Jonas had been keeping his predator-like gaze on me while licking his lips as I trembled there at his feet in fear. My Master's excuse for his actions caused the excited Elder to snap his head toward Master Peter with an expression of fury.

"I have every right to touch this property of yours by Haus law. I am to be familiar with your collar's favors by leash. In fact, I have paid for such pleasure. You were warned of this rule, Peter. You are the one in error here. I break no rules. I was kissing your collar and playfully feeling his flesh. There was no deep molestation going on. Check him. There is no penetration of any kind anywhere in his person. You we me punishment for this dishonor. As do you Leo. I demand to be made whole this very minute," Jonas bellowed out with his dark eyes lighting up like the fires of hell had been set in them.

I almost fainted at them words. Jonas was loudly calling out my Master claiming he was showing illegal public jealousy. He added Leo's name for aiding Master Peter in breaking the Haus rules by preventing him from enjoying his favored position with a future leash.

Most in the Haus were aware the expression "to be made whole" meant Jonas wanted to give both offending Dominants five lashes in the chains. This is the punishment for the crime he claimed had been committed against him. I couldn't believe my ears. Jonas's command outranked my Master's by miles. It became clear Jonas was planning to whip Master Peter, and the creepy Leo, that very minute.

I sat there staring with a dumbfounded expression at Master Peter. He was observably frightened by Jonas's loud announcement. My Master shot a look of disbelief at me. I shook my head too terrified to dare utter a sound. I was nothing compared to these men. I mean, that was pretty evident since I had just nearly been eaten for Jonas's supper. I sat there wondering if Jonas was sending me, and Master Peter, a brutal message with this display.

I understood that by punishing Master Peter for standing up to his taking such wanton liberties with me in broad daylight, Jonas was harshly demonstrating his true power in the Haus as an Elder. I thought maybe Jonas wanted to make it known that my Master could not protect me from his dark appetites, when, and wherever, his urges hit him. I realized if Jonas did this, it would also create a hesitation in Master Peter or anyone to call out Jonas the next time he demonstrated public affection of any kind with me or with any collar.

The other possibility, I thought, was that the Vampire had decided his blood lust was not completely sated by his light toying with the thing of his desire. Therefore, my Master's and Leo's flesh would have to do in my place.

Either way within only moments of Jonas's public outcry, the torture Masters come forward and hauled the indignant Master Peter and Leo off down the hall to the "thudding" room. I watched feeling nothing was real while the two Dominants were led away.

My Master, in true arrogant well-born fashion, shook off his Torture Master's grip. "Get your hands off me trash. I can walk without your aid. I been doing it since I left my mother's side, thank you very much." He then stormed down the hall and waited for the others to catch up and let him into the room.

Leo though was struggling and screaming that he was falsely accused of any wrongdoings. The torture Master had to have assistance from the one my Master denied to detain him. The two big black collar brutes dragged the fighting schwuler to join Master Peter and let the Dominants in for their punishment.

I watched the four of them go inside that door at the end of the hall, never bothering to try to stand up from where I had fallen. I shook my head trying to clear the fog from my brain. This couldn't be happening, could it?

Jonas's chuckling brought me out of my cloud of unreality. "You go rest like I told you, my love. I am going to teach your Master a few manners. I imagine when I am done with him, he won't be so quick to make you suffer for doing what he ordered. He doesn't get to make you pay for doing your job well. This is what he wanted, the power and control of the Haus using his

Priceless collar. Well, he got it. Now he can learn there is a reason the Elders can do what they like with a spent leash. You see Christian Axel; many a Dominant has attempted to pull this very shit of using their pretty boy or girl collar to get their hands around our necks. This attempt to earn favors and control this way has a little-known side effect. No Elder can own their own submissive, so we are allowed to prey openly on any leash in full public view we have enjoyed past or to come. That my dear is why no one likes to leash their treasures to anyone of us old, twisted fucks. This you finally understand my love?" He smiled with much wickedness in his expression, then yelled for someone to tell Vilber to come get me and take me home. The place was packing up with nosey Dominants as gossip travels fast in the Haus.

Jonas waited there, quietly grinning with pure evil, until Vilber came rushing down the stairs. Without any hesitation the brute hurried to me, grabbed my arms, then threw me over his shoulder like a sack of grain. I didn't say shit about this embarrassment. My thigh was killing me. Better to be carried like this than like a fucking bride in Vilber's arms. I was aware I could no longer managed the staircase. I really had overdone it like the doctor told me not to.

I hung over Vilber's big shoulders with my mind whirling in abject horror. The nightmare of my compromised position had finally reached my consciousness. Jonas had basically told me from this point on, until I could break my metal), I was subject to unwanted pawing, molestation, kissing, and likely worse in public. He was stating that no one could stop the Elder leashes in their lustful pursuits thanks to this fact. He didn't have to say it, but I had realized that questioning by a Dominant of any of the Elders attentions toward me could result in their severe punishment. Master Peter and Leo were discovering this the hard way. (Master Maxx chuckled and so did I. Hey, seeing a Master get a whipping, I was for that shit, hell yeah).

Since the Elders were the law of the Haus, who the fuck would decide if they went too far? Obviously, these perverted brothers would stick together if any complaint of bad behavior were lodged at them over perceived misuse of a spent leash. They could do as they pleased with me. They had the full authority and rights. Master Peter had handed me right over to them for this horror. This was bad. Fichen dich.

Vilber said nothing, nor did I, as he carefully returned me to Master Peter's apartment. He took me right to bed. I didn't fight, argue nor give any lip about that either. I thought I had done enough damage for one day. All I wanted to do was get in the bed and hide the fuck from the world under those covers.

I'd had my fill of excitement in those few crazy days. Hell maybe for a lifetime you know. Two killings, one penetration with a female, and more than a few from the males, four seductions, two trips outside with one ending in a gunshot wound, a blood transfusion, a wild dance, torturing Egon, near getting eaten by a Vampire, and now getting my Master thudded. Shit, and all this in only three days. It had been a very busy week for Mad Maxx. I was bushed.

My head barely hit the pillow and I was out cold. You'd think the fear of Master Peter's anger would have kept me at least a little alert, but I swear I no longer cared what happened to me. I had once again begun to feel the dark pull of thinking myself better off as food for the worms.

It just seemed all too complicated for my young mind to accept. There never seemed to be an end to the drama, danger, intrigue, unwanted affections, or harsh brutality in the crazy world all around me. I finally understood this shit wouldn't be over in a month or two. I had years of pain and terror coming. This knowledge was crushing my soul slow but sure. Truth is I never thought I would make it out alive or at least sane if I managed the impossible.

As I closed my eyes that afternoon, I can recall thinking, "Vampires, schwulers, statue fuckers, cross dressers, and fathers that fuck their sons. This is a fucking freak show and you, Mad Maxx, are the star attraction. Gott verdammt. I just want the crazy Earth to stop and let Christian Axel the fuck off this ride."

I have no idea how long I slept before Master Peter stumbled into the room. I pretended to be asleep even though my hypervigilant ears heard him the second he came home. I kept my eyes closed listening without moving a muscle while he cursed under his breath.

He was damning Jonas to the pits of hell, and for some reason bad mouthing Gretta and Leo too. I did my best to hold still when he crawled into the bed stripped of all his clothing. He reached out and wrapped his arms around my waist then pulled me roughly into a cuddle with him. I did my best to keep my breath even still playing unconscious, but my Master was no longer buying my act.

"Maximillian, this seduction business is a foul thing. I suppose I owe you an apology though there was no other way to do what needs to be done. Jonas and those perverts that call themselves the power of this Haus are hell bent to take advantage of my kindness to them. I allow them a taste of my joy and they abuse the privilege of it openly and without restraint. I suppose the only way to prevent this is to keep you hidden in this apartment as much as possible. Otherwise, well that shit that happened today will only get worse. I will send Vilber or Olaf for my required services. You my love are staying home." He buried his face in the hair on the back of my head holding me more tightly.

I opened my eyes in pure horror at his solution to my painful situation. If I could not leave that apartment then I could not seduce the last Elder Barnim, practice my thudding techniques, nor take over the council. I was in no hurry to be openly misused by the perverted Elders, but without their continued attention I was never getting out of my collar.

I sent out a desperate call to my brother Maximillian. This issue needed to be dealt with in the most horrid of ways. It would take both of us to do the unthinkable. We needed to seduce our own fucking father. I wanted to die with the sudden realization that unless we placated this monster in a most unnatural way, he could terminally interfere with our plans. Believe me when I say to you, I briefly considered taking a trip to the washroom and opening a vein. I thought I would have rather bleed to death slow than go through with what it would take to keep my Master out of my way.

This seduction of your Master Peter was the hardest thing I ever endured in my struggle to live to see another sunrise. The reason I chose to do it was simple. Somehow, I held on to the belief that no matter what terrible thing I must do, survival would mean I could eventually find my way to you Meine Liebe. I closed my eyes, took a deep breath, and opened them to see Maximillian had answered my call.

He nodded with a look of disgust that he understood what he had to do when the moment came. I let him know with my eyes that I would aid his burden by shouldering a bit of this heavy weight threatening to crush our heart. Mad Max was also there that night. Even that hateful sadist had a look of sympathy for the two Max boys that had to endure such a sickening fate.

I turned in my Master's cuddle to face him doing my best not to show signs of my growing turmoil within. "Master, there is no need to hide me out like a criminal from these men. I don't know why you even care if they stroke or kiss me in public. Everyone knows that they can bark at me but not bite after the one time. It is all show and nothing more."

Master Peter scoffed. "That is bullshit, Maximillian. You seem to enjoy the interests of these men that only bark. The Haus will think you are the flirt and me the cuckold."

I frowned. "How can you say that? I thought you said I should care not for what others say or think? Now you tell me their idle chatter bothers you. They are speaking with no information of worth or truth, this you know damned well. I am not a flirt and you're not the cuckold."

My Master shook his head and growled out, "I don't care what anyone says when I know it is a lie. Gossiping is mostly entertainment, and no one really believes half of it. Yet, I happen to see that look on your face whenever Jonas comes round. You have feelings for the man, don't you dare deny this. I also painfully know you no longer love me, and likely never did. The spark that was only barely lit between us has grown cold. I dare you to deny your noninterest behaviors in regard to my tender advances."

I sighed loudly. "Well Master, I won't deny any of that. I admit I have been coolly tolerating your affections. You traded me off like the whore and encouraged my seduction to hop in more beds. I know you told me this had to be done. You said we needed these men to get my metal broken, but knowing this didn't mean my belief about your true love for me was not bruised. I am flattered that you think my seduction skill is so perfect that you believe I find interest in the creepiest man in the world. However, that is all you are witness to. My affection for the Vampire Jonas is merely a stratagem against our enemies. The attention of one with his influence cannot be a detriment to this House of your Master. Allowing his lust to cool, now that could be deadly. I do believe that today, my emotional upheaval with regard to your true heart for me has been quelled. I no longer question your love for me, Master, and I beg your forgiveness that I was so shallow I ever did."

Master Peter's eyes narrowed in suspiciousness. "What the hell do you mean your emotional upheaval was quelled today and you no longer question my love? You speak in riddles. I warn you, Maximillian, I don't care for this deception you seem to be aiming at me."

I chuckled bitterly at that. "Master I am not trying to confuse nor deceive you. Today I saw you come to my aid even though you knew it could get you punished. Don't think that bravery went unappreciated by your unworthy Maximillian. I was terrified of Jonas's overzealous attack, and when I cried out for help, my beloved Master came running. I was taken with much romance when I saw you stand up to that brute without a sign of fear. Then, with honor you stood you ground and walked like a man to the room of thudding. I saw the fire in your eyes. I knew then and there, your love for me is pure, honest and true. I was shamed that my own return for such a fierce flame of passion was not even capable of enough heat to light a cigarette."

I could see the look of anger smoothing on my Master's face. "Ah, well, that is truth. What are you going to do about this inequality of service then? Where there is no interest, no affection can come of it. That is just my problem now, is it? I love my Maximillian with the heart of lion, and he loves me not back."

I shook my head smiling with much mischief just as Maximillian forced me out of the boy. "You are wrong, Master. You need not lock me in this apartment. I have found my passion for the one I love, and you are him.

The Haus will never believe again you are not the true holder of my collar nor my heart." I closed my eyes and leaned forward engaging my Master in a passionate kiss as I had with Jonas earlier that afternoon.

Master Peter moaned out as the engagement got more heated. With all my strength I faked my way through this entire nauseating scene of intimacy with my own flesh and blood. I faked sublime interest, wanton eagerness, and not so unlike with Xavier, even appeared happy to take all his lustful interest and more.

It helped me get past this horror by seeing the deep cuts and welts on his backside caused by Jonas's lash. I focused on the damage I intended to level on his flesh the second I was free of his hold. This aided my acting job more than you can ever know Meine Liebe, but by the time it was over I still felt used, angered, befouled, and disgusted with myself.

Ah, these nasty feeling you know well. Ja, Meine Liebe? Of course, you do little one. All children of incestuous sexual abuse do. I can tell you there is no need for self-blame. Not your fault. When you are too small and weak to escape the cruelty of the one supposed to protect you, how can you be the one wrong? That is insane to believe and if anyone else tries to lead you to think otherwise, you have my permission to punch them in their self-righteous, no nothing heads.

For true, it took me many years to finally stop blaming myself for this nightmare with my own father. Especially, since he led me to believe I had granted him permission, with the collar you know. That was bullshit, brainwashing, and so far from reality it is hard for me to even comprehend how I ever fell for such a lie. He never even was truthful about who I was submitting to nor what that shit even meant.

If I had tried to say nein, he would have beaten me down, collared me, and the consummation gone the same anyway. These parents that molest and rape their own Meine Leibe, they have no care for you or anyone but their selfish pleasures. They would do this to anyone. They see their child as an easy target because they're readily available and that kid got no one that has a close interest in his or her welfare. Very few in this world care for another when they are not of their own blood.

It was almost impossible for your worthless Master Mad Maxx to beat the many obstacles and people in his way to breaking the collar. Beating this father, your Master Peter, well meine Demonseed Frau, which has been so difficult I have yet to manage it. Someday though, you and me, together we will beat both Debbie and Peter. (I smiled and nodded at that idea while Master Maxx stroked my face with adoration in his eyes).

This bullshit shaming that Debbie has created in you, I intend to block. If you can only learn to trust my words, my wisdom Meine Liebe you too will learn to stop letting Debbie's sickness burden your soul. You are innocent of any wrongdoing, just as I was. We do what these Godless parents want, or we die, or even worse than death, be trapped in the metal.

Please remember there is nothing wrong with choosing to live. If things get harsh and your heart hurts to breaking, try thinking of all the babies we will have together. Feel the love and pride your HusDom has for his precious Meine Liebe who is stronger than he can ever hope to be.

I know you can focus on our dream of a life in a bright happy world to get away from this darkness, ja? I will even buy you the biggest house on the block, and pretty dresses that will make all the other frau's jealous with envy of meine beauty.

Ah, I know. This will bring your gorgeous smile. To sweeten the deal, I will build a doghouse in the backyard, and we leash Debbie and Russell to this. They can eat oatmeal from the dog bowls, and I will let you beat them every day for all these years of barking in our ears, ja?

That smile of your lightens my heart and brightens this room to near blinding. I swear though, you are a vicious little thing. Have I told you today just how much I love you?

Well, I do. How can I not? I fear if I don't, maybe you burn your Master Mad Maxx up in the house he builds for you.

Damn now, there is a truth that hurts. Ja she most likely hates you doesn't she Mad Maxx? He looked at me with curiosity then frowned and rubbed my hair while sighing. I just stared with a hateful gaze, angered at his teasing me.

Please don't look at me like that. I am kidding but then again, I am not. I know the fury in your heart, Meine Liebe. I know I would probably want to burn me up too. It is truth I have been most brutal and rude to you. Don't think I am not aware. It doesn't make sense to you right now that if I am not, you never get the chance to set that fire. One day you will understand every bit of this craziness.

I can only hope you will eventually love me for truth despite the harsh training I do to you now. Until then, I want you to know this is not the life I wanted, but it is the life I got. Remember that, on with this story, ja? He took a deep breath and hugged me tightly once more.

"That night, after Master Peter fell asleep most pleased at my return to appearing open to his attentions, I had to get the hell out of the boy. Neither Mad Max nor Mad Maxx would trade me places, so I just left the flesh sleeping there in his Master's spoon. Even though I had

left I still felt like I needed a shower as badly as the boy did.

Mad Max shook his head in disgust. "Well normally I would insult you at this moment, but there is no reason to add to the pain on it. You have my respect Maximillian. I want you to know I don't just say that because Jonas took my cane so I cannot beat you with it over any smart mouthing back."

I shrugged at that bullshit. "I suppose that is as close as I ever get to hearing a kind word from you. I take what I can get."

He nodded. "Of that there is no doubt, whore."

Mad Maxx scoffed, "Well that peace between us lasted about as long as I thought it would. A full second of no fighting, color me impressed."

I was too tired for Max's childlike behavior. "This is terrible. How the fuck can we keep our sanity with six of these horrors all running around putting their nasty hands on us? I never get any rest, nor have time to study as it is. We are going to fail at this. We haven't even captured Barnim, nor dealt with the horror leash of Drexel and Bladrick. Maybe we should go back out for a midnight stroll. See if the snipers shoot better in the dark."

Mad Max snorted loudly, "Did you hear that brother. Maximillian asks how we will stay sane. Hate to break it to you, but that battle was already lost. We went nuts a long fucking time ago. Look here idiot. there are four of us, maybe more. Personally, I think that qualifies us for a job as an astronaut, because we are practically in outer space as it is. Now that I have solved that worry for you, the question I have is did that acting job you suffer through save us? I don't trust Peter. He lies about everything. Maybe he extracts our dignity then locks us up anyway. We need another plan in case he tries to keep us penned in."

I shook my head while Mad Maxx shrugged. "There is no other fucking plan. You are the fool now, Mad Max. That rope work of this man is impressive. We maybe could sneak out a few times until the bastard caught us and bonded us to his bed. Do you think I seduce this Kinderschänder (child molester) because I like him to fuck me? Nein, we must make him sure the we are broken to his will. It is a long shot, but unless you can teach the boy to walk through walls it is our only hope."

While the three of us were arguing, Der Goldene Hund appeared. To our amazement he walked over and entered the boy. We stood there, our mouths on the floor. He never rode the flesh anymore, not since the stuffed dog was torn apart by our stepfather. I turned with an excited gasp and yes, there was Christian. He smiled at me lovingly then kissed my forehead. I snugged up doing my best to get as close as possible to the man I no doubt loved with all my little heart and always will.

I slipped quietly from Master Peter's grip. His beating and Maximillian's skills at the coupling had worn the middle-aged man to a place of deep sleep. I put my finger to my lips hushing the battling Max shards. This was a job for a Christian Axel the most powerful of us all.

I didn't make a sound while I dressed, then slipped from the room, and apartment. with great stealth I rushed down the stairs shooting a glare of extreme caution at Vilber and Olaf. They nodded but didn't make a sound as I tore off down the hallway. The silver and black collars dropped to a kneel as I limped passed. No one got in my way nor attempted to stop my rapid pace while I headed for the back staircase.

I didn't hesitate, pushing my aching leg with all my will right up those stairs. I headed for the top floor, my destination, Jonas's apartment. *I looked up at him in surprise while he shot a kind smile and ran his hand through my hair.* **Ja, the Vampire was who we had snuck out to see.**

It was a dangerous risk no doubt, but I knew that Mad Max was right. We couldn't trust Master Peter. It was more likely he would take our more eager appearing favors and still lock us all away from the world. He was

too jealous to ever buy our act no matter how well done it may have been. We had to break the collar no matter what it would cost us. To leave our Master's whim, to chance a worse outcome than whatever horror Jonas may extract from us, to equal the trade for his aid in this developing situation. Besides, he was the one that caused it.

I would have left this to the Max shards, but to fail meant a fate worse than death. I cannot stand the sex with men like Maximillian can. I hate violence against another that Mad Max adores. I am not a friend to pain that Mad Maxx is. This boy is my responsibility.

When the rough things come it requires one that can do all, at least for a short time anyway, that I just said without depending on another to tap in just in the nick of time, that is when Der Goldene Hund Christian comes.

This plea for help from this difficult Elder would require much skill deployed within a tiny amount of time. I had to keep this visit brief or risk being caught. In only moments I needed to present to Jonas my wicked charm, probable physical seduction, intense bravery, then a return to Master Peter's arms with stealth. I was not sure the Max shards were ready for this kind of accelerated and rapidly changing scene. No way I was chancing finding out the hard way either.

I made it to Jonas's door. I looked around and found the floor empty. This was good. I was relieved to have no witnesses to my midnight visit. I knocked on his door, holding my breath that he was alone. There was always the chance he was visiting someone, had company or was being entertained by another collar. (Hey, he is a sexy Vampire man. He can have anyone he wants with his kind of dark charm. I was not so conceited to think he was not tooling around with many other hearts. Christian laughed at that hard as did I.)

To my relief the Elder came to answer before my third attempt to hail him. I was starting to sweat thinking this was a waste of my time. He opened the door, and an evil smile lit his face immediately.

"Christian Axel, well, I hope I am not dreaming again. If I go into my bedroom right now, will I see me sleeping there or are you the real thing this time," he chuckled at his joke.

I laughed nervously. "Nein. I think this time you will find me in that bed if you go check." I flirted back while smiling with as much fake interest as possible.

Jonas's eyes went wide with shock. "Ah, then I need to say good night and get back in there." He began to tease that he was closing his door to run back to his room.

I grabbed the wood before he could shut me out. "Please Jonas, I need your help with a problem. I think I have a problem I mean, a serious one maybe?"

Jonas stopped giggling and his playful banter ceased. "This is about Peter, ja? He slapped you around. Gave you a directive to never see me again, perhaps?"

I looked around to make sure no one had slipped into the hallway. "If you would allow me to come inside. I would rather discuss this without the ears in the walls catching my drama."

Jonas flinched. "Ja. What the hell am I thinking? The beautiful boy of my dreams comes to my door in the middle of the night. He is desperate, alone, and begging to come in, and I haven't dragged him into my lair. Shit. The greatest of X-rated films starts just like this and I stand here scratching my head letting opportunity maybe pass me by. Get inside Christian Axel. Forgive my poor manners. I was just so surprised to see you is all." He pulled me inside and closed the door behind him.

I kept down my trembling as best I could. I dropped my gaze and got right to the point. "My Master, he thinks I am too free with my affections. He told me he looks the cuckold. His remedy is to keep me home and stabled. Jonas, I cannot do what I need to do if I am locked away in his apartment."

Jonas nodded. "Ja, I assumed that maybe his next move was to try to limit the damage he has done to his status. I assume you did your best to point out the errors in his thinking?" He crossed his arms and appeared deep in thought.

I took a deep breath and braced myself for his scorn. "Uhm, ja. I went even further Jonas. I did my best to seduce him and offered willing eagerness with his sexual affections." I felt my heart speeding up to my admission of engaging in such revolting behavior with my own motivation.

Jonas didn't even flinch, raise an eyebrow or appear affected negatively in the least. "Ah, that was a brilliant move. I assume it didn't work though or you wouldn't be here."

I shook my head and really felt shame to my next statement. "Well, I don't know that it didn't work. I left him well sated, out cold in his bed. I am here to trade whatever you ask to gain your aid in the event that when he wakes, my charms have worn thin. I need you to prevent him from keeping me prisoner more than I already am."

Jonas chuckled. "Willing to trade for whatever I ask. Well now that has possibilities. You have my attention, Christian Axel. So, when can I get this thing, I ask for in *return for me using my power to block Peter from chaining you up at home?"*

I took a deep breath. "Right now, if you wish, or whenever you say. I only ask your vow to come to my aid if in the morning I am not seen anywhere outside the fucking apartment."

Jonas laughed with a look of humor on his face. "My, you are much more aggressive than I thought you to be. I sort of thought you were just being dragged along the road to Dominant, but now I see a wolf in sheep's clothing before me."

I glared at the Elder Vampire with much fire in my gaze for a change. "You hear this. I will only say it to you once. I am not going to stay in this fucking collar, Jonas. You and all you jackasses calling themselves Dominants can do whatever the hell you want to me. I tell you this, better fucking hurry up and get your turn. Because when I break this damned metal collar, I will crush every fucking one of you that misused, betrayed, or caused me pain. This I swear on my Gott damned black soul. Pick a price and quit dicking around with me, Jonas. I am tired of this game of lion and mouse. You have me dead to rights. I am aware you can have me put in the ground, shot, whipped, bled into your tub, raped by fucking dogs or whatever you sick bastards do for fun at the expense of those that cannot defend themselves. Just get this horror you planned to do to me over with. Do you see me?

Because I am here just like you planned that I would be. That is why you did what you did today. You treat me like a stupid fool. I am a lot of thing Jonas, but a fool is not one of them. I want to live. I see more than you think I do. I am tired of your pissing with Master Peter at my expense. So, fuck me, drink my fucking blood, or kill me, but help me. I mean it. Speak now or I leave and fuck the lot of you. I walk out the Haus door and find my freedom the way I should have long ago."

Jonas stood there, his look of humor never leaving his expression. "Now that is the fire that proves you are a Priceless. I will name the price as you demand. I want to take your virginity as my Donor this night, right now. I want to taste you before the demons of your unimaginable fury that give you the forbidden powers settle down in your heated blood. You agree to this, and I will make sure that no lock is on any door in this whole fucking Haus that you don't have the key to open at will."

I glared at him feeling the urge to strangle this horrid man right there no matter what would happen afterwards. "Fine. Then let's do this. Maybe then you will stop fucking bothering me all the God damned time. I am sick of your setting off that twisted motherfucker that calls himself my Master. Don't you have a life?"

Jonas laughed, appearing more thrilled than ever when he heard an angry outburst at him. "Nein. Not yet.

Follow me Christian Axel. I intend to extract one this very night."

I shook my head in disgust, then shot a look at the worried looking Max boys. What a fucking life I had found for myself. Oh well, sucks to be me. Wait a moment, this time it was Jonas planning to do all the sucking, ja?

Chapter 27: Bloody Wedding

I followed Jonas to the back of his dimly lit apartment. All around the place were statues, art, and décor, all of it violent or grotesque in the theme of it. Even his furniture was the kind one would expect to see in the modern dark romanticism of a vampire.

The chairs of his living room were all high backed and richly decorated in red and black. His couch was velvet in a deep crimson color. I shivered slightly as I did my best to ignore the many gargoyles and bloody scenes from the paintings down that hallway. This place was creepy, Meine Liebe. I thought I wouldn't be able to sleep a single wink there if I had to. Yikes!

Then we arrived at the end of his long hallway to a door painted the same dark red as his couch. Memories of the torture chamber of Xavier's time with me filled my mind threatening to send me screaming the other fucking direction. I was full on trembling while that scary Vampire man turned around smiling with his toothy grin.

"Ah. I have waited too long for such an auspicious visit from the boy of my darkest dreams. You come inside and I will drink of your powers, Christian Axel, but this must be done willingly for it to work at its full potential. The legends say the demons that fuel your blood are tricky, and not easily captured in a single expression. I

wish to focus your mind. I need all the anger, the lust, all the madness that the circle of forbidden silver holds at bay unnaturally within you. I think tonight I will see the true soul of this boy come to me, when before I get only his masks. If this is the case, follow me. If this is not the real Christian Axel, then I warn you I will know it. It will be best if you find him quickly. I am not interested in the false ones." He stood at that door, his dark eyes blazing into my own.

I scoffed. "You are speaking crazy, Jonas. I told you here I fucking am. I think you're not only insane, but maybe you are deaf and blind as well. The only masks I see around here is the freaky ones you hang from the walls as your spooky art."

Jonas laughed loudly and deeply. "Ja, this is the boy Christian Axel that I never have met before this day. I offer you my greetings, dear love. I have waited some time for you to appear. Things got a little too busy for your others, ja? I must say your youth can wear a man out trying to keep up with your juggling too much."

I narrowed my eyes at that shit right there. "What is this you say? Juggling? You know Jonas, I have led a busy life since I first was hauled to this Gott forsaken place six years ago, but funny, since I meet you, things have been unusually stressful even for me. If I were a distrustful soul, I may think you had something to do with all of it."

Jonas shook his head clicking his tongue. "Christian Axel, I told you I wanted romantical love from you. That means you must learn to trust me, or we cannot be together. If I cannot have what I want of you, then you are worthless to me. I tell you I grant you my powers, and I brought you the leashes and powers of two others. I tell you I can break Peter's chains and even that metal around your neck. For all my honesty and holding up my end of this bargain I get distrust, suspiciousness, paranoia, and open discord. Now how is that equal service for equal service, my love?"

I growled at this insane man. "You play me the fool yet again, Jonas. Cut out the games, Gott verdammt. You sent the message loud and clear that you wished to see me just as you say. Well, surprise, surprise, here I am. The way I see it, you will take what I offer how I offer it, or Fick dich selbst (Go fuck yourself)."

Jonas smiled with much glee. "Perfect. The Priceless is now ready. Enter here Christian Axel, but you go first and of your own willpower."

I shook my head but walked inside that room mumbling, "Du bist verdammt verrückt. Wissen Sie das? Hat deine Mutter dich auf then Kopf fallen lassen? Oh, ich weiß, Sie wurde von einer Fledermaus gebissen, richtig?" (Translation: You're fucking crazy. Do you know that? Did your mother drop you on your head? Oh, I know she was bitten by a bat, right?)

310

Jonas broke out in riotous laughter at my grumbling to myself. "Christian Axel. I think you calling another crazy is maybe the funniest thing I ever hear. Your mad as the hatter, so I suppose you have the experience to point out my many faults. This I will give to you though; I still was not completely sure of your true priceless blood until this minute. I will need a moment to calm down my excitement. The real thing is here at last. I have waited so long." He held his chest then flipped on the lights.

I looked around the bright room. A large four posted bondage bed was in the center of the room covered in black sheets. There were no windows, just heavy rock walls like those of a castle. There was a fireplace built into the far wall. It looked well used with many ashes and an unspent log within it.

On the floor were black and grey tiles made to appear of natural stone with various black heavy throw rugs everywhere. A large black dresser with many drawers and no glass mirror sat near the bed. Next to that was a tall candle holder with a well-worn tallow sitting on it.

There was not another thing in this huge, poorly decorated room. It sort of reminded me of a tower prison cell where those of the royal blood of England would await their fates by the axe when condemned to death. I wondered if Jonas had meant it to favor this resemblance since I was aware he was a lover of medieval history.

311

I didn't care much for the look of that bondage bed in the center of this mostly empty room. I must say the possibility he planned to tie me down was not something I was thrilled about. I turned to glare at him with much irritation.

"Ropes will not be necessary. I told you I would come willingly. Leave me free of them and I thank you for the mercy of it," I spit out at him feeling even more anger rising within at his stupid smiling back at me like he was. I really hated that he had me stuck like this, literally.

Jonas nodded. "Well, that is not possible, Christian Axel. You cannot expect me to think you won't try to flee when this business begins. I choose to bond you for your own good this time. Maybe in the future though, after you're used to this, we can remove the restraints."

I roared at that, "You say you take a virginity from me, Jonas. I say I fucking grant my permission to do this. You use ropes anyway? Why? Because you plan to take my choice to say nein. I tell you right now I will not permit you to tie me down for this nightmare. I cannot tolerate yet another rape, fool. This is what Peter did to me. You are telling me you're no better than him?"

Jonas continued to smile coolly at me despite my increasing anger. "Ja. I am no better than him, Christian Axel. You walked in here willingly. Now I refuse to grant you any further choice. That is too bad for you. You'll get over this. In time, you won't even care anymore. You can hold still to endure my bondage, or I can knock you down. Either way, I get exactly what I desire. There is your fucking choice, Christian Axel." He laughed maniacally at that.

I shook my head, "Okay, ich verschwinde hier. Scheiß drauf. Wir sehen uns in der Hölle Jonas." (Translation: Okay, I'm getting out of here. Fuck this. See you in hell Jonas.) I turned around and attempted to leave. Motherfucker telling me I had no choice. We'd see about that, ja. I nodded my head in approval at Christian's statement glad he was running away from the Vampire man.)

Well, as usual I forgot how small and weak, I was compared to the mature Jonas. I made it to the door still muttering insults at him when he pounced on me. He grabbed me by my shoulders and flung me to his floor with a loud wail, and much fury.

I was stunned a bit by this sudden aggression, but I recovered quickly. I struggled to my feet, but the tricky vampire was on me in seconds. He flung me across the room like I was a nothing in weight.

I rolled across that stony floor finally colliding with the dresser. My hat flew off rocketed in the opposite direction from the rest of me. That dresser rocked back and forth from our meeting. I went to stand and something from the shelf above it fell onto my now bare head.

Whatever it was, it knocked the holy hell out of my skull. I fell back to my knees grabbing at my stinging, burning scalp, yelping nearly blind from that pain. Jonas took advantage of my momentary compromised state. He jumped on me from behind locking his grip under my arms tightly.

I kicked, thrashed, and screamed at him full of fury. "You let me go, Jonas, you motherfucker. I will kill you; I swear it. Unhand me. I withdraw my oath. I do not grant you a fucking thing willingly. Help! Someone help me. This cocksucker is trying to murder me. Gottverdammit, help me. Anyone? Damn you to hell, schwuler kindersolester (child molester)."

I admit for that moment I didn't give a shit about breaking my metal, nor that this monster could call the Guard on me. I was so full of my demons of fury if he had given me any quarter, I would have slit his Gott damned throat.

This uncontrollable anger was why I had stopped "cleansing the flesh" in the first place. Gerard had filled me too full of vengeance to manage without my Max boys. I thought I had enough time and rest from the days of that evil man's abuse to calm this problem down, apparently I was wrong. The fierceness of my need to retaliate had not settled a bit.

This was exactly what Jonas had wanted me to do. I didn't understand it at the time, but he purposely had triggered my symptoms. The legend of the Priceless was his reasons for such a cruel torture. He truly believes that only the blood heated by my demons is pure enough to grant him the power of extra years and keep him young.

Ja, this is his truth. You look at me like that, but I didn't say I believe that shit. I merely say Jonas does. Beware the perceptions of others Meine Liebe. They can be dangerous for your good mental and physical health. Ignore what others think or say about you, but do keep in mind when their beliefs are threatening to your safety, ja? I nodded that I understood his advice.

I realized he knew what hc was talking about. Afterall, he had learned it the hard way.

Jonas ignored my pathetic struggle to free myself of his hold. He dragged me to his bondage bed, and with some difficulty – hey I am a fighter, you know – he got me tightly bonded in his ropes.

I did all I could to make his life pure hell as he restrained me to helplessness, arms and legs spread eagled, laying on my back. I spit at him when I could no longer kick or punch him. He was sweating and his long hair was in a tangled mess from his heavy physical task.

I noticed he had not stripped me of my clothing. I wondered if he planned to just cut my throat without sexually assaulting me. I was kind of glad of that possibility, to be honest. I wasn't happy to be bled to death, but not having to endure another fucking from an old schwuler was at least a small mercy. My bar for gratitude was a bit low, but hey I was tied the hell up. Not like I could do anything no matter what his nasty plans with me were.

Jonas wiped the sweat from his brow and sat down on the bed next to me. "Well, you're quite the tiger, Christian Axel. You gave this old man a run for his money, ja? No matter, you are all set for this thing I have desired all my days."

I growled out in fury, "Oh? Then get to killing me, arschloch. I grow weary of your foul breath and ugly face. I'd rather be anywhere, even at the roots of the trees in the orchard than have to look at you another moment."

Jonas patted my injured left thigh, making me wail out in pain. "The young are always in a hurry to die. You will not die this night, my love. I take only enough to sustain me, neither a drop more nor less. You are almost ready. We have your anger flowing like the lava from a volcano, but we now require your lust."

I rolled my eyes at that. "Then you are the one who will get fucked, Jonas, not me. I can lay there and pretend I like it when you rape me, but I cannot fake lust where there is none. You can grow that hair longer, put on a dress and prance in it wearing lipstick like Claus all you like. Unless your cock falls off and a vagina grows in its place, not happening. Not ever. I already told you I do not find the man sexy."

Jonas nodded while breaking out in a wicked smile. "You sure? There is always a little interest in all humans if stroked the right way." He reached out and grabbed my manhood.

For the second time in my short life, I was sorry I wasn't varying my chastity device. I was not turned on by his attempts to gain my sexual desire, which was not why I missed the damned thing. It was because the idea of a man touching me that way was even more upsetting than the way they used me like the Frau. All Jonas managed to do was make me even angrier.

"You fucking cocksucking schwuler pig. Stop grabbing my schwanz. Why the hell can no one

317

understand that I am straight," I yelled, spitting out each word. I was about to blow a gasket at his manipulating my cock like dat.

After several minutes, the dense Jonas finally discovered you cannot make the heterosexual, a gay person any more than you can do the reverse. He could stroke my manhood till the end of time, all he would get was a tired wrist and an intensely pissed off Christian Axel.

He let me go with a look of terror in his eyes. "This cannot be. You really don't find me sexually attractive in any way?"

I groaned in pure agony. That leg wound was killing me and being bonded that way as you well know is not fun either. "I have been fucking telling you from the start. I am straight. Clear out your ears, you bastard. For that matter, I like my sex normal. You know, with a woman and a man without blood or wearing dresses. I sure as shit hate my father riding me like a fucking pony. What the hell is so wrong with me to lust for the natural way of enjoying sex? I am just not perverted enough for this fucking Haus, damn me. God fucking help me. Not even a single hair on my head is twisted like any of you freaks. No matter what you enforce on me, I will tolerate it only skin deep. But if you think you can ever tarnish my soul, you lose! I am still me. None of you can take that away, not ever." I was screaming this shit, all my secrets *like an idiot, I might add, by now beyond life and frustrated.*

I thought I would surely get caught by Master Peter by this time. I realized Jonas was taking too long to defile me, you know? I meant to get in, tolerate his fetish raping, and then run the hell back home. To my horror this crazy fucker was acting like I had all night for this nightmare.

Jonas sat there rubbing his face for a moment. "Damn. Well, your strong heterosexuality is a surprise, Christian Axel. Especially after all I know you have gone through. I suppose it makes sense when I consider it though. The legends say a priceless is meant to find his mate and make the Priceless kinder with his Priceless female. Of course, you would not be lusting after another male. This never occurred to me but is more than obvious. I have been witness to you looking at the females with unbridled interest in the hallways. There is no doubt your drive for breeding is powerful just as the rumors claim it would be. It is said this is all you will think about, dream of or desire, children, and a wife. A schwuler or pansexual Priceless would not be so heavily driven in mating with only the Frau. How could I have missed this? Shit."

I rolled my eyes. "Cut the shit about legends of the priceless and vampires. You see, here on the planet Earth, people stop believing in the fairy tales when they become adults. Gott verdammt, Jonas. Get to fucking me or let me go, will you? You are wasting my time. I need to get back to the apartment before my Master awakens. If I get caught, then the only legend of the Priceless they will become the truth is that I will be growing a fucking strong tree in the yard like all the rest of dem."

Jonas nodded. "You wait here. I have an idea." He rushed from the room leaving me there bonded like dat.

I screamed out in disbelief, "Wait here? Are you serious? Where the fuck else can I go, Jonas? I cannot turn into a bat to escape your ropes. You never bit me yet. Ficken Dich. This is crazy shit. Please someone kill me."

It seemed like forever before the schwuler Vampire returned. I was laying there cursing my existence for like the millionth time you know. I saw him come through the door and I began to prepare a string of insults to hurl at him for leaving me there to stress like that. My tongue was hampered almost immediately when I saw a beautiful black collar Frau come into the room behind him.

I dreamily stared at her without attempting to cover up my interest in the view. The woman shot me coy looks and covered her smile with her hands. I admit I even forgot that I was bonded in Jonas's clutches. See that was my problem with the Frau. They always made the idiot Maximillian stupid with lust for them, especially when

they were exceptionally good looking. To be honest, I didn't care. All women were beautiful in Maximillian's puberty driven eyes, so long as she was a girl, he was automatically her slave.

I no longer was interested in what Jonas was up to. He stood there next to the bed laughing at my sudden quiet and stupid grin while I stared at her in a full trance. It wasn't my fault I was so overtaken like that. The woman was a fucking vision of heaven. No more than twenty, long blond hair, deep brown eyes, well endowed with all the things the fairer sex should have. A credit to her gender I give her that.

I glared at my Master with a look of worry that he was talking about girls again. I eased away ever so slightly heading for the floor to avoid another potentially painful coupling with him.

Christian noticed my discomfort. He pulled me back toward him sighing loudly, "Where are you going? My lap is over here, meine Frau."

I trembled a little while stealing glances at his manhood, ever vigilant for any signs of his budding sexual interests. He saw my anxious watching of his boy parts.

He smiled gently at me then stroked my cheek. "Relax, Meine Liebe. I am well sated for now. You are safe as long as you don't wiggle that cute little bottom on my manhood to distraction, ja?"

I leaned back calmed but scooted my booty to his thigh while avoiding making any contact with his groin.

That made Christian laugh as he ruffled my hair. "You are adorable, Meine Liebe. How did this worthless man get so lucky to find such a rare gem? One day your beauty will rival the Goddess of Love herself. When that happens, I will be helpless against your charms. I already am hostage to them. What a glorious torture I suffer in your eyes, meine Frau. I will confess to you the second I saw you begged me to take you from here, my heart fell and shall never rise again. I would have robbed banks, killed people, challenged Gott himself, to possess you for my own, and that was before I held you in my arms. Just think what I would be willing to do now that you are my own blood bonded forever. I found you at last." He kissed the back of my head and squeezed me tight, making me cough like the little child I was.

He laughed out loud at my immature response to his romantic and deep affections. "When father time bring you the gift of maturity, will you feel the same I wonder?"

I looked up at him screwing up my face trying to appear serious. "I love you, Master. I really do, but I did hate you at first. I am sorry about that. It was wrong of me not to try *to understand you don't hurt me to be mean. You told me but I don't listen. I know I said I would burn you up, but I wouldn't, I swear it. I will burn up your dad though. You'll see. One day, I will make him stop hurting you."*

Christian suddenly looked incredibly sad. "Ah, my little bird, if you mean what you say, I can die a happy man right now. I don't need you to fight my battles for me, Meine Liebe, but the fact that you swear you would, that is love. Could the legends be truthful? I thought you were too young to feel the way a woman can, but now I wonder. The rumors tell us the love of a Priceless pair has no limits or boundaries. The Elder say it is pure and timeless which is why the blood bond can never be broken." He leaned down and kissed my lips while closing his eyes, appearing enraptured.

I stared at him while kissing him back, wondering if being bitten by a Vampire had made him into one (hey look I was nine, okay). He ended his deep kissing when he opened his eyes to see me looking at him with curiosity.

He laughed. "You looking for something in my gaze, meine frau? Dishonesty? An answer to a question perhaps?"

I nodded. "Yes Master. I wondered if Master Jonas bit you and now you can turn into a bat. Is that why you can sneak in on Debbie and Russell all the time? If you can, would you bite me so I can fly away from here? If you make me a vampire too, then I will come live with you in Germany. I just don't want to live in this basement anymore. I am not trying to escape you, I promise."

Christian's eyes went wide, then he broke out in bitter laughter. "Oh, Meine Liebe. This is the saddest and funniest thing I ever heard in my life. I was hoping this story would fill you with hope, but this is the wrong kind of it. Nein, Meine Frau. I cannot turn into a nasty old bat, nor can Jonas. Those are all lies about the fetish vampire people. Stories and tall tales Meine Liebe. Besides, do you think if I could turn into a bat, fly, and have the creepy Vampire powers of legend I would have let Debbie and Russell live? I would have done far more than just waste such things with sneaking up on those rat bastards."

I looked down at the mattress in much disappointment. "Oh. I guess I was being stupid. I apologize for my ignorance, Master." I sniffed feeling terribly upset that I had believed for a moment it was going to be as easy as a little bite to save me from my torture.

Christian gently raised my face by my chin, so I had to look at him. "It is not stupid to wish for magical powers when life is so harsh, meine Frau. You are a child. These beliefs of innocence are a blessing that nature gives to her little ones to help them deal with confusion in their environment. You are not ignorant. You are in pain. For that I beg your forgiveness that I not only cannot prevent

324

such a condition but am here to increase it. I will ask you to do your best to endure the burden I hand to you, and never forget that we have a destination of great hope to come from it. All things end, Meine Liebe, the good and the bad. It will seem like forever, but even this nightmare basement will someday be a memory. You see your Master Mad Maxx before you. Do you think he didn't think that his own torture in his metal would never end? Well, you see I wear no collar today. I sit with the most beautiful frau in the world in my lap, laughing at my silly antics from those days so long ago. One day, we will sit together with our children in our laps and tell them the tales of these dark days with our smiles of victory. Have faith little ones. Time seems to move slow when you're in pain, but father time is neither late nor early. He is always right on time. It is the perception of the one waiting on his ass that causes it to seem otherwise. Trust in me that I never tell you untruths and be patient. We cannot change circumstances, Meine Liebe, but we can change how we view it. That is what we do for you, and what happened to that idiot Maximillian. He stopped wasting his time trying to control the brutal world and learned to control how he responded to it. Only then did he become the Master Mad Maxx that holds you. This you understand, ja?"

I nodded, "Yes Master. I think I do. You want me to stop blaming myself and calling myself names. Then I can be a Mistress, right?"

He smiled at my childlike simplistic understanding of this most complex dilemma. "Believe it or not, every day you are getting closer to that very thing. Meine Liebe. In time all this horror I put you through will make perfect sense. Until then, you will cry, beg, and scream for me to stop. I cannot stop this though it is already too late for us both. You will hate me for all the horror I will force you into. For what it is worth, I hate myself for having to be the one that does this harsh training to you. That doesn't change the fact it must be done. I know you are strong enough to endure all that will come. It still pains me more than you can ever know to be incapable of making this all go away. I didn't cause this nightmare life you live. Your mother created the situation that led me to find you in the first place. You choose to ask for my brutal aid rather than die in this stinking hell hole. That alone is worth my respect. I cannot truly fix any of this insanity. I can only teach you how to survive it. However, your question does have me thinking. Maybe I will call Jonas tomorrow. I will ask if that old Vampire can shape-shift yet. If he says ja, well meine Frau I will meet you in the rafters hanging by our toes right After we kill our parents, ja?"

My eyes went wide and then both of us broke out in maniacal laughter. For several minutes we howled at his dark humor over my misconceptions about Vampires. When we finally calmed down, he returned to his story after a few more hugs and kisses, and my re-scooting my booty far from his lap.

"Jonas cleared his throat and waved his hand in front of my face trying to break my gaze of eagerness at that pretty Frau. "Ah, I think Maximillian likes you a great deal Emma. See the way you have subdued his demons meine beauty? This boy is helpless against your charms."

The gorgeous Emma giggled but kept her distance lingering at the entryway. "I think I like Maximillian back Jonas. I see you tell no lies. He is most uncommonly handsome as you said he is."

I wanted to say something kind to her over that flattery but all I could do was stare like the clumsy boy I truly was. This lack of response made both Emma and Jonas chuckle at me. It never once occurred to me that this girl was not the least upset to see me tied down in a bed, within a spooky room. You know it is amazing what those women could do to my good sense in those days. I should've at least questioned this weirdness but no. That stupid boy cared only that there was a female present and she was demonstrating interest in him.

Jou ever had a moment in your life where you would like to go back there and scream at yourself, "don't fucking fall for it you God damned fool." I nodded thinking of all the times I wished I could do just that.

Christan smiled then chuckled bitterly, "Well this was one of mine, which is for sure."

Anyway, much to my thrill Jonas pointed at the bed next to me. "Come sit here, Emma. Maximillian cannot see you way over there. I bet he would love to know you better." The Vampire backed away while that angel come and took a place next to me.

I could barely breathe. Her sweet smell overcame my senses. Her milk white skin seemed almost translucent in that dim lit room. I thought she had to be made of marble or perhaps ceramic, she was so unblemished and perfect. She had me in a spell and I never wanted to break free.

Emma shot a look at Jonas. "Can I kiss him, Jonas? If I do you will not tell anyone, right?"

I heard that. "Ja, you can kiss me, Emma. Jonas, shut the hell up. He tells anyone then I will kill him, I sweat it." I struggled trying to get closer to this beautiful woman.

She and Jonas really laughed at my sudden outburst while Jonas responded to her inquiry. "Ja, you can kiss him, Emma. This is why I bring you here. Kiss him all you like and touch him too if it pleases you. I don't think Maximillian will complain."

I shook my head wildly. "Nein, I never argue with you Emma. I love you with all my heart. I would even marry you this night if you would have me."

That made the girl swoon. "I would say *ja*, this very second too, if the Haus would allow such a match Maximillian." She leaned down and began to kiss my lips with vigor.

I closed my eyes and let her sweep me away with her passion-filled kisses. I felt her hand rub across my chest. This caused all my muscles to tense in wanton desire. I pulled hard, struggling with all I had to break through those damned ropes. I wanted to embrace this glorious woman and take her as I had Annette only days before. I was no longer thinking about my illusion of virginity, breaking my collar, or Jonas standing right there watching this whole scene.

Only Emma and her soft touch mattered to my hormone riddled brain. I moaned out in full thrill when she began tearing at my blouse unbuttoning it to get at my flesh with her stroking. Our kissing was getting more than a little heated. Jonas had been unsuccessful with his useless attempts to gain my sexual interest, but Emma did it in only seconds. I could feel my erection threatening to tear out of my breeches before she even ran her hands down my stomach seeking my manhood. She gasped into my mouth when she grabbed my cock realizing I needed no further stimulation. I was more than ready to grant her my favor if she would allow it.

She pulled out of our kissing to look down on my, uhm, interests. "I think you like me a great deal,

Maximillia," she chuckled nervously then shot a look at Jonas who had a big toothy smile on his face.

I panted out hoping she planned to do more than just hold me with that glorious hand of hers. "I told you I love you, Emma. Jonas please, I am begging you. Let me out of these ropes. I want to prove to Emma; I do love her. Let me out, Gott verdammt," I wailed out in frustration when the girl let me go and stood up, backing away.

I watched full of longing as she rushed out the door never looking back. I shot a look of fear at Jonas then back to the now empty doorway.

"Tell Emma to come back, Jonas. Did I say something to upset her? Damn me. Please get her to come back. I apologize for it. Let me go. I will chase after her and show her I am a man of honor. I didn't mean to scare her with my over eagerness." I was now full-on whining like a little bitch that the female of my dreams had fled without allowing for my couple with her.

Jonas chuckled and walked over to his dresser. "She will be back in a moment, Maximillian. You just watch that door for her. She had to get herself prepared for your lovemaking is all. It is the secrets of the woman she attends. I picked her just for you. I am happy she pleases you so much. I now see you tell the truth. You are straight, very straight. You find your lust with the female, not the male, and rapidly I may add. This is good to know, but not relevant to my interest in you as my lover. It only matters when it comes to my other interest in you."

I shook my head. "I don't give a fuck about a thing you say, Jonas. I want to speak to Emma. When will she come back? She is taking too long. I must get back to my Master's apartment and I desire to spend some time with her first." I kept seeking her return to the door as he told me to ignore his movements at that dresser.

Jonas laughed deeply and loudly. "Stop worrying about Peter. I took care of that when I got your Emma. We have all night if I wish it. You just relax and wait for the girl. She is coming. Do you see her yet?"

I growled out now quite irritated but still beyond interest in Emma's return. "You are telling lies. You cannot have taken care of Master Peter, but I no longer care about him or you Jonas. You can go fuck each other. You know damned well I don't fuckin see Emma because she is not here yet. Damn it. You go tell her I don't care about her makeup or if she is wearing fresh panties. This rushing off was not necessary. I am happy to take her as she is. I tell you she ran away. I upset her somehow."

Jonas sat down on the other side of the bed than my Emma had. "Well, you are full of lust that is for damned sure Christian Axel. Tell me what you plan to do to Emma when she comes back?"

I snapped my head to glare at that damned fool. "What the hell do you think I will do. I plan to fuck that girl if she will let me. I think her kissing says she will. Why are you asking such a dumb question? Surely you are not blind. I am ready for the mount." Jonas immediately looked to the crotch of my breeches.

"Ja. It would seem your more than ready to penetrate Emma. I can understand that. She is a pretty girl." He began to undo the buttons of his cuffs and roll up his sleeves.

I frowned at him in increasing anger. "If you understand that then what the fuck are you doing sitting there? Go get her or let me go get her myself. That girl was hot."

Jonas shook his head. "If you penetrate her then you cannot break Peter's collar, Christian Axel. It is your only virginity to offer as sacrifice for collar selection. You better think about that a moment, or do you no longer care?"

Now I was pissed. "Rat bastard. is that what this is about? You bring this beautiful princess in here to tempt me, so I trap myself in my metal? Betraying schwuler motherfucker."

Jonas's expression melted from humor to that of a demon. "If I wanted to do that I could without granting you the pleasure of penetrating anyone. With only a word you will be on your knees for all time. I bring that girl in her to raise your lust, and now I see your anger returns. You are ready for my own penetration despite all your best efforts to thwart me. I condemn you to be my lover and donor with this act I am about to enjoy. I have already arranged that your request that you offered for your fourth virginity be done. Time to pay up your end of this bargain."

I let out a yelp of surprise when he reached out with force and ripped my breeches down to my ankles. I then saw the thing he had retrieved from his dresser while he kept my attentions on the door looking for Emma. A lancet knife with a fancy pattern was cupped in his hand.

Before I could let out a word of dispute or inquiry, he clutched my right knee. In a single smooth stroke, he opened the flesh of my upper thigh with that lancet weapon. I wailed out in both terror and surprise at this vicious attack.

The blood began to well from my rather deep but short gash. Jonas dropped his head and began to drink my leaking fluid from the hole he made in me. I screamed and yelled for help while he licked and sucked at my wound. Fear had made me her bitch. I swear I nearly lost my mind from this scene right from a nightmare.

After only a few moments, which felt like hours to be honest, he lifted his head from my thigh. His eyes were closed, and an expression of ecstasy was on his face. I saw my blood on his lips which scared me even more than I already was. I yelled out in intense distress upon seeing this terrible thrill he was experiencing.

Jonas opened his eyes that appeared glazed with satisfaction and looked at me. "That was supernatural, my love. I never tasted anything so sublime as you. Now, for my consummation completion that marks you as my lover for all time."

I whimpered with near madness when the Vampire crawled upon the bed still holding that lancet in his hands. He took a position above me making me think he was about to cut my throat and finish what he started at my thigh.

Instead, he dropped down forcing his lips to my own kissing me in a frenzy heavier than Emma's a moment earlier. I had begun to cry despite my resolve to die with some honor. Hey, don't judge me too harshly for that crying shit, I was only thirteen. I know I keep bringing that up but when there is a kind creepy thing like a Vampire sucking your blood while your tied up, it can be a bit upsetting you know. I nodded with my eyes wide in terror at the idea of that Vampire man sucking my Master's blood. I would have been crying too.

I was sure he planned to kill me, **Meine Liebe,** but Jonas was about to do something I found much worse than that, at least at that time I thought so. Without any comfort of lubrication, nor kindness of gentle deployment he undid his pants and forced himself into me. The brute didn't even break his harsh kiss while he did it.

I of course was sent right to hell from that pain. No matter how accustomed you are to this kind of penetration, there is no natural lubrication. Without something to keep down the friction your tissues tear and blood with much pain is a given.

I realized too late this was the reason for his bonding me. He was aware I would never hold still and let him dry rape me like that nor let him cut me open either. I sobbed throughout the entire drawn-out couple of his harsh thrusting into me. Blood from the damage he caused finally offered some smoothness to the brutal act. While horrid for me it did thankfully appear to aid him into getting close to his climax.

I had no idea this was the marriage blood bonding ritual he was pulling here, but then again I hadn't done my fucking homework on what it meant to be his Donor, now had I? If I had, then I would have at least been a little less traumatized though I doubt I would have been so willing.

This was a painful lesson I will not soon be forgetting. If you must deal with an unusual fetish, make God damned sure you find out ahead of time what you're getting yourself into. I cannot stress that shit enough. Always do your homework first before you go making deals at midnight with Vampires on their home turf.

Then, just as Jonas reached his apex he lifted up and backhanded my tear drenched face with much force. My mouth was busted immediately. I felt the blood flowing down my quivering lips and chin. He let out a moan indicating he reached orgasm.

Then while still spasming in his climax, he forced his mouth back to mine. I had to endure his fresh kissing and his cleaning up the bleeding he caused with his tongue. I felt sick to my stomach from this gross bloody business, not including the dry sodomy. It was seriously brutal.

Jonas, filling himself to a point of pure satisfaction in all his lustful desire, allowed himself to collapse on me. I could barely breath under the weight of this grown man. I panted out still weeping like a child unable to find any words to express my disgust and terror over his bizarre sexual assault.

He must have come to his senses because he rolled off me. Jonas lay there next to me sweating and panting with his eyes closed and a smile on his face.

"Well, then it is done, Christian Axel. Now you belong to me for all time. That collar Peter put on you is bullshit. No matter where you go, I own your soul, and your blood is flowing in my veins. I share your demons and will haunt your dreams till the day you die." He took a deep breath as if this was the greatest day of his life.

Well, it was up there among one of my worst. "Untie me you fucking brute. You didn't tell me all this was involved in being your lover. I never agreed to any of this but I do agree you will haunt my nightmares forever you freak," I wailed out in pure despair at this horrible mess I was in.

Jonas opened his eyes and lifted himself to rest on his arm. "Calm down Christian Axel. This was just the deflowering ceremony. I will never be this harsh again. Next time, we can be together in a gentle fashion and the bloodletting won't have to be so dramatic. This was a onetime thing."

I glared at him with tears still burning my eyes. "Bullshit, you tell lies. Emma never came back. What the hell was that even about? You bring a woman here to torment me? You cut me and dry fuck me. Now you talk crazy shit about my collar not mattering and I belong to you forever. What the fuck? Let me out of these ropes. Look, I am still bleeding. Maybe you can drink it until my doctor needs to do another blood transfusion."

Jonas's eyes went wide with that. "What? A blood transfusion. When?"

I sniffed loudly and wailed out "Yesterday. Why the fuck do you care? I can call that doctor right now and he can give you all the blood you want. Just please untie me first."

Jonas groaned out loud. "You didn't tell me this. This was a waste. It is no good."

I screamed out in rage, "I swear to God if you don't let me out of these ropes right fucking now than I will show you wasted, you bastard. Who do you mean it is not good? Sure, seemed fine to you a few minutes ago."

Jonas nodded then began undoing his knots. "Christian Axel, we have to do this all over again. I cannot have your blood mixed up with another's so soon when I do it. I can overlook the recent couple with Peter since he is of your blood, but this blood transfusion, nein."

"You can go to hell, Jonas. I am never letting you do this again. In fact, I didn't let you do it this time. " I yelled out as he freed my legs at last.

Jonas let out a gasp, "Wait, who donated the blood for the transfusion?"

I growled out in pure irritation while he let lose my first arm, "My fucking father. Who else do you think, you monster."

Jonas smiled and breathed with what appeared to be relief. "You mean Peter, right?"

I pulled my second arm free and reached down to pull up my breeches. "Unless I have another one, ja. Maybe Felix and you lied to me. How the fuck would I even know. This is a damned insane asylum for perverts. I no longer believe a thing any of you weirdos tell me."

I jumped off the bed moaning out in pure agony from his attack, and my very pissed off left thigh, that gunshot was a bitch you know. I limped over slowly to grab my hat. I was leaving. I had decided this fucker needed to stay the hell away from me.

I couldn't believe I said it but at that moment I yelled at Jonas, "I would rather be the lover of Claus or even Master Peter. At least they are kind enough to use fucking lube when they forced themselves on me. You're not only a freak, but you also have no manners. When you rape someone the least you can do is offer a bit of fucking comfort, you rude bastard." I must say not one of my finest statements right there. Christian laughed hard at that, but I didn't think it very funny. Dry penetration hurts, nothing humorous about it.

When I went to bend down to retrieve my hat, that Vampire Elder came at me. Before I knew what hit me, he had snatched me into his arms grabbing my waist from behind. He dragged me kicking and screaming back to his bed. I was now ready to kill this bastard. I'd had enough of this horror, and to be terribly honest, he scared the fuck out of me worse than he had before this nasty situation.

Jonas held my arms so I couldn't punch him. Then pulled me in his lap my back to him in a snuggle hold. He did not encounter too much difficulty keeping me restrained despite my struggling. I was weakened by the pain of his rough couple and my gunshot injury not to mention spent from all my attempts to get out of his ropes.

"Now what the hell do you want. You got everything you asked for. Let me go, Jonas." I broke down into

another crying fit. I am not ashamed to admit this, I had a bad week as I told you already.

The Vampire laid his head on my shoulders sighing. "I cannot let you go upset like this, Christian Axel. You must calm down. We are lovers now, and lovers look out for each other. I realize I hurt you and likely scared you a great deal. There is nothing I can do about this. I apologize for not warning you ahead of time of the brutality of the deflowering of the fourth virginity with a blood bonding, but that is the way it is done in my sect. In time you will forget this rough business. I swear to you, I will never hurt you like that again. From now on only romance and gentle couplings you can be assured of that."

I shook my head wildly. "I don't want any couplings with you gentle or otherwise, Jonas. You see I am not interested in the man. I don't want you sucking my blood either. In fact, I want you to never touch me again." I was sobbing without any attempt to hide my tears by this time.

Jonas nodded his head that he had laid heavily on my shoulder "Ja, I know. Despite your current regrets, I must demand you keep your oath to me. I expect you to be the lover I asked you for. I understand you will never desire me sexually, but your heart can still be won without physical attraction. That is a prize I desire more than your return of interest in my lust. I can never return the favor of orgasm to you thanks to your need to keep your virginity. Thanks to that we cannot expect to enjoy an equal trade in our intercourse anyway. I accepted that unavoidable fact when I decided I wanted your affections as my lover. For a moment I thought this thing we did was ruined by your blood transfusion. However, since your blood was not mingled with another that has no kinship, this bonding we did tonight is valid. You belong to me Christian Axel. One day you will go into the world and find your mate. When you do, I will come and join her too in this blood bonding like we did this night. Then for all time your family will be my own. I can rest now with the knowledge that I am assured immortality through my beautiful Christian Axel and his loving blood bonded mate. Then the many children from your unions with her."

I was startled by his statement. "What? You did this so you can call me and my Frau family? You seek immortality through my children? Why do this to me and mine? Why not just choose your own mate, then make children with her?"

Jonas laughed at my ignorant question. "I am schwuler, Christian Axel. I desire the female the way you want the man. It will be a hardship for me to blood bond with your Frau only the one time. How can you think I would be able to overlook my disgust long enough to breed for a single kid, much less enough of them to find my immortality? Besides, I want the pure Priceless in my

342

pedigree. Only the rarest for Jonas. You see I have a taste for the macabre abominations of this world. Nothing on this Earth is more forbidden nor dark than the Priceless metal."

I did my best to quell my tears, unsure what to think of this strange reason the Vampire was giving for his unnatural affections toward me. "This thing you did to me. Are you planning to hurt my Frau this way?" I perked up my ears ready to hear this answer since my Master said he had promised my leash to this Vampire man.

Jonas chuckled. "The female has less stress over the penetration part of this ritual, Christian Axel. Nature has suited her with a powerful way to bleed without rough mounting. When you find her, I can wait to call in my leash rights during her woman's cycle. Then I can join her in intercourse during this moon phase and break her flesh just as I did your own. Her pain will be less but the blood bonding stronger than you or I can ever hope to achieve even if you had been a virgin in all ways when we did this. The Priceless female donor or vampire has more power than any man can imagine thanks to the magical uterus and ability to produce new life. I do not lust for the woman, but even I can respect the unlimited potential each one possesses within her. It has always been my curse to feel no sexual desire for the gender that holds the greatest supremacy and all the deepest mysteries of our race."

343

I narrowed my eyes in confusion. "You said my Master's collar no longer matters. What the hell does that mean? Are you saying that you can claim me away from my Master?" I shuddered a bit at that thought. Hey, I hated Master Peter, but this guy just drank my blood, raped me, and beat the hell out of me. Even my Master wasn't that fucked up. Okay forget I said that. Maybe he is, but in a different way. I mean, ah, fuck it. They are all bad. A rock and a hard place you know.

Jonas shook his head. "Kind of. What I did was lay claim to the rights of you as my own. If for any reason Peter were to die and you still wear a collar, you belong to me as my lover, blood bonded mate. There is no longer anything Peter nor anyone else can do to stop me from calling in my rights to your favors. That idiot Master of yours didn't blood bond, but then grants a leash to others that can do the same. He assumed none of us would dare to mark what he thinks is his alone by right. Most Dominants don't dare to incite such anger in one among their own rank, but you see Peter leashed you to one above him, didn't he? I am at the top of this Haus, and while I cannot own a collar outright, I can own a permanent leash. Xavier did this, you may recall. Always remember, anytime you share your collar with another, you risk such a possibility they will set their claims deep. The Haus allows up to four leashed Masters per collar. Well, your Master has found out the hard way this very night that he should not have tried to use you to climb the status ladder if he wanted you all to himself. This is another reason no one likes to leash their collars to an Elder." He started laughing with much wickedness in his tone.

I almost couldn't get a breath unsure what to think of this disturbing statement. "Huh? I don't understand. What is this you tell me about my Master? What do you mean the hard way? A permanent leash like Xavier, you mean, oh my God, nein. This cannot be."

Jonas spun me around forcing me to look him in his face. "But it is, Christian Axel. In fact, I had the Dungeon Masters haul Peter away when he came to my door with anger after awakening to find you missing. He was out of his mind with jealousy and knew where to find you. I had just returned to the apartment with Emma to find the dumb bastard kicking at my door demanding I open it so he could collect his collar. Well, I informed him of my blood bonding with you and my decision to enact my rights as your leash Master and husband. He grew more furious, which he is aware is not legal. He must share you with me like it or not until that collar of his is broken. When he refused to leave me to my favors with my prize, I sent him to be punished. The second offense for this kind of dishonorable behavior is three days in the Dungeon and another five lashes. Since you are currently without your Master's direction, you will stay here with me, your secondary Master and permanent leashed husband. This is done and there is no undoing it."

I began to silently weep at the horror he was saying to me. "But you had not blood bonded me yet! You lied to him. I told you I took back my oath. You had no right." I was not unhappy to hear Master Peter was being roughly handled but I was more than despaired to understand I would never escape this secondary nightmare of the Vampire over it.

Jonas nodded. "I assumed you would try to back out, Christian Axel. Well, I warned you I always get what I want. There is nothing that will stop me when I find my passion. I desire to have my Priceless family and I will fucking have it too. You belong to me, and now you know it and everyone else will too soon enough. I have collected one of a set. I will make damned sure you break that metal of Peters. You will go out and find your mate. Then when she is ready to break her own, I will bond to her too. My pair will be complete, and my life's obsession quenched at last. I grant you assured freedom, stop the incestuous abomination of your father's affections, and will see all your dreams of a Frau and children come to truth. I give you all this for only the price of your family granting my immortality in return. Now that is more than fair, don't you think Christian Axel?"

I looked at that Vampire full of fear nodding. "It sounds right, but somehow I feel you made a bargain with me that will not be balanced in my favor."

Jonas smiled his toothy smile full of wickedness. "You must learn to trust me, Christian Axel. After all, the deed is done. I don't believe you have a choice, now do you?"

That Vampire was right. He had made sure I had no choice.

Chapter 28: The Shattered Husband

"Jonas held me tightly where I had to look at him, granting no room for my struggle. "That is correct. You have no choice. We are blood bonded for life and there is no return once the blood has passed between us. You will be staying here with me for the next three days. Then you can return to that rude father of yours. He will learn to obey the rules, and little Christian Axel so will you. From this day forward you grant me my pleasure how, when and where I say without hesitation. I can be a generous man, but you cross me then you can expect brutality that would make this thing I did to you tonight seem like a nothing." His eyes blazed with fire from within as he opened his mouth to demonstrate he had bitten his own tongue.

I groaned out loud as I recognized the meaning of that gash in his mouth. He had mingled his blood with mine during his climatic kissing during his deflowering of my fourth virginity.

I looked at my Master in pure shock, unsure if I was understanding what he was saying. I thought he had just told me this Vampire man, Jonas, had done to him what Master Maxx did to me during our collaring ceremony.

My Master told me that cutting his boy part and mingling it with the blood from my booty during his rough sex with it made us married. He told me this "blood bonding" was for life and could never be undone. How could he be married to me if he was already blood bonded to Jonas?

Master Maxx saw my shocked look and patted my head. "You are wondering how I blood bonded to meine Frau if I was already this way with Jonas, ja?"

I nodded while screwing up my face in curiosity.

He chuckled. "The blood bonding can be done between two of the same gender and one or both of them can still blood bond to one of the opposite gender. You can blood bond to one of each, this makes sense, ja?"

I nodded but then became more confused. "Wait, Master you said that you leashed me to Jonas. He told you he wanted to blood bond to your wife, but I am already that way with you. He is not a girl. He can't do that horrible thing to me that he did to you." I smiled, feeling relieved that I would be spared that horror after all.

Master Maxx shook his head frowning. "That is usually true, Meine Liebe, but sadly not in your case. Damned Debbie, she soiled you too heavily for me to bargain this situation away. You see I took your last honest virginity when we blood bonded, and collared as is Haus law. This leaves you only the fourth secret virginity left to trade for the collar selection. This virginity is not one that most favor, so I had to take your case before the leaders of the Haus. Otherwise, you would be finished my love. Without any unpenetrated area, you no longer qualify to belong to the Haus. Your special nature as the legendary female Priceless has saved you and also condemned you. The Elders and Voting Council have bent the rules in order to accept your most coveted membership. Only Jonas was willing and remember he had demanded it by oath from me long ago, to accept the task of deflower your secret virginity. Worst yet, the only way he can is also considered a blood bonding. Jonas will save you from being sent to the circuit, but he will gain you in the only double blood bonding that has ever been recognized by the Haus. That bastard is the Head of the Haus now Meine Liebe. He can bend the rules to his favor, and in order to get that Priceless pair he wanted, he has done just that."

My eyes went wide. "What does that mean exactly? I mean, does that mean I will be married to both of you when he bites me?" I shivered at that thought.

My Master looked at me with pity and sighed loudly. "You are too clever for your own good, Meine Liebe. Ja, that is exactly what that means. Even if after you break that collar of mine, he has rights to your special services in the way he likes including that horrid blood fetish of his. At least until the earth swallows his vampiric ass up for good."

I whimpered in terror. "He blood bonded you, Master. You are married to him too. That is what he meant. He wants to be in our family by being able to make us have sex with him all his life."

Master Maxx groaned. "See you are very fucking clever. Apparently smarter than that stupid Maximillian. He didn't understand what that Gott damned vampire was up to. Here my nine-year-old Frau figures it out in only moments the thing that took me eight fucking years. A Frau already undone with my own blood bonding has figured it out. I thought we were safe since it is forbidden to blood bond with two of the same gender, but that old schwuler is not truly considered the male thanks to his lack of lust for females. Therefore, he is claiming the spot of the opposite gender blood bonding with you along with the requirement of your fourth virginity to do this unthinkable thing. Until the day that old bat dies neither of us can escape his bed and blood lust for our Priceless powers."

I hid my face in my Master's huge chest, breaking out into tears. "Don't let that Vampire do it, Master. I don't want him sucking my blood. I don't want him with us and our kids. He will hurt them like he hurts you. Like he wants to hurt me."

351

Master Maxx pulled me away from his chest and stared into my face with much sternness. "Meine Liebe, stop this weeping. Jonas is insane. No one lives for eternity. You and I have no powers of immortality. That is all a myth like the Vampire sleeping in coffins or turning into bats. We must do this thing, or you and I cannot be together. Worse, the Haus will sell you away from me forever without his help for this virginity. We have no choice but to tolerate his stupidity for a bit of time. Jonas is already an old man, meine Frau. He will die soon enough. If not soon enough for us then maybe he can have an accident, ja?" He smiled at me with an expression of pure wickedness in his gaze.

I stopped crying and nodded. "Yes Master. I understand. I won't cry anymore but I swear I will kill him myself after I break this collar. I won't put up with him hurting you, me, or our babies."

My Master pulled me into a tight hug. "That is meine little Demonseed Frau. It fills me with much pride to witness that she is already a lioness over the children of her HusDom. I almost pity Jonas when he meets his fate at our hands, Meine Liebe. We kill him together, ja? That bastard has tortured me for years and now plans to do the same to my family. Nein. You vow to me; we play his game until your metal is off your neck. Then we do what we must without regrets."

I nodded. "I promise, Master. I will help you kill that Vampire man the minute we are both free."

He stroked my back gently. "Rachel, I love you with all my heart. You just focus on your training, and one day soon we will have our family. All this horror of the Haus, collars, D/s, this basement, only a nightmare of things long in the past for us both. In you, I find all the struggle was worth the pain. Truth is, I believe we find hope and strength in each other. A love like ours can never be denied. Nothing will get in the way of our dreams. I ask the you be patient, trust me, and love me. If you can do these things we cannot lose."

I pulled back, sniffed, and wiped my nose with my wrist. "I will Master. I love you too." I smiled bitterly at him.

He rolled his eyes. "Well, you will need to learn some manners and hygiene, Meine Liebe. I must say that was disgusting watching you use your wrist for the handkerchief. What next? You brush your teeth with my toes perhaps?" He giggled while he poked playfully at my nose.

I swatted his hand away. "Do you see any tissues around here, Master? I didn't use the sheets because that would be gross."

My Master laughed out loud. "You are such a smart ass. No wonder I love you so. You remind me of me. Now sit back and we get back to the story? Or would you rather pick your nose and wipe that on the walls?"

I groaned. "I am listening, Master, and I don't do that. Are you trying to gross me out?" I sat back snuggling into his lap again.

He laughed even harder "Thank Gott you don't do that. Though, it bothers me that I tell you such horrible things about my life and you think my saying you wipe boogers on the wall is gross. Your idea of what is truly nauseating needs some work, Meine Liebe. Okay, where were we? Ja, the horrid night of my deflowering and blood bonding with Jonas. That was not a good night, I have to say."

"He laughed at my stupidity of walking right into his trap. Master Peter had taken two of my virginities when he collared me, but he never blood bonded. When this happens, the Dominant must report the "marriage" to the Head of the Haus, and the Voting Council for the record. It is how they make sure the rules are followed and those with such a bond are not accidentally double or triple blooded.

I was screwed, quite literally. I not only had to put up with the lustful advances of Master Peter, but thanks to this nightmare I was also Jonas's bitch. My Master had been beyond dumb himself to fight the Elder when he was notified of this horror. Even my idiot ass knew that interfering with the rights of a Dominant taking his pleasures with his blood bonded partner carried a heavy penalty.

Though in reality Jonas had cheated his way into this situation. I was not made aware of his truthful intentions. I also never granted my approval. It was also dirty business that when Master Peter was hauled away, I was still free to be saved from a huge mistake.

This is why before I blood bonded with you, Meine Liebe, I asked for your permission. You took my ring and agreed to marry me. I did give you the right to say nein, though I cheated too. You are far too young to have known what this meant, but under the circumstances, nothing could be done.

You see, I fucked up when I took your virginity to protect you from that Darrell. I knew eventually your Master Peter would discover my indiscretion. He is just that kind of bastard I assumed he would check. If he found this out before I did it formally – you know, reported it to the Haus – he would have reported you soiled and ended us both. That is why I completed it and had your Master Peter witness it before I returned to the Motherland and left you in his care.

I had to cover my tracks and save your collar from the tarnish I committed against you. You have no idea how much trouble the moment of anger at Darrell and Debbie cost me, though you did suffer terribly twice yourself. I had to beg for special permission to marry, blood bond, and collar my slave at a forbidden age. Again, the Haus wanted your membership so badly they bent the rules for us on all that too. It was a close call, Meine Leibe, and I still have nightmares over doing what I did to you, for what that is worth. (I nodded that I knew that feeling. His blood bonding and anal rape had terrified me I am/was not going to lie.)

Like you Meine Liebe, there was nothing I could do about this blood bonding. I was not too young to know better like you, but Jonas was a powerful Elder. I was aware his Elder brothers would side with him if I dared to point out his cheating me into his lifelong bond to me. Then I would surely bring down his fury at me for daring to call him a thief even though he is that bastard.).

I would have to deal with this humiliation and learn to live with it until I could find a way out of it, like that accident we discussed earlier. I shivered in his grip thinking of having to endure his bloody coupling and his sucking my blood.

Jonas scoffed at my observable distress. "Stop acting as if this will be a hardship for you, Christian Axel. You'll enjoy being my lover. Over time, this thing I enjoy will be nothing to you. I only require a feeding twice a month. It is not like this every time I want to make love to you. Now, I am tired. It is time for bed and tomorrow we go to visit Drexel."

I snapped out of my despairing feelings. "What? Drexel? Why?" I really began trembling over that name unable to handle jet another freak so close to this one.

The Vampire chuckled at my fearful gaze. "He wants to see you and I said we will visit him, that is why. We are to attend breakfast in his apartment by nine. So, off to bed we go. You wore me out. I need some sleep to let your Priceless blood do its job rejuvenating my old bones. Do not give me any trouble, you will not like it if you make me angry, my love. You know what? I think maybe for now, I will keep you bound up. I wouldn't want my disturbed Christian Axel doing anything insane, like taking an early morning stroll in the yard." He stood up hauling me roughly by my Master leash out of that room.

I had no choice but to limp behind him full of defeat. I swear I had intended to take that stroll he was speaking about. I wanted to die more than you can know. For that moment, I forgot about breaking my metal, dreams of a family of my own, and even that eventually I could be free to go out that door. All that I could see was endless nights of pain, terror, and humiliation, in Jonas's and my father's beds.

Jonas pulled me along to a black door in his hallway. He opened it to reveal his sleeping chamber. A large canopy bed was in the center of this richly decorated room. As with all the rest of his apartment everything was red and black. Even the walls, bedding, and sitting chairs were either midnight black or crimson red.

He had a bookshelf full of leather-bound books, and artwork that like everywhere else was dark themed. I won't lie, I found the look of his room unsettling and spooky without that Vampire in there. I noticed that at the end of his bed there was a large metal O hook welded into the frame. I knew immediately he intended to bond my leash to it.

I didn't bother to struggle when he padlocked my leash around it just as I assumed he would. When he came at me with the chains for my wrists, now that was a different story. I was in no mood for more of his bondage. I pulled as far as I could and doubled up my fists threatening him to come any closer. I was ready to knock him into his fucking precious medieval times.

Jonas chuckled at my aggressive stance. "Cut that out, Christian Axel. You come here and let me restrain those violent hands of yours. I cannot sleep worrying you will try to retaliate over our little misunderstanding tonight."

I growled out at him, "There was no misunderstanding. You took away my choice over bargains you made without granting me the right of full disclosure. You are a thief, liar, and rapist. You're the one should be locked the fuck up, not Christian Axel. You *fear I will kill you in your slumber because you Gott damned deserve it and you know it."*

Jonas shook his head while clicking his tongue. "Well, all that may be truth. I wonder do you realize if I am all those things, then likely I am even more the vile creature than you claim me to be? Want to find out how nasty I can truly be, or will you come over here before you really piss me off, Christian Axel?"

I got ready to swing at him. "Ficken dich, Jonas. You dare not kill me. Then what will you do for blood and rape? I will not endure your bondage any longer. Come any closer, I will hit you, I mean it."

That Vampire stood there coolly staring me down. "Oh? Well, you are right, I will not kill you my love. However, I can make your life a nightmare come to light. You see I can torture just as well as Xavier ever could. I was a Dungeon Master for twenty years my boy. Want to meet some of my nasty thudders or maybe my pinwheel? I hear you really enjoyed the rake a great deal. I have one. Want to see it? I am bigger than you. If you make me beat you down again tonight, I swear I will make it worth my while." He crossed his arms smiling with a look of victory.

I shuddered at that threat. "What? you would scar me up that way? Please, just leave me be. I cannot leave. You have me locked in. I swear I won't do anything but sleep here on the floor. I will never touch a hair on your head." I was now whining like a little bitch you know. Hey, that torturing shit with a pinwheel and rake is not fun.

Jonas shook his head with much sternness in his gaze. "I will not leave you unbonded tonight even if the Devil offered to give me back my fucking soul. I know you're capable of picking that lock. Don't play me the fool. Get over here and submit to me. Don't make me say it again, Christian Axel. I am not kidding. You're making me angry."

I dropped my fists and limped forward dropping to a kneel at his feet. My defeat to Jonas's will was complete. I couldn't get away, and another round with heavy torture I was not eager to endure. I cannot stand bondage, but that bastard had me cornered. I decided to fight another day by surviving this one with all my flesh intact.

He didn't say a word as he pulled me to the end of his bed. He then chained my wrists together around one of the legs behind my back. He effectively ended my easy escape from his restraints this way. Chains are painful to struggle in, and unlike rope there is no stretch nor give in them. He padlocked that chain closed. Houdini himself would have played hell to break out of that mess.

He stood up to admire me sitting there uncomfortably bonded to his bed. "This room has always been my favorite. I put all my prettiest things in here for my eyes to enjoy. Never has the vision been so pleasing as it is now. You're a beauty, my love. I am thrilled to possess the thing I have chased all my days at last. I can barely believe what I see." He reached out and took off my hat staring at me with adoration.

I glared at the floor refusing to gaze back at him. "Gute night, Jonas. Thanks for nothing." I barked out full of my demons.

Jonas chuckled with much humor. "Aw, you're adorable when you pout, my love. You will get over this disagreeable attitude. You better for your own sake. I will allow you to be irritable this once with me, but in the morning, I expect to see an eager, romantic lover or so help me Christian Axel, you will be sorrier than you are right now over making deals with me. Good night to you." He turned and went into his master bathroom to change for his slumber.

I immediately jumped from the flesh leaving that boy in his mindless trance. I called out to my Max boys for an emergency meeting. This was unwelcome news, and I was ready to lose my mind over it.

Mad Max, Mad Maxx, and Maximillian came to my call without hesitation. I stood there looking at them thinking of what I could do to survive this latest situation. Then it came to me. I needed to disengage Max and Christian from the others. Otherwise, we were particularly vulnerable to Jonas's trick of setting off our anger, and our lust for females like Emma.

I had the Max boys line up, then focused my mind. I reached into Mad Max's chest and pulled Christian and Max's essence free. I threw it on the floor into separate piles. I went to Mad Maxx and Maximillian doing the same. The piles of glowing gelatinous essence began to reform into the shards of anger/lust and peace/restraint.

The Max boys watched their bothers drying out in the air of the room becoming solid once more in stunned silence. We had become the six of us once more.

Christian comes too first shaken his head to clear his mind. "Now that was a wild ride, Der Hund. I never want to do that shit again. Having to live inside Mad Max and Maximillian, hell that other one too, yuck. That was not very nice, you know."

I nodded while chuckling over the angered faces of Christian's bothers over his insulting them. "Ja. It worked to capture us a big problem, I fear. Now take your brothers leash and wait for my command. I forbid either of you to ride the flesh until I figure out what to do about this vile situation. Understand me?"

Max stood up and took Christian's leash and handed his to his opposite shard. "Ja. This is heard loud and clear, Der Hund."

Christian snatched Max's leash from his hand with anger. "Ja I fucking hear you too. Come on Max, let's go find that sexy Emma. I want to look at her some more. This place is bullshit and the Vampire is more than spooky."

Mad Max growled out, "Wait here Christian. I come with you. I want to look at Emma too. You coming Mad Maxx? I'd ask you Maximillian but you're such a Frau, you'd likely bother our ears with chatter about her makeup and shit."

Maximillian scoffed. "Shut the fuck up, Mad Max. I will come with all of you too. I want to fuck that girl just as bad as everyone else does you know."

I shook my head and pointed at the tranced flesh. "Oh no, Maximillian. You take the wheel. Sorry brother, but the one that can handle this twisted shit needs to be riding the flesh tonight, and likely tomorrow too. Drexel is next. Go do your job."

Mad Max, Mad Maxx and Max/Christian giggled as Maximillian stomped his foot in frustration. "Seriously? I never get to do anything fun. You all treat me like I am nothing more than a door mat and pin cushion."

Mad Maxx taunted while the others really began howling, "We are not the ones doing that, fool. Can't you see who does this or did they finally fuck your eyes out?"

Maximillian come flying at Mad Maxx with a look of homicide in his eyes. I caught my wayward shard before he made his collision.

"That is enough of this shit. All of you, I am sick of this fighting among us. We should be working together against the ones on the outside not fighting within, you idiots. This is getting us deeper and deeper into this nightmare." I flung Maximillian across the room into the wall.

He slammed into it near shattering from the impact. That managed to scare the stupid out of all the Maxes and Christian.

They could see I was fed up with them all. "I created all you to help me. Thanks to your shortcomings we are blood bonded to a fucking Vampire man. I should not have been riding the flesh tonight, Maxes. That was exactly what Jonas wanted. He couldn't bond to any of you shards, he needed our core. Well, he got it. Shit, and despite your serious fuck up, you still are battling. The next one of you that hits his brother, I swear I feed you to Max and Christian for dinner. That is my final world." I turned around and left that fucking room to the Maxes to deal with it, I was done with it.

I got up and shook off my near shatter. "Der Hund is angry boys. I guess we better all call a truce or face the punishment for it."

Mad Max looked at the others then growled out, "Well? Get into the flesh then. You heard Der Hund. This is a job for you. Mad Maxx and I will watch your back in case the situation changes. This is bad. I never seen Der Hund so mad."

Christian sighed. "I have. Long time ago brothers. Look he is not kidding. No more fighting. If we lose Der Hund, we all die. Then it is schizophrenia city boys. Most of us would be shattered and only the strongest left to attend a mind full of monsters. Unless that sounds like your idea of fun, I suggest we cut this bullshit and work on getting out of here fast. Der Hund cannot take much more. I saw this happen before and it landed us in the asylum. Not fun."

I rushed over, then entered the flesh feeling the pain of all the injury Der Hund endured. I groaned out in agony as I attempted to get over the shock of this horror.

The Max boys and Christian looked at me with expressions of concern as I moaned out, "This is bad everyone. The Vampire was brutal. It is no wonder Der Hund is upset. Shit, this is worse than when Master Peter collared us."

The Mad Maxx gasped, "Holy hell. That bad? Okay, Christian, Max, go find Der Hund and see if you can calm him down. Mad Max and I will stay here with Maximillian." Mad Max nodded that he was in agreement.

Christian and Max took off after Der Hund while the Max boys hung around in the corners of that room keeping watch over the groaning boy.

Jonas came out of the washroom in a bathrobe with a bandage and antiseptic sprays. He knelt next to me. I had broken out in a sweat as the pain of my injured legs, and, well, you know, don't you Meine Liebe? Dry sodomy is something that causes much discomfort that tends to get worse before it ever gets bedder, ja? I nodded my head as I frowned at that most hideous fact.

The Vampire gazed at my contorted expression. "Ah, you're not feeling too good are you, my love? Well, I apologize for that. That is the way it is done. Nothing I could do about that. However, we need to treat that virginity wound to prevent infection, ja?" He tugged and worked till he got my breeches down far enough to expose his lancet wound on my right thigh.

I groaned lightly but said nothing while he attended my minor injury, then bandaged it up. He checked my gunshot wound and with great care changed the bandages on it. It had bled through again during all my struggling.

He let me know none of my stitches had been torn out this time, much to my relief, but I would need to stop being so "rough." I just sat there glaring at him with hate over that bullshit. He called me rough. Can you believe that shit? I shook my head with my eyes wide in disbelief.

My silence appeared to be unnerving to him. "You haven't said anything since I left for the cleaning up after our blood bonding, my love. Something on your mind?" He looked me over as if seeking the answer to come from somewhere but my fucking mouth.

I nodded. "Ja. I would like to request the mercy of a shower. I need to clean up from this business too, Jonas." I grumbled out with some irritation leaking into my tone.

Jonas shook his head. "Nein. I cannot allow you to remove the evidence of our blood bonding until it has been witnessed."

My eyes went wide in shock. "What? Witness? I don't understand?"

The Elder Vampire smirked at me. "That is why we go see Drexel first thing in the morning, Christian Axel. He is to witness I have blood bonded you. First, he will make sure you have given me your secret virginity. After that, he will want to see the proof of our life contract by checking to make sure I have consummated it to orgasm with the blood coupling. Then you can take your shower, my love." He patted my leg, still grinning.

I closed my eyes feeling full humiliation at this latest indignity "This is a fucking joke, right?"

Jonas chuckled full of humor. "Nein. That is the way it is done. A blood bonding Dominant can get any Dominant a level above to witness but I am an Elder. I have to get one of my brothers since there is no level higher than me. You would do well to recall that if you plan to say a thing about my taking a few short cuts to get your compliance. Are we clear, Christian Axel?"

I nodded keeping my lids closed tightly, "Crystal, Jonas. Though you need not threaten me. I will give you no further issues. I see you have me caught tightly. Struggling will only bring more pain than I am already in."

Jonas reached out and grabbed my face so fast it made me open my eyes in horror while gasping, "Where is Christian Axel? This is a mask I saw before me. You call him back here now."

I shook my head full of fear. "I don't know what you are speaking about Jonas. I am Christian Axel. I wear no masks. Please let me go. I cannot be anyone other than who I am."

Jonas glared at me looking hard into my eyes. "You cut the bullshitting me. Which one are you? I wish to call you by the correct name. Answer me mask or I swear I will bust your pretty face up." He reared arm to back hand me.

I yelped, "I am Maximillian. Please stop this. Jonas didn't hit us. What the hell. I didn't do nothing."

The Vampire smiled and dropped his aggressive stance. "Ah, you are the one with the submissive and special services skills, ja?"

My eyes went wide in surprise. "Uhm, I suppose? What is this game all about? You're speaking in riddles, Jonas. You can see with your own eyes that I am Maximillian, your blood bonded lover. This you say yourself, ja? I wear a silver pleasure submissive collar do I not? One can assume I am a submissive. I am well trained and compliant. Therefore, my skills in the special services are above the mark."

Jonas nodded with a playful expression breaking out on his face. "Okay Maximillian. I understand this mask. What is the name of the one that enjoyed the thud on Egon? That was neither Christian Axel nor Maximillian. Wer is das? Wie heißt er? (Who is that? What is his name?)."

I shrugged, "That is me, Jonas. You know damned well that is me, Mad Max."

Jonas smiled even more. "Now we are getting somewhere. Okay I know you Christian Axel, Maximillian, Mad Max, and do you have any other names?"

I scoffed. "I only have one name Jonas, Maximillian. You call me a name that was taken from me. Others call me a name that is untruth. I say to you my name is Maximillian given to me by my father when he collared me. You know this already. You are making my headache with this confusion. I beg you to stop this endless questioning. I think you are tired or maybe losing your mind."

Jonas looked deeper into my eyes. "Ha, you say I am losing my mind. That is funny Maximillian, coming from one with so many of his own in one head. There are others in there with you no doubt. The legend says you will have many backs to carry the heavy burden of the forbidden metal. I was told Justus had ten of him. I doubt only the three of you exist. Your load is much heavier than his was and you have not killed yourself yet. Maybe you have ten too. Maybe more. It is simply fascinating to witness this changing, like you do. Sooner or later, I will see all of these personalities you have. You cannot hide them forever. I will enjoy getting to know all them intimately. I admit I look forward to the pleasure of studying you." He stood up and got into his bed.

I shot a look of terror at the Mad Maxes. They returned my concerned gaze. This was not good. This Vampire man seemed to know about our shards. Der Hund needed to be warned. Mad Maxx took off to find him. We needed his wise advice and quick. If this Jonas could see us, then maybe he could shatter us too. This situation had gone from disturbing to an emergency in only a single conversation. Jonas turned off the light leaving me in the darkness of that creepy room to consider my compromised situation.

Der Hund returned with Christian, Max, and Mad Maxx hot on his heels. I told him the situation, and Mad Max helped verify this. I watched in terror as our core stood there confused, unsure, and frightened. That behavior made all of us uneasy. No one could figure out what to do.

Finally, Mad Max stood forward. "I beg you Der Hund, allow only the three of us to work together as one. I see no other way. You need a shield, and though I am a selfish bastard I realize if this sonofabitch gets to you again, we are all doomed. Maybe you could merge us together the way you did with Max and Christian. Fuck I cannot believe I am saying this shit."

Der Hund narrowed his eyes then smiled at Mad Max. "You're brilliant, boy. You have a great idea."

I whimpered at the idea of having to eat or be eaten by my brothers. "Please Der Hund, I don't want to be consumed nor consume the Maxes."

Der Hund chuckled, "There is no need. Come to me all three of you."

I stepped from the flesh and knelt before Der Hund with the Max brothers. He closed his eyes then reached down and pulled up Mad Max and Mad Maxx. He put them back-to-back, then he called to me and enjoined me with my brothers. Next, he placed Max and Christian into our center. They were protected completely by the three of us. No one could reach them without getting a Max brother first. We three were tied together facing outward with our backs guarded by the ever-vigilant eyes of the other two forever watching behind us. He then stood back smiling with joy to admire the new shard of the Master Mad Maxx.

Der Hund let out a yell of thrill, "The answer was there all along. We cannot control what is going on around us, but we can protect each other like a well-oiled machine. No matter what comes from our environment, you boys will turn like a wheel, smoothly taking command of the boy. Max and Christian will offer their good advice into your ears but be protected from getting out or others getting in by you, my shield shards. I will stay outside and watch for need to shatter or merge further but I think this time we got this right at last."

Mad Max growled out from his ropes, "This sucks Der Hund. I cannot even move like this."

Der Hund laughed. "Then you better get into the flesh quick. You will work with your brothers and do your jobs. Each will experience what the others do, good and bad, but only one can control at a time. Learn your roles or be destroyed and replaced by one that can. Now go." He pointed at the tracing boy.

We at first had some difficulty working together enough to get far, but eventually we made it to the flesh. All of us crammed inside, together for the first time since the days of Gerard's straight razor attack. We had forgotten how cramped it could be inside our head. This you understand ja, Meine Liebe? I nodded and rubbed my forehead recalling my own shards and our many arguments over the last few months.

After some initial arguing and struggling to get comfortable, all of us fell asleep with the flesh. It had been a long grueling day and a hard night. We needed the rest.

The sun rose and before it seemed a second passed Jonas was yawning loudly awakening from his slumber. The hypervigilant ears of the flesh awoke all of us. There was a brief confusion as to who would run the front and those that would guard the back.

Eventually, as we listened to Jonas head to his washroom to empty his bladder, we decided I, Maximillian, should manage this witnessing of the blood bonding bullshit. I was a little pissed to get that nasty task until Max reminded me all of us had to deal with the experience of the flesh the way Der Hund had fixed it. I felt better about it. After that though, the Mad Max brothers couldn't pick on me anymore. We all were in the shit now good, bad, or ugly.

Jonas came out of his washroom naked. We just sat there glaring at him with a bit of hatred Mad Max was crowding me, damn him. The Vampire saw that we were alert. He chuckled while opening his walk-in closet to collect his clothing.

"Tomorrow, I will expect you to attend all the services of your station, my love. This morning I think it wise I keep you bonded until the formal announcement of our blood bond is recorded. I told you I will give you no further choices and I meant this. I do admit I look forward to enjoying the luxury the pleasure submissive grants his lucky Master. It has been far too long since last I had such an arrangement." He began to pull on a pair of boxers and black trousers.

I started without an expression shift. "Oh? You have no silver collar for a long-time then?"

Jonas stopped dressing and gazed at me with curiosity. "Nein, I never had a silver collar. I only enjoyed a few leashes over the years as well as playthings such as the tarnished headed to the circuit. You're the only blood bonded as well."

I raised a brow at that. "Why did you never collar your own pleasure submissive? Then maybe you would not have been seeking to take things that belong to another, ja?"

That must have pissed him off. "Your inquires are quite rude this morning Maximillian, or are you Mad Max? Christian Axel perhaps? He is a smart ass like this."

I laughed manically. "I am the Master Mad Maxx fool. You, Claus, Drexel, Bladrick and Peter spread the silver too thin. I broke it already. Thank you for freeing me from my metal. You are indeed a man of your word."

Jonas's eyes went wide in what appeared to be fear. "Uh oh, this is true madness I hear speaking with your mouth, Christian Axel. I forgot to ask if you take medication maybe?"

I narrowed my eyes at this weirdo. "For what? I need no medication. Why is it so hard for you to understand I run this fucking Haus. I will have you drawn and quartered for treason against the king, fool. Np, I know. I will have you nailed in the yard before the rising sun. You'll turn to dust, right?" I began to giggle at that insanity right dare. I giggled with him over that funny idea.

Jonas cringed at my bizarre statements of grandiosity. "I suppose I should have figured out how to turn the madness off after I brought it on. Shit, okay, I gag you, then we go see Drexel, ja?"

I laughed wildly at that. "Why? Nein. He fucks the statues, ja? Well, no one can hold still like the Master Mad Maxx can. Watch this." I immediately pulled in and went to sleep turning off the flesh.

I came to when I heard the Haus doctor telling Jonas that someone had a catatonic fit. His voice sounded far away when he said he gave me a shot for some reason. I was groggy but awake when the Vampire came to stand over me looking down appearing upset for some reason.

I looked up at him and smiled. "Why am I in your bed? Did you grant me bed privileges, but I have forgotten? I suppose I overslept. I apologize for that. Did you set the alarm?"

Jonas nodded his head, appearing stunned for some reason. "Ja, I granted you bed privileges, Maximillian. I didn't think to set an alarm, but I am glad to see you have awakened at last."

I stretched a bit feeling very tight and tense. "I suppose you will be wishing to visit Drexel now. I get up and follow you right away." I sat up yawning, still trying to loosen my irritated muscles.

The Vampire pushed me back down into the bed. "Maximillian, we missed our breakfast with Drexel. He came down here though and witnessed my blood bonding

377

with you anyway. He was more than a little impressed with your staring trance. You never responded no matter what he did to you. I had to check to make sure you were still breathing. I thought for a moment I would have to restrain that horny bastard when he checked you for the blood and my seed and you never moved, nor blinked though your eyes were wide open for hours. Drexel was squealing that you are a living statue worthy of a museum. He must have asked me twenty times when your Master Peter was out of the Dungeon so he could call him to make his deal for your leash. I must say I never seen that man more eager for anything in his whole creepy life. How did you do that Maximillian?"

I shrugged. "Do what? I don't know what you are talking about. If Drexel is pleased with his witnessing though I think this a dream, can I please take a shower now Master Jonas? I beg your mercy on this request."

Jonas frowned. "You don't remember any of it do you? Oh, meine Gott. You are mad. I mean truly mentally ill, not just a rumor of it. Peter has collared a schizophrenic. What the hell."

I looked at this idiot with a bit of irritation at that nasty statement. "They call me Mad Max over some stress issues I had after they killed Ryker. I am not schizophrenic. I appreciate you not insulting me like that. Anyone can have a nervous breakdown. I was bottoming out and it got a bit out of control is all. I cannot call you out because you're my better, but I would ask you to never be so rude as to use that word around me again."

Jonas kept staring at me, appearing surprised. "Alright, I won't call you that. I suppose maybe you just a bit freaked out over last night is all. I must ask though, why do you think you are dreaming all this. Can you not tell if you are asleep or awake?"

I shrugged. "Because you say Drexel come and examined me. I confess I can sleep deeply. I was very tired, but no one could sleep through that kind of probing from that perverted schwuler. The only answer to this dilemma is this must be a dream. I still would like to have that shower though. That is if you would be so merciful. I would greatly appreciate your generosity in such a delicate matter. If you cannot be that kind, then let me say I really need to visit your washroom for another reason. My bladder won't hold much longer, and these sheets seem to be too nice to be soiling." I yawned again wondering why the fuck I felt so damned stiff.

Jonas nodded. "Ja, you can take a shower and use the restroom After you answer another question for me."

I blew out my breath feeling my bladder may burst before he got done with his weird interrogation. "Ja? I am listening. Ask and I will do my best to please you with an answer you desire."

The Vampire nodded then looked close at my face. "How many people are in this room right now?"

I chuckled at that weird question. "What? You have lost your mind, Jonas. You, me, and the doctor. I assume Drexel too since I can hear him but not see the schwuler. Can I go to your bathroom now? Seriously I am about to piss myself." I was truly about to lose my water.

Jonas's eyes went wide in fear, but he backed up and nodded. "Ja, go ahead Maximillian. I will wait here for you."

I relieved myself. Thank Gott, my back teeth were floating you know. Then happily I took that shower. I must have scrubbed half an inch of my flesh away trying to get rid of the Vampire stink. Yuck. Anyway, I got out and dried off listening to Jonas speaking to the doctor and Drexel.

I silently went to the door to listen in on their conversation. I heard them speaking in whispers, saying that lie that I had schizophrenia again. That was pissing me the hell off. I couldn't believe these fuckers. They rape you, stick their fingers everywhere while you're sleeping and tie you up. They think I am the one nuts. Ha, I think not.

I yelled through the door at them. "You better shut the fuck up. I can hear you." They quieted down immediately which made me giggle a great deal.

I went back to putting on my clothing when those rat bastards started up again. I was like Fichen Mich, you know. I hurried my dressing and ripped that door open ready to kick all their asses for calling me that fucking name.

I yelled out, "I said shut the fuck up. I am not schizophrenic, you cocksuckers, so stop calling me that."

Jonas flinched in a startle at my sudden rushing from his bathroom and roaring out like that. He looked around the room then back to me.

"Maximillian, my love, there is only me here. I am not saying anything. Who are you yelling at?" His expression was one of pure terror.

I looked around to see where the others were hiding. I knew this was just another mind game of this vile Vampire man you know. I couldn't see anyone else, but I could hear them all the same. I glared at that rat bastard with much fury.

"How are you doing that? You have them hidden in the closet, right? Why are you fucking with me. I gave you everything you asked for. Enough of these stupid games you play with me, Master Jonas." I was near ready to kill this monster over this cruel tactic of his. Those men were still yapping.

Jonas shook his head with what appeared to be pity in his eyes. "Sonofabitch, you're hearing voices, Maximillian. You have shattered. Shit, I was too fucking late. Just like Gott damned Justus. Fuck, I cannot wait another lifetime for another Priceless to show up. What the hell am I going to do."

I roared out in full fury, "You are speaking in riddles again, Master Jonas. You're pissing me off, you know. I hear voices alright. I am going to your closet to tell your friends they can come out now. This trick is not working."

I rushed to his closet and tore that door open with such force I almost ripped it off. I looked inside, but no one was there. I ran out of the room to his living room. It was empty. I then chased them voices down the hallway back to his bondage room. It too was without a living soul. I felt the sweat breaking out on my brow.

Jonas walked into the room behind me with his gaze to the floor appearing terribly upset by my behavior. He watched me, sighing loudly while I tore around the room wild in a panic. Gott Verdammt, I couldn't find out where he was hiding those people, but I was still hearing their voices.

Chapter 29: Dungeon Honeymoon

I ran around that room sure that Jonas had a tape recorder or something working the sounds of those men. I looked under the bondage bed and in that fireplace too. It was starting to really get on my last nerve listening to them call me names and accusing me of being schizophrenic like that.

I finally got fed up with them. "Shut the fuck up. That is not true, and you all know it. Stop calling me that, Gott damn it. You are a bunch of rude bastards. You know I can hear you. I said shut up," I yelled out covering my ears trying to drown their voices out of my thoughts.

Jonas stood by the door watching me. He kept looking behind him which began to make me think he was hiding something, you know. I pulled my hands off my ears glaring at that rat bastard.

"What are you looking at, schwuler? You got those men in the other room, don't you. What fucking game are you playing now? Tell them to shut up, Jonas, or I will kill every cocksucker that utters another word. Are you listening to me Vampire? I have had enough of this shit. You call Claus. Have him come here. I want to speak to the cross dresser. I will take this case right to the top. You

384

cannot torture me when I do nothing wrong. Why are you doing this to me?" I was getting myself a bit worked up. I admit that but I was tired of hearing all that shit those fellows were spouting about me.

Jonas started to look a bit nervous. "Christian Axel, you listen to me. You need to relax, my love. These voices you're hearing are not real, I tell you. There is no one here but you and me. It is your own mind playing the games with you not your lover Jonas. I swear this."

I had to laugh at that bullshit right there. "Oh, you swear this, huh. I would believe you like I would believe the sky turned purple. You are a liar and a rapist. You call Claus, I mean it. I want a second opinion. I don't agree with anything you say. This is not regular. Stop it, damn it. I can hear you. You don't have to yell. It hurts my ears. Why do you keep mocking me? Stop repeating every fucking thing I say and get Claus. I mean this Jonas. You're really pissing me off." That stupid bastard was saying everything I was like a fucking parrot. You should have heard that shit, Meine Liebe. I was getting really tired of it. I nodded. I hated it when Debbie and Russell did that crap to me too.

Well, that Vampire kept turning up his radio recordings. It started to get so loud the fucking walls were shaking with the bass of it. I couldn't figure out why the hell he needed to listen to his music that loud. It made me anxious. My muscles were stiff enough already you know.

385

I started to try to work them back to smoothness just in case I had to fight, which I thought was likely since Jonas was still standing there staring like a fool.

I paced back and forth, stomping my feet. That helped me feel a bit better but still I couldn't calm that strange fear inside my head. I started rubbing my hands together and stroking my hair, yelling for those men to shut up there speaking loudly about me.

I am not ashamed to admit it, this loud music, the men yapping, and the walls shaking like that was scaring me a bit. The sweat was pouring down my face. That bothered me too, making me feel cold, and somehow unreal. I wiped it over and over but still more water poured down my forehead. This had to stop. I wondered if maybe Jonas slipped something to me, or if that shot I heard the doctor say he gave me was messing with my head. That had to be the answer, someone had drugged me.

I looked at the Elder Vampire. "What did you do to me? You slipped me a pill. Did Drexel do this or the Haus Doctor? You all think you're so smart. I got you figured out. You drugged me. Maybe you did it when we danced. That is why I am here isn't it? You fucked with my head, gave me a drug then brought me here. That's it. I have had it with the lot of you. Always speaking bullshit and lies. You call that doctor now. I want the antidote. Hahahaha. I know what you did. See, I figured out your riddle, Jonas. This is all just a dream. It is not real.

You're an imagination. Call my mother. Tell her that I am not falling for this. Agnette is a fucking fool. You all are. I am better than any of you. Go ahead, turn into a bat. I will not pull off your fleas. I think you deserve them for drinking all that blood you stole from the innocent people of the city. You're a week Dracula man with parasites. No one likes you, Jonas. They think you're creepy." I began to laugh maniacally at the idea that he had fleas in his long hair.

My eyes went wide. "Travis had head lice one-time Master. They cut all his hair off because they would lay eggs on his head. It was super gross. Did Master Jonas have to cut off all his long hair too?"

Master Maxx nodded while looking at me with seriousness. "Well, that is the problem with the Vampires you know. They are nasty. Jonas never cuts his hair no matter how many fleas he gets. I told him to, but he never listens to me. It is truth anytime there is poor hygiene you can get bugs. If you keep wiping your nose on your wrist, you'll get them too. Then I cut all you hair off to get rid of dem."

I shuddered. "Okay Master. I won't do that anymore. I don't want my head shaved."

He giggled., "I think you'd be cute with a bald egg for a head? Nein? Oh, okay. just use something besides your wrist, ja?"

I nodded. "Yes Master. I apologize. That won't happen again. Thank you for your mercy."

Master Maxx's expression changed to that of confusion. "What mercy? I told you I show no mercy to you. Stop asking for it, Meine Liebe. You know I worry about your mental health. You seem to forget an awful lot. Anyway, what were we talking about?"

I narrowed my eyes wondering if he was funning me. "You were mad at Jonas for playing his radio too loud, Master."

He nodded while smiling. "Ah, ja. That was the day he drugged me up or something. You know I have never figure out how he does that shit without me knowing it. Anyway, as I was saying..."

"Jonas, he let me fume and rant for a bit over his slipping me drugs. Then he asked me to calm down yet again. Now I was getting tired of all that pacing, hand wringing, and the noise. I decided fuck it; I was getting some peace one way or another.

I remembered that he had that lancet blade in his dresser. You know the one he cut me with to drink my blood? Ja, I decided to cut off my ears. That would end me having to hear those men calling me schizophrenic. They weren't shutting up. I couldn't find them to make it stop. It made sense at the time, but I admit maybe I should have thought that idea out a bit more. He laughed nervously and shot me a look of concern. I nodded that maybe cutting off his ears wouldn't have been a smart move, but hell I thought about cutting off my tongue. Oh, never mind.

I ran over to rifle through the drawers. Jonas yelled at me to stay out of his things. I ignored him. This was his fault anyway. If he didn't want me to look in his dresser, he shouldn't have left it out in the open after he drugged me.

I ripped out the compartments throwing them onto his floor. I found the lancet almost immediately. I grabbed that damned weapon and opened the blade. There was no hesitation. I went right for my left ear since I am right-handed, it was easiest you know.

Well shit, you'd have thought I grabbed Jonas's own cock then threatened to cut it off. He come running at me knocking me into floor with much force screaming for me to put down "the knife." I was beyond pissed at that. First, he turns the radio full blast and then he won't even grant me a fucking hat to drown out the sounds. I was

389

only trying to make the noise shut off. There was no reason for him to go nuts like that.

I still had that knife in my hands when I hit the floor from his pushing me. I growled out in frustration but decided it mattered not where I cut the damned things off. The floor, standing up, whatever.

Jonas leapt on me grabbing my wrist that held his lancet. "Give this to me, Christian Axel. You're having a psychotic fit. What are you doing? Leave your ears alone. Shit, you cut your head already. There is blood everywhere. This has gotten out of hand. Fuck, I need help here. Someone help me." He started screaming for help like a maniac. Master Maxx started laughing, and so did I.

He wrestled that knife away from me. Then he started punching and backhanding me in the face. How rude can a person be? I tried to defend myself from his blows, but that man was a lot bigger than me. He nearly knocked me unconscious for no reason at all. That Jonas was the brute to be so cruel.

I couldn't move from his stunning me that way. I felt him get off for a moment. Then he came back and grabbed my leash. I could barely see the schwuler through all the blood caused by his smacking me around. I thought he was about to drink my blood again. This was unnerving. I couldn't even imagine all my life having such a brutal lover to bear. I began to wail in terror with the visions of his beating me up every day to satiate his fetish desires.

Jonas was panting and sweating from his attack on me. He pulled hard on the leash demanding I stand up and follow. I didn't bother to mind him. I could do anything but wail and scream in pure fright. I just knew he was taking me to his bathtub to drain me dry of my fluids for his sick pleasure.

When I refused to stand, he backhanded me. I cowered and covered my head to protect myself from his abuse. He didn't hit me this time. Jonas grabbed my upper arms and started dragging me across that room. I kicked and flailed, screaming bloody murder you know. Jonas ignored my wild attempts to get him to let me go.

When he got me to the entry of that room, I reached out and grabbed the door jambs. I was hanging on for dear life. I wasn't going to have my throat cut without a fight. Jonas roared out in anger when he couldn't budge me.

Then he let go my arms knelt down and grabbed me by my neck. He took me into a sleeper hold near choking me to death. I clawed at his arm, but he wouldn't call off his pressure. The room started going black and I grew weak from lack of air.

I may have passed out, but if I did it was only for a moment. I felt Jonas lift me to my feet, but I was too groggy from his breath play move to fight him off me this time. He gripped me under my arms and dragged me to his room. I come back to my senses fully to find him bonding my hands behind me with that damned chain of his.

I immediately got angry fighting him with all I had left. He pushed me to my face and pinned me there with his knee in my back to finish his restraining.

Again, I could barely breathe from his weight on me. "Let me go cocksucker," I stammered out with much fury.

He said nothing back. I heard the padlock close over my hands. That really set me into a wailing fit. I hate bondage, you know. I was more unhappy about his drugging than chaining me up like that. This bastard wasn't kidding when he said he could be a monster. I wondered if he was taking me downstairs for torture next.

Jonas grabbed my arms making me stand up despite my screaming like I was. "Christian Axel, stop this noise. Now I command it. You will follow me in silence, I mean it, or I will make you sorry you were ever born," he roared out while backhanding the fuck out of me.

I won't lie. I was in a crying fit by this time. I assumed this was the end of us for sure. Why else would he bond me up other than to cut my throat without a struggle? I did shut up my wailing, but I sobbed quite loudly over this sad death I was condemned to. Who would have thought Maximillian was the murder victim of a Vampire? I wouldn't have believed such a fantasy if you had warned me in advance.

Jonas stood there watching my weeping, appearing confused as hell. "hat the fuck? This is schizophrenia. It has to be. Fucking Peter. He collared the shattered but told no one. This is a disaster. Shit if I call the Haus doctor, they will take you away Christian Axel. Worse, he will report this to the Voting Council. Sonofabitch, what can I do to fix this before someone finds out? You cannot break your metal if you are reported to be mentally ill boy. I want my Priceless female. You have to get her for me. Ficken mich. Gott damn it, what the hell am I supposed to do.

I shook my head still crying like a little bitch. "Where is Master Peter Jonas? He has not come back for my leash yet. He won't be happy you're cutting my throat. Why do you do this to me? I am not even that big. You need a larger collar to feed you. If you let me go, I won't tell anyone you drugged me up, nor that you play your

393

radio so loud. I don't want to die in your bathtub. I just wanted a shower. I apologize for that. I will never ask for such a thing again. This is terror. Call Master Peter, will you? Tell him I left the stove on, I think?" I was a bit confused from the drugs he gives to me you know. I nodded recalling that medications can make someone a bit groggy.

Jonas stared at me hard. "I can take you to your Master Peter if you want Christian Axel. Will you stop crying and wailing if I do?"

I felt a twinge of hope that maybe the Vampire wouldn't kill me after all. "Ja, I shut up, I swear it. Please, I beg you. I don't want to burn down the Haus and I think I left on the stove. I won't burn down the Haus if you take me to see him, I swear it. They put you away for burning down houses. Ryker was not fair you know. I had to stop him. He was trying to trap me in the metal. Why did you drug me up, Jonas? Won't you get high when you drink my blood?" I was feeling very strange by this time, something was wrong, but I wasn't sure what.

The Elder grabbed my collar leash. "Stop acting the fool and follow me. We are going to see your Master. He must know how to fix this. Otherwise, you would already be gone from this Haus. Your mad as a hatter, Christian Axel. That fucker never told me. If I had known, I would have been much more careful with you. I thought you were only in the initial stages, but you're fully insane. I have a few words for that sonofabitch, let me tell you. I cannot unblood bond, but now I am stuck with a Gott damned schizophrenic for all my days. Shit!"

I shook my head angered that he kept using that word. "I am not. Stop saying that, Jonas. It is not true. You take me to my Master. He will clear all this up. I need to turn off the fucking stove. You drugged me. You shouldn't have done that, Jonas. When will this shit wear off? I need to study for a test, you know. I am sure to fail it on this acid trip or whatever you slipped into my blood."

Jonas groaned out loud. "I didn't fucking drug you, Christian Axel. Just follow me. Keep that mouth shut. Don't make a scene. I am taking you to Master Peter, understand me?" He grabbed my face and made me look at him.

My eyes went wide in fear "Ja, I can hear you. Stop hitting me, brute. I do what you say without all the abuse. Are you going to turn off the radio first or do you always play your music so loud?" The walls were still shaken with that heavy base of his.

He shook his head while sighing. "Ja, I always play it that loud. Come with me Mad Maxx. You're beyond my help no doubt. Peter should have a plan or your toast boy.

Why the hell is this happening to me." He began walking, pulling me along behind him.

I growled out. "Nothing happened to you, Jonas, you bat bastard. I am not fixing you any toast either. Get it yourself."

Jonas dragged me to his front door then roared out. "I said shut up. Not another word. You're making no sense, you crazy sonofabitch. Your mouth is going to get us caught. No sounds out of you, that is a directive."

I glared at him but didn't say another thing. I heard his fucking directive loud and clear. It was a stupid one, but that is the Dominant for you. I never could figure them out. I followed behind him in high protocol while we went down the stairs headed for the dungeons to see Master Peter.

All around us silver and black collars fell to their knees as we passed them. That seemed very funny to me for some stupid reason. I began to giggle about it. Jonas turned and shot me a look of warning. I shrugged at him because I couldn't stop the laughing no matter how hard I tried. Oh well, he shouldn't have gotten me so high. You know that stuff makes you laugh at dumb shit like dat.

Other than that infernal laughter I was mostly quiet for the entire trip to the bowels of the Haus. When we got to the narrow steps that lead to the holding cells Jonas turned around. He backhanded me till I nearly fell down the stairs.

"Stop that insane laughing. There is nothing funny about any of this. Plus, it is giving me a headache," he yelled out as he reared back and hit me again.

I did my best to stifle that sound, but I confess a few little chuckles escaped. Jonas would stop briefly then turn around and glare when I did that. His threats made me try harder to control my mirth. My head was near a bloody pulp as it was. More of his punching, I certainly didn't need.

Finally, we arrived at the cells. Jonas told the Dungeon Master to lead us to Master Peter then "get lost" till he called for him. That fellow led us down the long hallway with his keychain crashing into his hip. That sound was making me cringe.

I spent almost four years in this concrete prison. I was not happy to return to it, trust me. when that bastard stopped and unlocked the door. I stood there hating him with all my soul. He nodded at Jonas then tried to rush past me with his head down.

I yelled at him, "I hope you die cocksucker." Then began to giggle at my fury statement.

The man turned looking at me in a startle while Jonas jerked hard on my leash. "I said leave us, Hemmel. This is not your business. Keep moving. Maximillian, I told you to keep your trap shut." He again backhanded the fuck out of me, then dragged me harshly into the cell.

Master Peter was laying on the cot, he had too since there is nothing else in those cells but a commode, you know. He didn't even bother to sit up nor look at us as we came inside with him. I dropped to a kneel behind Jonas thankful for the rest. My head was killing me after the harsh beaten it had taken.

Jonas spoke first. "You think yourself clever, do you? I hope you are proud of yourself for this trick. This is maybe the foulest thing I ever seen pulled in this Haus, and I have seen some shit in my day. This Priceless collar has deceived me."

My Master turned his head staring at us harshly then snorted, "What are you speaking about, Jonas? Didn't my collar please you? Oh wait, I apologize, I forgot. You blood bonded that which is mine. What is the matter? I must assume you didn't enjoy your legal lover's favors if you are here. The boy, my Maximillian, looks like he certainly enjoyed a great deal of yours. He is a fucking mess, Jonas. What the hell? He will do whatever you want without beating him up like that, you know. What is wrong with you? Can you not control your collar without using force? That is a surprise. I assumed your being an old Dungeon Master, you'd know how to gain compliance without resorting to violence."

The Vampire spit on the floor. "Fuck you, Peter. Why didn't you tell me?"

Master Peter laughed loudly "Tell you what Jonas? I don't know what you're complaining about. You stole my collar for your own lustful interest and now you're upset. Why? I don't have any idea why you are here. Leave me to suffer in peace, thank you very much."

Jonas roared out. "You are a bastard. You know damned well why I am pissed. Your Maximillian is schizophrenic, Peter. You have been hiding this fact. How the fuck did you do it? Xavier? Did you pay off the Haus doctor maybe?"

My Master sat up in his cot glaring at Jonas with hate. "He is your Maximillian too, if I am to understand why I rot in this cell. You are the fucking fool, Jonas. You took him from behind my back. I didn't get any chance to warn you to be careful with this collar. This is what you get when you pick another's pocket. If you steal what is not yours, then it is your problem when the haul is not what you expected but the punishment brutal."

399

Jonas roared out. *"Can you fix this shit. If anyone finds out, then he cannot break that metal. You know the rules."*

Master Peter scoffed. *"Ja, I can. Obviously, I managed to sneak him past even your vigilant radar, didn't I? Why should I help you, Jonas? You fuck with my Maximillian behind my back, then have me whipped and caged like a criminal. Give me one fucking reason I should do a damned thing for you."*

Jonas jerked my leash hard sending me nearly face first to the cell floor. *"Here is your reason, Peter. You let anyone see this madness, then he is no good to you either. Do you think I don't know what you're up to? I want that female Priceless too, you know. This fucking collar is the key. He is broken like all the others, but somehow you got him past the Guard this long. You do it again or so help me I will…"* My Master interrupted him.

"You will what, Jonas? You exiled me, then you lost Maximillian, didn't you? You have all this power, but you cannot prevent the others from finding this collar shattered, can you? You think you know me, but you don't know shit. A female Priceless? There is no such a thing, fool. I am only interested in Maximillian because he is a treasure. One day he will break his collar and be a great surgeon. I had hoped only to use his favors among the Elders to make sure that silver was judged Dominant, but you took it too far. Now, I dare not leash him out

again. He is leveled Priceless. without the aid of the Elders and the Council. There is no way they will vote unanimous. The way I see it, thanks to your greed and lust for a myth, he is already trapped in that metal. It no longer matters if anyone sees he is shattered. Take him back to your apartment. Enjoy him all you like Jonas. better hurry though, the Guard will hear his screaming at the voices. Then they come and get your forbidden lover and shoot him in that busted head of his." My Master shot me a look that appeared disgusted.

Jonas chuckled sounding full of wickedness. "You are great at hiding this insanity I hold on a leash, but terrible at deceiving me about your motives for it. You damned well are seeking that female just like me. You can deny it all you like, but if you must please know I heard about this contract of yours with this boy. Now, why I wonder would you want to control his special services after he breaks his metal? Ah, and that language in the contract, let me see if I can recall it. Ja, I remember. He must find a "blood bonded Frau" and produce children before he can be free of Master Peter even after being judged Dominant. Well, isn't that interesting? Why the hell would you be so interested in Maximillian by putting a foot to his back to hurry and produce young? I suppose his choice of female to breed these children with matters not to you, huh?"

Master Peter crossed his arms and glared at Jonas with open hostility. "You are a nosey bastard, Jonas. That boy will go to medical school. That is expensive you know. How he pays me back for it and my request for price is not your business."

Jonas nodded, "Ja, normally I would agree with you it is not. However, in this case I believe we are seeking the same thing. I am right and your irritation over my discovery verifies that. I will say this only once. Your desires and mine are not in conflict, Peter. You can work with me on this, and we both get what we want, or you can be my enemy. You take the later, then I say prepare to be moving out of that cushy apartment. You can also say goodbye to all your aspirations for power. I will crush you without care."

Master Peter and Jonas stared at each other for several moments in silence after that threat. Then my Master sighed loudly. "Okay, Jonas, I see you're a worthy opponent. I would rather have you on my side than against me. I will call in the favors I have used to hide this schizophrenia, but only if you and I come to a full agreement on the future of this Priceless business. Your blood bonding him behind my back was dangerous. Look at how you set off something that I had under control. You must agree to never do anything to him without checking with me first in the future. Also, I want out of this dungeon."

Jonas smiled then shot a look at me. "I think we can come to a reasonable agreement Peter. I am glad to see

402

you are indeed as clever as I now understand you to be. I will call Hemmel and get you released. What of Maximillian? We cannot have him behaving this way in the open. I barely got him here with all that infernal laughter and yelling at voices. I had to beat him down just to get him to stop screaming."

Master Peter looked at me with concern. "Ah, that bad, this time. It would seem the disease is progressing faster than I expected. Okay, no matter. I will call my outside contact to come treat him. Tell Hemmel to bring a strait jacket for this collar. Make him think this is for punishment. We give him my cell here and leash him to the wall till the symptoms calm, ja?"

Jonas nodded. "Brilliant. Consider it done. I leave him with you while I get that strait jacket and secure your release." Master Peter stood up and took my leash while Jonas took off out the door of the cell.

Master Peter stood there in silence for a moment waiting till Jonas was out of earshot. "I should beat you down for fooling with this man behind my back, but I am sure he'd have found a way into your blood sooner or later. Shit. I suppose with your issues, it is not a dreadful thing to have Jonas in our back pocket, ja? I do hate to share you with him though. No worry, once you break that metal, I will have that bastard killed. He has a lot of gall."

I smiled at my Master. "Did I leave the stove on? I don't mean to burn down the Haus, you know. I just keep forgetting to turn it off. Can I get to my bed now? I don't feel good. Tell Jonas to turn down his radio. The noise is hurting my ears. He is busy recording this conversation, did you know dat? He can read my mind so be careful about telling me any secrets. He will hear them. That Vampire was trying to cut my throat, but he drugged me up too heavily. He can't drink it because it is tainted, you know."

Master Peter gasped. "Huh? Oh shit. Jonas is not lying. You have shattered, Maximillian, you are making no sense. We have no stove in the apartment. What is this shit about being drugged? Oh, meine Gott. I thought Jonas was being hysterical over your little freak out, but this is truly schizophrenia. How did this happen? Nein, this cannot be. What the hell am I going to do? There is no fucking cure for the Mutter of Madness. I am ruined."

I giggled uncontrollably, "Call your doctor friend Master. He can give me the antidote. I have nothing wrong the Kings doctor cannot mend. It is just blood poisoning you know. However, can you please turn down that radio? I don't like that song, and I wish you wouldn't mock me like dat." I began to mumble to myself there in my kneeling.

Jonas returned with the strait jacket. They unchained my wrists and my Master told me to hold still while they

404

both strapped me into that damned thing. Then they padlocked my leash to a small hook in that concrete wall, forcing me to stay on the cot. Then the two of them stared at me for a moment while I glared back.

Master Peter spoke first. "Be still till the doctor gets here in a few hours. We will take you home after he sedates you and we can sneak you home without discovery."

Jonas nodded his head. "I agree, but Maximillian comes home with me. I am not done with him Peter."

My Master scoffed angrily, "Seriously Jonas. Look at his face. You cannot even tell what color he is under all those shades of black and blue. He needs rest, damn you."

Jonas frowned. "We can discuss this elsewhere, I think. I am not willing to fight in front of this lesser. You know the rules. Come to my apartment. We need to work out details of our arrangement anyway, if you can behave like the gentleman."

Master Peter growled out, "I am a gentleman, Jonas. I never beat up thirteen-year-old mentally ill boys. I also never fucked one over so bad they needed a strait jacket."

I watched the two of them leave closing that heavy steel door behind them.

These cells, you know, are solid like your basement here. I kind of find it ironic I find my blood bonded Frau in a similar cell to the ones I spent many years in myself. The Gotts have a sense of humor, I guess.

I groaned and nodded. I thought God had to be one hell of a nasty bully. I say that because I thought what he had allowed Debbie, Russell, Peter, and Jonas to do to me and my Master Maxx was funny to him, I would rather not know the fellow. Just saying.

The moment I heard the area quiet of any life. I took a deep breath and stepped out of the boy. I called the others out too to wait for Der Hund.

Der Hund rushed into the room. "Brillian work. I swear I believed that shit myself. You're a genius."

The Max boys all patted that fused Shard on the back-smiling with much joy all thanking him for getting us the fuck out of Jonas's apartment. Three days my ass. Nothing like a little symptom exaggeration to literally keep everyone the fuck off you. We all knew Der Hund needed the break from Master Peter and Jonas's lusting. The added bonus of them believing the boy too daft to

understand their plotting was icing on this slice of deception cake.

Der Hund spoke up. "Okay, okay boys, calm down. Time for celebrating when we break the collar, ja? For now, ChristMax has bought us a moment to do some thinking without all that nasty sex shit. You know that doctor will be here soon with sedatives and drugs. That will help dull the pain of our existence, so bonus there, but that doesn't help us with keeping our thoughts clear. Master Mad Maxx was a wonderful shard to handle this Drexel. You all bound together negate each of your powers. ChristMax here works wonderfully to create the illusion of madness. You may now spilt into your own shards."

The shard ChristMax split apart immediately. Christian and Max giggled at their wild behavior in the center of our core the Mad Master Maxx. The three Maxx boys had cancelled each other out allowing the fused Lust/Anger and Restraint/Peace shard to melt together. They spun like a top, shifting rapidly from all the emotions day contain. The temporary insanity of hearing voices, agitation, paranoia, memory loss, confusion, delusions, and the ability to not feel pain was the result. We had finally learned how to control how we responded within rather than trying to control the outside while fighting each other, you know.

This was something we recalled from the night we frightened Olaf and Vilber in Xavier's chains. Lunacy scares people. When people are afraid, they leave you the hell alone. We reached inside and simply allowed our emotions to run amok. That led to sheer madness, at least on the surface anyway.

It was a calculated risk, but to be honest, Meine Liebe, one more brutal couple, gross sex act or foul molestation, we would bust a gasket for truth. This had to be done. With a break from the schemers, we could at last do a little of our own.

Master Maxx winked at me while I giggled at his great crazy act. To be honest, even I believed him nuts. I was so glad he was only faking it. He was faking insanity, right?

"We agreed that Maximillian would ride the flesh and give the rest a break. The plan was now to pit Jonas against Peter while seducing the rest of those schwulers behind both their backs at any cost. Then when our metal was history, we would find our mate.

When the female priceless of our dreams was found, we would share our story with her. She would be made aware of all the things we learned from the Elder, and our father's plans. This woman of ours would join us in the deception to beat them all.

On the glorious day that Jonas and Peter found their graves, she and I would run away from this life of brutality. We would settle far from all this pain, and insanity forever. Hand in hand, she would grant me the gift of a family. I would grant her my undying love and protection in return.

Then when our children and their children grew in number, she and I would grow old in each other's arms. When the sun sets on our time here on Earth, we would leave with the knowledge that we left it better than we found it. That was our plan. This is the dream I find in you, Miene Liebe.

I nodded. "I want that too Master. Do you promise it can happen? We will have a happy life far away from the Haus, Debbie, Russell, Master Jonas, and Master Peter? No more pain or torture forever?"

Master Maxx hugged me tightly then said while smiling with great kindness in his eyes, "I have faith that you and I will find a way to make our dream happen, meine Frau. We are the legendary Priceless blood bonded pair. Anything is possible when you're a legend, Meine Liebe. You see Jonas, he is seeking the magic of immortality from us. Peter, he desires the fantasy of power our struggle creates. They are both fools. You and I have no such enchanted things in our blood. There is only one thing we possess in a supernatural amount, meine Frau. That mystical ability to love deeper than the size of our souls. That is what makes us unbreakable. So many have stolen from our flesh, Meine Liebe, but no matter what they have tried they never reach our hearts. If you could see inside there, you'd find your face etched within my walls. I live only for you, and one day you will live only for me. We belong to each other for all time. That is the real secret of the Priceless pair. Nothing more and nothing less."

I smiled at the idea that he had a picture of me inside his heart like a locket. I looked at him closely. He giggled then poked me in my belly making me laugh too.

"What are you seeking in me now, Meine Demonseed Frau?" He narrowed his eyes, still smiling playfully.

I kissed him on his lips quickly then sat back. "I was drawing your face with my eyes, Master. I will have to color it in later, but I already pinned it in the walls in my heart too. I want to have it for when you have to go away, to help remind me why I am suffering."

Mad Maxx's face suddenly contorted to a look of pain which frightened me as I watched his eyes fill with water. I yelped when he reached out suddenly and grabbed me holding me tightly while he began to loudly sob. I was very frightened by his behavior, so I held still, unsure what to do. I thought I made him angry. I had never heard anyone this upset when no one had died.

It was several minutes before he calmed to a quiet quivering. He held me laying his head on my own. I whimpered full of terror thinking I was sure to be thudded harshly for whatever it was I said wrong.

He heard my sound of fear and pulled me back. I stared up into his red, puffy tear drenched eyes, bracing for his backhand. He lifted his hand, and I flinched as he rubbed it gently down my cheek.

"I am sorry, Meine Liebe. You touched my black heart with what you said. I don't know how I can continue to torture you when I hear the purity of your childish love for your worthless HusDom. I want so badly to steal you from this Debbie and take your far away from all this brutality. I cannot even free myself, but I spend all my days thinking of ways to save meine Frau. You're just a little girl, and I want to protect you in the way any good father would. However, you're not my kind. Your meine blood bonded mate. This makes me more insane that the only woman I ever known so intimately is one that is not one yet. Tell me, how can I keep doing what I must when I love you so much it kills me each time I have to be cruel to you?"

I looked at the floor thinking about his question for a moment then smiled. "I can pretend to be a brat if that makes it easier, Master. I am not afraid of your slaps or your chains. Well okay, yeah, I fear your torture. I want you to know as long as you love me, and it makes you proud, then I am happy to endure it for you. I want to have

411

your dream too. If it means I must cry a lot and get thudded till I am fifteen, then I think I can do it. I still don't like the sex stuff though."

My Master laughed till he choked. "Ah, I love you more and more every minute, Meine Liebe. You're so strong for a little one. I think I asked this once, but are you sure you're not a midget instead of a young girl? He laughed at that. No matter. You do make me proud. I tell you I can love no other nor do I want to. I will also say, you are a brat. There is no pretending with you. Oh, and too bad about not likin the sex stuff. You're not getting out of that. I like it a lot. You didn't mind it that much earlier I noticed." He laughed while he ruffled my hair and I slapped away his hand rolling my eyes.

He rolled me to my back and tickled me until I had to use the yellow bucket or soil the sheets. He took his own nature break then picked me up, snuggling me close, while carrying me back to our spot on the mattress. He rubbed my back while he began his story again rocking me slightly, letting me listen to his words, and his heartbeat. There was no doubt the strength of our unusual bond had now become, unbreakable.

"The doctor Master Peter had been using from outside the Haus arrived about two hours or so later. Maximillian had entered the flesh and the rest of us hung around, just in case, you know.

I sat there glaring at the tall man with Jonas and my Master. He came toward me and I tried to back up, appearing afraid of him. I noticed I was drooling a bit. I assumed this happened when all of the Maxes and Christian have left the boy uninhabited.

When the flesh was mindless. He could not swallow that spittle that leaked down my chin in rivers. I would have wiped it away, but it is kind of hard to do with a strait jacket on? The doctor saw my anxiety at his approach. He backed up asking my Master and Jonas to "restrain Maximillian" for his exam.

The brutes come at me causing me to wail out in fear. I didn't know what they intended to do. This was some scary shit, with all the rubber gloves, doctor bags, and who knows what he intended to shoot me up with this time. Ugg, I do hate the shots when I don't know what poison they are putting into my blood stream.

Jonas and Master Peter held me down while this man looked into my eyes. He asked Jonas a lot of questions about what I said to him. Then he asked about any stresses I had to endure lately.

I yelled out before Jonas could answer him on that. "I would think getting fucked without lube while a vampire sucks your blood after being shot for going outside is pretty fucking stressful, you filthy sonofabitch. Get your

413

Gott damned hands off me pig fucker." I was being honest is all, though I admit I couldn't prove the doctor liked to screw the pigs. He looked like one of those perverts to me.

Master Peter slapped me harshly. "That is enough Maximillian. You hold still and let this man examine you, or you will get a thudding. I mean it."

Well, that calmed my ass down. I was in no hurry for a tawsing from my Master. He is real hell with that thing. Mad Maxx may like that shit but Maximillian will pass.

That doctor spent some time looking me over. Then he pulled out a tissue and wiped the sweat off his brow while shooting nervous looks at Jonas and Master Peter.

Jonas growled out appearing to become impatient with the man. "Well? What the fuck can you do about this insane bastard? Do we have to hold him down till we are old men or what?"

The doctor frowned. "This is definitely a psychotic onset of some kind. This boy shows some signs of schizophrenia but doesn't appear to have enough of the symptoms yet to make that call. I will say, I personally think that is what we are looking at though. If it is, the disease, in time will tell. You can expect increasing paranoia, delusions, and hallucinations if it is the mental illness. It will worsen and last more than six months. If it is stress causing this break from reality, then it should calm down in one month or less. I warn you though if it lasts for three, then we have an atypical schizophrenia but not the pure illness. That too can be a tough thing to treat."

Master Peter groaned. "What the fuck exactly are you saying? Does Maximillian have schizophrenia or not?" Jonas nodded his head.

The doctor shook his head. "I am saying it is too soon to tell. This break seems to have come fast. Acute breaks after stressful events usually have a better prognosis than those that onset slow over many months. Have either of you noticed Maximillian withdrawing, talking to people not there, losing weight, showing anger outbursts with sudden acts of aggression toward others, crying fits, acting paranoid, or believing wild tales? I can see he is dressing oddly, that is quite the outfit he is wearing. When did he start favoring such archaic fashion?"

Now that pissed me off. "Are you serious? You're worried about my fashion sense? This bastard over here thinks he is a Vampire and the other one put a fucking collar on me and makes me call him Master. Did you know they raped a thirteen-year-old boy that straight? You call me nuts. Help, someone help me. These people are crazy. Master, call the fucking cops. Why do you stand there? I am not the sick person in this cell. Did you know they will not let me leave? They shot me. Is that not insane," I yelled at the top of my lungs struggling trying to break free of these crazy men.

Jonas backhanded me with force. "Settle down, damn you. Doctor, calm this boy. I cannot take any more of this shit."

The doctor grimaced. "Hitting Maximillian is not advisable. I would ask you both to try to use restraint. He is in obvious mental pain. I will give him something to quiet him, but I warn you both, this may only be the beginning. Peter, I will keep this out of the records as long as I can, but if this is schizophrenia onsetting, I can do nothing for him, nor can you. He will need to be institutionalized. He is noticeably young. An onset at this age is tragedy. He will be lost to all of us."

Master Peter closed his eyes and Jonas sighed, appearing upset as well. "How long till we know if, you know, this is the end for the boy," rasped out my Master.

The doctor shook his head, "I will give him some medication to calm stress. We wait, watch, and if there is improvement in a few days or weeks, then we can rule out the worst of the possibilities. The only thing I can be sure of Peter is that Maximillian is significantly mentally ill. He is going to need mental health assistance and I would suggest keeping him from anything that he could injure himself or other with for a while."

Master Peter stared at Jonas. "Oh? How the fuck do you suggest we do that doctor? You say to keep the stress down then tell us to keep him restrained? With Maximillian one equals the other. Some of us would have known this had they bothered to speak to me before they went doing stupid shit with a weak-minded boy."

Jonas scoffed at that. "If people would not be hiding truths from everyone, things would not have gotten out of hand."

The doctor went to his bag while Master Peter and Jonas argued cryptically with each other over who was more at fault for my situation. I watched in silence as that skinny man pulled out a tube of something and filled a syringe with it. That medicine seemed to be sort of green to me with weird sparkles inside it. I began to fear that maybe this was the mind-altering stuff Jonas had given me earlier.

He held the needle into the air telling Master Peter and Jonas to roll me over so he could administer this crap into my backside. Fuck that I thought. You know, I had already started thinking this guy wasn't even a doctor. Nothing in that whole fuckin place was ever what it seemed; you know.

In the Haus, I had learned that the girls that say they love you are looking to kill you. Your Master is really your father. The Vampire is your husband. The door guards, oh, they are your only friends. Of course, they would shoot you if you tried to get past them. No hard feelings, right? The children are slaves used for pleasure and then they are fertilizer for the Orchard. If you say nein, they torture you. If you say ja, they torment you. No matter which way you go it is the wrong way. Everything is upside down and there is no escaping it. So, this guy, well I knew right away he was a fake, was like the rest of them.

I started to struggle with all my might. Fighting and cussing the lot of them with every fucking foul curse I could come up with. I think I even made up a few of my very own. That doctor did get his injection into me, but not until after I gave all three of them a taste of my boots.

It only took a few minutes for that shit to work on my senses. The room began to sway, and the light grew dimmer. I could hear them whispering around me to each other. I kept on hearing that fucking word again, schizophrenia, which was bullshit. I was faking this insanity the whole time.

To Be Continued in "Prince of the Elders".

Alexandria May Ausman began demonstrating severe psychotic episodes while still in her teens. She was abandoned by her family after being diagnosed with Paranoid Schizophrenia at age sixteen. Forced to struggle with this devastating illness alone, she has suffered medication resistant symptoms, numerous hospitalizations, homelessness, exploitation, and an uncaring mental health system.

Despite the hardships, Alexandria managed to raise two healthy children to adulthood and has four beautiful grandchildren. She obtained a bachelor's degree in psychology and held a job as a child abuse investigator. In

2003, she began a career as a diagnostic psychologist while working towards a Master's in psychology.

Alexandria never forgot the experience of 'slipping through the cracks.' She worked tirelessly to help people suffering severe mental illness and/or all types of abuse have access to necessary services for over seventeen years.

In 2017, she was published and became a professional model of "goth fashion.' and won the World Gothic Models contest in 2018. She holds the title of World Goth Queen for life.

Alexandria began writing several series of fictional novels after a catastrophic return of psychotic symptoms in 2019. She obtained the Killer Nashville Falchion Award as Best Southern Gothic writer in August 2023, and is a finalist for her book Delusion of the Collar and the Key.

Today, Alexandria is retired, and homebound due to crippling symptoms of Schizophrenia. She currently lives in Tallahassee, Florida, with her loving husband and a loyal support dog.

www.ingramcontent.com/pod-product-compliance
Lightning Source LLC
Chambersburg PA
CBHW071639260626
47170CB00001B/162

* 9 7 9 8 9 8 9 0 0 4 8 4 3 *